LOLA AND THE MILLIONAIRES

Part One

KATHRYN MOON

Copyright © 2020 by Kathryn Moon

Lola & the Millionaires, Part One

First publication: June 11th, 2020

Cover art by KellieArts

Font art by Lana Kole

Editing by Meghan Leigh Daigle

Formatting by Kathryn Moon

All rights reserved.

No part of this book may be reproduced in any form or by any electronic or mechanical means, including information storage and retrieval systems, without written permission from the author, except for the use of brief quotations in a book review.

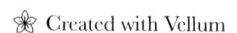

❀ Created with Vellum

The unauthorized reproduction or distribution of a copyrighted work is illegal. Criminal copyright infringement, including infringement without monetary gain, is investigated by the FBI and is punishable by fines and federal imprisonment.

Please purchase only authorized electronic editions and do not participate in, or encourage, the electronic piracy of copyrighted materials. Your support of the author's rights is appreciated.

This book is a work of fiction. Names, characters, places, brands, and incidents are the products of the author's imagination or used fictitiously. Any resemblance to actual events, locales or persons, living or dead, is entirely coincidental.

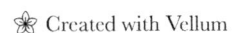

❦ Created with Vellum

To the beta babes, of course!
Jami, Ash, Helen, Kathryn, Desiree
You took the best possible care of Lola and of me!
Thank you

A Note on this Omegaverse

There are NO shifters in this book.

Aside from the unusual human biology, this Omegaverse is not a paranormal romance. These alphas, betas, and omegas are *not* shifters. This is an alternate universe to ours, with an alternate human biology that includes animalistic traits adapted to a romance premise. There are fancy penises, mating instincts, pheromones, and bonding marks, as well as a slight hierarchal social construct. Alphas are considered powerful and prone to leadership and they form family packs, omegas as the precious and sexual glue that holds those packs together, and betas are the average and normal.

Lola's story does deal with themes of the aftermath of sexual abuse and emotional trauma. If you find yourself uncomfortable reading such material, please proceed with caution (especially where you see large chunks of italics, which are flashbacks.)

Lola

1

"Gin and tonic. Want me to leave it open?"

I shook my head at the bartender. "Close it."

This was my third glass of the night.

Time's running out, I thought, scanning the length of the bar. Women like me lined the glossy black bar top, the high polish reflecting the flashing, spinning lights from the dance floor. We sat on our stools like jewels in their fastenings, while the rest of the club patrons pushed around our shoulders to catch the bartenders' attention.

A man leaned forward around me as I took my bill, signing my name on the line and digging a bill out of my bra to leave for a tip.

"Tequila on the rocks."

The man at my side twisted as the bartender nodded back at him. Narrowed eyes latched onto me immediately, studying me with cursory interest. He was good-looking, or at least good-looking enough to catch someone's eye. He had a lean frame, blue eyes, mussed light-brown hair, weak chin, and patchy stubble. A different week, and I might've smiled and encouraged him to chat me up a bit. Tonight I was in the mood for something else.

When he started to smile, I shook my head and spun my stool to turn my back to him, taking a sip of my drink and wincing as it burned in my throat. Henry, the bartender, had really upped the gin on this one. I would have to make sure I didn't finish it. Which meant I had even less time.

Come on, Lola, just pick one.

Normally I liked this club. It was one of the few beta-only night clubs in the city and by far the classiest. I could come here and be safe from the oppressive pheromones of alphas who were looking to settle for an eager beta when what they really wanted was the rare jewel, the omega. I'd been one of those betas just a year ago, secretly wishing I might develop into an omega like some magical fairy tale transformation. That I might be precious, rather than run of the mill. But I'd learned the cost of an alpha's attention finally, even if it had taken me twenty-five years to realize the truth.

And now I'd found my safe haven. Philia was a little shelter against the weight of alphas and omegas on my mind. And if that wasn't enough, the music was always good for dancing, the drinks were strong, and the men who showed up looking for women were either hot, well-dressed, or both.

Tonight, though, I was losing interest. Either my routine—sit at the bar, no more than three drinks, always leave alone—was getting old, or it was just an off night at Philia. I took another bitter sip of my drink and slid off the stool before Mr. Tequila On The Rocks could brush up too close against my back.

My timing was shit. As soon as my feet hit the floor a body collided against my back, sending me stumbling forward, tossing my drink up and walking directly into the splash. Two large, warm hands grasped my hips to keep me from falling on my own face, and they pulled me back against a broad chest. I jerked away from the touch, adrenaline spiking and making my heartbeat ricochet in my chest.

"Shit, I'm so—"

"It's fine, I—"

I spun and stumbled back to blow off whoever ran into me, only to find my words drying up on my tongue. *Fuuuuuck, pretty*, my brain declared. Which was correct and also kind of an understatement.

"I'm sorry," he finished, smiling as his eyes took equal interest in looking me over as mine did with him.

Short, inky black hair framed his masculine beauty. He had dense stubble growing over his tan jaw and thick eyebrows over dark eyes. His features were broad, and he had a mouth designed by God herself for kissing, with full but not plump lips. Latino or Hispanic I guessed, looking at eyelashes that women would've paid good money for from a beauty store.

Now we're talking. This was what I was in the mood for. Even if I hadn't known it a minute ago. It was like I'd been waiting for this absurdly handsome man to walk into me.

"It's my fault for not looking," I said, shrugging.

On my chest, a trickle of gin and tonic slipped down beneath the low collar of my dress, curving over one of my breasts and catching the stranger's eye. He leaned in, one hand reaching up to cover my shoulder, his thumb pressing over the sticky alcohol on my skin. *Don't flinch*, I ordered myself. The touch was hot and provocative, but he wasn't gripping me tight. I was safe.

"Let me buy you another drink," he said into my ear, and I could finally make him out over the heavy thumping bass of the dance floor. A warm voice with a natural rasp that raised goosebumps over my skin. His lips almost brushed my earlobe, a little trace of heat and damp breath on my skin.

Drowsy, languid arousal washed over me as I took in a deep breath. Fresh laundry, a little citrusy, pure beta. Not that I expected anything different at Philia, but there was no reassurance like the biological. Here was my mark for the night. This guy was handsome, and he was tall and broad-shouldered, and he was *safe*.

Or as safe as any stranger might be. He wasn't an alpha.

I tipped my head, letting my cheek brush his until I caught his eye. At least neither one of us was pretending not to be interested.

"How about a dance instead?" I asked.

His eyebrows raised and his smile grew, revealing deep dimples. "I never say no to a dance. You sure you don't want the drink?"

I shook my head. It didn't matter that I didn't finish my cocktail. I didn't need to now. I'd made my plan for the night and I *never* drank to get drunk.

Control was something I refused to give up, especially over myself. I pushed the now empty glass back onto the bar, brushing my chest against his. His hand on my shoulder slid down my arm and over to the open back of my dress, fingers digging in lightly for a moment. I ducked my chin to hide my smile as I let him lead us to the dance floor.

Men were kind of easy. Skin usually did the trick. Eye contact always helped.

It was a formula I followed.

1. Drink until I'm buzzed enough to lose the constant tremor of anxiety that hummed in my chest, but not drunk enough to start remembering the past.

2. Find a safe beta target.

3. Reel them in.

4. Get laid. Try to burn off the frustration that clawed through my veins. That clenched my teeth together into a grimace and made my jaw ache. That burned in my eyes so hot, I thought I might scream until my throat was raw. That I might just keep screaming until they buried me in the ground.

5. Go home and try to sleep.

We wove through the crowd of dancers, pressing closer together. I ran a hand up his back, amused at the smooth texture of his suit. Maybe he'd just gotten done for the day at whatever finance job he had in the neighborhood. Either way, the tailoring looked good on him and the quality was high. Maybe I'd make him leave it on just so I could hold onto that high thread count whenever we found the dark corner we'd be using later.

I spun and turned my back to him, his hands cupping around my hips, fingertips settling in the grooves of my hip bones. The music rattled the floor beneath us as I found the rhythm, pleased when he followed it without hesitation. None of that boring dude posturing, where he just stood still and I rubbed up against him. This guy and I were moving together;

our bodies had been designed for the connection. I reached my arms back, palms holding onto his shoulders, and rested my head on his shoulder, a soft scratch from his stubble against my temple.

Our hips curled together, and one hand remained squeezing my hip as the other meandered up to my ribs in a slow caress that left a ticklish, prickling path on my skin. Sweat gathered on my back, the press of the crowd and the heat of the man with his arms around me making my blood rush in my veins. Slowly, tension unwound from my muscles. My mark was a good enough dancer that the more I relaxed, the stronger his lead was until I was loose and following the coaxing guide of his hands. I shifted my feet apart, and his leg filled the space. His breath was hot on my neck, his hands gripping tighter with every slow roll of our bodies in unison.

His thumb stroked against the underside of my breast and my eyes widened, surprised by the intense pound of desire that answered the light touch. I pulled away, just for a second, and he was ready as I spun to face him. He pulled me flush against him, and now the leg between my thighs was something to grind against. I gripped at the collar of his absurdly fancy suit, running my fingertips along the silken underside, and tipped my chin back to meet his eyes.

The flash of colored lights was reflected back at me in his gaze, as well as my own face. My lips were parted on a pant and my eyes were hooded, arousal plain to see. I tore my stare away, watched the undulating forms of the other dancers over his shoulder, frowned at the edgy need racing through me. This was *more* than I usually found on these excursions. More desire, more chemistry, and that carefully measured leash of control I held was starting to slip from my grip.

And then his head dipped down, lips skimming over my throat as his fingers dug into the curves of my hips and ass, drawing me tight against the ridge of arousal between us. I moaned, and I don't know if he heard it in the thunder of bass and moaning lyrics around us, or if he felt my breath, but he sipped softly on my skin, tongue flicking out to taste over my pulse.

For once, too much felt *good*. My eyes fell shut and my forehead landed on his shoulder as we moved in tandem. A few shifts of clothing and we'd end the mimicry of sex in exchange for the actual physical act. I was as impatient to move onto the next part of my routine as I was greedy to savor the sensuality of so much touching, so much closeness with another person.

This was why I did this. This is why I braved the panic attacks of being out of my recent safety zones in favor of the anonymous contact in over-crowded clubs. I missed touch. I missed intimacy. This was a poor woman's charade of the two, but it was better than shivering in my bed all night trying not to think about *them*.

I rocked against the thigh rucking up the hem of my dress and my panties slid wetly against my skin. Shit. This guy had to be feeling how badly I wanted him by now. Not that I wasn't feeling the same from him.

We lifted our heads at the same time and all I needed was one look from those blacked out angel-eyes of his to know. I surged up, and his arms circled my back as his eyes slid shut, our lips colliding in a perfect meld. No clumsy confusion, just out-and-out deep kisses, tongues stroking together as I rode his leg like it could get me to the crashing point I was craving so badly. It probably could, if I was patient.

I was never patient.

I pulled away, felt his groan vibrate against my lips, and then grabbed his hands from my back, dragging him through the crowd with me. His brow was faintly furrowed, his smile curling as I led us off the dance floor and toward the dim and twisting hall, past the customer restrooms and around the corner.

Employees Only. The private restroom that was always open and never occupied. Until I walked in with whatever man I'd grabbed for the night.

I pushed in with my shoulder, finally far enough from the

pounding music to hear his easy laugh, the chuckle rasping in my ear like a tongue between my thighs. It turned quickly into a moan as I pushed him against the back of the door, pinning him there by those perfect shoulders of his and taking his mouth again, rubbing my body against his in a desperate bid for friction.

"Fuck, gorgeous," he muttered, before losing track of whatever he planned to say as I sucked on his tongue.

This was the tricky part. Some guys wanted to *get to know you*. Plenty were usually happy for a quick anonymous fuck. But sometimes the sweet ones wanted to know—

"What's your name? I'm Le—"He shuddered as I bit his lip, grasping the back of his neck with one hand and holding our mouths together.

Finally getting with the program, he let out a soft, muffled, growl and gripped my ass in his big hands, spinning me to the door with a soft slap of my skin against the surface. I wrapped my legs around his hips, a high breathy sigh escaping my lips as he rubbed the stretched crotch of his pants against my lace underwear.

"Fine, we'll save that for later," he said, laughing.

There's not gonna be a later, I thought. "Condom?" I asked.

He raised an eyebrow. "I can honestly say I wasn't expecting this."

I resisted the urge to scoff. No one came to Philia without at least hoping to get laid. Instead I pulled out a dollar bill and passed it to him, nodding to the machine over his shoulder. He laughed again, that wicked sound that made my stomach flip and my panties wetter, and scuffed his hand over his dark hair.

The thing I liked about the employee bathroom was that there were a few lights out overhead, so it was dim but not dark, and that none of the employees bothered walking all the way back here so it was always empty. Also, it had a fantastically open countertop that was never soggy with soapy water.

My mark for the night went to buy us some protection and I crossed to the counter, waiting until he turned around so he could watch in the mirror as I flipped my skirt up and shimmied my underwear down. He crossed the small room quickly, eyes tracking my hands as he flipped the condom packet aimlessly between his fingers.

"Here," he said, holding out his free hand.

I grinned and turned, hooking my panties over his finger and watching him tuck them into his back pocket.

"For safekeeping," he said, smile big and close to laughing.

"Mhm, obviously," I said, tugging him closer and nipping at his lips, softening the bite with a quick lick of my tongue. I wasn't normally this into kissing, but most men didn't have mouths so obviously made for the act. If it weren't out of my routine, I would've begged for this man to get on his knees for me.

"I meant what I said, about not expecting this," he murmured, nose brushing against mine as he crowded me against the counter.

"Will you be offended if I admit I came here pretty much for this reason?" I asked, glancing at him from under my lashes. What did he want me to be? Shy and innocent? Or a vixen?

"Me specifically?" he asked, stilling and frowning.

What? I laughed and frowned at him. "Why would I be here for you specifically? I mean, after you crashed into me, yeah, you specifically."

He relaxed and shook his head, smile returning. "Right. Dumb question. Come here."

Hmm, maybe the fancy suit wasn't from the finance district. Maybe my handsome mark for the evening was one of those low-key famous people? Either way, I was less interested in that than the fact that I was pretty sure his lips had extra muscles for how perfectly they clasped and took control of mine. The awkward puzzle of his question passed with one kiss after another until I was panting and clinging to him.

"You wet for me, gorgeous?" he whispered, and I shivered at the rougher edge of his tone as he grew more aroused.

"Find out for yourself," I answered, desperate to be touched.

He hummed, smiling into the kiss and holding me with one hand at the center of my back as the other delved under my skirt, brushing like feathers against the inside of my thighs. Higher and higher his touch skimmed, refusing to be hurried even as I squirmed closer. The second he touched my sex, we both moaned, his fingers sliding through generous moisture and my hips bucking into the touch as it echoed up into my heart, making it thump twice as fast.

"More," I moaned, hands stroking over his chest, tugging the crisp gray shirt loose from his pants, fumbling at his belt and then back up to his collar to undo the top buttons.

"Christ, you're soaked. Lemme taste," he hissed, hand drawing away and up to his lips.

I watched, breathless, as his tongue flicked out to taste the shining slick I'd left on his fingers. His thick eyelashes fluttered and he groaned, sucking hard on his own digits until I tugged his hand away and replaced his fingers with my tongue, fucking it into his mouth and whining at our shared taste.

His hand immediately returned to my pussy, stroking and dipping inside as I blindly tore at his buttons. Even the stretch of his fingers was good, and I rocked into the intrusion, encouraging him deeper.

"Condom."

"Counter."

"Put it *on*," I said, laughing.

We leaned away from each other, both of us grinning, and my heart clenched. Why was this guy making me feel more than the others? Making me giddy and laugh, and more than just helping me scratch an itch that was less about desire than mastery?

"This first," he said, sliding one finger deep inside of me, hissing as I clenched around him. I shivered and tried not to collapse completely as his thumb brushed against my clit, making me stiffen and cry out. "Yes, that's it."

I whined and shuddered as he repeated the careful touch,

the sensation both sharp and gentle, the beginning every bit as delirious as the coming finale.

"Enough," I gasped.

"Not nearly, gorgeous. Come on, you like that?"

It was so simple, but I *loved* it, my body rolling as it had on the dance floor as he pumped one finger, and then two, all while slowly rolling my clit under his thumb. His other hand stroked up from my hip to my breast, working it gently through the fabric, gripping briefly and testing my cry as he squeezed tighter.

"Yes!"

I was so close and I wanted to draw some of the reins back. I leaned forward, pushing aside the collar of his shirt to suck on his throat. And then I saw it, a set of shining crescent scars facing another. I froze just as he crooked his fingers inside of me, drawing out a stuttering and surprising orgasm that left me crumpling forward into him, his arm curling around my back and drawing me to his chest.

"You want our mark, don't you, beta bitch? Yeah, you want to pretend you're good enough to belong to an alpha. Except you're not, and you know that, don't you?"

"Stop! Stop, stop. Let me go." I gasped and pushed at his chest, his hands immediately retreating and then grasping my shoulders. Ice shot through me like knife wounds as I fought my way free from the beta's grasp.

"Hey. Hey, what's wrong? I'm sorry! What happened?"

"Nothing," I said, trying to catch my breath and knowing I wouldn't find it. Not while he had his hands on me. Not while I was stuck in this shitty little bathroom with him. "Let me go."

I twisted and squirmed, my eyes fixed to that mark on his throat as I pulled myself free of his hold. He stilled, and I glanced up into his eyes briefly, and then immediately back onto the scar. The bonding mark. The bonding mark *only* an alpha could give. His hand reached up to cover the scar as his eyes widened.

"Oh, this? It's not— We're not like that," he said,

although I could hear the lie in his voice, the rickety wobbling notes.

"I don't need to know what you're like. I just need to go," I said, my own voice hollow as I rounded him carefully, waiting for him to strike, to grab at me again. Fuck.

See Lola? It doesn't have to be an alpha. You can always be at risk. Now look at what this routine has gotten you into.

"Seriously, wait, please. Let me explain," he said. He held himself back, hands raised and open, non-threatening. He didn't need to do anything to be threatening. He had *that mark*, which meant that somewhere out there—maybe not in the club, but probably not far—was an alpha with a claim on this beta.

I rushed for the door, let out a brief, terrified whimper as he lunged to follow me. The sound stopped him, my back braced against the door and my entire body trembling, waiting for him to strike.

"I would never *hurt* you," he said, eyes huge. His lips were still bitten pink with my kisses, and his fingers were still shining with my release.

Stupid. Stupid, stupid, fucking stupid.

I slid to the side and opened the door, ignoring the twist of my heart and the flinch in his gaze, before rushing out into the hall. I ran down the hall, refusing to look over my shoulder, the lines of the walls seeming endless as my heart rate started to speed.

Breathe. Breathe you fucking idiot. Breathe. Just breathe.

I shoved my way through the crowd, pulling my coat check ticket from the small pocket at the front of my dress, and spared a glance behind me. No sign of him. There was a brief, contrary pang of disappointment, but it evaporated quickly, my heel clicking against the floor as I waited for them to bring me my purse. People were passing me, brushing up against me, and every point of contact was excruciating. My own skin fit wrong as I tried to hold onto the remaining threads of calm, to keep breathing, to pretend that the ceiling wasn't crashing down on me.

Fucking stupid.

I avoided the coat check girl's fingers as I took my purse, rushing for the exit as I drew up the app on my phone to call a beta-only cab. I was never coming back to this club. Never risking another chance meeting with that beta.

It might be time to give up the routine altogether if I could stand it.

I marched two blocks in the dark, in my heels and my skimpy dress and my old leather jacket, meeting the cab outside a nearby bodega.

"Look at her, arching like an omega for that bite. Never gonna fuckin' happen, Showgirl."

"How's your night goin' gorgeous?" the woman asked me from the driver's seat, making me twitch at the endearment. It hadn't sounded so cheesy and unfamiliar on his tongue, but now the word was abrasive.

"Long," I said, and there was a tense pause before the woman nodded and turned the radio on. The music was soft and moody, and I slunk down in my seat as we passed Philia, my eyes growing wide, panic rising in my chest. There he was, standing outside the doors between two of the security guards, scanning the sidewalk with wide eyes and a brow furrowed with worry.

With my *fucking panties* in his fist.

Lola
2

I stared at my blaring phone the next morning, waiting until the last possible second to swipe.

"Hey," I said, frowning at the crack in my voice. After my failed attempt at Philia ending in a shattering disaster, I hadn't really gotten any sleep, which sucked considering it was my—

"Congrats! It's your first day at *Designate*," David sing-songed, voice too loud and echoey. He was on speakerphone, probably Bluetoothing it from his car service.

"I hadn't forgotten," I said, lips twitching. "Just like I hadn't forgotten to set my alarm, in case that's why you called."

Not that his call would've done the trick. I hadn't had my ringer on in over a year.

"I'm calling because this is a big day, Lo," David said, losing his attempt at chipperness. Which was good because David was acerbic through and through, and chipper just came off as manic on him.

"I'm not gonna fuck this up, I promise," I said, staring at my reflection in my bathroom mirror, trying to force the disappointed weariness off my features by will alone. When that failed, I flipped open my makeup case. When in doubt, paint it on.

"I didn't—I know you're not!"

"I know you went out on a limb for me," I said, and David huffed. "I'm gonna rock this for you."

"*Lo*…Jesus. Look, did I point their team to your old web series? Yes. But that's it."

"You put my application in."

"Only because you were about to miss the deadline."

I raised my eyebrow and then smirked when I remembered he couldn't see me. "Thank you," I said, slow and sincere.

I really needed this job. I really needed *any* job now that I'd finally put the bulk of my savings into this new apartment. It stung a little that in my attempt to get out of David's hair, he ended up having to find me not just any job but my actual *dream* job in the Beauty Department of *Designate Magazine*.

"Ehn. Literally no one in this industry got in on merit alone, okay? We all knew *someone*, so I'm your person. I'm good with that. You just need to be good with that too."

"I'm good with it," I lied, faking brightness.

"So there's gonna be a car waiting for you."

"David!"

"I'm not doing it *every day*. Just be glad I didn't send flowers to your new desk."

I blinked, staring down at my sink and waiting for the bout of teariness to pass. "You just wanted to make sure I wasn't late."

David scoffed again, but this time there was a little laugh mixed in. "Dinner tomorrow."

"Dinner tomorrow. No fucking flowers, David."

"No fucking flowers," he said, imitating me in a gruff, nasal tone. He was quiet for a beat, and I was ready to hang up when he said, "Your mom would be proud of you."

Low blow, David, I thought. And probably not the target he was aiming for. "I'll see you tomorrow," I said, and then ended the call.

My mom would not be proud of me. Relieved maybe, just to see I was employed again after a year of hiding in David's guest bedroom. But luckily for my mother and for me, she'd missed the past five years of my life. Still, if there was one thing my mother would want to say to me, it wouldn't have to do with pride. Pretty much the opposite.

I told you so.

She'd warned me about alphas, about what they wanted from betas, and I'd tried and failed to prove her wrong over and over again.

And then I'd gone to the Devil's Noose that night, with my best friend Baby.

As if summoned by my thoughts, my phone rang again, this time with Baby's name across the screen. I dropped it on the counter, flipping it to speaker and ignoring the twinge that always hit my heart when I dealt with Baby. Baby, who had undergone that magical—okay, rare but biological—transformation I'd always dreamed of. One day she was a beta, and the next night at a dive bar in Old Uptown, she was a newly perfuming omega.

"Putting my face on, babe, what's up?"

"HAPPY FIRST DAY OF WEEEERRRRKK!" Baby screamed through the phone, the horrible shrill tones bouncing around the ghastly drab pink tile of my bathroom.

"Dear god," I muttered.

"Hi, sorry, I love you. What kind of look are you going for?" Baby rattled at rapid-fire. "Bold and daring? Pristine and angelic? Classic noir?"

"Alive," I said, dabbing primer onto my face. "Tell Chef not to give you so much caffeine straight away in the morning, you're supposed to pace that shit."

"Nah, I just tell each of the guys I haven't had any yet, so they bring me fresh mugs to bed," Baby said.

I squawked a laugh. "Oh, the privilege of a lazy omega with a devoted pack."

"Damn straight," Baby said. "Late night?"

I hummed, and she hummed back. It had taken us a while to find our ease after Baby found out she was an omega—the blessed minority to be coveted and cherished and adored by alpha packs—and not a beta as she'd assumed for twenty-five years. I'd always wanted to be an omega and desperately craved the approval of alphas, so the sting when I'd first learned that *Baby* had been granted my wish was keen and sharp, cutting through the camaraderie between us. It didn't help that while she was going through the deliriously happy process of getting to know her pack of alpha bikers, I was going through a personal hell with another.

Baby didn't approve of my new weekend routine, but she definitely wouldn't have approved if she knew I was doing it alone, and not with a small group of other betas like I lied and told her.

"It was a bust though," I said. "How's the crew?"

"Same, same," Baby said. "Wanna get lunch soon? Maybe somewhere fancy Downtown? My treat!"

More like one of her alpha's treats, but Baby and her guys were always very careful to keep her alphas out of my way. Sometimes Seth, her beta, would join Baby and me on our lunch dates, but mostly they let her hang out with me alone.

"It's a date," I said.

"Yay. Okay, I'll let you focus on your wing liner," Baby said. Baby mostly skipped a makeup routine, which was good because she could injure herself and three others with a liner pencil.

"Love you, babe."

"Love you, Lo."

I sighed as she hung up and rolled my shoulders. Okay, so we were mostly back to normal. I still got a bit tense, but I didn't want Baby to carry that for me. My mistakes were on me.

I glared at my reflection again. Limp blonde hair. Hollow cheeks. Lips chapped from nervous biting and picking. I couldn't decide if I was the before picture in a self-improvement ad, or the after image from a serious wreckage.

I used my foundation to paint on clean, even skin, hiding away the dark circles under my eyes from lack of sleep and the bouts of acne on my chin and forehead from stress. Despite getting a job as an assistant beauty editor, I was planning on keeping it low-key. I wanted to go in and get my work done at *Designate*. I wanted to earn the place David had found for me, but I didn't want to catch a lot of attention. At least, not from my appearance.

Because there would be alphas at *Designate*. The head of my Department was an alpha, although I'd been hired in my interviews by a team of betas. But it was a major magazine, and even the CEO of the media company that owned *Designate* was an alpha, not that I expected to run into him in the offices. I'd learned my lesson when it came to alphas. I was done being one of those betas who chased after a pack that couldn't care less about me.

DESIGNATE WAS LOCATED in the Stanmore, one of the tallest buildings downtown, not to mention one of the most beautiful old Art-Deco buildings in the country. It'd been the same location for the magazine for over sixty years, and the magazine was as much a part of the history of the building as the building was to the city. I stepped inside and allowed myself a good twenty seconds to gawk at the angled chandelier, the gold framing details, the intricate tiling of the floor, to just *enjoy* that I was here—not as a spectator but as someone who worked in the building. Then someone bumped my shoulder, and I let the moment pass.

I was early, thanks to David's car service, dressed in a simple black dress that was designed to hang loose and formless, and I blended in with the sea of men and women in business attire and wool trench coats that squeezed their way into the building. I didn't know the full rundown of the offices in the Stanmore, but I did know that under the five floors *Designate* occupied was a well known and entirely beta run legal company.

I wiggled my way through the crowd, breathing through my parted lips to avoid the few faint wisps of alpha pheromones I caught, and headed for the security desk. The woman behind the gorgeous stone counter was a bulky beta woman who took a remarkably unhurried look up from her newspaper after I cleared my throat.

"I'm a new hire for—"

"Name?"

"Lola Barnes," I said.

A few clacks of keys and a screeching old printer at work later, and the woman passed me a flimsy cardboard square with a barcode across the bottom. "That'll get you up to your floor, and they'll manage the rest. If you don't have your pass by tomorrow, you can come to the desk for another. You check-in at floor fifty."

I blinked and took the temporary key card, resisting the urge to make the snarky comments hovering on my tongue. I slipped through the turnstile with my pass, tucked the card into my pocket, and headed for the elevators, wincing as I stared at the crowds. The people in the lobby were packing themselves into the carriages like sardines in a can. I may have been early to work for *Designate*, but the rest of the building was filling up quickly.

Just breathe.

I dove onto an elevator at the last second, everyone shifting by tiny increments to make room for me, a briefcase jammed against the back of my left thigh. I held my breath as the door slid shut in front of me and wiggled my hand over to hit the button for the fiftieth floor. I took tiny breaths as the seconds passed until I realized I was in an elevator with no one but other betas and then relaxed. I didn't like being crowded, but the elevator was gradually emptying and I was able to actually slouch against the wall, well out of reach of the last four occupants when we reached the fiftieth floor.

The doors parted and I stepped out, breathing deeply for the first time in minutes. I was alone in the beautiful hall, the heels of my shoes echoing against the marble floor. I turned and watched the elevator doors shut behind me, finally able to admire the incredible Art Deco scrollwork engraved in the polished gold.

I was here. I was at *Designate*, and I was an assistant beauty editor on her first day.

The hall was a soft shade of periwinkle with faux pillar molding accented in cream and gold. Every detail—from the intricate floor tiles grouted in brassy gold, to the swirling crown molding—was pure decadence. Ahead of me, beautiful cherry wood doors with crystal glass panes waited to be parted. One of the elevators ahead of me chimed, and I started forward before I was caught ogling.

And then my feet stalled, the heavy whiffs of sensual masculinity and bright startling champagne filtering out of the elevator. Alphas, two of them, stepped out together, and shock froze me in place. It'd been a long time since I was in close quarters with an alpha, but that wasn't even the only reason I was so startled.

The first of the pair, tall with silver streaks running back from his temples through dark brown hair and crows feet at the corner of his eyes, was Matthieu Segal. *The* Matthieu Segal, CEO of the global media company Voir. Voir owned *Designate* along with a half dozen other major magazines and outlets, and this was the man in charge of all of them. Next to him, dressed in a dapper velvet jacket and wearing shoes that had a trim of gold along the sole, was the exquisitely handsome and polished Cyrus Cohen. Also known as my immediate boss, the Head Beauty Editor of *Designate*.

Cyrus' head twitched in my direction, sunlight glowing on the deep brown of his skin, and I had the urge to dive and hide, but it was too late. He spun to face me, and I tried to force the terrified expression I was no doubt wearing off my face. His eyes narrowed as he took me in, and Matthieu Segal slowed and turned on black polished shoes, staring at me over the high collar of his tan wool coat.

Look at her like this, it's pathetic really.

I shivered, shaking old voices out of my head. I tried to force my steps forward, even as every muscle in my body clenched, desperate to run away.

Matthieu Segal took one step back as I managed one

struggling step forward, and Cyrus's narrow stare suddenly broke into a shining smile.

"You're my new hire aren't you?" he asked, eyes brightening. He glanced at Matthieu. "Told you I needed to be early today."

I forced the barbed wire in my throat down and dipped my head once. "Lola."

"I'm Cyrus, you're in my department." He stepped forward, and my whole body gave a brief flinch until Matthieu's hand landed on his shoulder and held him in place.

"You're David's cousin," Matthieu said, mild voice low and hinting at a French accent smoothed by a long stay in the States. "Welcome to *Designate*."

"Let me show you around," Cyrus said, taking the cue from Matthieu's restraining hand and stepping back to offer me space to walk past them both to the office doors.

I took one steadying breath and forced my feet to move, nearing them both as Matthieu backed up and made more room for me.

"Enjoy your day," he said, gray-blue eyes watching me briefly before turning and jerking his head to Cyrus, encouraging him to walk ahead of me.

What had David told them? He couldn't have said more than he'd known—that I'd gotten myself mixed up with cruel alphas, and afterward had barely been able to bring myself to leave David's apartment for months. But David had promised not to say anything on the topic at all, so maybe Matthieu Segal was just good at reading body language, or maybe I was projecting terror more obviously than I realized.

"You're coming in while we're in the middle of a few projects, which might feel chaotic at first, but I think it'll give you a good picture of the way we work. I saw your video series and I'm excited to have you at the table for our planning sessions," Cyrus said, walking almost sideways toward the office doors.

His excitement was palpable, matching his tipsy scent and

contrasting strongly against Matthieu's more subdued and grounded presence.

"I've been a subscriber of the magazine for as long as I can remember," I said, pushing the muscles of my own face into some semblance of a smile. Both alphas pushed a door open, and I focused on the receptionist at her clean cream desk with the lush bouquets on each corner, rather than their imposing and potent energies on either side of me. "I'm looking forward to being a part of the process."

"Mr. Segal, Ben is upstairs, ready for you. Good morning, Mr. Cohen," the receptionist greeted, a beautiful, young beta with a blue-black bob cut and electric pink lipstick that paired nicely with her pale skin.

"Morning, Daze. This is Lola, my new beauty assistant. Will you get her set up and then bring her over to my wing?" Cyrus asked. I stiffened as my coat shifted, Cyrus' hand landing at the base of my back for a soft beat. "I'll see you in a bit, Lola."

Daze, which was probably some kind of nickname but suited the preternaturally pristine woman, rounded the desk with a beaming smile.

"Let me take your coat, and I'll give you the tour," Daze said.

CYRUS WAS EQUALLY AS exuberant as I reached the beauty department's long row of offices, but this time his energy was absorbed by the three other editorial assistants in the room with me. *Designate*'s beauty-halla, as one of the other assistant editors called it, was the kind of spectacularly compartmentalized, stunningly organized, thoroughly stocked makeup inventory my dreams were made of.

I was trying to follow the line of conversation at the large conference table littered with highlighters and blushes and mascaras and lipsticks and palettes for days. Except my eyes kept drifting to other corners of the room. The canisters of brushes. The fridge of face masks. The turning mirrors with varying levels of magnification.

"It's like going to the toy store when you were a kid, isn't it?" one of my new coworkers asked. *Betty*, I reminded myself, a redhead I was mentally referring to as 'queen of blending' due to her impeccable contouring and perfect smoky eye. She looked a bit like she was waiting for someone to turn a camera in her direction, rather than the person who was planning the photoshoots, but a year and a half ago and I would've been the same if I'd worked here.

"I want to be everywhere at once," I said under my breath. "There are some brands here I've never even seen in person before." And certainly never tried, given how pricey they were.

Betty nodded and grinned gleefully. "And we're the lucky bitches who get to sample it."

"I thought *Designate* was aiming younger," I mentioned. "Can our audience really afford Rubenesque?"

Betty's grin faded to a frown, her brow tangling at me, but Cyrus answered me from the other end of the table.

"Probably not. You're right. It's one of the issues we're struggling with lately. Now that we're cruelty-free, our options are narrowed. We don't get Rubenesque's advertising money if we stop featuring their products, but telling our subscribers that the best powder foundation is sixty bucks a pop isn't winning us a lot of popularity from the leading indie beauty influencers."

"*Designate* is about *high-end* beauty," Zane, our only other male at the table, answered with a roll of his eyes. "High-end is high prices."

Cyrus' lips twitched at me, and one of his shoulders shrugged softly. He had perfect bone structure and a clean-shaven head, and his skin shone just enough to hint at a bit of product, the gloss offset by the faint shadow of a beard over his jaw. His eyes were slanted, almost catlike, eternally teasing, and the table was quiet before I realized our stares were locked together, the pair of us smiling.

Knock it off, idiot, I hissed at myself, jerking in my chair and looking down at the layout on the table, a mock-up of "Products to 'Zest' Up Your Routine" with a theme of citrus names to the colors.

"Do you always do this segment on a white background?" I asked, tapping the mock-up. I knew perfectly well they did, and it'd been a major pet peeve of mine. The hissing voice at the back of my head told me to keep my mouth shut, but for once, I stifled it easily.

"It's the only way to see the colors accurately," Betty said, a little drone in her voice. Apparently, I hadn't impressed her by questioning Rubenesque.

"To see them against white," I said, shrugging. "But a lot of these products are sheer and they're going to interact differently on everyone."

Cyrus' lips pursed and he spun the mock-up to face him. "We've done photoshoots before on skin tone differentiation in looks."

"What if it's not on a model though?" I asked, sitting up. "What if you just split the mock-up into like…four, maybe six quadrants and show it that way." I spun my stool and jumped up, quickly crossing to the foundations and grabbing up a handful. "If you match the sections to Lissie's magic bases that claim to blend so well, then you can add even more product to the feature."

"Going solely Lissie might piss some of our companies off, but we could follow that general premise," Zane said, looking to Cyrus who was watching me with a heavy stare. "Grab the best foundations for each tone range."

I focused on the others, relieved to see no one resented my sudden interruption in the planned mock-up. This was it. This was why I wanted this job. I *had* been a subscriber for years and for at least half that time, I'd had ideas I wanted to share.

"Okay, so we present this to Wendy on Thursday. Get those colors set up stat," Cyrus said, pushing up from his stool. "Zane, you, Lola, and Betty sort out the colors. Keep it simple, try and duplicate across the different shades, make the products as versatile as possible. Corey, Anna, keep on their asses and start planning your new copy. Keep the 'zest' in theme... Oh, and note Lola on the sheerness, that kind of thing. If it looks good, we can make ourselves a new regular layout."

He headed for the door without another look, and Betty clucked her teeth and offered me a reluctant but genuine smile. "Not bad, newbie."

Lola

3

The next day, I finished a soft brush stroke on the thin plexiglass layer covering our warm mid-tone, implying plush lips. It had been a last-minute suggestion of mine before we made our new product-feature mock-up to add a face, and I'd had to demonstrate with a thin black acrylic before anyone really took me seriously.

"Admit it," I said, smiling at Zane. "You thought I was gonna draw the equivalent of an emoji."

Zane snorted, shaking his head and then whipping his long, surfer-blond hair back over his shoulder, folding his arms over his narrow chest. "Just be glad you're earning your keep," he said. "For about a week, Cyrus thought the magazine would just go ahead and cut your position. Wendy still thinks we're over-staffed."

"Wendy thinks the magazine's dried up in general," Betty mumbled from my other side, and Zane hissed at her.

My eyes widened, and I stepped back, letting them step in and make their careful strokes of color and product. "She's the Editor-in-Chief."

"She *loves Designate*," Zane assured me over his shoulder as he twisted a brief smear of vivid, blood-orange lip gloss above my implied pout and then rested the bottle and brush artfully alongside. "The magazine's just had a lot of tension since Segal was hired for Voir."

"Like the cruelty-free change?" I asked.

"No, that was Wendy," Betty said, and I nodded, but neither of them offered to elaborate.

"Okay, I think that actually looks very compelling," Zane said, voice prim. "I'll take the shot. Are you guys getting lunch in the canteen?"

"I'm meeting up with a friend."

Betty hummed. "You go on ahead then, Lola. I'll make sure Zane here eats his green vegetables."

Zane snorted, going to pick up the nice camera and positioning it over our work. I got the distinct impression I was being shooed out of the room so they could continue whatever gossip they'd hinted at in front of me. Which was fine. I had a feeling I'd probably hear all of it before long anyway, and I was more interested in seeing Baby.

I grabbed my coat from Daze—short for Daisy, and probably a better fit for the somewhat spacey but charming receptionist—and headed down to the lobby. Aside from Cyrus, and the brief run-in with Matthieu the day before, I hadn't been in contact with other alphas in the building. And while Cyrus might have had the heavy scent of an alpha, he seemed relatively laid back and from what I could tell, only dealt with us in the group setting. I could live with that. I was determined to.

Baby was bouncing on the balls of her feet in the lobby when I got downstairs, dressed in shredded jeans and an oversized t-shirt that I knew probably reeked of one of her alphas. At her side was the handsome beta, Seth, or 'Bomber' to match the cut of the leather jacket he was wearing. They stood out sharply against all the wool and black and suits of the Stanmore, but they were both so good looking you could almost believe they were models on their way up to *Designate* for a photoshoot—pre-hair and makeup and wardrobe.

Baby held her hands out for me as I exited the turnstiles from the elevators, knowing I wouldn't be comfortable enough for a hug in this crowd. I gripped her outstretched hands in a soft, quick squeeze, and then tucked my hands into my coat, glancing over to smile at Seth to avoid seeing Baby's slight fall in her smile.

"You look so cool and professional right now," Baby said, grinning. "Do you like it? Is it fun? Do you like…is it just like going to the makeup counter together?"

I laughed, remembering the days of going to the department store makeup counters to get our faces done before we went out for the night, back when we didn't have the money to buy all of our products. "Um… It definitely *could* be," I said. "But mostly it's a lot of proofreading each other and playing around digitally editing our mock-ups. Where do you wanna get lunch?"

"Okay, so I know I said fancy, but—"

"But we love our greasy dives," I said, nodding, and Baby beamed at me.

"There's this sort of retro, semi-hidden soda shop nearby with cheese fries that have perfected the ratio of spud to dairy."

"Sign me up! Are you playing bodyguard?" I asked Seth.

"Long as you don't mind," he said, grinning. And I was pretty sure he meant it too, but I wondered what his alphas would have to say if they found he left Baby unchaperoned in the city.

"'Course not. Lead the way," I said.

"I'M JUST REALLY proud of you," Baby said softly, her shoulder brushing against mine.

My stomach was overfull, and it turned dangerously at the innocent contact. Seth was strolling down the sidewalk behind us on our way back to the Stanmore, and Baby was close to my side. I could practically feel her vibrating with the desire to lean in, and a small part of me was just as needy for the touch. I was hardly ever comfortable enough to be touched casually now, and the strange habit of hook-ups on the weekend didn't sate my secret craving for a decent cuddle.

"Thank you," I said, glancing at her and smiling, feeling the weight of her stare, her study.

"Not just about the job," she said.

I nodded. "I know, babe."

"If you're ever up for it, you could come to the Plaza," Baby said, taking my hand as I stiffened, my eyes fixed to the golden doors of the Stanmore. "Super mellow night. Pack only, I promise."

"You're always welcome, and our crew knows how to behave themselves," Seth offered, his hands stuffed into his pockets.

"I'll think about it," I said. It was not happening. Not any time soon, at least. It wasn't just that it was a pack of alphas. The Howlers…they knew too much about me, about…

Buzz and Indy.

I disguised my shiver of disgust by pulling my hands from Baby's and rubbing them together in the cold. We'd finally made it back to the Stanmore, and as much fun as it had been to pig out with Baby—she still made me snort with laughter, still was one of the easiest people to talk to about nothing and everything—I was ready to escape the soft cloud of her perfume, and the way heads turned as we walked together to stare at us, trying to pick out who was the precious omega.

"Gonna get back in there," I said, offering her a smile and bracing myself for what I knew was coming.

Baby teetered, brilliant green eyes wide and hopeful, but she held herself back until I nodded. Then her arms were around my neck, my face full of her sugary and floral-scented hair. My throat was strangled, but I passed my hands over her back in a semblance of a hug as she squeezed me tight.

"I love you so much, Lo."

"I love you a shit ton, babe," I said, making her laugh and release me.

Seth was waiting, gaze warm and fond on Baby, but he spared me a quick, crooked grin before he drew her into his side like he'd clearly been waiting to do the whole time we were together. I wondered if he got very much time with her aside from when their alphas weren't around. Was he always on the fringes, waiting for scraps of affection like the rest of us betas? I waved goodbye and headed upstairs to *Designate*, heading directly for the workroom to see if the others had put the mock-up together while I was on lunch.

Instead of finding the others, I found Cyrus alone in the room, hands braced on the worktable, pages spread out under his focus. I tried to back out the door, but he was already looking up, eyes curling up in the corners with warmth and lips stretching in a smile.

"Lola! Come here," he said, waving me closer and looking back down at the new mockups.

I hesitated, but what kind of excuse could I give him for refusing? I crossed to the table, deciding it was safe to face him with that space between us. Better than moving to his side. He looked up, a slight line digging between his brows as he realized where I was, but it passed and he spun the pages for me to look.

"This is your work. And two days of it too," he said, tone friendly and warm. "It's impressive."

I stared down at the mockups, the clean lines of the six layouts cleverly trimmed to show the overlapping product that worked between one tone and another. My smile grew, fed by the almost giddy scent of Cyrus across from me.

"Is it good?" I asked. I thought so. I liked the subtle difference in my ink sketch faces, and I liked seeing the way the shades from the makeup had varying results from one sample to the next.

"It's our best this year, easily," Cyrus said, leaning in. "And I'm not too proud to admit that this is the kind of concept I should be pushing, not my assistants. You're getting the credit for this."

I was keenly aware of the lingering haze of Baby's perfume hanging over my shoulders and in my hair as Cyrus stared at me. And while his focus was intense, he didn't seem to be showing any of the usual alpha signs of arousal or aggression, signs I knew intimately.

"Good," I said, nodding, and he grinned.

"Good. There's a photoshoot we have planned this Friday, mostly of Zane's arrangement. I'd like it if you came with me and him." My eyes widened, and Cyrus waved a hand between us. "Don't stress about it. I want you to observe, but someone will probably ask you to get a coffee or two."

"That's fine," I rushed to say. Coffee fetching had been more along the lines of what I'd been expecting in my first week, so I wasn't about to act like I was too good for it now.

A magazine shoot. With models and lights and professional makeup artists and the *clothes*. For a moment, in pure excitement, I forgot that I was alone in a room with an alpha I barely knew. A pure laugh, bright and surprising, rose up from my throat as my cheeks stretched and filled in the biggest smile I'd worn in months. When I looked up, Cyrus was at my side, my breath catching and muscles tensing, the laugh dying on my tongue.

"Way to make a splash, Lola," he murmured.

Cyrus was tall, towering over me and making me tilt my head back to look at him. When he reached out to squeeze my elbow, I skirted back, his fingers barely skimming my skin. He was already backing away, heading for the door, and my heels continued to carry me back as my breathing came in soft gasps.

Control, I chanted mentally, stretching the word to match my slowing breaths. Betty had said that Cyrus was perpetually flirtatious but never crossed any line with his employees. A touch on the arm might be overly affectionate for a boss, but he hadn't lingered or squeezed the way my old boss at the restaurant usually did.

"Get your shit together, Lola," I muttered, twisting away from the door and moving to reorganize the products we'd pulled for the mockup.

"AMERICANO FLAT," I said, passing Zane his coffee with a

quick nod, before heading over to the lighted booths where the models were getting their makeup prepped.

The rest of my first week had passed more or less as I'd expected. I learned my way around the photo editing programs we tended to use, practiced writing copy, and did the more basic assistant tasks I'd been prepared for like shipping products we passed on back to the companies. No one had blinked on Friday morning when Cyrus called me with Zane to head to the photoshoot, and I was relieved to see that the beauty editing team wasn't as catty and competitive as Betty said the fashion editors were.

I dropped espressos and non-fat lattes off to a few models who were busy holding still for their artist before taking the last over to our big star of the day—Rakim Oren. There was a massive alpha, taller even than Cyrus and twice as broad, hovering against the wall facing Rakim, but he made no move to stop my approach and kept his ice blue eyes over my head. My hand was shaking slightly as I neared the omega, a heady cloud of chocolate and caramel scented perfume hanging around him. It was a mouthwatering sweetness, airier but possibly even richer than Baby's.

Rakim Oren was one of the most famous and recognizable omegas in the world.

He was stretching in front of the mirror, tan brow furrowed and neck arched as if he was inviting an alpha's bite, his crystalline green gaze glaring at his own reflection in the mirror.

"Honey and soy," I said, resting the coffee cup on the only available inches of the counter, ready to back away.

"Is it just me or does this look crazy uneven?" His voice was smooth and coaxing, more masculine than I'd expected against his innocent, open features. He had dark short hair, curls damp against his forehead, and a dense but close beard.

I glanced down at his shoulder and frowned as I stared at the splotchy, rushed cover-up of foundation on his skin. It looked cakey, the sponge marks probably as clear as whatever they'd been used to cover.

"It's…yikes, yeah."

Rakim sighed and rolled his eyes—eyes that took one look into a camera and made a company hundreds of thousands of dollars. "It's Courtney. I swear she leaves everything to post. Like, we didn't hire a makeup artist so someone could airbrush me invisible in photoshop, Courtney."

My lips twitched, and I was ready to make my escape again when I saw him reach for a foundation that was a shade or more too light for his skin to really blend.

"Not that one," I said.

Rakim Oren's hand froze over the bottle and his eyes slid to mine, a dark brow arching. "That's the one she used."

"And now you're splotchy," I quipped, sighing as his lips curled. I pointed to two of the ignored options. "Blend those together and then powder with the one she chose."

"Do you know what you're doing?" he asked, narrowing his eyes at me.

I looked him over, more objectively. The lights on the mirror were good, but the ones for the shoot were warmer, and makeup was picky in high-resolution. Courtney, whichever of the women dressed in black that was flitting around the room, was right that touch-ups could be covered in the post-editing, but Rakim was right that it could also be done correctly beforehand.

"I do," I said, nodding.

"Okay then, you do it," he said, relaxing back into his seat.

"Oh! No, I didn't mean. I can't—"

"Cy!" Rakim called over his shoulder, and I stiffened as Cyrus looked up from his tablet and crossed to us.

"What's up, hun?" Cyrus asked, his alpha instincts making him stand taller and broader in front of the omega.

"Who is this lovely creature, and can she do my makeup that Courtney has attempted with the subtlety of an axe when a butter knife was called for?"

I snorted and choked on my stifled laugh as Cyrus just

gave Rakim an indulgent smile. "This is Lola, our new girl," he said warmly. "And she certainly can't do worse."

Cyrus gave me a brief, warning glance. Not unfriendly, but more like 'I vouched for you, so don't fuck it up.' The big alpha, the one who was dressed all in black and I was pretty sure was wearing a holster under his tailored black jacket, had moved a little farther away and was watching but without suspicion.

"Fix me, Lola," Rakim said, sweetening my name into a long rounded plea.

Cyrus was already returning to his corner of the room, calling over his shoulder, "Ten minutes."

Fuck. Ten minutes gave me no room to hesitate.

I lunged and grabbed up the supplies, and Rakim grinned and settled deeper in his chair, letting his head fall back to expose his throat and shoulders to me, his thighs spread open in front of him. Courtney had done a good job on his face at least, getting the dewy, fresh look that'd been assigned to the shoot, so all I had to do was correct her coverup on the omega's shoulder. His outfit was hanging up at the corner of the booth and there wasn't a shirt for the look, just a jacket and a patterned scarf and slacks. It wasn't until I had my foundation choice mixed and was stepping up close, that I realized the need for the coverup in the first place.

This wasn't a tattoo cover. Rakim Oren had a bondmark.

"Oh."

"Yeah, it's like, not a secret, but since no one wants bondmarks in shoots, it's not general public knowledge either," Rakim supplied.

I pressed my lips together and grabbed a wipe, erasing Courtney's clumsy work, revealing the shining crescents of the bite. I picked up a new sponge and set to my own work, using long smooth strokes to follow the line of his musculature, instead of the usual pressing dabs. It left more room for error generally, but also allowed for natural shadow. The ridges of the scar might catch some light or shadow, but that would be easier to photoshop out than bad coloring. When I moved to repeat the process on the other shoulder he raised his eyebrows.

"So they match. It's close, but nothing will ever be one-hundred percent perfect," I said, concentrating on being even.

Someone called five minutes in the room, and I grabbed a brush to blend and then powder, picking up a quick bronzer and highlight at the last moment and using it to soften the last line where I ended my work.

"You *do* know what you're doing."

"I used to do a lot of live video tutorials. No photoshopping in post," I said, smiling.

Rakim's stare was an almost tangible pressure on my skin, and my lungs were full of his perfume, the scent growing stronger with every minute passing.

"You didn't want to be a makeup artist?" he asked.

I did, kind of. I also wanted to work at *Designate* and study and influence new trends. Mostly though, I hadn't worked in a year, and I was happy to just be back in the world that I loved.

"Apparently, I can be both," I said instead, catching his glittering smile. "All done."

At the same moment, one of the assistants called for Rakim to be dressed.

"Thanks, Lola," he said as I dropped poor Courtney's supplies back to the counter and left to join Cyrus and Zane.

I flashed him a quick smile and then ducked out of the way of the fuming brunette whose work I suspected I'd just corrected.

"Show off," Zane muttered as I reached him, the snap in the tone balancing perfectly between irritation and teasing.

Cyrus just winked at me and returned to watching the room in its busy work.

Lola

4

The photoshoot went late, and while Cyrus told both Zane and I that we could head out whenever we wanted, Zane didn't budge, and neither did I. It was somehow both dull and thrilling to watch. A lot of time was spent waiting, rechecking, retouching, reorganizing, and then the room would work twice as fast to compensate.

Rakim was done early, escorted out by his giant of an alpha security guard, the privilege of being the star of our models for the day. I wondered briefly if the alpha security was actually Rakim's bonded alpha, but dismissed it quickly. The big guy was too professional and showed none of the usual hovering and possessive alpha behaviors. Another sickly sweet omega female was early to leave, and I wasn't surprised it was the beta models who were called to stay late. Kind of typical.

Cyrus parted ways with us when we finally left the room after eleven, and Zane grabbed his coat and headed for the elevator as I went to grab my purse.

"It's club night!" he said, shimmying his shoulders at me as I headed for our group office.

I debated briefly asking him to wait, joining him for the night. Except that would expose my habit, and even if Zane was after the same thing—a temporary hook-up for the night—there was something vulnerable about letting someone else see that side of myself. Plus, I was still a little shaken from my last attempt.

I was alone in the elevator on my way down, when it stopped two floors below mine, doors parting.

Oh god, please no.

As if I'd conjured him by thought, standing in front of me was the handsome beta whom I'd run from just days ago. He was stepping inside the elevator, facing me directly, even as his eyes grew wide with shock and recognition.

"You—" he gasped before he was cut off.

"Lola!" Cyrus was at the beta's back, and the only possible worse thing than ending up in an elevator with this beta for fifty floors was the new reality of the four men entering the carriage.

I would be in this elevator with my handsome stranger beta, my boss, *his* boss Matthieu, and another unfamiliar alpha. Already my heart was pounding, knees buckling, and I slid toward the corner, my arms folding around my stomach protectively. Cyrus was speaking to me, or speaking about me, but all I could hear was rushing, gusting wind—no, my pounding pulse. My lungs were frozen, refusing to take a breath, and the unfamiliar alpha—tall and blonde and classically handsome—brushed against my shoulder, making me shudder and press against the wall.

Suddenly the sound of the elevator was crisp again, Cyrus' honeyed tone falling to silence as four pairs of eyes fixed to my trembling form.

"Lola?"

The beta's hand raised and stopped Cyrus from stepping closer at the same time Matthieu's did.

"Give her space," the beta said. The alpha who'd brushed against me backed away with the others to the opposite wall.

Hold her down. I tried to swallow down the tangled trap of memories rising up.

A high-pitched ringing in my head burned in my ears and then settled, revealing the soft, low whine vibrating in my throat. The elevator was cloying and heavy with alpha scents—sticky champagne and smooth velvet warmth and something heavy and sweet.

"Lola," the beta whispered, stepping between me and the alphas.

"Leo," the blonde alpha warned in a gentle tone but stopped as the beta's hand went up to quiet him.

"You're all right," the beta said softly.

"Look at her, fuckin' desperate for that knot isn't she?" he hissed, laughing as he watched Indy push my thighs back and open until I cried out at the pain of the stretch.

"She's gonna fuckin' scream for it? Aren't you, Showgirl?"

I swallowed, turned away from the men in the elevator, darkness flickering over my gaze, and pressed one hand to the polished gold interior of the elevator, trying to brace myself against their voices, Buzz and Indy. The alphas who'd toyed with me for weeks before I'd run from them. My own reflection was clear in the metal, wide-eyed and shaking, the warped shadows of the men at my back twisting on gold.

Be normal. Control. Get your shit together, you fucking idiot. I swallowed my next whimper, fixing my gaze to the corner of the floor where I couldn't see any of the men out of the corner of my eyes or in the reflection.

Again, darkness flickered, but this time I realized it wasn't my memories or my panic attack.

"Oh Jesus, not now," muttered one of the men.

It was the fucking power in the building.

The elevator jerked, and my already weak knees gave up. I slid to the floor as the lights flashed and the elevator stopped.

I whimpered against the bare pillow, rocking my hips back as if I could force Buzz deeper.

"You think you get my knot? You think you deserve that? You're a fuckin' beta, Lo," he laughed, skirting back from me. "God, look at you, tryin' to bare your fuckin' throat for me. Don't think so, babe. You're just ass."

"Lola, take a deep breath for me."

"Open wide, bitch, that's it."

The small space was full of burnt marshmallow and pine

sap, and I gagged, jerking as a warm hand brushed over the back of my neck.

"It's just me," the beta, Leo, murmured. "You're safe."

"Oh no. You're not getting away. You wanted a knot, you're fucking getting one."

Breathe. Breathe, idiot. But I couldn't, all the air had gone out of the space and I was surrounded by alphas, no matter what Leo said about being safe. I clawed at the smooth tile of the floor, another thin whine squeezing out from behind my clench teeth.

"Caleb."

"I don't think I sh—"

"Caleb," Leo repeated, voice sharper.

Fingers bruising around my wrists. Teeth snapping and grinding and pinching skin, but never biting. The horrible pressure of their smells and their bodies. Hadn't it been sweet for a few days? When had it stopped feeling good?

I thrashed as I was pulled into a pair arms, one hand digging—

—Pulling hard at my hair as I sobbed—

And tucking my head against a warm throat.

A hand clamped over my nose and mouth, muffling my voice until I couldn't even breathe.

Gentle warmth coated my throat like syrup as that dense, soft scent turned me limp and languid...

Trying to catch my breath on the lumpy bed, tears and spit wetting the sheet beneath my cheek. It was time to go, wasn't it?

"You're mine now, Showgirl."

I WOKE, my head pounding, my body aching like I'd strained every muscle all at once, and there was the beta.

They called him Leo.

"You're safe," he said immediately, rising up just slightly to hide the figures behind him. "They just got the elevator down to the first floor, and the doors are about to open."

I leaned forward, thoughts foggy, and didn't try to fight him as he helped me to stand. I wasn't doing it on my own. Not after an attack like that, that was for sure.

I knew they were watching, the alphas. I swallowed my moan at the understanding. Cyrus Cohen and Matthieu Segal had watched me *completely lose my shit*. Or had heard it. I wasn't sure if the blackness from the power outage had persisted or if that had been part of the panic attack.

"You're safe," Leo whispered again, a thick arm holding me close to his side.

I wasn't wearing my heels, and my head drooped to glance down at the floor.

"I have them," Leo said, showing me my shoes linked in his fingers. "I'm going to walk you out."

"There's a car waiting." Matthieu's voice, his accent sharper now, stopped abruptly as I flinched.

"I'm going to walk you to the car, and I'd like to make sure you get home safe," Leo said. "That's up to you, though. Is that all right?"

The doors opened, and to complete my humiliation, Rakim Oren and his massive security guard were there waiting in the lobby.

"I love this old building, but I hate this old build—Lola?" Rakim stepped forward, and Leo ushered me around him, my stocking feet sliding along the smooth floor.

"Rake, hold up," Cyrus said, a firm and heavy weight in his voice I'd never heard before.

I could barely keep my head up, and it was easier to let it drop and avoid the throbbing, pulsing shine of the chandelier lights of the lobby.

"You want your shoes, or you want me to carry you?" Leo asked. There was something so sweet and careful in his tone that made me feel twice as vulnerable. I held out a weak hand, but instead he bent, those large familiar hands maneuvering me into my heels as I balanced against his shoulder.

"What happened? Is she okay? Are you okay?" Rakim whispered to the others. Suddenly, it clicked.

Leo's bite. Rakim's. These men were a pack. Not just a pack, but the kind of fairy tale arrangement of handsome and wealthy alphas I'd imagined as a little girl. Men in black limos who showered gifts over their omegas, who took trips around the world and drank champagne and dressed to impress. The kind of men I'd trimmed out of magazines and pasted into my school notebooks so I'd have something to distract me from my algebra.

Leo caught me against his side as I wavered, my embarrassment thick and thorough, shame rushing up my cheeks.

God, I hoped I was fired. Or maybe I would just ensure it, by *never facing these men again*.

"One more minute, Lola," Leo coaxed, all but carrying me through the lobby and out the doors.

The car Matthieu promised was waiting, a sleek and simple town car—a bit longer and grander than the kind David used—and I fell into the back seat, sliding over to make room for Leo, who paused in the frame of the open door.

"You'll let me come with you?" he asked.

My blink was slow and drowsy, my nod heavy, and he sighed and slid in after me. There was a patient pause before I realized I needed to give the driver my address, and I slurred it out.

"You're okay," Leo said, reaching slowly to me.

I was too tired, too defeated to move, and when his hand cupped my cheek, thumb brushing through a wet track of tears, I leaned into the touch instead of pulling away. He drew me into his chest and I collapsed with something that was too ashamed to be gratitude. More like acceptance. I needed to be held, whether I wanted it or not. Leo might've been claimed by an alpha, but at least he *wasn't* an alpha.

"You're okay. You're safe," he murmured.

I might've been safe. I definitely wasn't okay.

I was ruined.

I WOKE IN THE NIGHT, head still aching but no longer foggy, and stared at the figure I was pressed flush against. I was vaguely aware of coming back to my apartment, of Leo carrying me up the three flights of stairs. I couldn't remember if I asked him to come inside or if he'd offered.

He'd left the light in the hall on, the door to my bedroom partly open so the room wasn't dark.

We were both still dressed. He hadn't even touched my tights or the vest I wore buttoned over my blouse. His skin smelled like fresh laundry, but when I ducked my head I realized his shirt had that heavy, comforting smell. It was from his alpha, the blonde I hadn't recognized. The one I was pretty sure had bundled me up just before I'd fallen unconscious, taking the painful edge off the panic attack.

I slid out from between Leo and the wall of my tiny bedroom and headed for the bathroom, washing my face and finding an abandoned t-shirt and sleep shorts to change into. When I returned to the bedroom, Leo was still there, eyes squinting and blinking slowly.

"You don't have to stay if you don't want to," I whispered.

"I'd like to stay, but it's up to you," he answered, pushing up on one elbow.

I hadn't slept next to someone since…since I'd started up with Buzz and he'd still been pretending to be sweet. There was a big difference between hooking up with a nameless Leo in a club bathroom and lying next to him all night.

But I knew what I needed, and for once I listened to the impulse.

I slid onto the bed and accepted Leo's open arms as an invitation to return to where I'd been cuddled up against his chest. His sigh warmed the top of my head, and I tugged one of the abandoned blankets to cover my bare legs.

"Will your pack mind?" I asked, testing my theory about who those men were to each other.

"My pack is all very glad to know I didn't leave you alone tonight," Leo said, one hand stroking my back.

I fiddled with one of the open buttonholes of his shirt, my

body confused between the tension of lying next to someone, of being held, and the exhaustion still lingering at the edges.

"I'm sorry for running," I said.

"I understand, Lola," Leo said. "Believe me."

I nodded. I believed him. He knew exactly how to handle my panic attack, did his best to help me fight it, and then had perfectly managed the aftermath. Which meant he was probably familiar with the process.

"Just rest," he coaxed. "If you're up for it, we'll talk in the morning."

My throat tightened briefly, and Leo's touch soothed me through the sudden bout of tension until I was curling closer. While he was here, I was going to soak up the comfort in a way I hadn't allowed myself to do before. I was going to pretend I was just cuddling a guy. Just normal.

WES

5

The first time I saw Lola, she was sitting in a dark doorway at the crack of dawn, in the diciest area of Old Uptown. She was in front of an old rundown building that still had it's 'MOTEL' sign hanging, now dark with only the 'No Vacancy' neon lit beneath. There was what looked like a dive bar on the first floor, with a few beer brand signs hanging in the windows. Lola was there, shivering, pale skin peeking out of a slit in the knee of her dark jeans, and she had a grease mark on the elbow of her thin, long-sleeved shirt. Vivid purple hair was piled into a tangle on the top of her head, and there were dark circles under eyes and bruises on her chin and throat. She was visibly trembling in the cold, and I turned the heat up to high as I drove up to the building, trying to warm the car for her.

"She says she'll be waiting on the sidewalk for you. But Wes, whatever happens, please don't leave without her in the car."

The old motel looked deserted, with crooked blinds hanging in the windows above and black paint covering half of the large bar windows. Lola's eyes didn't even blink as I pulled the car to the curb, her stare vacant and dazed. I glanced at the dark windows of the building. It didn't look like anyone was up if they were inside, and it didn't look like anyone was around to stop me taking this girl somewhere safe, but I pulled my handgun from its case and tucked it into my holster just in case. Favors for friends—like this errand was for David—didn't usually call for firearms, but one look at the girl crumpled in the doorway, and I was prepared to push back if anyone gave me any trouble.

Lola twitched as I stepped onto the sidewalk, shrinking back into the shadow of the doorway, her head lowering submissively.

"David sent me."

"Oh. Right." Her words were slow but not slurred. I reached out a hand to help her up and she shrank away, pulling herself up by clinging to the grimy archway.

She reeked of alpha, and I tucked my hands behind my back as they fisted impulsively. The scents on her were harsh and sticky and sweet, and there were too many to pin down. I backed away from her, giving her room to walk in her heavy slouch, and opened the back seat door for her. She slid in and I saw the red scratch marks over a bite shaped bruise on her throat, my stomach turning queasily as I stared at the discolored but unbroken skin.

I was tempted, briefly, to lock her in the car and break down the doors so I could hunt down every single one of those filthy scents. But that would get messy, and I didn't have any backup. I didn't know what I'd be walking into, either. Instead, I shut the door behind her as gently as I could and headed for the driver's seat.

Lola was directly behind me, pressed to the door, her forehead against the glass with her back to the motel.

"There's water, if you need it," I said, tipping my rearview mirror just a bit so I could see her on the bench seat behind me as pulled back into traffic.

Take her to the police station, I thought. *Or the hospital.*

I could tell David where to meet us. Maybe not the police station though. She deserved to make that choice and not have someone haul her there. I glanced at the mirror when she was silent. She was still shivering and I realized she was probably in some form of shock. Shit. What did I have?

We pulled to a stop at a red light, and I glanced down to the passenger seat floor where my 'go bag' was waiting for unexpected trips with Rake or for work. I leaned and tugged the zipper open, fishing out a black sweatshirt and draping it over the side of the passenger seat.

"Cold?"

Lola looked at the fabric as I started to drive again, her stare empty. Just when I thought of pulling over, bundling her into the sweater, cracking open a bottle of water, and tipping it to her bitten lips, Lola reached a hand out and dragged my sweater to her lap and then up to her nose. I released a silent sigh as she took a deep breath and then dove under the hem of the sweatshirt until it swallowed her completely, messy purple hair reappearing through the neck.

Her arms wrapped around her middle, fingers just peeking out of my sleeves, and someone behind me honked. I'd taken my foot off the gas.

Focus, buddy, I reminded myself. I wasn't any good to this girl if I got us into a car accident.

"Where are we going?" Her voice made my fingers clench around the steering wheel, warm and quiet and a little raspy.

I blinked hard, clearing my head and telling my hindbrain to go fuck itself, *now was not the time*.

"Your cousin David asked me to take you to his apartment," I said.

Her head drooped against the window again and I listened to her rustling into a tight ball in the seat, and then the quiet crack of plastic as she opened a water bottle. Good. I stared hard at the brake lights of the cars ahead of me as Lola gulped down water and sat in continued silence for the rest of the ride.

Give me their names, I thought to the young woman in my backseat. I could turn the car around after getting her to David, maybe call up a few of my guys who wouldn't mind helping me out with a side project like this one.

But what if she went back? They did sometimes. My own mother had, plenty of times. In that case, Lola might be better off without my interference. Not in the long run, but… I could keep an eye out for her.

The drive ended, and somehow I didn't feel ready. Lola

was though. She'd gotten antsy in the last few minutes, as if the shock she'd been suffering was fading and she was realizing that she was alone in a car with an alpha she didn't know.

I frowned as I parked and Lola squirmed out of my sweatshirt.

"Hang onto it," I offered, like a fool.

"No. I…I don't have any money to tip you," she said, dropping my sweatshirt to the seat and frowning at her own empty hands.

She thought I was a cab service.

"It's covered," I said, so she didn't worry.

She nodded and exited the back of my car, heading for the front doors of David's apartment without a glance backward. I watched her from the curb until she stepped into the elevator, and then fished my sweatshirt from the backseat. I wasn't sure if I wanted to save it, or burn it.

I STARED out the lobby doors as Leo followed Lola into the back of Matthieu's hired car. She'd been fine earlier, and it'd been good to see her again after all this time, as if she were more to me than a random favor to a friend. I didn't care that she didn't remember me; the less she remembered about those assholes who hurt her, the better. She was blonde now, still beautiful. While I'd watched her with Rake during the photoshoot, I thought she'd seemed…well, like whatever had happened to her hadn't left deep scars.

Now I knew that wasn't true, and I regretted deciding to let her go and not burning down that hell hole where I'd found her when I had the chance.

"What happened?" Rake repeated. "Is she claustrophobic?"

"Maybe," Cyrus said slowly, his own stare fixed on the dark car pulling away.

"She's scared of alphas," Matthieu answered. His jaw was

a hard line, lips pursed, and I suspected he'd known that much about Lola even before the elevator had broken down. "I suppose the power outage didn't help," he added, and Caleb hummed with agreement.

"Leo will make sure she gets home safely," Caleb said.

I would've offered to do it myself. I'd done it before, but Rake and the others would have questions, and I'd never told them about my quick errand for David. When he called in a favor with Matthieu and Cyrus for his cousin, I'd wondered if it was Lola.

"I wanted to ask her to be my new Courtney," Rake mused. "My Courtney upgrade. I think I still will."

"Come on. Let's get to the car," I said, wondering if it would do Lola any good to get tangled up with the members of my pack. If it would do *me* any good, when the stunning beta was rightfully terrified of alphas.

Lola

6

one, I thought, staring at the dent of the pillow the next morning. And then a cupboard door clicked quietly shut in the kitchen. My eyebrows bounced up. *Not gone.*

Leo was in my kitchen.

I stayed in bed, debating whether I was brave enough to face him after the humiliating reality of the night before, or if I could wait long enough and he might leave without making me face that talk he'd offered.

Except with the sounds, came smells.

Curiosity conquered cowardice, and I padded out of my bedroom. On my small breakfast nook table—the only table for dining that could fit in my tiny apartment—sat a coiled up black leather belt and silken tie stacked neatly together.

Leo had his back to me as I entered the kitchen, his white shirtsleeves rolled up tan arms as he poured batter into a waffle iron. Which was weird because…

"I don't own a waffle maker."

"You…*didn't*," Leo said slowly, glancing over his shoulder with innocent, wide eyes. He was still wearing his white button-down, the buttons generously open to the middle of his chest, revealing tan skin and dark hair, neatly trimmed.

I also definitely hadn't had fresh strawberries or heavy cream or the coffee that was brewing in the machine or the sausages cooking in the skillet. The skillet was at least mine.

"I may have made an order while you were sleeping," Leo said, shrugging his shoulder. "But I had a craving."

A craving that couldn't wait for takeout?

He closed the waffle maker and turned to face me, leaning against the fridge. "So, first I should explain," he said.

My eyebrows bounced in surprise. I was pretty sure, of the two of us, I was the one who needed to do some explaining.

"When you and I…met, at the club," he started. "I meant what I said, that I don't usually, um…rush into situations like that."

"Because you have a pack," I said.

Leo's eyes flicked up to the ceiling, head shaking back and forth. "Yes. Well, yes and no. I am bonded to an alpha. I have a pack. We just aren't…most of us aren't really exclusive to the pack. I, *personally*, just tend not to be in much of a rush. But you…you are very compelling." He gave me a sheepish smile with those perfect deep dimples, his five o'clock shadow now firmly entering the denser territory.

I frowned and stepped forward into the kitchen as Leo turned back to the waffle maker, spinning it on it's stand to grill evenly.

"I think I knew that there are packmates that maybe aren't bonded, but I've never heard of bonded mates being…"

"Open? Yeah, I suppose it's not common, but it works for us at the moment. We're very devoted to one another, bonds or not. But for some of us, our sexual affairs extend outside of the pack. Caleb, my alpha, would never question me if you and I had had sex that night. I love him, he loves me, but his bondmark is just a visible part of our connection. It isn't a warning to others or a leash to keep me in line." With that, Leo's eyes found mine, trying to read something from my still expression.

"Okay," I said.

That doesn't mean he doesn't own you. It doesn't mean he wouldn't be angry with me for sleeping with you, I thought. Maybe he wouldn't show it right away. Buzz had seemed…not affectionate, but not cruel at first either.

Leo sighed, even though I hadn't said another word. "The sausages are probably done. Do you like sausage? These are chicken."

I rarely ate breakfast anymore, and if I did it was usually just something carb-y from wherever I stopped to get coffee, but I wasn't turning down this feast. I divided the sausages in the skillet between two plates as Leo pulled the golden waffle from the iron and cut it in half before starting a second.

"I…" I hesitated over my plate, a smile flickering as Leo loaded my half of the waffle with strawberry slices and a thick spoonful of whipped cream. Huh. I didn't own a hand-mixer either, but there was one in my sink now. I shook my head to clear it and looked up at Leo. "Yesterday, it caught me off guard to see you. But I also…I have a hard time being in close quarters with alphas."

Leo's gaze was steady on mine, flicking down briefly to watch me bring a bite of waffle up to my lips. His lips stretched as I let out an involuntary hum of pleasure as caramelized sugar and fresh fruit and dense cream sang together in harmony on my tongue.

"And the power fritz didn't help," Leo said, and I nodded. "How's it been working with Cyrus? He's so used to being infectious and impressive, I guarantee he hadn't noticed you were uncomfortable until last night."

"It was all right, though," I said, lifting my chin, my tongue flicking out to catch cream at the corner of my mouth. Leo's stare tracked the movement, and I marveled at the slight widening of his pupils. "He hasn't been aggressive or anything."

Shock flashed over Leo's face, eyes widening, before vanishing quickly. "He wouldn't," he said. "Cyrus isn't…well, let's just say if he wanted to be aggressive, he'd get your permission first. They're…my pack's not like that, Lola, I promise."

I shrugged and turned away, crossing to my small counter

that separated my minuscule kitchen from my marginally larger living room. "It makes sense, if they already have their omega," I said.

I pushed myself up onto the counter with one hand and had another bite of food as Leo studied my bare legs with an absent interest.

"I understand why you'd be wary," Leo said. "I've had my own negative experiences with alphas. It was part of why I opened Philia."

I was sitting on my counter, a bite of waffle dripping cream hovering halfway to my open mouth, when his words sank in. "*You* opened Philia? Oh my god, that's why you asked if I was looking for you specifically?"

Leo blushed and crossed the open space between us, his hip pressing to my knee. He set his plate down and pushed it aside, his hands coming down slowly over my thighs. "I own the club and…I'm a partner in a real-estate firm. I thought for a second maybe you knew who I was. Rake and I have had issues in the past with people kind of tracking us down… wanting a way into our pack."

I coughed at the thought and then pushed my own plate aside. I looked at Leo and raised an eyebrow.

"I'm guessing you'd believe me now if I said that was definitely not the case?"

Leo smirked, and I watched the shift of his mouth with growing interest. "I believed you before. But yes, I can see now how unlikely that would be. I do have a question for you though," he said.

I was busy drinking him in by sunlight, the slight wave in his rich black hair and the soft dent beneath his full lower lip. I nodded for him to continue.

"Is my pack going to be an obstacle if I want to see you again?" he asked.

His fingers on my thighs gave the faintest encouragement to open, so light I could've ignored the suggestion without any effort. I parted them slowly, and Leo filled the space until the sensitive skin of my legs was bracing against the soft fabric of his pants.

His question sank in slowly, and I found myself tensing slightly as I gave it thought. Could I get involved with a man who was bonded to an alpha? Sure, I was already in regular contact with one alpha from his pack, but that was a simple arrangement. Cyrus was my boss, there was no question that in our relationship, he held the power. What kind of demands could Leo's alpha make on me if I was in a relationship with the beta?

Leo was patient, he didn't push or speak a word while I thought, but he raised one hand from my leg and brushed his fingertips up my jaw. My eyelids fell shut and I leaned into the touch. God, I hadn't realized how totally touch starved I was until this morning.

"I…"

I needed to say 'no,' to put myself squarely out of reach of this pack, even if that did make it impossible between Leo and I. Since when did I really want a relationship, anyway? I had my weekend hookup habit for a reason.

Except that reason was that I didn't want anyone to see what a complete disaster I was, and Leo had already witnessed that for himself. What was he even still doing here?

"They won't touch me?" I asked. What was I doing? Leo couldn't promise that to me, not if his alpha didn't want him to.

"No one is going to touch you without your express interest, Lola," Leo said, his voice taking on a rough edge. My eyes opened and found a deep groove between Leo's eyebrows, his jaw ticking. "I know you don't know them. You don't really know me. But I can promise you not one of my pack would ever disregard your comfort or consent."

"This would just be between us?" I asked in a whisper, my eyes burning.

He dipped his head, gaze holding mine. "Just us."

I sighed out, breath trembling. I wanted this. I wanted someone to *see* me.

You're going to shatter this time.

I leaned in and Leo was there, his nose grazing against mine, foreheads touching. For a moment, we just breathed together. I hadn't had anything but brief club quickies for a year, no hesitation and no lingering. My whole body felt like a raw nerve waiting for a blow to hit and to prove that snarling version of my mother's voice in my head right. Leo waited, one sticky thumb stroking the inside of my thigh, his other hand cupping my neck gently.

I tipped my head back and our mouths slid smoothly together, soft puzzle pieces shifting closer and blending sweet, brief movements into a slow series of kisses. There was fruit and cream and sugar on our lips, and a little taste of mint on his tongue as it swept against the seam of my mouth and then retreated again. His hand on my thigh shifted to the back of my hip, pulling me to the edge of the counter until we were flush from chest to hips. I slid my arms over his shoulders and crossed my legs behind his back, waiting and curious to see if the mood would escalate.

Leo hummed into the kiss, and I thought I could feel him stirring with arousal against the thin material of my sleep shorts, but neither of us took it any further than the decadent, drugging kisses. Gradually, kissing turned back into breathing, and I turned my head to feel his stubble scuff against my cheek.

"Are you sure?" I asked.

"Hm? Which part?" His voice was rough and low, and it sent a light shiver down my back and warmth pooling in my core.

About me, I thought.

"That this is okay," I said instead.

Leo huffed, and his breath raised goosebumps on my neck. "I'm sure. More than. We'll take it slow."

I nodded. Slow was good. Slow gave plenty of time for warning.

I HAD LEO'S NUMBER–ALONG with a waffle maker, which I hadn't really settled on how to process—when he left that afternoon. I also had a serious case of beard burn on my lips and neck, and a frustratingly stubborn case of arousal.

My phone rang while I was in the bath, trying and failing to—ahem—handle the arousal issue on my own. I huffed and sagged in the cooling water. I should've talked Leo into fingering me again. He almost kind of owed me one anyway, since the last orgasm had been spoiled when I freaked out at the sight of his bondmark.

I gave up on my 'relaxing' bath and wrapped myself up in my fluffy robe, rushing to my bedroom to catch the call before it dropped.

"David!"

"Are you all right?"

I gaped at my empty bedroom. "I…" Was David somehow suddenly aware of my inability to get myself off? And if so *why?* And how fucking *awful*.

"I spoke to Cyrus."

"Oh. God, really?" I grumbled and curled up on the foot of my bed, glancing at the still dented pillow where Leo had slept. I flopped down into the spot and rolled my face into the mattress, breathing in his clean smell and maybe huffing that warm alpha tone too. Just a little. It was harmless if I never intended to have any contact with him, right? "I'm okay," I mumbled, still holding the phone to my ear.

"Don't be embarrassed."

"Too late. My boss called my cousin—who got me my *job*—to tell him I had a panic attack."

"Actually…I called him. I just wanted to see how you were—"

"Oh my god, *David*," I whined, squeezing my eyes shut as if that could prevent me from dying of embarrassment.

"He said you'd already made yourself invaluable. That you'd probably just entirely reshaped one of the department's regular layouts *and* you stood out for the team at a photo-shoot," David said.

That shut me up at least.

"It wasn't until I was ready to hang up that he mentioned the elevator shutting down and…everything. He said Leo got you home okay though?"

"You know Leo?"

"I know them all. Mostly Cyrus and Rake and Matthieu, but I've met them all. Lola, you're okay?"

"Yes. Yes, I'm okay. I'm debating coming down with the stomach flu—"

"Please don't do that."

"—but I am actually…fine." I rolled over in the bed and blinked up at the crack in my ceiling when I realized I was telling the truth. I'd had panic attacks while still staying with David and barely left my bed for three days. "It wasn't actually being in the elevator with them. I was just surprised, and then the dark…"

"They're…they're a good pack, Lola. I wouldn't have gotten you that job working for Cyrus if I didn't trust him completely. And I was right anyway, he speaks very highly of you."

I actually smiled at that. "I did have a really good first week, panic attack notwithstanding."

"Come over for lunch tomorrow and we'll celebrate it. Or commiserate."

"Deal."

I hung up lighter and a little relieved. Cyrus had led with everything I'd done well this week instead of my meltdown. That was a good sign, right?

My phone chimed in my hand, and I lifted it to see an alert for a text that must've come in while I was still in the bath.

UNKNOWN - 6:46
missin u

I frowned at the screen, and swiped open the text, not sure what I was expecting to find. There was nothing else but the message, and no clue whom it was sent from. Cool dread trickled down my spine and I forced it away.

It wasn't… It wouldn't be from them. Buzz was dead. Indy was gone. They'd let me walk out of their clubhouse.

And 'missin u' definitely didn't seem like the kind of sentiment I'd have gotten from either of them. Maybe if the creepy anonymous message was 'you dumb bitch' I would worry, but this was probably some kind of weird baiting bot. I deleted it and pushed my phone face down on my bed.

Maybe my bath couldn't relieve my tension, but I was pretty sure if I could find my batteries, I knew what would do the trick.

Lola

7

I considered calling in sick on Monday, just to avoid running into Cyrus or Matthieu or…anyone really. Even after David's call, I was flushing red every time I thought about collapsing in the dark elevator, whimpering and whining like a pathetic creature waiting to be kicked.

Downside number one to agreeing to testing the waters with Leo was that he could tell my boss I'd been well enough to text him a picture of waffles—I was experimenting—the night before.

Instead of wallowing at home, I decided the best armor I could wear was a good face of makeup and a fierce outfit.

I had my shit together.

I was living on my own again.

I had my dream job, even if it was a little bit gifted to me. That was okay because I *was* earning it.

Cyrus wasn't even in the group office when I arrived in my dagger heeled boots and crimson red wrap dress, but I got an approving chin dip from Zane and an 'ooo' of excitement from the girls.

"Guess what makeup artist got booted from Rakim Oren's fashion week entourage?" Zane asked me as I took my own seat at the long table.

My eyes widened. "Wait. Courtney?"

"Courtney," Zane said, waggling his eyebrows at me.

"Way to go, *killer*," Betty said.

My lips twisted to fight my smile. "Okay, I do feel bad though."

"Don't, she'd been with him for years and she was getting lazy. There's no room for error on a fashion week catwalk anyway," Anna said with a wave of her hand. Anna reminded me of myself a year ago. She had highlighter yellow hair, and today she was wearing a vintage, sequined green jumpsuit that clashed with her vivid red eye makeup. Looking at her in all her technicolor glory, I missed my own purple locks.

There was a rap on the door, and I was still smiling when I saw Cyrus hovering there. My smile froze for a beat as his eyes met mine, and I might've imagined the flinch on his face for how quickly it disappeared, but it made my gut freeze all the same.

"We've got a quick meeting in Wendy's office," Cyrus said.

"Oh god, Lola, thank fuck you look decent today," Betty blurted out as the whole team scrambled out of their chairs.

"Delicate as ever, Betty," Cyrus muttered, but this time when he looked at me there was genuine humor and friendliness.

Maybe I had imagined the flinch, or maybe Cyrus was disgusted by my show of weakness, or maybe he was pissed that I was getting involved with his pack. The evidence was gone now, though, and he took the lead of our group with his back to me as we marched to the elevators and rode them up to Wendy's office. He did keep everyone else between us in the elevator ride though.

Quit overthinking it, idiot. Be professional.

Wendy Thurman was every bit as polished and perfect as anyone might imagine a fashion and beauty editor to be. She was tall, statuesque, with deep honey-colored skin and pin straight salt and pepper hair down to her waist. She was wearing high waisted pants, her hands plunged into the deep pockets, and a romantically tailored rose-colored blouse. If she wore makeup, it was imperceptible, but she was flawless so

I suspected she just had an extremely precise routine. No one had perfect pores without a little extra help.

She wasted no time, and I'd barely made it into the room before she addressed us. "This is good," she said, pointing to a projection on the barren white wall of her palatial office.

It was a polished version of our product feature layout. And my ink drawings were still there.

"If this doesn't get drowsy over the next few issues, and you keep focusing on product versatility, it'll be your new format," Wendy continued. Her tone was abrupt and her voice a bit naturally raspy. She pressed a button on her remote and a new projection was up—the images from the photoshoot on Friday. "This, however, was deeply uninspired. Try a little harder, Cy."

"Got it," Cyrus said with a simple nod.

It wasn't until I saw Corey's shoulders drawing in, that I realized my own were raised high. Wendy Thurman was a beta, and she was talking down to Cyrus like he was...

Like he wasn't an alpha.

It made me edgy, but I was surprised to find that Cyrus seemed calm. His bubbly scent was muted, but it wasn't souring either.

"And this," Wendy said, pointing to the photo of Rakim. "Which of you lent your helping hand on this one?"

Now Cyrus stiffened, but I didn't see his hand spreading behind his back in warning to me before it was too late, and my own hand lifted in the air.

"New girl," Wendy said, narrowing her eyes at me.

"Lola," I said.

"Lola gave us the idea for the new product feature layout," Cyrus said quickly.

He was sticking up for me. I braced myself as Wendy rolled her eyes. "I'm not looking at the product feature. Lola, are you a makeup artist or an assistant beauty editor?"

"Assistant beauty editor," I said, lifting my chin, ready for whatever this powerful woman wanted to throw at me. But I winced when she turned back to Cyrus.

"Cyrus, do your assistant beauty editors do our models' makeup?"

"Rakim insisted—"

"Is Rakim your boss?"

Finally, Cyrus' impenetrable cool calm cracked, just the softest scoff at the back of his throat before the sound was cleared away. "No, Wendy, he is not."

He's his omega, I realized. This wasn't really about me doing Rakim's makeup, it was about Rakim's influence over Cyrus?

"I let him bring his personal makeup artist onto my shoot, I expected him to actually *use* her, and not start rearranging everyone's job description," Wendy said.

I pinned my lips shut and so did the rest of the beauty department, Cyrus shifting in finite twitches.

Wendy sighed and turned away from us all, clicking her remote again and bringing up another fashion shoot, one edgier than before that must've been done before my arrival.

"This isn't awful, but it doesn't *change* anything. Doesn't add anything. I'm not impressed," Wendy said with a shrug.

And just like that, whatever battle had just taken place between Cyrus and Wendy over me, or maybe over Rakim, passed. Wendy picked apart a few more projects from the team, praised the cover feature, and I wondered that everyone seemed so relaxed after she'd finished telling us that she was disappointed in all but two of our efforts for the issue.

"Cy, Lola, give me a minute," Wendy said, just as everyone made a move to head for the door.

"Brainstorm," Cyrus told the others, turning and offering me a quick and tight smile in support.

Wendy slid behind a vast glass top desk that looked as if it might be there for the sole purpose of making her appear more imposing. Cyrus pulled out a chair for me, stepping away and offering me space as he took his own. Wendy sighed as the glass doors to her office swung shut with a whisper.

"I apologize for overstepping my role," I said, deciding I'd rather draw the first bullet than be left watching Wendy pepper Cyrus with them.

Wendy waved her hand. "You're not really the one who overstepped though, are you?" she asked, but she was staring at Cyrus instead of me.

"Wendy, come on. Are you really mad that Rakim fired his *own* makeup artist?" Cyrus asked, relaxing back into his chair and filling the space with languid limbs. The pose feigned relaxation, there was an edgy tension in the air around him, as if he were trying to restrain his own alpha presence.

"After going to the trouble of making me hire her for the time? Yes, Cy, I'm pissed," Wendy bit out. She collapsed back into her own chair with a huff and glared at Cyrus. "I'm going to be even more pissed if he poaches the new assistant beauty editor *you* wheedled me into hiring. No offense, Lola, you did good work. You were the neck down on his shoot, yeah?"

I nodded, and her lips pursed.

Cyrus turned his head to smile warmly at me, and I was so distracted by the discomfort of the conversation that I forgot to be startled by him. "It was flawless, didn't take a single spot of touch up in post."

I sat up a little straighter at that and then ran the conversation back through my head, turning to Wendy. "Sorry. Did you say poach?"

"Rake hasn't gotten a chance to talk with her yet," Cyrus said gently.

"Well, he had the chance to send me an email," Wendy snapped back.

"He only wants her for the week until he can find a replacement for Courtney," Cyrus said. "I heard your review of our department, Wen, I'm certainly not about to lose Lola."

"See that you don't," Wendy said, offering Cyrus a poisonous grimace in the disguise of a smile.

"Umm…" My eyes bounced between the pair.

Cyrus sucked in a breath and shrugged some of their peevish war of words off his shoulders. "Right. Sorry. Rake is coming in at lunch to talk to you. He…he hasn't had the best experience with unfamiliar makeup artists and—"

"As an omega," Wendy cut in bitterly.

"—he's sought after enough that as long as his artist can pick up the plan from the lead artists for the catwalk shows, he can bring someone of his own choosing. He was hoping you'd be interested," Cyrus added gently, holding my gaze.

My lips parted in an 'o' but I didn't miss the brief glare Cyrus and Wendy shot one another. There had to be some kind of history there, I just couldn't quite piece it all together. I pushed that aside and focused on the offer and what it meant for my job.

You're going to fuck this—I slammed the door on the voice in my head and glared down at my own hands. Could I do this? Backstage at fashion week would be no joke, and it wasn't as though I'd spent the past year preparing for high-pressure situations.

Could I really turn it down though? Backstage. At. Fashion. Week.

"What if…what if I got permission to take close photos of the makeup looks while I was there?" I asked, turning to Wendy, whose eyes narrowed. "We could do a trend page on it. Or even a layout where we try accessible versions," I added to Cyrus.

Wendy's laugh was soft and her smile was genuine, changing the sharp angles of her bone structure into something classical and beautiful instead of so intense. "You know, Lola, I was really looking forward to firing you after two weeks. I'm a little annoyed with you for being this useful. Sure. Cyrus will get you a decent camera from tech."

Cyrus was beaming again for the first time since we'd entered Wendy's office, and she was turned away from the shine on his expression.

"Cyrus, try not to coast on this next issue, if you don't mind."

"I'll gamble," Cyrus agreed with a dip of his head, which sounded like a dangerous promise to make, but it didn't make Wendy frown.

I rose as he did, and Wendy's form of dismissal was to turn to her phone, so I followed Cyrus quickly out of the room. We walked past Wendy's assistants and out to the elevator in silence, and it wasn't until the elevator arrived that Cyrus paused, frowning.

"Oh. Should I—"

"It's fine," I said, even though anxiety spiked as he stepped into the small space with me. "I'm sorry—"

"Don't. God, definitely don't, not after you just sat through World War Wendy with me," Cyrus said, sighing and slouching against the wall opposite mine.

"Is she…"

"She's usually worse," Cyrus said, groaning and rolling out his shoulders. His alpha scent was unfurling in the space between us, teasing a flush to my cheeks as if I'd been sipping on champagne. "But she liked your work and it softened her up."

Cyrus laughed at my face. Shit, if that was Wendy 'softened up,' I'd hate to be in on the meeting where she was having a bad day.

"Are you…all right?" Cyrus asked. "I know your first week ended on a…sour note."

I fidgeted in place, and the elevator dinged as we arrived on our floor. "Embarrassed, mostly," I said.

"Don't be," Cyrus said, gesturing for me to walk ahead. "Rake's going to show up a little after noon to sweet talk you into helping him next week. You were seriously interested in that, right?"

I nodded.

"Good. Your suggestion to catch the looks backstage was a stroke of luck too," Cyrus murmured as we neared our office. "We'll keep your fashion week adventure on the down-low for a bit longer though, to keep Betty off your ass."

I snorted and glanced back, blinded by Cyrus' gleaming grin.

CYRUS ARTFULLY MANEUVERED the rest of the team out of the office for lunch while I double-checked some copy for Corey. I caught a whiff of Rakim from the hall before I even saw him walking up the mirrored glass hall to the office. His big alpha was with him, broad in his black suit, squared features arranged somberly. They exchanged a soft word, and then the alpha returned in the direction they'd come until he was out of sight. Rakim caught my eye as he stood in the doorway, holding a bouquet of plum and pink blooms in one hand, and a takeout bag in the other.

"I come bearing bribery," he said, eyes vivid under the bright natural lighting of our office.

My mouth curved into a smile without my permission. Rakim Oren had charm down to a science.

"Full disclosure, when Leo helped me pick out the flowers, he said to tell you they were partly from him too," Rakim added, walking through the room, an aimless eye scoping out our product counters before he came to sit in the chair next to mine.

When his knee grazed mine, I slid back an inch, and he glanced down to the spot, eyes narrowing. He looked up again, smiling brightly, but I thought there was a hint of curiosity or dissection in his gaze, and I forced myself to stay still and not try and lean away from the aura of omega perfume that hovered around him.

"I thought I probably couldn't go wrong with peanut butter and jelly sandwiches," he said, dropping the flowers and paper bag down on the counter. I scooped up the bouquet as if it might act as a shield, while Rakim folded down the paper bag and brought out two foil-wrapped sandwiches.

"You say peanut butter and jelly, but I feel like you mean

it in an artisanal way," I said, watching him unwrap a hearty looking coarse bread that oozed with fresh strawberry jam.

"Guilty," Rakim said, smiling. "Cyrus texted to say that my surprise was kind of spoiled?"

I nodded and looked down at the flowers in my arms. They were deeply fragrant, but they still didn't stand up against Rakim's rich perfume. Omega perfume didn't have quite the same effect on betas as it did alphas, but I did find myself with a soft aching in my stomach, almost like hunger.

"Wendy told me this morning that you wanted to borrow me. I'm not sure I'm qualified, honestly," I said.

"Wendy hates me, so I'm sure she did the worst job ever selling the idea," Rakim said, waving his hand through the air as his tongue slipped out to lick away jam from the corner of his mouth.

He hadn't shaved recently, and his beard was growing dark and dense and soft looking. He had the effortlessly casual and stylish look down—a weathered leather jacket on his shoulders over a t-shirt and wool pants rolled up slightly to show off his dark, laced boots. It was meant to look approachable, but I had a feeling that the price tag on even the t-shirt would've made me gape.

"Here's the honest truth," Rakim said, setting his sandwich back on the foil and sucking his thumb clean in a way that made me clench my thighs, his own good looks entirely to blame instead of his scent. "I never used to bring my own crew to these kinds of events, but I was getting...not harassed exactly, but..."

"By alphas," I said.

He looked up and met my gaze. "No. Betas, actually. Like I said, not *harassed*, but I was dealing with a lot of people getting into my space, trying to cultivate relationships to find an in with one of my alphas. Sometimes it was physically uncomfortable, but mostly it was emotionally exhausting." Rakim shrugged.

"To have people trying to take your alpha's attention?"

Rakim frowned and shook his head. "No, it's not...We've

all had relationships outside the pack, myself included. That's how Leo joined us. I just don't like being *used*. The men in my pack are all grown-ass adults, they can find their own fuck buddies. And someone pretending to be my friend isn't going to automatically find their way into our home."

I looked down at the bouquet in my lap again and swallowed hard. Did he think I was—

"Oh, shit, no! I didn't mean it like that," Rakim rushed, reaching out and grabbing my wrist before I could pull away. "Sorry, no. Look, I'll be professional now. I was already considering asking you to jump in for fashion week before…um…"

"Before you knew for certain I wasn't chasing your alphas," I supplied for him, knowing he would've heard the full details from the rest of his pack by now.

"Ye-yeah. I guess I just didn't want you to think I was a stuck up fashion diva the way Wendy probably made me sound."

He sounded sincere; he looked it too, holding my gaze. His fingers were still wrapped loosely around my wrist, thumb swirling over my pulse, and the touch was somewhere between intimate and friendly.

"About Leo," I started.

"Lola, honestly, I didn't mean it like that—"

"But he is part of *your* pack—"

"He is, and your relationship together won't change that," Rakim said, with a firm and gentle certainty.

I blinked and pulled my hand free of his. He hadn't meant the words as a warning, but I needed to take them as one. Did I really want to get involved with someone who would always belong to others first?

"This got…off track," I said, putting the flowers on the counter and fussing with one of the folded edges of the wrapped sandwich. "The only makeup I've done for you was a cover-up."

Rakim sighed and stretched taller in the desk chair. "True. I suppose I figured if you didn't think you could do it, you'd let me know. You didn't seem like someone who would take the opportunity if you knew you'd bomb it. And it's not like there won't be teams of other professionals on hand."

I sucked in a deep breath and straightened my shoulders. "Okay. I *do* think I can do it."

Rakim's smile wasn't quite as bright at Cyrus' but it went all the way to his eyes, making them glitter. "Awesome. There's going to be a car at your place Friday morning at, and I'm so sorry about this, but the ass crack of dawn. Like four-thirty. But if you text me your coffee and pastry order, it'll be waiting for you. I'll talk to Wes about getting us beta security too, so you aren't stressed out. There will be some alphas backstage, but they usually give me space anyway, out of respect to my pack," he rattled off, eyes rolling.

I swallowed hard and stared at my unwrapped sandwich, any appetite cooling as I wondered if I'd landed myself in a position I wasn't really prepared for.

Lola

8

"*Look at you. Just desperate for this dick, aren't you?*"

"*Fuck. Yes, Buzz, please. Ah!*"

"*That's it. Hold yourself open like that, beta. Wanna see how deep I go before my knot stops. I bet you wish you could take it, don't you? You wish you were a sweet little omega with a pussy that just ate me up.*"

I whined and spread my thighs apart as far as I could, trying to prove to him that I could be good, even if I was just a beta. Buzz was on the bed beneath me, arms raised and head propped up under his hands as he watched me stretch my sex for his gaze, the muscles of my thighs screaming with exhaustion even as I pushed to prove to him that I was what he wanted. His sticky, smoky-sweet smell was so thick in the air, I had a hard time catching my breath.

I whined as his knot stretched at my opening, but I couldn't force myself down to take him in, and he just laughed as I retreated.

"*So close. You're never gonna do it though. You think you love alpha dick, but you can't take the knot, can you, beta? Bites and knots are for omegas, aren't they?*"

"*I can do it,*" *I gasped, sinking down and trying to push past the stinging stretch in my core. I sobbed with frustration, and then Buzz's hands whipped out, gripping my hips and holding me in place, pain threading out from my core as he tested my limits.*

"*Wait!*" *I cried.* "*Wait, please!*"

"*You want my bite, beta?*" *he growled.*

"*Buzz, stop!*"

"*You want it?*"

His fingernails felt like claws in my side, and when he turned us over, the mattress was like sandpaper against my back. I tried to squirm away, to grab the edge of the bed to pull myself away, but Buzz snarled and dove down.

I screamed as his teeth sank into my shoulder, a blaze of pain sudden and boiling on my skin, the bite wrong *on me. He retreated only to move to my breast, repeating the sudden snapping of his teeth in sensitive flesh, tearing into me.*

"Stop. Please, please, stop!"

"Betas should know their place, Lola," he whispered, lips crimson. His teeth bared, and he lunged—

"MORNING."

I landed clumsily inside of the town car on Friday morning, my eyes wide as I stared back at Leo.

"What are you doing here?" I asked, catching my breath.

The sky was still a dark shade of lavender as I'd tiptoed out of my building, concerned about waking any of my neighbors at a totally ungodly hour even while knowing that the screams from my nightmare would've already done a thorough job.

"I wanted to see you," Leo said, smiling. His eyes still looked a little heavy-lidded, and I wanted to slide across the seat and burrow into the soft haze of his dark sweater, but I was still suffering the phantom bites from my nightmare. "I volunteered to get your coffee."

There were two paper cups in the car's holders at the center of the back seat and a paper bag sitting on the floor by Leo's feet. I closed the door behind me and the car pulled away from the curb.

"C'mere for a second," Leo murmured, arms extended.

I hesitated, the twisted up nightmare version of my first night with Buzz still lingering in my head. It wasn't a real memory. Buzz hadn't ever tried forcing his knot, that had been Indy's personal favorite way of tormenting me. Buzz had preferred to refuse me his knot, knowing how badly I'd wanted to impress him. And no one had ever bitten me—instead, they'd used the mention of a bond like a tease and then turned it into a weapon against my own insecurity.

"Lola?" Leo asked, sitting up, eyes seeing too much on my face.

I pushed across the seat and gave into my initial impulse, nestling against Leo's chest. He bundled me up in strong arms and hummed happily as I tucked my face under his jaw.

"You okay?"

"I think my nerves about this week kind of messed with my dreams," I admitted.

Leo hummed and shifted us until I was perched properly on his lap, held close and securely. "I can't honestly say I know what you're going into with fashion week. I check out some of Rake's runways but avoid backstage. I *do* know, however, that both he and Cyrus have absolute faith you're going to crush it."

That did make me smile a little. Working with *Designate's* beauty department this week had given me more confidence in my job and my knowledge of makeup.

"I was going to try and take advantage of this alone time with you, but how about I make up for that later, and right now you and I just catch a few more minutes of the sleep we sacrificed getting up this early?"

I didn't think I could sleep after my nightmare, especially not while being held by someone. But I did like the idea of just resting in the quiet like this with Leo.

"Did you really get up this early just to ride with me to the tents?"

"I arm-wrestled Rake for it," Leo said, and I snorted. "I'm serious. He's trying to play it cool, but he has a crush on you."

I stiffened, and Leo nuzzled against the top of my head. The omega was interested in me?

"Hey, what's that? Alphas, I get. But Rake?" he whispered, picking up on my discomfort.

I swallowed down the truth and forced myself to relax. "I like this, between us, and I'm definitely not in it to come between you and your pack. I just need things to be...separate," I said. "I know it's not just us, but—"

"I understand," Leo said, reaching one hand up from my waist to run his fingers through my hair. "Just us."

I winced. I was totally the 'other woman,' which was the last thing I wanted. I especially didn't want to be another beta in Rakim's life who tried to wedge themselves between him and one of his pack.

But with an omega, came alphas. Even having lunch with Rakim, I'd walked around the rest of the day with a lingering whiff of his perfume.

The night Baby's perfume had come in, I'd gotten one decent hit of her scent on my skin when I hugged her. And then I'd landed myself in an alpha's bed. Buzz's.

And that one had been a hard trap to untangle myself from.

So Rakim could bring me flowers and hire me to do his makeup in an emergency. He might be stunningly handsome and delightfully playful company. But it was hard enough being friends with one omega and keeping my boundaries safely in place. Rakim seemed like he was the kind of persistent that would make boundaries impossible.

"Lola, you're so tense, you've got *me* worried," Leo said softly, pressing a kiss into my hair. "What can I do?"

I coached my limbs into softening, my breaths into slowing. "I'm fine. Tell me about your week."

LEO WALKED me to the tent security, my hand in his, but there was an awkward kind of quiet between us ever since he'd teased me about Rake. He stopped me before I joined the line, tugging me closer with a gentle twitch of our linked hands. He was frowning, eyes scanning my face, and I was almost relieved at the thought that maybe I'd ruined things between us already.

Relationships were already a complicated addition to my life, and getting involved with someone in a pack was the worst kind of idea, wasn't it?

"Hey. Don't stress about anything but the job, okay?" Leo said.

I nodded and found him bending down to me. I arched to meet him in the kiss without thinking, a soft gasp on my lips. Had I forgotten how easy it was to kiss Leo in the past week? Apparently, because I found myself leaning in and opening to him, the restless worry of the morning evaporating with every pass of his lips over mine.

"Maybe I should've started the morning like this," he whispered as I melted into his chest.

"Maybe," I agreed. "Sorry I was off while we had time together."

"Forgiven. Sorry I added a bit of worry to your plate," he answered.

I smiled and stared up at him. The city was blue around him, dawn only just making a commitment to brighten the day. I took a greedy pass of my hand over his chest and wondered how hard it would be to steal his sweater. I was pretty sure it was cashmere and it felt like actual heaven on my skin.

"Rake's gonna try and talk you into going to about fifty after parties with him," Leo warned. He raised an eyebrow, "You're welcome to claim a date with me to get out of them, but for the sake of realism, I would advise *actually* having the date with me."

"Ahh to keep up the illusion," I said, and Leo's grin grew at the same time as mine. "Noted."

He snatched another, rougher kiss from my lips before backing away. "Break a leg, just not Rake's. He's a terrible patient."

I bit my lip as I waited in the short line to get inside, giving my name and showing my I.D. My stomach was flipping, and it wasn't just nerves about the first day of fashion week. Life was turning into kind of a rollercoaster. I'd woken up, sweaty and shaking from my nightmare, only to rocket quickly between comfort and safety with Leo to instant insecurity, and then back to feeling happy and giddy.

Granted, I'd spent the last year in a massive extended low point. I was generally out of practice with dealing with fluctuating emotions.

"Lola!"

Rake was already here, shirtless and in low slung sweatpants, standing with a group of models. I rushed over to him, and he stepped out of their circle.

"Sorry, you're not late or anything. I'm just excited to see you. Come on, I'll introduce you to Maureen, she's doing the makeup on this show and a few others I'm in this week. She'll give you some resistance to start with, but when she sees you know what you're doing, you'll be golden with her. She hated Courtney anyway."

My eyes were on Rake's shoulders as he led the way through the narrow curtained-off backstage of the tent. He had a tattoo on the back of his shoulders, a flower digging through the muscle of his back, thorns piercing the skin and petals dropping down his right side. The blooms looked almost like a rose but with rounder petals, and I wanted to reach out and trace them with my fingers.

Rake was still talking, mostly pointing people out and their significance. I noted his dresser, Diane, an older black woman with a warm smile and a beautiful pile of box braids like a crown on her head, as well as our two massive beta security guards that followed at a comfortable distance. Everything else I let filter through. Rake was chatty, and I wasn't sure if it was caffeine, nerves, or just him naturally, but he didn't seem to mind my quiet, so I sipped my coffee and followed him through the crowd.

"Rake the rake!"

"Maureen, my dream," Rake cooed back to the petite

round woman with the bottle red hair and the oversized black square glasses.

"You're the new Courtney?"

"I'm the Lola," I said, and Maureen smiled, the gap in her teeth winking at me.

"I want dark thick brows, make his beard look as bushy as you can, and everything else keep it good and washed out. Ashy even, if you can get it on this golden boy. You brought your own kit? Good, use it if you need it. They give us products, but I won't tell the marketing team if you need to fudge a bit. There's reference up on the board there," Maureen said, pointing to a work board that had model's pictures pinned above their looks, as well as a few inspirational photos to match the fairly old Slovak looking line of menswear. "We're not in a rush, and if he's ready too soon he'll just smudge himself when all the girls try to cuddle up to him. Keep an eye on the time, and use your best judgment."

"Got it," I said, with one simple nod.

Maureen hummed and narrowed her eyes at me through bottle thick glasses. "We'll see."

"You'll love her, Maureen, just wait," Rake said as the makeup artist waddled away.

"That was Maureen Weiss," I said, watching her leave. "She was like the definition of a runway look while I was growing up."

"I know," Rake cooed, brushing shoulders with me briefly. "She's great. Less up in the ego of the world than a lot of names as big as hers." I waggled my eyebrows at him, and he laughed. "Okay, yes, I am a little up in the ego. Come on. Let's grab a decent corner spot and chill before it gets really crazy in here."

"OHMIGOD, RAAAAAYKE, I'VE *MISSED* YOU."

"Rake! Finally, I've been texting you forever."

"How's the *fam*, how's Cy?"

"How's your bae, Caleb?"

"How's the delicious Matthieu?"

Rake's eyes slid to mine as I finished powdering his face and got ready to define his eyebrows and beard. He didn't move a single muscle, but I could see it in his stare. *See what I mean?* My lips twitched.

One after another, assistants, models, and maybe even lighting directors—but all betas—stopped by the booth where I was prepping Rake. Each of them gushed their greeting to him, managing one to two cursory questions about him before turning the inquisition onto the subject of his alphas.

"If anyone acted like that with Baby, I'm pretty sure she'd stab them in the tit," I said as another hopeful left us to our work.

"Baby?"

"My best friend. She's an omega," I said.

"Oh! Baby...hmm, that seems like the kind of name I'd remember. What pack is she with?" Rake asked, pouting as he racked his brain. Because usually the packs that found omegas were full of significant alphas.

I tapped his forehead gently to remind him to smooth it out and started on his eyebrow. "Howler. I doubt you know them, they're a motorcycle crew in Old Downtown."

I pulled my brush quickly away as Rake's eyebrows shot up. "I'm sorry, you're best friends with an omega in a biker pack, and you didn't tell me? That's so fucking cool! How hot are those alphas? I bet they're like, just the right amount of feral, aren't they? God, imagine their..." Rake trailed off at the sight of my face.

"I haven't really spent any time around them," I said. Just the one night when Buzz and Indy had dragged me to the Howlers' bar and Baby and I had sat on opposite sides of a table, pinned between men with their hands holding us still. It might not have been the Howlers' fault, but I hadn't gotten the *best* first impression of the growling and rugged pack of bikers.

"How long has she been with them?"

"A year."

Rake winced and his face went blank, letting me get back to work. "Your best friend's been with a pack for a year, and you haven't spent *any* time around her alphas? Sorry, I know that…I guess I just thought maybe it was better for you around alphas you knew."

I worked in silence, finishing both eyebrows and deciding my approach on his beard. He must've let it grow out for this show, it was nice and thick on its own. But I could fluff it up and make sure his skin underneath would keep the shadow too. In the back of my head, Rake's question about my tolerance of alphas circled. I was managing to be around Cyrus pretty well, although he was rarely like what I expected from an alpha.

"Bikers are kind of a sore subject for me too, I think," I admitted softly.

Rake blinked. I wondered if Maureen would be pissed if I used a little mascara on those dense eyelashes of his.

"How come no one ever asks about your other alpha?" I asked.

"Wes? I know, right?" Rakim answered. "I mean, I think it's a bit that he aims more to blend into the background. I bet most people don't know he's part of our pack. And the ones who do probably just think he's my guard dog. But Wes owns his own personal security company, and he and Matthieu trade up old classic cars for fun."

"You think it's about the money for them?" I asked, nodding my head to the swarming activity behind us, thinking of all the men and women who'd tried to claim Rake's attention.

"Some. Or just about how likely they are to get their photograph printed somewhere. Or maybe it's just about…"

"Alphas," I supplied when he wouldn't.

Rake shrugged. "Some people chase them. Not something you think about, I guess."

"Are you assuming I'm naturally terrified of alphas? I wasn't born scared, Rake. I used to chase them," I answered.

Rake's slack shock was in the corner of my eye as I drew a sharp line along the edge of his beard for the makeup. "And then one caught me, and I learned my lesson," I said.

Rake gasped softly, and I turned my focus to the outline of his lips, forcing him to hold still and not speak, leaving my confession in the empty quiet between us.

Lola

9

Rake was one of the season's busiest models, and some of his bookings were at clubs or hotels around the city. It wasn't the first time I'd done a makeup look in a cab—I'd pinned Baby down more than once when she showed up under-dressed for a night out—but it was definitely the craziest. Three days in, and I was getting used to carrying around wisps of Rake's omega perfume. It was clinging to my hair, it coated my palms, and he was kind of touchy so there were traces of it around my waist and shoulders. I'd been edgy and anxious about it at first, but none of the people with us backstage seemed to notice or care. Rake wasn't the only omega around, and I was mostly surrounded by betas who couldn't have cared less if he was.

"God, Lola, this is incredible," Rake said, turning his head side to side to admire the golden laced look I'd just finished up for his ritzy studio show. He was cloaked in metallic jacquards, layer after layer until it made his shoulders hang a little heavier, but he looked regal and almost godlike.

"I was worried this one was out of my depth, actually," I admitted, brushing a little excess gold dust out of his dark hair.

Rake stood from his seat, almost chest to chest with me, and I swallowed as I remembered that he was just tall enough to hover his face over mine. The taste of chocolate truffles clung to my tongue as we shared breath.

"Pretty sure nothing is. You're a goddess," he said, his

hand reaching out of the deep sleeve to cup my throat. The warm golden rings on his fingers stung against my skin as his thumb stroked briefly along my jaw, my lips parted on a soft gasp.

"Models in line please!" the stage manager called.

"Gonna talk you into going out with me tonight," Rake said, winking briefly with glittering feathered lashes, before leaving me at the mirror as he left to stand and wait for his cue.

I hadn't called in my date with Leo yet, mostly because I'd been so exhausted at the end of every day, it was easy to make firm cases to Rake for not going out. But I didn't want to use Leo as my excuse to avoid spending time with one of his packmates, and David had taken me to a couple of fashion parties a few years ago when I was fresh out of college and begged him to share his cool Uptown world with me. Maybe it was time for me to test the world out a little. Rake didn't seem like he'd leave me to the wolves at a party, and I was sick of staring at the still-packed boxes in my apartment.

I grabbed up the digital camera *Designate* had lent me for the week and went up to the line of models, taking a few close shots and clips the magazine could use. Rake pursed his gleaming lips at me for one, and then turned and faced the curtain, his face sharpening into a predatory intensity he'd wear down the brief runway.

The close space near the curtain was crowded, omega perfumes mixing with some of the beta model's manufactured fragrances until it all blended together into a kind of white noise for the senses.

"Kill it," I offered the group in a whisper, catching smiles from a couple of the other models who'd seen plenty of me at shows in the past few days.

I turned and headed back to the mirrors to clean up my station and pack up. Halfway there, my steps slowed. There was a woman sitting in Rake's chair, tall with a silver bob and pale eyes. She picked up one of my brushes and brought the soft end to her nose, sniffing lightly, before those eerie eyes flicked over and locked on me. Nude pink lips stretched in a predatory smile, and my throat tightened.

I couldn't smell her from here, but I could guess. She was an alpha. Rake's soft touch from a moment ago suddenly seemed to burn on the skin of my jaw, and I fought the urge to run from the room. She could follow if she really wanted to.

Maybe she was only a friend of Rake's, or maybe she was someone in charge of the show. I reminded myself that I had a good working relationship with Cyrus, who was also an alpha, and forced myself forward. All I had to do was pack up my gear, and then I would find myself somewhere quiet and removed to wait for Rake.

"Lola, isn't it?" she greeted as I reached the station.

I nodded when my tongue refused to budge in my closed mouth.

The alpha stretched out a thin and elegant hand. She was dressed in a low cut black jumpsuit, her skin perfectly even and smooth, with just the slightest hint of wrinkles around her eyes. She could've been anywhere from her late thirties to fifties, wealth tended to warp age from what I'd seen recently, and that steel-gray hair was a little too perfect to be natural.

"Odette," she said. "I own the building."

I didn't really want to take her hand, but there wasn't any reason not to. I held my breath as I got the first whiff of her alpha scent, heavy jasmine, cloying in my lungs.

"It's a beautiful space," I said, shaking her hand and pulling away quickly as one of her sharply manicured nails scratched gently at my wrist.

Odette smiled thinly at the compliment, her eyes tracing me from head to toe. "Are you one of Rake's collection? Or… let me guess, *Cyrus'* flavor of the month?"

"I'm sorry?" I heard her perfectly, but the words were so unexpected, I didn't know how to process them.

Her smile flattened to a patronizing sympathy. "Oh, Lola. That pack runs through their side pieces like they're upgrading their smartphone model." She stood, and I was so stunned at the implication, I didn't move out of her reach. Jasmine scratched down my arm, and her fingers took a tight but not painful grip around my wrist, nails resting their dagger tips over my pulse. "A beta as sweet as you deserves to be cherished, don't you think?"

I flinched at the sound of my designation on her tongue and tried to back away.

"Whatever attention they're spoiling you with will dry up before long, darling," Odette murmured, head bending and crowding into my personal space.

"Please let go," I said, my whisper breathless as I tugged on my arm.

Odette's cheek grazed against mine, and I gasped at the blatant scent-marking, body frozen. "They don't hand out bites to their toys," she whispered in my ear.

"Odette."

I jumped at the soft bark and stumbled backward as Odette's grasp on my wrist vanished. My back hit a firm chest, and two hands settled on my shoulders. A scorching wave of subtle sweetness and dense warmth like wool velvet washed over me, and I whimpered at the familiar alpha scent.

"Matthieu," Odette said, eyes wide. Her lips parted and a tinkling laugh escaped. "You have to be kidding me. She's not your type at all, is she?"

I swallowed my panic and held it tight in my chest. Matthieu's touch on my shoulders was soft and he'd stepped back an inch. If I wanted to run, he wouldn't stop me, but I wasn't stupid. The chase would be a temptation to Odette and right now, between the two of them, I knew which alpha was the lesser evil.

"You've always had boundary issues, Odette, but scent-marking like that?" Matthieu's voice was beautiful and easy, and I'd never smelled an alpha scent like his before. There was something coaxing about it as it surrounded me, an enormous armchair inviting me to sink in and dream the day away. I wavered, and this time when my back hit his chest, neither of us moved.

"Well naturally, if I'd thought she had any kind of *bond*—"

"I need to pack up," I murmured, a little dizzy between the two opposing alphas.

"Of course," Matthieu answered, moving around my side and putting himself between me and Odette, forcing her to back away. "Enough toying. Leave her be," he added to the other alpha, a growl tucked away in the words.

I put my things away in their cases on autopilot, leaving all the wipes and quick washes Rake would need to clean up.

"Moved on from Carolyn at last, Matthieu?" Odette called.

Matthieu didn't answer her, and I heard the soft click of heels retreating as I hyper-focused on tucking my brushes into their holders. My hands were shaking, and he backed away until I could barely see him in my periphery.

"Would you like me to take you to get some fresh air?" he asked softly.

I jerked my head in an uneven nod and looked up to the mirror. He was standing behind me, eyes watching the room. He looked casual for the event in a v-neck sweater and black slacks, and I wondered if he'd come to be a spectator, or only to meet up with Rake. I stood up straighter, and his eyes flicked to meet mine in the mirror. Matthieu seemed especially unreadable to me, his gaze was warm and interested, but it seemed more watchful or concerned than the appetite Odette had shown.

I turned to face him and his head ducked, tipping in a gesture for me to follow him. We went in the opposite direction as Odette, passing a hospitality table where Matthieu grabbed two bottles of water. He led and I followed out of the studio's backdoor and down a long, mirrored hallway. It occurred to me that I didn't know the building and couldn't really know where Matthieu was taking me, but just as my wariness started to creep back in, we reached our destination. Matthieu opened a tall glass door out onto a screened-in balcony, and I sighed as the first gust of sharp, chilly air hit my face.

Matthieu lingered back at the door as I crossed the open balcony to the screens, stopping and leaning against a pillar. The city air was sooty and smelled like exhaust and maybe a bit like the garbage bins in the alleys, but it was a welcome reprieve from everything that still clung to my skin.

"I'll make it clearer to the security that you're to be as much a priority as Rake is," Matthieu said. He joined me by the screens, a comfortable arm's stretch away, and held out one of the water bottles.

"That's not really necessary," I said, cracking the lid of the bottle and gulping it down like I'd been wandering in a desert, washing away the chocolate and jasmine.

"Anyone in that room could've seen how uncomfortable she was making you. Wes would've stepped in, but he thought it might be better for you to lessen the number of alphas you had to deal with…"

My cheeks flushed, and I wrapped an arm tightly around myself. It was like having a massive open wound exposed to infected air, knowing that this whole pack was not only aware of my weakness, but paid it enough attention to let it affect how I interacted with them.

You shouldn't interact with them at all, I thought. This was the cost of getting involved with Leo. The cost of my position at *Designate*. My working for Rakim this week.

"She marked you in the hopes of irritating our pack," Matthieu said.

"I could tell," I bit out.

He was quiet for a long stretch, and the heat on my face grew worse. The scents that now marked me—my neck, my shoulders, my cheek—were tangible brands.

"I apologize if my stepping in added to your discomfort," Matthieu said with careful precision, his usually soft accent turning crisp with unease.

I groaned, propping my elbows on the ledge and pressing my face into my palm until my eyes burned with the pressure. I took a deep breath, and there was Rakim's perfume against my nose so I tore away again.

"No. You… I appreciated you stepping in, thank you." I looked at him and he was watching the street below, hawkish nose outlined in a thin glow of sunlight, the groove in the center of his chin marked in shadow. His head dipped in a light acknowledgment.

Older men weren't usually my type, or at least not one with the gap between our ages like Matthieu and I had, but he was…*appealing* seemed like the right word, but somehow not enough. I could imagine him twenty years younger and my age, and somehow I was pretty sure I preferred this more weathered version. Or maybe I was just falling back into nasty old habits. He was an alpha, and I badly wanted their attention.

"I'm going to go…wash up. Would you tell Rakim I'll see him in the morning?"

"Of course," Matthieu said, and he turned and made it to the door before me, opening it and standing aside. *Like a gentleman.* "Leo is watching the show. I'll let him know where you are."

"Sure," I said, but I was already hurrying down the hall, leaving Matthieu and his slower pace well behind me.

I stopped before reaching the back of the studio and sliding into the unoccupied restroom. I splashed cold water on my face, but all I smelled in the water in my palms was chocolate truffles and heavy jasmine. I turned the water to hot and pumped soap into my hand, lathering it up to the cuffs of my sleeves at my elbows. Remembering Rake's touch on my jaw, Odette's cheek against mine, I bent over the sink and splashed my skin again, added soap to scrub away the scents and my makeup for the day.

The bathroom was beautiful, with patterned marble and gleaming brass, and there were fluffy towels waiting in a tidy pile for guests' use. I took one and lathered it with soap, scoured it over my face, my jaw, my throat, and down to my collar. Matthieu's dense scent was light on my shoulders and when my ponytail swung down to tickle my nose, Rake's perfume was there. My breath hitched as my heart started to hammer in my chest. I washed my arms again, my face too until my skin was pink and my eyes were red and watering, and then I started over until the water was burning hot and my skin stung from the friction of the towel.

I gasped and braced my hands against the cool marble, water steaming in the sink, towel soiled from my makeup, and mascara shadows dark beneath my eyes.

"You fucking mess," I whispered at my reflection, face twisted in frustrated disgust. I wanted to strip my clothes off, tear my hair tie out, and scratch away every last whisper of any scent, even my own pale beta notes.

"Lola?"

I bit back my moan as a light knock sounded on the door. Leo. I bent in half, resting my forehead against the cool of the edge of the counter, and tried to control my breaths.

One look at me, and Leo would know. Maybe not all the details, but he'd know I'd fallen apart again. How many times could I reasonably expect a guy to put up with my bullshit before he packed it in and gave up the pretense?

I hadn't locked the door behind me and it opened slowly by a few inches, and then Leo was sliding inside. I didn't move. I was waiting for him to look his fill, and then turn around and leave.

He crossed to me, hands pulling me up gently by my shoulders. I kept my eyes on the running water as he looked me over, watched his hand reach over and turn the taps off with a numb and vacant attention. I hissed as his fingers turned my face to his, his touch against the spot where I'd scratched myself pink trying to wash away Rake's perfume. I stared at his five o'clock shadow and then raised my eyes slowly to his, struck by the solemn and sorrowful empathy in his gaze.

Just give up, Leo.

He winced when he saw the red mark on my jaw and his hands retreated from me. I sighed, but instead of leaving me in the restroom alone, Leo shrugged his large coat off his shoulders and draped it around mine. It was warm from him and I shivered inside of it, my eyes growing wide.

"Think about what you want to pick up for dinner. I want to sit on your couch and eat takeout tonight," Leo said.

"Leo," I whispered, a crack in my voice.

He opened his mouth, probably expecting me to protest. But god, I was too fucking tired for that. I threw myself at his chest and he let out an 'oof' of breath before his arms surrounded my shoulders.

It didn't escape me that he smelled like that lovely, warm alpha of his, but it was so familiar on him that I almost thought of it as *his* scent. I tucked my arms into the sleeves of his coat and tilted my head back, my eyes falling shut as his head bent, and his lips pressed to my forehead.

"Just pizza," I said.

Something wild and abrasive that roamed constantly under my skin went still as Leo smiled in answer. "Just pizza it is. We'll have it delivered."

Lola
10

I couldn't be certain, but I was pretty sure Matthieu ran interference with Rake while Leo helped me grab my things from my station before we made a quick escape from the rapidly crowding backstage. We rode in quiet in the dark car, but it was peaceful instead of tense, and Leo didn't ask if I was all right. Either he didn't want to make me uncomfortable or he was learning the truth—I was never all right.

I used to be.

But it wasn't pizza waiting in the brown bag in front of my door when we got back to my apartment.

"I hope you don't mind. I called in a favor," Leo said, bending and grabbing the bag. He opened the bag and pulled out a bottle of…shampoo. I blinked at it. "It's scent canceling. They make it for omegas and Rake's used it before, but I used it for a while… Well, we'll get to that."

I stared at the bottle. There were others in the bag too, a whole collection from the size of it. "Which of them brought it?" I asked.

"Caleb knows the brand, but it was probably Wes that brought it here," Leo said.

I swallowed and unlocked my apartment door as I processed the information. This was probably going to be how things went. Whatever happened to me, if one of the pack was there to witness it, the others would know. They were a *pack*, so that was probably a given. I needed to decide if I was okay with that.

But the decision seemed unexpectedly simple.

"Will you tell them I said thank you?" I asked, stepping aside for Leo to join me.

His shoulders dropped in relief. "Of course, don't worry about it. I'll put them in the bathroom, yeah?"

It struck me all at once, the roles this pack had already found themself taking in my life.

Cyrus sticking up for me against Wendy. Rakim's playful flirtation and teasing. Matthieu stepping in against Odette. Caleb, who I hadn't really even spoken a word to, scooping me up during my panic attack, his scent putting me under. Leo's eternally patient dedication to caring for me despite our time together consistently colored by my *fucking issues*.

Leo had told me from the beginning. These men weren't out to hurt me. I was starting to believe him and, more than that, I was really sick of being the problem. I rolled my shoulders, imagining the heaviness of the afternoon dropping to the floor.

I watched Leo's back as he headed toward my bathroom by the bedroom. "Yeah. Actually, I wouldn't mind a shower."

"Sure," he said, over his shoulder as he slipped through the door. "I can order for us and pick something asinine for us to watch. Unless you prefer artsy shit?"

My lips quirked at the offer and I slipped my comfortable sneakers off, tiptoeing down to pause in front of the bathroom door.

"That sounds good. Or you could join me?"

Bottles of scent canceling body washes and sprays and hair care and perfume went clattering across my tiny sink counter as Leo fumbled the bag in his surprise. He whipped around, head cocked, and I fought my laugh at his stunned expression.

"In the shower?"

I raised my eyebrows. "That's where I was thinking of heading for my…shower, yes."

Leo swallowed, and his surprise settled into a slow-growing smile. "Are you going to wear my coat?"

I laughed and shrugged out of his coat. "Pretty sure this beauty is dry-clean only, so no?"

I tucked it on the hook on the other side of my bedroom door before returning to the bathroom. It was tiny, and together Leo and I barely fit in the space. I had a tub that I just managed to fit into, but it would be a squeeze with Leo. Which was kind of the point, wasn't it?

"How about this shirt?" I asked, tugging lightly on his button-down. "How's it do in the shower?"

"Oh, no, this is silk. It prefers natural rainstorms," Leo said, reaching for his buttons.

I squirmed on my tiptoes as I watched him start to undress, happy the game I'd started was shifting the mood away from the shadowy one we'd been carrying since he'd found me after the fashion show.

"Your socks?" he asked, lips twitching.

I laughed "My *socks*? Yeah, they're cashmere." They were fucking cotton. I took them off and shucked them outside of the bathroom. Leo pulled his shirt off and my hands stroked a greedy pass up his chest, tracing the grooves of muscle with my fingertips.

Leo wasn't a huge guy, but he was bigger than I usually went for. Instead of intimidating, it made him feel sheltering, like I could lean into him and let him block out the world for me. My hands trailed back down to his hips and I stepped closer, Leo's gaze darkening. I plucked at the waistband of his trousers.

"What about these?" I asked.

"Buffalo wool," Leo said, the dry teasing turned into an almost growl as his voice lowered.

I snorted. "Buffalo?"

"Mhm. Very specific washing instructions. Better not risk it."

He grunted as I reached to the front of his pants, one of my hands reaching down to cup him through the 'buffalo wool' while the other undid the top button. His cock jumped against my palm and Leo stumbled against me, our bodies bumping together. He slipped his fingers under the hem of my sweatshirt, skimming over my skin, and my breath caught.

"This looks expensive too," he said, raising my shirt up my waist, although his eyes were focused on mine, watching my reaction.

"Priceless heirloom," I agreed in a whispered murmur, undoing his zipper.

Leo's head dipped as I raised up to my toes, our mouths meeting in a sloppy, starving kiss. Leo moaned as my busy hands dipped beneath the waist of his boxer briefs, teasing at the base of his cock until he pulled my sweatshirt up over my breasts, and I had to abandon the kiss and my playing to help him pull it over my head.

"The bra is basically solid gold, very heavy in the water," I rushed out as Leo threw my sweatshirt out to the hall floor.

He laughed and then caught my waist, dragging me up to his chest, his head dipping and mouth sucking hotly along my jaw.

"Fuck, finally," I sighed, eyes falling shut and neck arching. I moaned as his teeth nipped, my body shuddering with a strange combination of arousal and a reflexive kind of terror. But Leo soothed away old memories of snapping teeth by licking and kissing over the spot until I was trying to actively climb him, body desperate for friction.

"Question," he rasped.

"No question," I whined, rolling my hips against his as my toes slipped on the tile. "More mouth."

"Condom?"

Oh. I went still in his arms, and Leo kissed my pulse gently before lifting his head.

"They're around somewhere," I said, frowning and relaxing in the circle of Leo's arms around my back, eyeing my bathroom dubiously. "I only moved in a month ago, and I kind of haven't settled yet."

Leo's smile hinted that he might've noticed as much. "Is it

ungentlemanly of me if I admit I was planning on maybe seducing you tonight?"

I grinned and shook my head. "Not if it means you came prepared."

Leo's hands slipped up my back to undo the clasps of my bra. For a man living with five other men, he was pretty good at that. "Shower before or after?"

Any scents left on me from the day were phantoms now, maybe a few stray traces of Rake. But I was safe here with Leo. I shrugged my bra down my arms and said, "After."

I stifled a squeal as his hands slid down to cup my ass, lifting me off my feet and pulling my legs around his waist. I wrapped my arms around his shoulders and bent my head to his lifted one, taking his lips in a series of slow, needy nibbles and presses. My back hit the doorframe of the bathroom and Leo hiked me higher, pulling his mouth from mine and wrapping it around the tip of my right breast.

"Oh, god!" I arched, pushing myself against his sucking lips.

This was what I missed with all those bar hookups. I never really undressed with any of those strangers, never got this much attention. I forgot how good it felt. Leo was both gentle and thorough, his tongue twirling around my nipple until it was tight and aching.

"Pants off," I gasped, my feet pushing the legs of his pants down. Leo swapped breasts and I ran my hands up into his short, dense black hair, gripping it tightly.

Fabric hit the floor and Leo pulled away, his lips and my breasts shining from his kisses. "Your turn," he rasped. "You order the pizza, and I'll grab the condom."

I nodded and Leo lowered me to my feet, but I held his face in my hands, taking another long kiss from his mouth, hips rocking against his and stirring up the growing erection he was sporting.

"Get moving or I'll fuck you here in the doorway," he whispered, biting my bottom lip and soothing his tongue over it.

We parted in the hall. I'd dropped my bags by the door, and my phone was tucked away in there. I hopped down the hall, wiggling my way out of my skinny jeans until I was left only in my panties, rifling through my bag and digging out my phone.

"Toppings?" I called.

"You. On me."

I snorted and ordered us extra cheese and pepperoni. When I turned, Leo was prowling down the hall, buck naked and stroking his cock in his hand.

"You are fucking gorgeous," he said, eyes drinking me in.

"Ditto," I whispered, eyes widening.

Couch sex for the win, I thought as Leo joined me in the living room. He had a condom packet in his free hand, and he tossed it to my coffee table next to my couch before sinking suddenly to his knees in front of me.

"Leo?"

His fingers hooked into the waistband of my panties, and he pushed me backward until I was leaning against my front door and he was kneeling between my parted legs.

"I've been thinking about how you tasted on my fingers for three weeks, gorgeous," Leo rasped, peeling my underwear down my thighs. "I need a refresher. Step up."

I swallowed hard as he tugged on my underwear around my ankles. He was so ridiculously beautiful, those huge dark eyes staring up at me, dense muscle in strong lines down his back. I raised one foot and then the other as Leo took my last scrap of clothing off. My eyes trailed to my living room windows, wondering if anyone would or could see us like this, but the lights were off, just the orangey glow of flickering street lights outside lighting the room, and the apartment building across the street had its blinds down, mostly.

Leo stole my attention back as he pulled my hips forward and dragged one of my legs to drape over his shoulder. He kissed my thigh by his cheek and scuffed it softly with his stubble.

He looked up at me again. "Put your hands in my hair. I

liked that. Wanna know when I do something that feels good for you."

I slid my fingers into that black silk gratefully and whimpered as Leo pulled me to his mouth, pressing a soft kiss directly against my clit, a warm feathery thrill rushing through me in response. When his tongue slipped out, leaving a hot trail from my clit down to my opening, my hips kicked and my knees buckled.

"Fuck!"

Leo hummed, tongue lapping up my quickly accumulating arousal, shoulders wedging my thighs open and helping to keep me upright. "How much time do we have, gorgeous?"

"Wha-? Um…thirty to forty-five—oh, fuck, Leo!"

Leo hummed against my core as my hands fisted in his hair. His tongue was pressing up inside of me, and I gasped. Fuck. I thought I'd gotten eaten out before, but those guys were *wimps* and Leo was divine. His hands guided my hips with a gentle suggestion, and in a moment I was riding his tongue as it teased me open with the most sinful nudges and caresses.

"Oh, god, Leo, please. Please."

I prayed more in a three-minute time span than I ever had in my life combined, my whole body tensed in a curve as I waited for the onslaught of filthy perfection to crest. Leo's nose nuzzled against my clit, his tongue fucking me and lips slurping at the fruits of his efforts. I cried out, tugging on his hair, making him groan, my own shiver following like a sexual domino effect riding out between us.

"Harder," I whispered, almost ashamed of the word, of the rough edge that I feared even as it took me over into ecstasy every time.

Leo moaned against my skin and one of his hands left my hip to wedge between us, replacing his tongue at a deeper angle. My voice was high and cracking, and then Leo dove in again, lips clasping over my clit, sucking hard on the spot until I bowed forward. My body lost its strength and its balance in the wave that rushed up my spine and over my head, and if it weren't for Leo fastened firmly on my sex, I would've fallen right to the floor. He held me up, two fingers fucking into me as his lips continued the assault. I shouted through clenched teeth, vision flashing and pulse pounding. My hands slid from his tortured locks to brace myself against his shoulder, and Leo softened his touches as I shuddered through the aftershocks.

I was ready to push him to the floor, settle myself on top of him, and ride him to the same spectacular finish he'd gifted me, when he pulled back and pressed me back to the door as he stood. I was weak-limbed as he gathered me to his chest, but I jumped when he needed me to, leaning in to suck my own flavor off his sweet lips.

"Goddamn, gorgeous," Leo whispered.

I hummed my agreement as Leo carried me with shuffling steps toward the couch. He stumbled and I caught myself, finding my feet under my shaking legs, and marching forward, backing Leo to the edge of the couch and then pushing him down by my grip on his shoulders.

"I'm going to get addicted to your taste," he said, bouncing against my cushions, his cock bobbing against his stomach and leaving a drop of pre-cum on his muscles. He was thick for a beta, which meant he'd feel like a stretch for me for sure. I couldn't wait.

"I'm afraid I'm going to enable that habit of yours," I said, grinning as Leo leaned forward and pressed a kiss to my mound, reaching around me to grab the condom. I settled my knees on either side of his hip as he fumbled with the packet, rushing to tear it open. "Can it be like this?" I asked, nibbling on my bottom lip.

Leo looked up, the condom halfway on and his eyebrows raising. "You on top? Like I told you, that's my topping of choice."

I laughed and covered my face briefly with my palms. What a perfect, wonderful dork.

When his hands reached for mine, I gathered them together in one loose grip and then scooted closer on the couch, pushing his hands behind his head and against the wall.

"Just for fun," I said, so he would know this wasn't something I was afraid of. I just wanted to watch his face as…

I took his cock in my free hand, bending so my face hovered over his. His tongue flicked out to wet his lips and he hummed, finding my taste still there on his skin. Then I fitted him against my opening and our eyes locked as I sank down his length in a slow rocking rhythm.

"Fuck," he whispered, our panting breaths mingling as I rolled my hips, a whine caught at the back of my throat. "Too much?" he asked.

"No. No, shit, you feel so good, Leo." He wasn't too much at *all*, he was perfect, like he'd been designed to nestle inside of me, make me feel like a completed puzzle.

Leo's smile was soft and his eyes were hooded as one of his hands slipped free from my grasp, cupping my jaw. I nuzzled into his palm and together we sighed as I took him to the hilt, rubbing myself against his base.

"Good doesn't even begin to describe," he said, and I nodded, my eyelids drooping.

I gave in to the urge, pressing my forehead to Leo's and letting my eyes shut as I started to ride him. The drag of him was full and swollen inside of me, making sure I felt every fraction of movement between us.

"Let me touch you."

I nodded and my palm flattened against the wall as Leo started a thorough exploration of my body with his hands, gripping and stroking, falling to my hips to urge me faster for a moment before sliding up to roll my breasts against his palm. His breath was on my neck, our faces close but resisting the urge to kiss again so we could focus on our bodies connecting.

"I knew as soon as we started dancing. I knew it would feel this good."

I kissed his jaw and then sucked on the spot, discovering the flavor of him all over again, sweet and clean. I hadn't had a clue. If I had, I don't know that I would've flown from that bathroom, alpha bite or not. Remembering the moment, I leaned back and found the scar on his shoulder, tracing it with my fingertips. Leo held his breath as I bent my head, confused by my own impulse to press my lips to the spot. The kiss was slow and Leo moaned, his throat exposed as his head fell back, bobbing with a swallow.

"It feels good?" I asked.

"Your mouth anywhere feels good, Lola," he rasped. He swallowed again and then added, "Yeah. Bi-bite a little?"

My steady rocking on his lap paused as I considered the request, and I smiled as Leo twitched inside of me. I opened my mouth and set my teeth over the marks, biting gently.

Leo's response was immediate. His cock throbbed and his hand flew to my hips, tightening as he started to buck beneath me. I moaned and bit harder, and Leo released a slow, plaintive howl of pleasure, his hips racing and cock fucking roughly into me.

I pulled away and Leo gasped as I wrestled us down into the cushions until he was flat on his back. I dove down again, this time scratching my teeth against a new spot, higher on his throat. Leo groaned, his fingers digging in, fucking me from below as I latched, sucking against his skin and grinding back into his thrusts.

What the hell is wrong with you? the nasty voice whispered.

"God, Lola, don't stop."

Nothing, I answered for myself, sliding one hand between Leo and I to toy at my own clit. Our bodies came together with wet, noisy smacks, and Leo's arms circled my back, holding me to his chest as he drummed inside of me, my fingers trapped and working myself into a desperate frenzy.

"Come. I gotta feel you squeeze around my cock the way you do my fingers, gorgeous," Leo gasped. "Come for me."

I released his throat, shouting and thrashing as lightning whipped through me. Leo growled as I clenched around his still thrusting length, and I bucked and rode out the electrifying pleasure until my muscles went loose and limp and useless.

"Fuck. Can I—?" Leo sat up, still rolling into me, and he tried to turn us.

He wanted on top.

"Ye—yeah, you—" I cackled with laughter as Leo's attempt to roll us over ran out of room on my narrow couch and we slid clumsily to the floor.

I bounced on my back against my hardwood floors, but it was a soft landing. A moment later, I was breathless and Leo joined me, spreading my thighs open and sliding home again. My sexed-up sweaty skin slid and stuck on the floor as he settled over me, fucking me desperately with a tangled furrow on his brow, eyes fixed to my face.

"Do it again," he rasped.

"Bite?"

"No. Come again, Lola."

"I-I can't—"

Leo reared back, changing the angle of his thrusts, and his fingers found my clit, merciless and rough against the sensitive nerves. I shouted, chest rising and eyes squeezing shut, and a moment later Leo's mouth was on my breast, sucking hard and biting with his teeth, drawing a line of pleasure directly from my breast to my cunt. I throbbed around him, my hands skidding on the smooth floor as he fucked me, every bucking roll of his hips driving me squeaking against the floor.

My legs circled his hips, and Leo was fast and rough between my thighs. His fingers took my clit in a pinch, and the fire in my blood was sudden and explosive. I came with a strangled scream, arms pulling Leo against me as he lost his wild pace with a series of deep, sharp kicks inside of me. He twitched on top of me as we went limp together, our breaths loud and uneven.

"Holy. Shit," I breathed, eyes opening huge to stare up at my ceiling.

"Tell me that was romantic," Leo said. "I promised myself we'd be really romantic when it happened."

A gasping giggle escaped me. "You fucked me against my front door, on my couch, and my *floor*, Leo. It was about as romantic as it can get."

He puffed against my throat, his body heavy but pleasant on top of mine.

A soft knock sounded on my front door and the pair of us stiffened.

"Um. Just gonna leave this out here for you guys. Uh. Go team?"

I stared in shock at Leo and mouthed slowly 'Oh my god.'

"Thank you," Leo answered to the delivery guy standing on *the other side of the door*.

"Yup. Yup. Have a nice night! Nicer night! Have a nice time!"

Rapid footsteps faded down the staircase and the laugh bubbled up from deep inside of me, a sudden floating happiness in the wake of three orgasms and the most absurd finish to sex I'd ever had. Leo's laugh met mine and I gasped as he pulled out of me, leaving a wet kiss on my mouth.

"Stay there."

"Naked on my floor?" I asked, more giggles rising.

He grinned, kneeling over me. "Just for a minute. I'm gonna take care of the condom and grab us a sheet to curl up in and that pizza."

I sighed as he pushed up onto his feet and ran down the hall to the bathroom, deciding that sex on the floor was enough floor exposure for me, and I could wait just as easily on the couch. I was sitting up when Leo returned, streaking down my hall and tossing me my bedding.

"You are not going to open that door—"

He did. He opened it naked.

"No one's out—oh, shit."

He dove back in and shut the door, locking it behind him as he grinned at me. There were two red marks on his skin from my bites, and his hair was sticking up at odd angles from my fists. He joined me on the couch, sliding into the open spot I made for him in my tangle of bedsheets and comforter.

"Someone was coming up the stairs," he said, breathless and grinning.

"You're a little bit crazy," I said, snuggling into his warm chest and draping my legs over his, tucking the sheet over my breasts for makeshift modesty.

"I'm a little bit deliriously happy," he said, leaning in and kissing my shoulder before pulling the hot box of pizza onto our laps.

God, that smelled good.

"Now I just need to stuff my face so I've got energy for us to do that again," Leo said, opening the box. My stomach let out an audible growl as I was hit by a waft of greasy, cheesy, salty ambrosia.

"Before or after that shower I haven't had yet?" I asked.

"During?" Leo suggested, eyebrows ticking up.

"During is good," I nodded, taking a slice from the box, my mouth watering as the cheese made a perfect stretch from the center.

DURING WAS EXCELLENT. After the shower, with a couple hours of sleep and wandering, greedy hands was even better.

"I am thoroughly impressed with your range," I said, my cheek on Leo's heaving chest.

"My range...of motion?" he asked, catching his breath.

"Mm. That too. I meant your range of sex stylings."

"Sex *stylings*?"

"Yeah, you know. Rough and fast, fucking me across my living room floor? Check." I made a little checkmark in the air with my fingertip and continued. "Better stamina than my building's hot water tank? Check. Slow, intense, gropey bedtime sex? Check."

Leo caught my finger and drew my hand to his lips,

kissing my palm. "Just so you know, I was going for 'passionate' not 'gropey bedtime,' but thank you."

I curled against him, pressing my giddy smile into his shoulder. This all felt so *good*, I sort of couldn't believe it was happening to me.

It can't last.

My smile settled and I closed my eyes, hoping the post-sex haze and another few hours of sleep might shut the nasty voice in my head up for a while longer. Instead I found myself thinking of Rake and what he'd said about the betas who chased his pack.

"Hey, Leo?"

"Hm, what's up, gorgeous?"

"How long do you think we can do this?"

"I mean, I thought I was being pretty optimistic bringing six condoms, but if I need to run to the store, I will."

My lips twitched with another smile, but this time an ache followed in my chest. "I mean...if I can't be around alphas, how long can it last?"

Leo let out a long sigh, and I shook my head.

"Fuck. No, erase that question. I don't know why—"

Leo turned and hauled me against him, his arms wrapped around my arms and my waist in a trap that bordered on distressing. But I held my breath and waited for him to speak, knowing if he let me go right now, I would probably run to the bathroom just to force space between us.

"I'd be lying if I said I wasn't hoping that with enough time, if we took things at your pace, that you might find yourself comfortable around my pack and I wouldn't have to make any decisions like that. I..."

"You're bonded," I whispered, and Leo nodded, his chin on my shoulder bumping against me.

"Is that... Do you think that you'd be comfortable trying to be around them occasionally? Or do you know, right now, that's never going to happen for you?" It wasn't asked with any judgment, and I wondered what he would say if I said I knew for certain I never wanted to go to his home or be around his alphas.

He might lie and say we could work around it, he might even say that and *believe* it, but I knew it was impossible. So instead, I tried to imagine myself lowering my guards. Not for everyone, but for Leo and his pack. I liked Cyrus, and there was something…comforting almost, about Matthieu.

"You don't have to answer now," Leo said. "I know it's probably something we should've thought about before tonight but I…it wouldn't have changed how badly I wanted you."

It might've kept my heart from breaking if we fell apart sooner rather than later though. Except I didn't want to think about not having nights like this with Leo again. Not having someone really *see* me the way he had when he found me earlier.

"I think that I should try to be more open to your pack if that's what you want, or they want, or—"

Leo's hands turned me to face him, and he sat up on his elbow. We could barely see each other, there was just a little light from the hall bathroom.

"You mean that?" he asked, voice rising with hope.

I nodded. "Yes."

"Lola…" His head dipped and I met him in the drowsy, licking kiss. "Hmm… I think you must like me."

I laughed, and the slow trickling tension that had risen during the conversation faded away again.

"I definitely like you," I answered in a whisper, and I demanded another kiss, and then another, until we were coaxing each other to sleep with lazy grazes of our lips.

Lola

11

"I know what you're going to say. But Lollipop, my queen, my goddess, please just consider. It's the last day of fashion week. It's gonna be the best, biggest, most amazing after-party, and I really think you've got to congratulate yourself and come with me. Now before you—"

"Sure, I'll go," I said.

"I'm sorry, you'll fucking what?" Rake asked, makeup smeared over his face and down his neck as he dropped his third wipe to the counter and gaped at me in the reflection of the mirror.

"I said I'll go to the party," I said, shrugging and trying to keep my smile under control.

Rake's eyes narrowed and he huffed. "Damnit, Leo already sold you on it, didn't he?"

I laughed and finished packing up my stuff before grabbing the wipes from Rake's hands. "He did, but you were doing a *really* good job, so don't feel bad. Let me do this."

Rake 'pfft'd but the sound died off as I turned his chair to face me and tipped his chin up, washing away the remaining streaks of makeup with gentle, thorough sweeps.

"Leo's been walking around all day every day in a total daydream. Day-sex-dream. He's very smug about how well laid he is, basically," Rake muttered as I washed around his lips. "I'm super jealous, by the way."

"You have a pack. Fuck your alphas," I said.

"I'm not jealous of *you*, I'm jealous of Leo getting to sex you up."

I blushed and shook my head. Rake's brand of flirtation was more aggressive, and I wasn't really sure how to respond most of the time. Especially not when we were this close together and he was lounging back in his chair like he was just waiting for me to climb onto his lap, those glass green eyes watching my every move.

I blinked and leaned back, aware of the warmth in my cheeks. It'd been a few nights since Leo had stayed over at my place, and I was surprised by how *eager* I was to have him back in my bed. I'd kept my bar flings in a careful and strict routine, and those had been messy and brief. Even before meeting Buzz, I usually had a craving for sex and once it was satisfied, I was good for a few weeks until boredom set in again.

Now, it was different. I wasn't craving the release so much as I was craving the time with Leo; the touching and teasing that led up to sex, the connection during, and the gentle pause on the spinning world as we curled up together after.

"Your dopey happy expression isn't *quite* as bad as his, but it's close," Rake said, but his smile was fond as he stared up at me.

I ignored him and grabbed up a jar of oil cleanser. "Brought you this. Want me to put it on you?"

"I will take absolutely any excuse to have you touching me," Rake said, slouching down in his seat and throwing his head back.

I snorted and stood behind him, scooping some of the solid oil from the jar and warming it on my clean fingers before massaging it onto Rake's face. He held a small groan of pleasure behind his lips, his eyes falling shut as I spread the oil over his skin, working out the last of the makeup left.

"I hope he's paying you extra for the spa treatment."

I looked up into the mirror to find David standing behind me, and I grinned as I continued to spoil Rake.

"You know I never skimp," Rake mumbled, a dreamy smile painted over his lips.

"Hey, I'll be done in a minute," I said, turning my cheek to accept David's kiss there.

David was about the same height as me, comparatively short to the models running around backstage, and I'd always thought he dressed more like a lawyer than a fashion buyer for some of the best boutiques in the city. He preferred for his look to be called 'classic,' but I noticed even he'd stepped it up for the week's festivities, wearing a bold patterned jacket in a subtle shade of plum.

"This is for you," David said, hanging a black garment bag from the mirror we'd been using. "And it's a gift, not a loan, so I had it altered for you."

"David, I said—"

"Don't bicker with me, Lola. Just take the dress."

"Fine. Thank you."

"Ohhh, can *I* bully you into accepting presents too?" Rake asked, and I glared at David, stepping away and wiping my hands on a rag.

"No. Go wash up. I'm gonna put my own makeup on before changing."

"Start by giving her your swag bag extras and then work your way up to outright purcha—Ow, Lola!" David jumped out of the way as I pinched hard on his arm for encouraging Rake. I glared at him and he glared back, but I was pretty sure I caught the sneaky bastard fighting a smile.

Rake slipped away, grinning at me over his shoulder, and I rolled my eyes.

"That's cute. Rake usually lets people flirt with *him* not the other way around," David mused.

"Don't encourage him," I answered, taking Rake's seat.

Rake had been more careful around me this week. Vocally, he took every opportunity to come on to me, but physically he held back. Once again, it must've gone through their pack's rumor-mill that I was twitchy about being scent-marked. This time I was a little grateful. With Rake restraining himself, I found that I could set our interactions on my own terms of comfort. If it was a post-nightmare morning, I stayed restrained. If it was the end of a long and successful week like this one, maybe I'd let go a little at the party. I knew Leo liked the idea of Rake and I hitting it off, and I did crave that glittery feeling the omega's attention left me with.

"Why not?" David asked. "He's an omega, not an alpha. Now, aren't you going to even peek at the dress?"

My smile was tight-lipped. "Show me!"

"WOW."

Leo didn't actually say the word, but I watched his lips form it as his eyebrows rose up his forehead and he looked me over head to toe, twice.

I blushed for the fiftieth time since I'd put on the electric purple faux-wrap dress David had brought for me. It fit like a glove, the wrap creating a deep-v collar with the skirt parted over one thigh.

"Told you. Total wet dream," Rake murmured behind me. He jogged down the front steps of the hotel our last show had been at, leaving a brief kiss against Leo's cheek before murmuring something in his beta's ear.

Leo's smile spread, his eyes still on me, and then Rake left him to slide into the waiting limo. I caught a brief glimpse of long legs inside of the limo, and then Rake shut the door. We'd meet him at the party with the others, but Leo had arranged for us to ride separately. I wondered if it was a pain, if I was making Leo and the others jump through hoops to accommodate me, and then I forced down the doubts in my head for a minute and stepped down the stairs.

"It's the dress," I said to Leo as he continued to stare.

"Bullshit," he answered, grinning. "You're doing that dress favors. Let me take your bags."

"You're looking especially fashionable tonight," I said,

passing Leo my work bags gratefully and then looping my arm through his.

"I promised Cyrus and Rake I wouldn't embarrass them tonight. They say my sense of style is 'chronically dull,'" Leo said, grinning as if the idea of annoying his packmates entertained him.

He was wearing a brown leather tailored coat with the sleeves pushed up to his elbows, deep blue shirt, and skinny black tie peeking out against his throat. His pants had a soft sheen to them and a faint stripe, making his legs look long above his boots.

"You'll have to tell me if you get bored," Leo said. "I sell these people beach houses, but I never know what to say to them at parties."

"Baby and I used to get David to sneak us into events like this so we could mooch off the open bar," I admitted.

Leo grinned and opened the door to the short town car waiting for us. "I had a catering staff refuse to serve me another pastry puff once. Party finger food is my weakness."

I slid into the back seat giggling, and when I looked back I caught Leo watching the gap of my skirt rising up my thigh.

"We could skip the party too," I said, grinning at him.

Leo's cheeks darkened as he ducked and followed me into the backseat, setting my bags down on the floor. "I'm not saying I won't try and convince you to sneak out early with me. But no, let's do this. You deserve to celebrate your success this week too. Rake said you've got a good buzz going with the community."

My eyebrows bounced. "I do?"

Leo mimicked my expression. "You did your first ever hired makeup artist work for Rakim Oren during fashion week. Yeah, Lola, you impressed people. Fuck, you're gorgeous when you blush. Come here, I've missed you this week."

I fell into Leo's waiting arms, shivering against the cool leather of his jacket while taking greedy kisses from his mouth.

"Mphm." He leaned back briefly and stared at my mouth with a quirked smile. "You taste like lipstick."

"You're wearing some now," I said, pecking my lips against the purple smears of lipstick I'd left on Leo's mouth.

"Cold?" he asked, passing warm hands over the goosebumps on my arms.

"A little. I didn't think David was gonna pick something this…exposing for me, and all I had with me was a hoodie."

Leo reached around me and pulled a massive blue scarf up from the seat, wrapping it around my shoulders with a soft smile on his face. It smelled like alpha, specifically Caleb and his warm soothing smell, and I decided not to protest. Maybe it was Caleb and Leo's connection, or maybe Caleb just had an especially relaxing pheromone, but he didn't put me on edge the way other alphas did. And the scarf was as soft as a cloud.

"Now we look like a set," Leo said. "I've got your lipstick on, and you've got my scarf. Now come here and make sure the color is even."

LEO and I stood close together at the bar, watching a pair of tipsy models do an improvised pole dance on the spinning carousel. Two pairs of teetering high heels were abandoned at the edge of the ride, and there were a couple security personnel with careful eyes on the girls to make sure neither was injured.

"They're having a nice time," Leo reasoned with a shrug.

"This is why jumpsuits became trendy," I said with a nod as one of the models did an enthusiastic high kick. I caught Leo's side-eye and shook my head. "Don't even suggest it. I have a strict no flashing the public policy."

He grinned and leaned in, kissing the corner of my jaw.

The party was located at a high end, rooftop club downtown. The music was heavy, and the dance floor was crowded with more models posing as their personal assistants stood aside taking photos for social media. The bar was open, and there were snack trays drifting around the room, and photobooths, and—inexplicably—a conga line running the length of the room led by someone in a full-body rhinoceros costume. There was a zebra somewhere too, so maybe it was a zoo theme for the evening.

"Another drink?" Leo asked, nuzzling against my ear.

I leaned my hips back against his, warmth pooling in my center as Leo's hands squeezed my hips. I set my glass down on the counter and eyed it briefly. That was my second of the night, and if Leo ordered me another I'd be at my third, my usual self-prescribed limit. But would it be so bad to be buzzed? Leo wasn't going to let anything happen to me, and even if he was looking in the other direction…

My eyes slid across the room to where most of Leo's pack were clustered together in a private booth. My gaze landed on Wes, the big alpha in charge of protecting Rake, and he twitched, staring down at his own glass of alcohol, one that hadn't seemed to diminish at all in the hour we'd all been at the party. With Rake tucked between Cyrus and Caleb, the three of them together a beautiful blend of fashion styles, Wes' attention seemed to be drifting more towards me. It didn't feel predatory, more like he was so used to being protective and now I was the object of his focus.

"I'm gonna wait a bit," I decided, turning to face Leo. "We can sit with them, you know."

He didn't even ask who I meant, his stare immediately flicking over my shoulder to where his pack was. "We could go dance too. I don't want you to feel stressed tonight."

"Thank you," I said, leaning in to kiss his chin. "But I think it's weird that we're avoiding them. If I get uncomfortable, I'll let you know. Why don't we ask them to dance with us?"

Leo's smile was slow and sultry. "Gorgeous, you're going to do a terrible job of discouraging Rake if you let him see you dance. You dance like sin." I blushed and shook my head, but Leo's fingers squeezed my hips again, drawing my attention back to him. "But if you want to let go with us both a bit, the others will make sure no one gets so much as a glimpse."

My lips pursed as Leo and I stared at one another. Was he saying what I thought he was saying?

"No one can resist Rake for long," Leo murmured, his gentle stare stripping me down to the secrets I tried to keep even from myself.

"I like him," I admitted, and Leo nodded. "But I'm not here with you, just to—"

Leo's head dipped, mouth slanting over mine, and for a minute I let go of any thought of alphas or omegas or designations at all. It was just Leo and I, his clean scent washing away my anxieties as it filled my lungs.

"Never doubted that," Leo said, his forehead against mine. "Just know that I'm not going to discourage you from getting closer to anyone in my pack. Especially not Rake. He and I share more than an alpha. We're, you know, lovers too."

I nodded and kissed him again, holding on to the moment of us. Just us. I didn't know if I had it in me to relax with Rake, to open myself up and let down some of the densely constructed walls I'd been sheltering in. But I knew that my longevity with Leo would likely wither if I resisted any connections I had with his pack.

"You have me, Lola. Either way," Leo said.

"Okay. Good. Then I don't want to be a wedge between you and your pack," I said, stepping back and pulling one of his hands into mine. I tugged him in the direction of the booth, and Leo followed, smile stretching over his purple-stained lips. He'd wiped my lipstick away once already, but this time I thought I'd let him leave it.

"There's my conquering hero," Cyrus said as we reached the table.

I smiled and leaned back against Leo's chest as I realized that maybe I'd been a little bit preemptive about dipping my toes in with the pack. The table was strong with alpha and omega pheromones and Wes was a massive revelation. I hadn't caught much from him before, but the sweet sex and sea mist fantasy that was curling around me was such a surprise, it left me weak in the knees.

And Rake said betas weren't hounding this alpha?

You don't chase alphas anymore, remember?

I did remember, vividly. But I was definitely…appreciating Wes' scent at the moment, although I couldn't bring myself to look at him at the same time, as if he might be able to read my reaction on my face.

"Where's Matt?" Leo asked.

"With Carolyn," Rake said, nose wrinkling briefly, he glanced at me. "That's Matt's girlfriend. She's lovely, but she says Matt's enough testosterone for her in one sitting."

Meaning she took Matt without his pack. Rake's slight pout stiffened my resolve to try and not monopolize Leo away from his pack so much. Even now, Caleb was looking at the pair of us like someone had placed a buffet of confectionary treats in front of him after he'd just found out he was diabetic.

"I was going to drag Leo out to dance with me, but I could use some backup," I said.

I didn't miss the sudden surprise over their faces, although Rake recovered fastest, pushing softly against a stunned Caleb's shoulder.

"Count us in," Rake said, all about shoving his alpha out of the booth. Cyrus followed with a grin, but Caleb paused as he stood off the bench.

Leo's alpha was a full head taller than me and he bowed slightly in front of me, blonde hair falling into his pale eyes.

"You're sure?" Caleb asked, as quietly as he could in a hall full of pounding music and fashion industry moguls shouting at one another to be heard over the melee. I realized then that Matthieu wasn't the only one with an accent. Caleb was British on top of being stupidly handsome.

I nodded, swallowing as the space between us seemed to grow hazy. Caleb's effect on me was almost like a sedative drug, and I fought not to swoon into him.

"Odette's around somewhere," Caleb said, standing up

straight and staring over the heads of the crowd. "We'll keep her out of your hair."

It was Leo who stiffened, not me, at the mention of the female alpha, and I twisted in his arms to catch his stiff expression.

"She used to be...I was part of her collection," Leo said in my ear.

His dark eyes locked with mine and I recalled all the moments he'd read me so easily, empathized with my anxiety regarding alphas, known exactly the right thing to do or say as I fell to pieces. He'd been through his own version of trauma with an alpha. And now...

I glanced at Caleb, at Cyrus and Rake shimmying their way to the dance floor, Wes waiting at our backs with a hawk's gaze on the crowd. He had an alpha. He had a pack.

Maybe...

I shook the thoughts out of my head, leaving a brief kiss on Leo's jaw and then sliding under his arm against his side as we followed the others to the dance floor. Nearly there, Caleb's eye caught on a couple at the bar, waving them in our direction.

It was Matthieu with a woman I assumed had to be Carolyn. She *was* lovely. Stunning and tall and curvaceous, with billowing red hair, and the kind of graceful beauty that came on with maturity. She smiled indulgently at Matthieu and sighed as he stepped away from the bar, allowing him to pull her in our direction. Matthieu looked so totally different I might not have recognized him on my own. He was in a simple white t-shirt and torn up jeans, the opposite of the dress-to-impress looks we were surrounded by, and his hair was a little wilder than what I'd seen at the office. He looked less like a CEO and more like a former model or designer. No, he looked like a musician, I realized, like he had been before starting his own music magazine decades ago.

"We won't keep you long, Carolyn," Rake called to the knockout redhead.

She smirked at Rake and narrowed her eyes. "If you want

to wear these heels on the dance floor, we can trade and then I'll be happy to join you for as long as you please, Rakim."

Rake's chin lifted at the challenge, and a moment later I laughed as he stepped out of his shoes and lifted them to hold in front of Carolyn's nose. "As a matter of fact, I'm amazing in heels."

Carolyn's smile hardened, and I looked past her to see what Matthieu thought of the aggressive teasing between his omega and his girlfriend. His eyes caught mine and there was laughter creasing the corners that I answered with a smile. Carolyn pressed one hand to Matthieu's shoulder for balance and unbuckled her stilettos, taking Rakim's short boots and sliding into them with a sigh.

They looked like clown shoes on her, and the heels didn't fit Rakim at *all*, but he strutted away in them with a slight wobble that made me snort. Carolyn followed him in an awkward stomp, lips quirked in a smile that seemed more determined than sincere. I caught the first whisper of her soft floral scent as she passed me. She was a beta, and I was a little shocked that she was willing to challenge her boyfriend's omega.

"Matthieu's girlfriends never like Rake," Leo said in my ear.

Matthieu trailed after the two, hands in his pockets and shoulders sliding between flailing dancing models. His head turned and his eyes caught mine again, head tipping in question. Was I coming?

"Does Rake ever like Matthieu's girlfriends?" I asked Leo.

Caleb caught the question and he smiled at me. "He tries," he said, shrugging. "Come on. We'll have to put ourselves between them before Rake gets it in his head to challenge Carolyn to a dance battle."

I checked behind me and Wes was still there, bringing up the rear from a close but not crowding distance. I offered him a smile, and he looked so startled by it that I'd almost turned around before his cheeks twitched in answer. Leo pulled me along by my hand, the music growing louder as we worked our way to the heart of the crowd. It was a low tempo groove, one that was easy to raise your arms and swing your hips to without having to worry about impressing anyone.

Leo's hands found mine in the air, his chest against my bare back as we swayed closer to his pack. Rake broke out from between Caleb and Cyrus, framing me at my front. He paused a few inches away and raised his eyebrows. He was even taller than usual thanks to Carolyn's heels, and he waited in front of me, matching the beat of my twisting hips easily as he waited for permission.

I nodded, stepping in with Leo at my back, and Rake met me halfway, his hips barely grazing against mine. One of his hands settled on my hip, the other slipping back to Leo to pull us closer together. Leo took my hands and draped them around Rake's shoulders, holding them there with one touch while his free hand cradled Rake's hips. The three of us moved in liquid unison, and with one deep breath I was drowning in Rake's perfume, my head back against Leo's shoulders where I fit perfectly.

"Sin," Leo said in my ear, kissing my pulse.

Rake watched my eyes as his head dropped, resting his forehead against mine, his grip firm on my hip. I could see the alphas out of the corners of my eyes, Caleb and Cyrus dancing together on one side, Matthieu spinning Carolyn on the other. I smiled as I thought of Wes looming behind us all, serving glares to anyone who tried to join our close cluster.

Rake's scent drowned out any others, and if I closed my eyes I was alone with him and Leo. I relaxed in their holds, and Rake's cheek brushed nearly to mine. I leaned into him, letting him mark me. His breath puffed against my skin.

"My Lollipop," he said, lips against my ear, tongue flicking out to taste and making me shiver.

We stayed like that for three songs, until my body burned and my chest was tight with a new kind of discomfort. Rake's hands never traveled, although Leo's did plenty until my skin was so hot, I was ready for him to peel me out of my dress right on the dance floor. When the third song ended and Rake leaned back, my eyes finally opened again.

His pupils were blown black and his tongue flicked out to graze over his bottom lip. I resisted the urge to lean in and steal my taste back from him, to catch some of his own. His chest heaved and he pressed forward once, let me feel the girth of his arousal against my stomach, and then he turned and dove between his two alphas. Caleb caught him in his arms immediately, and Cyrus was ready, taking Rake's face in his hands and pulling their mouths together in the rough and demanding kiss of an alpha.

I twisted to face Leo who looked smug and aroused.

"Take me home," I said, breathless.

Lola
12

"...Yeah, but he's not showing any of the usual symptoms, you know?" Zane mused to Betty, waving a carrot stick in punctuation. "Like, he hasn't started wearing a pocket square again."

"Whose pocket square are we judging?" I asked, pulling out the open chair at the cafeteria table with my coworkers.

My photos from fashion week had gone over great with the team, and we'd spent the next week replicating some of the looks—easy to do when I had firsthand knowledge. Zane and Betty pulled me into their tiny clique, completing my orientation at the magazine and digging for details of fashion week. I knew it had to do, at least a little bit, with them wanting to keep an eye on the successful new girl. Their attitudes were still supportive, rather than competitive or shady, and I probably had Cyrus' determination to use the team as a complete unit to thank for that.

Betty and Zane exchanged a calculating look, and Zane shrugged briefly before Betty answered me.

"Cyrus', kind of. I think his pocket square phase was just a fashion thing, *but* he does tend to get a little extra when he's dating someone new," Betty explained to me. "And now he's about a month overdue for a fling."

My eyebrows bounced. "You guys keep track of his romantic life?"

"Not *intentionally*," Zane assured me. "Cyrus is just... totally lacking in subtlety when he's fallen in love. He gets more than usually giddy about it all, and like…*whistles?* Buys us lots of lunches, brings pastries in the morning, that kind of thing."

"Romance is his drug of choice," Betty said with a nod.

"He's…a lot different than most alphas," I said, pushing my grain salad around in its bowl. The Stanmore's cafeteria was a culinary wonderland, with several booths set up around the room, one entirely devoted to a rotating calendar of award-winning chefs.

Betty and Zane exchanged another look heavy with unspoken gossip before Zane leaned forward, pushing his tray aside to whisper across the small space to me.

"Their whole pack is totally bizarre. Like, an *open* relationship pack? *With* an omega?" Zane hissed. "Rakim Oren must get off on shutting down his alpha's relationships or something."

"He gave Wendy, what? Like, two months before pulling the plug on her and Cyrus?" Betty muttered, and Zane nodded.

My head reeled at the new information, this twisted up version of Rake and Leo's pack. "Wendy and Cyrus?"

"Mmm. That was an explosive year at *Designate*, let me tell you. I swear I thought Wendy was going to cut Beauty altogether," Zane said.

I tried to imagine laid-back Cyrus with brutal Wendy and was surprised to find it was kind of easy. It also explained a lot about the meeting I'd sat in on between them. And Rake's nerves about how Wendy would paint him to me. I didn't buy the way Betty and Zane were talking about Rake though, not after spending the week with him. Instead, I wondered what Cyrus was thinking, getting involved with his boss.

"Did Mr. Omega of the century hiss at you every time you looked at one of his alphas, Lo?" Betty asked, and Zane snickered.

I swallowed and tried to keep my expression neutral, even though I realized I really didn't like my nickname on Betty's tongue.

"I didn't really run into them," I lied, and hoped there weren't any photos floating around of the party I'd been to on Saturday night. "And he's...we got along okay, but I don't know that I got a real glimpse of him in that setting and everything." Lie. Rake was a sweetheart and I was already missing him.

"What was the pay like?" Betty whispered.

That, at least, I could boast about. I grinned at them both and nodded. "Extremely generous."

"Well, we can't fault him there," Zane said, shrugging and raising his bottle of kombucha. "To eccentric omegas, and to Lola buying the first round of drinks tonight."

"Here, here!" Betty cried.

I bit my lip as I laughed. Damn you, Leo, for being out of town. Where was my excuse to get out of *this*?

"YOU LIVE IN A SHIIIIIIT NEIGHBORHOOD, GIRL," Zane cried, far too loud for the late hour. He was hanging out of the back of the ride-share we'd ordered from the club. His hair sat high on the top of his head in a ponytail I'd given him when he'd gotten sweaty dancing, and it swung forward, giving him the hysterical impression of bangs.

I giggled and tripped over myself, catching my hand on the railing up to my door, the neighborhood spinning around me. "Shhh...people are sleeping."

"Mmmkay. Be good, killer," Zane said with a wave before throwing himself back into the seat, the door slamming like a gunshot behind him.

I hummed and rolled my shoulders back, trying to take steady steps up to the front door, as if I could conjure sobriety by willpower alone.

With Betty and Zane, my three drink limit was obliterated. I'd done my best to ward them off, but by the time we left Philia—my request—I was well and truly drunk. I pulled open the downstairs door and tsk'ed at the broken lock. David had pressured the landlord while I was signing the lease to have the street door's lock fixed, but two months in and it had yet to change.

I slid against the stairwell wall as I dragged myself up to my floor. The lights overhead flickered and I paused, drawing in a deep breath and wondering if I could sleep like this, or if the nightmares would swallow me up if I was too weak to fight. I dug into my purse for my keys and undid the three locks, pulling out my phone and checking the time as I stepped inside. Was it too late to call Leo? His voice would settle my woozy heart before bed.

There was a message waiting, my phone screen the only illumination in the room as I shut the door behind me.

UNKNOWN 2:21 AM

u bein good showgirl?

My heart stopped and my phone slipped from my fingers, crashing to the floor with my purse. The room was dark, and my free hand hovered over the light switch, afraid to flip it and find I wasn't alone.

"Look at you, Showgirl, look at the mess we made of you. Filthy girl, we sure made you scream."

I heaved, bile surging up in my throat, and I raced to the bathroom through the dark, imagining the sound of feet chasing me with the crash of my heels on the floor. My knees hit the tile with a jarring ache and I threw up into the toilet, vomit burning like acid in my throat. Tears were already gathering in my eyes, and I braced myself for the panic attack.

Just breathe. Just stay awake. Get the lights on, Lola.

I was sick twice more before I was able to drag myself to the wall and flip the switch. In the half-second between my touching the switch and the light coming on, I imagined him standing there. Indy. Tall and skeletal, sneer stretching his lips, tattoos over his fingers as they dug into my throat.

The bathroom was empty, I was alone, surrounded by mildewy pink tile. I wiped my mouth with toilet paper and ignored the scratch in my throat as I wrestled my way out of my strappy heels. There was nothing like terror to sober you up, and adrenaline was racing through me, setting all my senses to a hyperalert state.

I was used to this. I could manage this. I sucked in a breath, and two more gasps came with it, my chest heaving and struggling as if I were running out of air. I pulled myself up on wobbling legs and braced myself against the doorframe as bright lights flashed at the back of my vision.

Breathe, Lola, I coached myself, although the voice was softer and lower, almost like Leo's. I turned the light on in the hall and held my breath, my ears ringing as I listened for any stirring in the apartment. I tiptoed into my bedroom and flipped the switch, tried to scan the room to see if anything was out of place or moved, but my vision was still dizzy from drinking. I stared at the dark space under my bedframe, and at my partly open closet door, and waited to find the courage to check them.

Was he here? Had he snuck back into the city, the *state*, just to frighten me? Buzz was dead, but Indy was still out there, and now I knew for certain he hadn't forgotten about me.

I sank to my knees and lowered my head to the wood floorboards, my breath skittering out of my chest as I saw the cardboard boxes stuffed beneath my bedframe, and remembered there was no space there. My closet came up empty too.

One by one, room by room, I turned on all the lights and reassured myself that I was alone. Indy was taunting me from an unknown number, but he wasn't *here* in my apartment.

He doesn't know where I live. He never did.

I was safe. I was safe. I was alone, and I was safe.

I didn't sleep. Hours passed until my trembling left me sore and achy. The sky was turning gray and pink and I was still balled up on my couch, watching the door, and then the windows. My phone was in my hand and I debated calling Leo, or even Rake or Baby, a hundred times at least. Instead, I sat in my tiny apartment with every light on and waited for daylight. I was too scared to get into the shower, and when dawn came, I changed my clothes at racing speed, the sensation of eyes watching me impossible to shake.

I kept my phone close by, looked at the text every minute, half-hoping and half-afraid it would disappear.

When the first car horn of the morning blared on the road, I gathered up my purse and headed for the police station.

"SO YOU CAN'T REALLY DO anything?" I said, sitting across the desk from one of the local officers.

"It's…not a threatening text." The woman wasn't unsympathetic, or at least she was going to the trouble to try and appear sympathetic.

"Indy is a threatening man," I said, raking my fingers through my hair in frustration. "I have a restraining order filed against him."

"But you don't have proof that this *is* from him," the officer said.

"That's… 'Showgirl,' that's what he called me," I said, my stomach sour at the nickname.

The woman's eyes narrowed and her lips pursed and I huffed a sigh, knowing exactly what she was thinking. Who *didn't* try to call me Showgirl?

"Look, I *am* going to pass this on to the detectives for the case. I just can't do anything for you right now. It would take a lot more than something as innocuous as what was sent for us to pull the strings needed to find out where that number came from and what towers the text pinged." The woman leaned forward on her elbows. "The asshole is tryin' to rile you up, but he's not giving any sign of intent, okay? You just keep ignoring him."

"Because he's going to keep texting," I supplied, staring her directly in the eye. "And I just have to…cope?"

"Yes," the officer said with a sharp nod, some of the sympathy vanishing out of her expression. "Cope. Report it.

Hope that the investigation continues to develop without you ever hearing anything from any of us again except 'ma'am, he's in custody.'"

She's got bigger problems than reassuring a beta who landed herself into hot water with an alpha, all because she wanted a rough fuck and someone to tell her she was important.

I swallowed and nodded at the officer, grabbing my bag and hugging it against my stomach as I pushed my chair back.

"I wish you the best, Miss Barnes, honestly," the officer said, her gaze wincing.

I continued to nod as I left her desk. The station was busy and loud, and I was heading for the stairs when my phone buzzed in my bag. I wanted to be sick all over again, and I reached my hand into my purse as if I were expecting my phone to jump and bite me.

Leo.

I sagged with relief and swiped the screen without thinking.

"Hey."

"Hey, gorgeous! I know I said I'd come grab you for breakfast, but my flight was canceled and the others are all filling up. I've chartered one for later today and I should be in by—"

"Get yer fuckin' hands off me, you goddamn motherfuckin'—" I shrank in on myself and pushed for the stairs as someone coming in with officers started to struggle and fight.

Leo's voice cut off abruptly at the sound of the fight in the background, and he was quiet as I made it to the staircase, the door banging shut behind me and cutting off the man's cursing. "Lola? Where are you, gorgeous?"

Lie, I thought. *Lie, and say it was a TV show.*

"The police station," I whispered, weariness suddenly crashing down on me. I hadn't slept a wink. All the adrenaline of my panic was used up, and I was getting teary-eyed all over again now that I was leaving the police station with nothing to show for it. What had I expected, really? For them to magically track and jail Indy with just one lousy text?

"You're what?! Lola? What's happened? Are you all right? Lola?"

"I'm okay," I said, but the words were completely undermined by the sudden crack in my voice as a sob worked its way up my throat. I forced it down again and stumbled down the steps.

"Lola," Leo breathed over the phone. "Tell me what happened, gorgeous."

"Um, no, I really am okay. I just...I got a text message and it—they can't do anything about it. He's not even in the state. It just flipped me out," I said, my voice tightening to a squeak. "Tonight is fine."

Leo sighed audibly, and the animal inside of me that wanted to *run, run, run* nearly made me hang the call up.

"You aren't hurt?"

"I'm not hurt."

"You know he's not in the state?" I made a soft strangled sound at the back of my throat, and Leo continued. "Okay, Lola, you can say no, of course. Wherever you'll be comfortable, that's where you should go. But if you'd be willing to, I'd like for you to go to my house. Rake's in town. I can even make sure the house is yours by yourself if you want. You'll be safe there. But if you'd rather go to your apartment, I'll be there as soon as I can. I'll try and get an earlier flight."

It was on the tip of my tongue to refuse, to return to my apartment and try to force myself not to just sit and stare at the door all day. But that stupid broken lock on the street door was taunting me. And if Rake was in town, he would be the kind of distracting presence that might get me to think about something else for five seconds. And I missed him. I missed Leo too, and the thought of being in his space, being surrounded by him in some way, was so tempting.

"I'll...I'll go to your house, if you're sure that's okay," I said. I'd made it down to the first-floor lobby and I stared out at the street, listening to Leo's soft sigh.

"Definitely okay, gorgeous. I'm texting you the address."

"Thank you," I whispered over the line.

"God, don't thank me. I wish I was there with you."

I puffed a watery laugh. No fucking kidding. I would've given anything to have had Leo's hand in mine while I sat across the desk from the officer. It scared me how easy it was to depend on him. Now all I wanted to do was to go somewhere that had traces of him.

"I'll be home soon, okay?"

Lola

13

Leo's house hadn't seemed like a daunting thing, really. Even though I'd never been there before. Even though our relationship was still fairly new. Maybe I'd pictured something like David's lovely apartment, something almost familiar. I hadn't forgotten that Leo lived with five other men, but my brain hadn't bothered painting a picture of what that might look like until the cab I'd grabbed pulled up to the six-story brownstone, sitting on the corner of a quiet neighborhood that surrounded a community park.

Please let this secretly be a handful of apartments, I thought, staring up at the vast old brick building that looked as though it might've been a school of some kind at one point. The gate of black iron fence was cracked open, and I wondered if Leo and his pack didn't worry about locking it or if Rake had left it open for me.

But it wasn't Rake who answered the door when I rang the bell.

"Oh." I stared up at Caleb with wide eyes, the tall alpha hanging back in the open doorway.

"Hello, Lola. I'm sorry, Rake hasn't made it back yet and Leo was a bit frantic so I didn't want to worry him. I can leave now that you're here, though," he said in a breathless rush, reaching up a tan hand to comb back golden blond strands. He was dressed casually in a rumpled button-down and jeans, with his toes peeking out from under the frayed hem.

"You-um, no. No, you don't have to go," I said, standing frozen on the front step. "I—it's your house."

Caleb nodded and winced at the same time. "I don't want you to be uncomfortable. I don't mind."

I caught my breath and looked over my shoulder. The cab was already gone. Not that I really wanted to leave. I faced Caleb again and shrugged. "I don't want you to leave on my account. I'll be all right."

Caleb stepped back, and between his courtesy and the absolutely *massive* old oak door, I had plenty of room to step inside. It was just that once I was inside, I would be alone with an alpha I barely knew.

But *Leo* knew him. Was bonded to him. I badly wanted to believe in this pack being different than my experiences with alphas, for Leo and Rake's sake.

I stepped inside, and with one glance away from Caleb, I was suddenly too stunned by where I was to care who I was with.

"Oh!"

It was definitely not a series of apartments.

It was…breathtaking.

The floor was made of small boards cut and angled into a diamond pattern. The walls were a deep shade of natural gray, textured in panels. It took me a moment of gawking—at the works of art on the walls and the greenery filling the open space and the contemporary lighting that warmed the space—to remember the name for the room I was in. A foyer.

This pack lived in an enormous house and they had a *foyer*. In the city. Until I was eleven, my mom and I had lived in an apartment without a second bedroom. When we moved, the second bedroom hadn't had a closet.

"The downstairs is really for show, business entertaining. I can… You're welcome to go anywhere you want, or I can show upstairs to the family areas. They're rather less intimidating," Caleb said. For all the rasp Leo had naturally, Caleb was entirely smooth and clean. He was *super* fucking British too, his words arching prettily even as he rambled at my back.

"Is it all this pretty?" I asked, studying the delicate, golden light fixture hanging above me, all angles and fine round bulbs.

"Oh? Do you like it? Thank you, I—yes, I think it's all quite nice."

I remembered then that Leo had mentioned in passing that Caleb was an interior designer. And then, with a sudden and humiliating wave, I realized that Leo lived *here* and he'd voluntarily spent the night in my shitty apartment.

"Fuck," I whispered. I closed my eyes, and my body wavered.

I heard Caleb's step, just the one, like he was prepared to catch me if I fainted or passed out or whatever this was.

"Let me show you upstairs to the den," Caleb said gently. "Rake will be back soon. And Leo's about to try and commission a flock of birds if it'll get him home any sooner."

I shook my head and swallowed. Maybe I needed to go. This was all too much, and I was only *standing in the foyer*. If I saw any more of the house, I might seriously lose my shit. And that wasn't what my relationship with Leo was about. Logically, I'd known he and his whole pack were wealthy as fuck, but I'd never in my life seen wealth in context as clear as this. It wasn't ivory pillars and crown molding either, it was pure, contemporary, thoughtfully considered class. This place was *sexy*.

"Is it me?" Caleb asked. "I can't tell if I should go or shepherd you somewhere to sit down or—"

Caleb's persistent panicking at having me standing in shocked silence did the trick. I giggled nervously and pulled my hand from my face, scrubbing it lightly over my eyes first.

"Sorry. I haven't really slept, and today started all wrong. I'm okay." I turned to face Caleb and tried to offer him a reassuring smile, but both he and I were too nervous in front of the other for it to be believable. "Upstairs would be nice."

Upstairs would probably be *divine*, if I weren't so totally overwhelmed it made it impossible to enjoy. Caleb sighed and nodded, walking carefully past me to give me plenty of breathing room. No amount of Leo's reassuring that his pack was different than the alphas I'd known would ever be as effective at calming me as Caleb's blatant concern for frightening me. Or maybe that stereotypical British awkwardness of his was just really soothing.

I followed him out of the foyer and into an enormous open room, twice as tall as the first room I'd been in, and clearly designed for open entertaining. The walls were a deep navy, and there were giant teardrop chandeliers hanging from the ceiling over spacious couches. On the far end of the room sat a full wet bar and a reading nook with shelves as high as the ceiling and a terrifying sliding ladder. My eyes bugged, but I bit my lips as Caleb all but jogged for the stairs, as if he might lessen the impact of the dramatically lavish room by shortening my exposure to it.

It failed. Intimidated didn't even begin to describe the feeling. Staring up at Caleb's back, I watched as his shoulders drew in while he hurried up the wide slatted stairs toward an enormous, sensually detailed oil painting of a fallen angel with glossy black wings and exquisite tanned skin. The angel reminded me of Rake. It probably reminded them all of Rake. Hell, it probably *was* Rake. Maybe he'd modeled for the artist.

"All of this is your work, isn't it?" I asked. Caleb stopped on the landing, and paused there he looked almost like he was being embraced by the angel behind him. It made me smile, and I gestured to the room—the intricate paneling and the sparse and open planning of the furniture, the metallic accents set against flat dark colors.

Caleb nodded and looked over my head. "It's almost a showroom, I suppose."

"It's beautiful."

His shoulders relaxed, and I followed him up the rest of the way. The second story *was* a little less imposing, or maybe it just seemed that way after having stood in that gorgeous downstairs living room. The stairs ended on a small landing full of small potted trees and ferns, sitting in front of the window that faced the street. Caleb led me from there into what must've been the den. The floorboards cut off as the room sank down by two short steps covered in dense looking cream carpet. Plush couches faced the open wall holding a large screen over a long and low fireplace. On the opposite side of the room, paneled glass revealed an open plan style dining room and kitchen beyond, and there were curtains on either wall ready to be pulled shut over the glass to make the den feel close and cozy. Closest to me, and most attention grabbing, was a luxurious looking contemporary hammock hanging from the ceiling, cushioned and covered with slate-gray, velvety suede.

"Can I get you anything?" Caleb asked me as I stood, still dumbstruck, looking at the glass case bookshelves behind the deep couches, everything in dark and warm neutral tones. "Water? Or something to eat? Leo's sort of the cook of the family, but he usually leaves us leftovers so we don't all starve while he's gone."

I slipped my sneakers off on the floor, afraid to muss the room, and looked to Caleb. He was hovering nearby but out of reach, with his hands behind his back, and I wondered which of us was more scared of the other. I was starting to think it might be him, at least of frightening me.

"Thank you for…doing whatever it was you did in the elevator," I said.

Caleb's eyebrows jumped over his vivid blue gaze, and I could've sworn he was starting to blush. "Erm, of course. It's… Rake calls my scent 'Xanax.' Um, here," Caleb padded down into the circle of furniture, pulling a blanket off the back of a couch and bringing it to me, standing at the bottom of the short stairs so that I towered over him. He was so classically handsome, so traditional looking, and I pictured Rake and Leo and Cyrus around him, how he would compare with their more unique beauty. It would be a buffet of handsome.

"Curl up wherever, wander. The kitchen is just through there, and you're welcome to anything. Rake will find you when he gets back, it'll probably just be a few more minutes."

I took the blanket from his hands—it was buttery soft against my fingers—puzzled by the offer until I got the first whiff of his drugging, syrupy scent. "Thank you."

Caleb nodded and passed me, heading for the stairs. I was a little surprised he was just leaving me with the run of his house, especially a house like this one, but he was right. All I wanted was to curl up. Except I almost called him back when I was left in the room alone. I wanted Leo, or Baby, or maybe even David.

David. That's who I should've gone to like this. Not my new boyfriend's, *alpha pack*, fucking fancy as shit house. I breathed out a long sigh, and then lifted the blanket to my nose, inhaling Caleb's scent deep into my lungs. Drowsiness hit me like a wave, tension I was so used to carrying unwound out of my muscles with the first hit of his pheromones. Xanax indeed.

I padded down into the ring of couches and headed for the largest, L-shaped one, diving into the corner and wrapping the soft blanket around me up to my chin. I settled into the cushions, drinking in the room around me, wondering what the rest of the house might look like. My blinks grew longer, heavier, and I let Caleb's drugging aroma carry me down towards sleep. Just for a few minutes. Just for…

"WHERE'S BUZZ?" I whined as I woke to Indy's hand on my skin, my back on a bare mattress. The room was dark and it smelled different, none of Buzz's sweet and ashy fragrance. Not Indy's pine either.

Maybe they were letting me just sleep tonight?

Someone coughed, someone in the dark, and I stiffened. I tried to sit up, and two hands pinned my shoulders.

"Indy?"

"Lola, wake up."

"You just relax, Showgirl. It's gonna be a long night."

I sat up with a gasp, taking deep gulps of air. My skin was sweaty and sticky, and the blanket around me was too hot.

Gentle fingers reached for the back of my neck and I skittered away, spinning to face—

"Hey, it's okay. It's just me," Rake said, an uncharacteristic worry in his eyes.

I took another deep breath and the nightmare, the old memory, faded away. I was at Leo's house. I had fallen asleep on the couch. Caleb's scent was on my tongue, and it replaced the mildewy flavor of the dream. Rake held his hand out in the space between us, and I peeled myself out of the tangle of the blanket before sliding my hand into his and squeezing back.

"What time is it?" I rasped.

"After one. I got back, but I didn't want to wake you so I've just been keeping you company," Rake said.

I blinked and looked around the room. The TV was on, muted with the captions running. I'd arrived at the house before ten in the morning. Had Rake really just been sitting with me for three hours?

"Are you hungry?" he asked.

I was. My stomach felt hollow, and I realized I hadn't really eaten anything aside from a few appetizers with Zane and Betty last night. I wasn't even sure if I'd thrown those up. Mostly though…

I frowned and stared at Rake. "Is there any way I could… take a shower here?" I was greasy and disoriented and exhausted, and nothing sounded better than trying to rinse the night off at the moment.

Rake smiled and stood from the couch, still holding onto my hand. "Of course. Come on, I'll give you a little mini-tour on the way to my rooms."

'My *rooms*,' he'd said. As in multiple.

Fucking rich people.

RAKE 14

Lola had that adorable, rumpled, 'I just woke up from a nap' look going on, complete with a pout I wanted to suck on. She'd *also* just had a nightmare or the start of one, and I was trying to keep it in my pants and not be my usual thirsty self, for her sake.

"Don't be intimidated," I said as I led her through the house, up to the fourth floor.

"Seriously? How could I not be?" she murmured, wide eyes drinking in every detail.

Caleb had done a good job melding six very different men's tastes into one home, compromising on rich neutral shades as a unifying palette and then letting us all dictate the styles in our own private spaces. But there was really no disguising the fact that we lived in a big ass house in the middle of the city, and we liked nice things. I was an omega. It was in my DNA to want to be a bit spoiled by my surroundings, after all.

"Do you each have your own floor?"

"No," I said through a laugh, adding privately, *we each have our own wing on one of three floors*. I shared with Caleb, and Leo tended to spend more time on our floor than his own top floor that he shared with Matthieu. Wes and Cyrus had the fifth floor, but Cyrus also tended to sleep on the fourth floor with us. "Do you like it though?"

"It's gorgeous," Lola said softly.

Was she being quiet because she was uncomfortable or

because of whatever had happened? Leo hadn't given me much to go on in his messages, only that Lola had a bad night and he wanted her to be at the house if she was up for it. Was it nightmares? Or something more?

"So, here's my space," I said. "I've got a few nest areas tucked around the house for when I'm kinda stressed but this is…"

I cleared my throat and watched Lola, trying to hold my rambles in my chest. Was it okay that it smelled like me in here? I knew my perfume stressed her out, but at the party she'd let me all but coat her in my scent while we'd been dancing.

Thinking of coating Lola in my scent was definitely *not* what I needed to be focused on at the moment.

"I like these window walls," Lola said, facing the tall wall in front of my bedroom that was made of wrought iron and glass panes.

"Yeah, we all like open spaces, but those allow me to curtain them off when I'm getting closer to heats." Her eyes trailed around my work space to where I had lights set up around a chaise lounge.

Fuck, Rake, move her along so you don't have to explain you take naughty pictures of your packmates for a hobby. Jesus, you're a mess.

"Uh, bathroom's through here," I said, walking her through the window wall's narrow doorway. *Fuck, my bed reeks of alpha sex. Fuck, why didn't I take her up to Leo's rooms?* "I—I can go and get you something to change into, if you want?"

Rake, you dumbass, is that a sex toy sitting on your side-table? It definitely was. It wasn't like we usually bothered putting them away. I was shuffling around like a weird version of a sheep dog, trying to guide Lola to the bathroom while blocking out the sight of my mess of a bedroom. I opened the bathroom door for her and watched her eyebrows bounce up.

"Um. Yeah. It's kind of…dramatic," I said, looking in at the glossy bathroom with the enormous jacuzzi tub directly front and center. "Shower's in the corner there."

Probably left some plugs in there too, just to totally traumatize the poor woman, I thought.

Lola nodded. I couldn't tell if the circles under her eyes were old mascara or the actual shadow of lost sleep. I wanted to attach myself to her side until Leo arrived, and preferably after too, but she wasn't talking or telling me what she needed, and I didn't want to push her. It was a shame she was so skittish around my alphas, because Caleb or even Matthieu would've been exactly who she needed right now.

"I'll be right back with some clothes and to check on you. And I'll get started on something to eat for us, okay?"

She nodded again, her arms cradling her stomach. I'd seen her do that before, and it made me want to lift them up and slide underneath, wrapping her up in my own. I swallowed and left, racing toward the elevator I'd intentionally avoided showing to Lola. Caleb said she'd nearly passed out after walking in the front door, so maybe it was better if no one mentioned the personal gym or the infinity pool.

I grabbed a few things from Leo's room. A t-shirt and a cashmere sweater, and decided Lola would be better off in my own boxers than Leo's. And maybe I just wanted her in some of my clothes too.

Except when I made it back to my rooms, Lola was still standing in the middle of my bathroom, fully dressed. Her eyes were watery as they met mine.

"I can't shake the feeling that he's watching me," she whispered.

My heart fully stopped beating for a moment, my gut turning to stone. Not for the first time, I wished I was an alpha, that I had the power to claim someone like Lola or Leo who had been injured by alphas and make sure no one ever fucking touched them again. Except in this instance, it was a good thing I wasn't an alpha.

I set the change of clothes down on the counter and crossed to Lola, giving into the impulse to pull her to my chest, relieved when her arms circled me and her hands clung to my back. "We've got a smaller bathroom around here somewhere. Or I can stay and join you, and we can do a bath instead?"

I tried to hold onto my calm when Lola nodded. "Stay, a bath sounds nice," she said, and my stomach did a little flip.

I nuzzled the top of her head, marveling at the way she loosened in my arms. So an omega perfume wasn't a total hard pass then? That was a relief. I'd been trying to be a good sport about her and Leo's relationship but, if I was honest with myself, I wasn't used to not getting what I wanted.

And I wanted Lola.

"I'll get the water started," I said, and Lola nodded, her hands going to the hem of her shirt as I pulled away.

You have to be on good behavior though, I reminded myself. Not just because Lola was shaken, although that was the first and most important reason. The other was that I wanted to know for certain that Leo would be okay with it if I made a serious move. He and I had shared a fling before, but it was obvious to everyone in the pack that his feelings for Lola were a big deal. Their connection wasn't about burning through temporary lust.

And I had my own secret hopes when it came to a relationship with Lola.

Those were long game though.

I turned the water on, and it rushed to fill the giant basin as I hunted down a few things to throw in. Some aromatherapy oils for relaxation, my favorite dense bubble bath. I frowned at the water and wondered if Lola was a glitter bomb kind of girl. I didn't mind being a little extra, especially when I was just chilling at home, but this seemed like a kind of somber day. I picked a deep blue bath bomb instead and then shook my head at myself.

Just throw the whole damn bath department in, Rake.

"Smells good."

I jumped as Lola stepped up to the ledge at my side, bending and sticking one delicate, pale foot into the churning water. I swallowed my own tongue as I turned and watched her sink into the water, rounded hips devoured by greedy water. Not that I could blame it. I wanted to be the thing that was surrounding every inch of Lola's naked skin. Her waist was tiny, but her tummy was slightly rounded and I wanted to hold her against my chest, feel her breasts pressed to me as she gasped for breath.

Get. Sex. Off. The mind.

Easier said than done for an omega, but I pushed myself away from the ledge of the tub and tore my eyes off Lola's skin as I hurried to undress and join her in the water. Her gaze was shuttered as I sank into the water, and I tried not to worry about whether or not she was as interested in my body as I was in hers. When she immediately moved to curl into my side, I gave into the triumphant feeling in my chest, even if it was accompanied by an excruciating awareness of her skin against mine.

"Sorry. Is it okay if I…?" she asked, sneaking under my arm.

I wrapped it around her shoulders and pulled her flush against me. "Of course. I'm glad you came here." Lola's eyebrows raised, and I fumbled. "I missed you this week. I was trying to think of excuses to have you around again."

Some of the hollow shock Lola'd been wearing since she'd woken from her nap was replaced by a pink blush over her cheeks.

"I should probably start pampering you then," she said.

"How about this time it's my turn?" I held my breath as Lola offered me a shy smile. We were up to our shoulders in bubbly water, the taps turning off automatically when it was full and the jets still running. I pulled Lola gently between my parted legs and then reached for the extendable shower head attachment.

She nodded and I switched it on, running warm water down over her head, carefully brushing her strands back, feeling her sigh and soften in front of me.

"You're good at spoiling someone," she said as I turned the water off and grabbed my shampoo from the ledge.

"Lollipop, I haven't even started," I said, the dark purr coming out in the words unintentionally.

It didn't scare my girl off though. Instead, Lola relaxed into my chest, letting me work an oversized handful of shampoo into her blonde strands. I wondered if she felt the slight hardness of my cock against her back. She had to, didn't she? She didn't seem to mind. She hummed as I dug my fingers into the roots of her hair and then down the tight muscles of her neck.

Lola needed a massage. Could I give her one without getting a massive erection? Probably not if she was going to make those cute noises at the back of her throat.

Don't think about sex.

Lola would make a good omega. A girl like this, sweet and a little vulnerable, talented too, was the kind of personality alpha packs would hand over their nuts for. It was acid in my stomach to know that someone had abused those qualities in her.

My pack wouldn't.

For the first time since I'd met Leo—back when Odette had still held him pinned under her boot—I found myself wanting to encourage my alphas to take in a new pack member. I'd told Lola I hated it when betas came sniffing after my alphas, and here I was wanting to matchmake them with her. But I wanted her closer, not just stealing time with her while we waited for Leo to return.

I finished washing Lola's hair, and she floated away from me. The hot water that took her place against me seeming cold by comparison.

She faced me, hair wet and plastered down her neck to her shoulders, lips smiling. Those *were* dark circles under her eyes. Ones she'd always taken care to cover around me before and I wanted to see erased.

"I have a crush on you," I blurted out.

Lola's smile bloomed, and a soapy hand reached up from the water to cover her face for a brief second before lowering again.

"I know. I have a crush on you too," she said.

I grinned back at her and took the soapy hand, tugging her through the water. I leaned in, and Lola's nose bumped against mine, our smiles too wide for the brief meeting to be considered a kiss. She settled, and her lips pulled softly at mine until my smile vanished with a low moan.

This girl. This fucking girl needed to be mine, one way or another.

Lola
15

"Lola," Leo rasped in my ear.

I opened my eyes to find Leo crouching in front of me. I leaned into his touch as he pushed strands of hair out of my face.

After the bath with Rake—which left me in a dizzy, happy haze of soft kisses—and a lunch laid out by a mysterious fairy whom I suspected was Caleb, I fell back asleep, this time on the hammock with Rake while watching something in French. Apparently, it was Rake who was into the 'artsy shit' Leo had mentioned.

"Hey there, gorgeous," he whispered.

"Hey. You're home."

He leaned in, and my eyes shut as he pressed a kiss to my forehead. "I'm home. Fuck, it's good to see you. I've been so worried."

"No, it's… I'm fine, Leo, honestly. The text freaked me out just 'cause…" I shook my head, and Rake stirred behind me.

"What times'it?" Rake mumbled.

"After eight," Leo said, smiling at his omega. "You two wanna come upstairs with me? I brought pasta, and I won't tell anyone if we eat it in bed." My lips quirked at that, and Leo ducked down for a quick kiss. "Do you have your phone, gorgeous?"

"It's on the table."

"Would you let Wes look it over? He might be able to track down where the phone was when the text was sent."

I frowned and pushed up on the hammock, Rake's arm slipping from around my waist. "The police said—"

"The police have to use legal channels," Leo said, picking up my phone from the table. "Wes doesn't. But it's up to you."

He held my phone in his open palm and I picked it up, swiping it open and changing the lock settings. "So he won't need the passcode."

"Thank you," Leo said with a sigh.

I combed my hair back with shaking fingers and shrugged. "Thank *you*. Thank Wes. I'm just... I'm okay. If it's better that I go back to the apartment—"

"No!" Leo and Rake both said at the same moment.

"I want you here," Rake said.

"So do I."

"The others..." I started, and Leo shook his head.

"They...they're all glad to have you here too, they're just trying to stay out of your hair."

"It's their house, Leo," I said, frowning. "They don't have to hide from me."

"Come on, let's go upstairs. Eat carbs. We're all being way too considerate, worrying about how everyone else is feeling. Time for some omega selfish self-care lessons," Rake said.

He slid off the back side of the hammock and Leo caught me as it swung in the other direction, pulling me to my feet. "Take the elevator up, I'll be there in a minute."

"There's an *elevator*?" I said, gaping at them both.

Rake shook his head at Leo. "Babe, we were trying not to spook her."

"The house is six stories, seven with the garden floor, of course there's an elevator," Leo defended with a baffled smile. "I take it you haven't mentioned the pool?"

"Leo!"

"Oh, Jesus," I said, covering my eyes.

"You are such a troll," Rake said to Leo, trying to stifle his laughter as he came and wrapped an arm around me. "Come on, Lola, he's just real estate bragging now."

I hadn't seen the elevator because it was at the back of the house, but it was a beautiful old cage elevator with soft dark velvet paneled walls. It was a small and romantic space trimmed in gold, and Rake and I fit comfortably inside, but it could probably have fit five at a squeeze. It was full of the scents of the pack, but after spending the day in the house I was starting to get used to them, almost as if they were background noise.

"Wes is good, and I don't think he's ever met anybody who doesn't owe him at least one favor. He'll track the asshole down," Rake said, hand stroking my back absently.

"I don't want to find him, I just want to know he can't find me," I said.

Rake's fingers squeezed gently on my side as the elevator slowed and settled to a stop. As soon as Rake opened the elevator gate, I gasped.

"So this floor is an addition that Leo and Matthieu came up with. They like their open spaces."

There were two dividing walls running down the hall on either side of us, but the wall opposite us was entirely glass, and the ceiling overhead was made of thick glass bricks, letting in light but warping the view.

"Matthieu's side is to the left, Leo has the right side." Rake held my hand in his as he pulled me down to the doorway that led to Leo's suite. The space was surrounded by floor to ceiling windows, some curtained and others hanging open to reveal a balcony around the outside of the building, dense with greenery.

"Leo came up with this place?" I asked.

"He found the property. Matthieu and Caleb picked out an architect to redesign the space with Caleb's input. Caleb wanted to be sure it didn't feel like one of those sterile contemporary lofts everyone has."

'Everyone' they knew at least. I hoped Leo hadn't told any

of them about my shoebox—cardboard walls included—apartment.

"Bed's this way."

Rake's bed had been massive, which I guess made sense as the omega, but I was surprised to find that Leo's was equally so. The mattress would fit Rake, Leo, and I with plenty of room to spare. For the first time since Leo had mentioned his pack being open to outside relationships, I wondered what those relationships looked like. Was Rake used to sharing with Leo and his alphas? Did they regularly bring in beta girls like me to play around with?

Not like you, that's for sure.

I couldn't imagine it. If Leo had been looking for easy sex to share with his pack, he would've run the other way after getting to know me.

The bed was on a platform in front of a windowed wall with wood slat shutters that were angled, striping the sheets with sunlight. Rake crossed to the bed, crawling on his knees to the center and then flopping face down. I smiled at his sprawled form and joined him, kneeling just out of reach.

"How did you meet your pack?" I asked.

Rake rolled over, his thin t-shirt rucking up his stomach slightly, and rubbed his hand over the stubble on his jaw. "Um, through the Omega Center. But Wes, he worked for a different security company at the time, and he didn't have a pack. I was his first assignment, and we just… It's weird to say it because I know what people think of omegas and their alphas, but Wes is like my brother. He's not my alpha because he throws me into heat or I put him in rut. He's my family. He's who I trust to keep me safe, to keep my pack safe too. So he joined the pack when I did."

"Baby met her pack through the Omega Center, but she was a late bloomer. How does it work when you're still a teenager?"

"Right," Rake nodded, wiggling backward into the pillows and waiting for me to join him. I settled against his side before he continued. "So I started kids' modeling when I was fourteen or so, and my perfume came in a year later. The Omega Center advised that I quit modeling and just worry about school until my maturity hit, or at least get a beta security team if I insisted on modeling. But I liked Wes when I met him. He was cool and just out of the military, the kind of badass a teenage boy is inclined to look up to," Rake said with a smile.

"So I hired him and a beta. Eventually, when Wes and I knew that my perfume wasn't an issue for him and his pheromones weren't for me, we just flipped off the Center and kept working together for about five years. Baby didn't get to go through it, but like...maturity kind of just starts as this general sort of itch. Like little mini heats popping up for ten minutes where suddenly, you wanna just rub up against any available surface. One day, when I was twenty, I popped a boner in a swimsuit photoshoot."

Rake grinned with me. "I know. I was twenty. Pretty embarrassed. And Wes wouldn't let me fuck the lighting team, so we left the shoot and headed back to the Omega Center. They opened up their magical binders of alpha scent cards, and I found three packs I liked. This one was the only one where the alphas didn't seem phased by the idea that I wanted to keep working. And Matt and Wes immediately got along, while all the other packs acted like Wes was a threat to their authority as my alpha. No thanks," Rake finished with a wave. "So yeah it's been...eleven years now."

I rolled to my back and squinted up at the ceiling. "It sounds kind of...businessy."

"Yeah. I had a romantic period when my perfume first showed up where I thought I'd meet my pack on my own. But...well, let's just say it was good I had Wes during that time. The Omega Center isn't always the most unbiased or natural way, but it is safe. And yeah, there were some growing pains at the beginning, but I can't imagine being in any other pack now."

"You would've scared off any other alphas by now," Leo said, entering his bedroom while carrying a tray stacked with takeout boxes that made my mouth water with the smells of garlic and tomato and butter. He toed off his shoes and I folded my legs beneath me to make room for him to sit across from me.

"Baby got her perfume while we were at a biker bar in Old Uptown," I said.

Rake snorted. "God, what a mess. Wait, was it the bikers she ended up with?"

I sucked in a deep breath. There were worse ways to start the story, after all, and after this morning and them opening their home to me, I kind of owed them the truth.

"No, it was a different pack," I said, watching as Leo parceled out cloth napkins hastily wrapped around silverware to each of us. "She met the beta of one of her alphas there. Seth had his alpha's scent mark on him, and he was there to discuss a truce between the two packs. He smelled Baby, and she smelled him and that alpha scent and…knew immediately, I guess. He figured out what was happening, and he took her to the Omega Center."

"Aww. And then she ended up with his pack? How cute," Rake said. He cracked open a box of ravioli and took a deep breath before releasing a moan.

I glanced at Leo and found his eyes on me, watchful and waiting as if he knew what I would say next.

"I didn't realize she was perfuming, and I'd hugged her and then went to dance. That was the night I met Buzz."

Both men were quiet, and Rake lowered his fork back down into the pasta. *Dumb. Should've waited until you were done eating.* But I wasn't sure I could keep food down and tell the story at the same time.

"Um…I was…I was kind of always trying to chase after alphas back then," I said, voice thinning to a whisper. "And I didn't know about the perfume that night. It was just the first time an alpha had responded to me in that way, with so much *focus* and *interest*. I don't know what he thought, that I'd bought a hit of perfume or whatever, but…he kept me around for a few days. And it was kind of exciting, and mostly he was...not sweet, but he was *intent*. And then one night, it just stopped and he told me to leave and went to look for a new fuck buddy. I saw Baby's text on my way out and realized what happened."

"This is the asshole that texted you?" Rake asked, brow furrowed. "What a dick."

I shook my head and forced myself to breathe through my pounding heartbeat. "I went to see Baby as she was packing up her apartment, and she... I asked her for her sweatshirt and she let me take it. I figured Buzz knew I wasn't an omega, it wasn't like I was trying to *fool* him I just—"

"Oh, gorgeous, hey," Leo murmured, pushing the tray aside and crawling forward to wipe away tears I hadn't noticed running down my cheeks.

"He didn't bother playing nice after that, and I don't know why I was so determined to stay," I said, high and breathless.

"Lola, alphas have a pull. I've been there," Leo said, putting his hands on my knees and giving me a comforting squeeze.

"Wes will find him," Rake said to reassure me.

"No. Buzz is dead."

"What?" Leo asked, leaning back, face paling with shock.

I groaned and covered my face with my hands. Rake's palms settled on my shoulders, cupping them gently.

"When I tried to get Buzz's attention again, he... He was the president of his motorcycle club, the Hangmen. He said he wanted to watch me with Indy, his Vice President. The pair of them...they called it sharing, but it was more like taunting and I...I just put up with it. The whole time. I was basically living there, begging them to be awful to me," I pushed my hands back, holding my hair away from my face, but I couldn't bring myself to make eye contact with either Rake or Leo. "They wanted me to see Baby again. I think they wanted to know if I could get her to come back to their clubhouse, but she was already with her pack so they made me go with them to see her."

"What happened?" Rake asked.

"Lola, you don't have to—"

"We went. I...hated being there. Baby stayed with her pack. I left with them. They were angry, one of the Howler's betas had pissed Buzz off. He left me with Indy and...I think someone spiked my drink. I—" I couldn't tell them everything. I didn't remember, I didn't *want* to remember that night. "I left the next morning. A few weeks later, the Hangmen were raided by the police. They'd been trafficking women out of the city and when the police caught up to them, Buzz was shot. Indy disappeared. He's the one who texted me."

I sat up straight, and Rake's touch slid away. There, that was done. It wasn't everything, but it was the shape of it and...

"Lola, gorgeous, look at me," Leo said, waiting through a long silence before I could bring myself to raise my eyes. His hand came up and cupped my chin to hold me under the gentle pin of his stare. "You are safe here. You are safe with me and Rake. You're safe with our alphas too; they won't ever touch you like that. Those men, those complete scumbags? They're not going to ever touch you again at all. We will make sure of it."

"It's my own fault."

"No, it's not," Leo said firmly.

"I took Baby's scent."

Leo's eyes rolled lightly, but it was Rake who spoke. "You think betas haven't grabbed hugs from me and tried to catch an alpha's attention? An alpha can tell the difference. Those guys were predators, plain and simple."

"If I hadn't been such a desperate wh—" I said, my fingernails digging grooves in my palms as my fists tightened in frustration.

"Hush. No, Lola." Leo rose up on his knees, scooting as close as my folded legs would allow. "I know what you're thinking and I've been there, I have. But this isn't about designation, I promise you. You gave those fuckers something they didn't deserve, and they abused the opportunity. That's not going to happen again, okay?"

I stared up at him and Leo's palm covered the side of my throat, his thumb pressing to the corner of my jaw.

"Okay?" he asked.

I didn't know how to answer. How could he know? What if I grew weak again, needy for attention, approval? But Leo looked so certain. He'd come out of his relationship with Odette and found himself in an amazing pack. Was he just assuming I could do the same because he had?

"Lola," Leo pleaded, brow furrowing.

I nodded, leaning into his hand. "Okay," I said, mostly because I hated seeing Leo in any kind of pain.

Leo sighed and bent to me, his lips against the top of my head, deep breaths ruffling my hair.

"Is it okay if I text Wes what you said about the Hangmen and the charges? If there are warrants out for Indy, it might help him track through any leads," Rake said.

"Do it," Leo said, muffled by my hair, not waiting for me to respond.

I checked my cheeks, but they were still dry after my initial tears. I felt...kind of hollow. It wasn't exactly a relief, and I didn't feel unburdened. More like by sharing what had happened with Rake and Leo, I'd sort of carved myself open to be inspected.

Leo shifted, and within a minute and a few clumsy twists and shuffles, his back was to his padded headboard and I was cradled in his lap. He didn't speak, and when Rake finished texting he settled his head against my hip in silence, his hand reaching back to cup around Leo's ankle. Second by second and minute by minute, the hollowness seemed to ease. No one offered me any platitudes or pity. Every one of Leo's breaths against my skin was gentle and reassuring enough on its own. Rake's frown was thoughtful, but every few minutes he would nuzzle his cheek against me.

I was safe here with these men, and if I could hold onto this, maybe I *would* be all right.

MATTHIEU
16

The house was eerily quiet with Rake and Leo locked away with Lola, music missing from the kitchen and the pack all keeping to their own quarters. Rake had gone silent from the group chat after delivering the biggest blow yet.

Indy, Vice President of The Hangmen MC. Wanted for sex trafficking.

It was both too much and too little information about the skittish young beta who'd caught the eye of…

Well, our whole damn pack.

I left my own rooms, trying and failing not to look in at Leo's as I headed for the stairs. The lights were off and I couldn't hear any voices. Was she still here? Probably. I couldn't imagine Leo letting her leave after hearing a bomb like that.

Was she one of the…

I swallowed and shook my head, hurrying down to the third floor. Sure enough, Wes was in his office, desk light on and casting a beastly shadow against the wall, a monstrous version of the gentle giant slouched in front of the computer screen. Thin glasses reflected the screen's glare, and Wes didn't so much as twitch until I pulled a chair up to his side and sank down, staring blindly at the information on the screen.

"Anything?"

"A lot. Not much useful yet. I couldn't get in to locate

where the text might've come from, but I've got a guy on it," Wes said.

"And no one's spotted him?"

Wes sighed and leaned back, rolling his shoulder and then reaching up to dig his fingers against his forehead. "Honestly? They caught sixteen men. A few more died in the altercation. There were plenty of bulletins posted about this guy, but as far as I can tell, not a lot of work has gone into tracking him down. A fuckin' year of moving around and getting good at hiding. Or getting lazy, if I'm lucky."

"A year," I echoed. Lola had lived with this for a year.

"A bit more than, yeah. How is she?"

"How should I know?"

Wes grunted and nodded, crossing his arms behind his head and closing his eyes. I wanted to urge him to work, to do more, to find the bastard, but Wes *would*. And I knew shit about tracking someone through the internet.

"Do you think it's good…her being here?" Wes asked.

I tore my gaze off the meaningless screen to stare back at him. "For her or for us?"

Wes' frown deepened. "Us? I meant for her, but why would you…"

"I think she is safe here, and if she's not uncomfortable, then yes. It's good for her. For us?" My head wobbled, and I reached up to scratch at my chin. "If Leo was not a part of our pack, he would marry that girl before the year was up. But what if she can't bring herself to become a part of a pack with alphas in it? He can't, he *wouldn't* leave Caleb and Rake. So will he lose her? Will she lose him?"

"We're not like this guy. She'll see that."

"Maybe," I said.

Wes huffed and sat up, head shaking. "No, Matt. Look at this shit." He moved his mouse and tapped his keyboard and up came a window with more familiar contents. A criminal record. Joseph 'Indy' Franks. He sneered at me through a small photo on the screen, gaze pale and skin pocked. He had a shaved head and sharp, thin features.

"Battery, battery, sexual battery, robbery, drug possession, five more counts of battery," Wes rattled off.

"*Fils de pute*," I hissed.

Wes, used to my slips back into French, just hummed with agreement. "Yeah, but I wouldn't blame the mother. Did a little research, and his dad stayed clean, but some of the other pack fathers were nasty pieces of work on their own. So trust me when I say, we are *noticeably* not like this fucker."

I wasn't sure it would matter. Or I was…trying not to be optimistic. Wes was watching me carefully, and I shook my head. Better to admit it to him.

"Okay. So she stays with Leo and, let's be honest, Rake too. She gets used to the rest of us. I…"

"You're attracted to her," Wes finished bluntly. I glared at him, and his eyebrows jumped. "Oh, I'm sorry. Am I supposed to be shocked? She's fuckin' gorgeous, Matt. I'm not immune either."

"You don't think that's a conflict?"

"Are you incapable of keeping your shit together if she isn't interested in you?" Wes asked.

"No! Well. *No*. But also, I don't know. It wasn't an issue with Leo."

"It might've been," Wes said with a shrug. "I mean, no, you're not attracted to Leo. But you and him get along. You have similar tastes in architecture, in food. Before Leo, Rake dated plenty of other men and women that you didn't like. Do you like Lola?"

"I don't know, it's hard to tell." *Yes*, although I suspected that was the base hindbrain physical attraction talking. I liked her work for the magazine. I liked that, despite all the challenges it presented to her own personal comfort, she was making an effort for Leo to be more open to the pack. She was terrified of alphas, but she was trying. My own girlfriend, Carolyn, didn't even like sitting at the same table as my pack during events. But I didn't really know Lola, and the problem was that I *wanted* to.

"I worry that any interest I might have will make her

uncomfortable," I said. "I shouldn't even be wondering about this. Carolyn…"

"Carolyn has never wanted a place with us, just you," Wes finished for me. "I suppose you're right. Lola's a long way from being ready to look at this pack as a whole. I don't know what that will mean in the long run. Speaking of Carolyn, how did she take you canceling your dinner plans?"

I shouldn't have been surprised. Wes kept track of us, it was as much his job as it was his role in the pack. "Reasonably," I said, and Wes huffed.

Carolyn took everything reasonably. It was why our relationship had worked as well as it did for as long as it had. She was comfortable in her independence, preferred our relationship outside of the bounds of my pack, and seemed to have no concerns about what that meant for us long term. Hell, it had *been* long term now, three years and counting. In the absence of a partner who wanted to be a part of my pack, having one who was happy to continue in a perpetual state of dating and living separately was a blessing.

"Do you think you'll find him?" I asked, staring at the face on the screen again.

"Honestly? Probably only if he continues to harass her. The bolder he gets, the easier he should be to find. But…"

But none of us wanted that for her.

"I'll find him," Wes said, voice darkening and eyes narrowing at the screen.

I nodded. Wes was usually too modest for his own good. If he was determined to find this little shithead, then he would.

"I'll leave you to it. But don't forget to sleep," I said.

Wes leaned forward in his seat and ignored me as I got up from my own. He knew his own limits, but he'd probably push them anyway. I couldn't blame him. I'd come running to the house at Caleb's message, knowing perfectly well there wasn't really anything I could do.

You're starting to sound like a mid-life crisis, I warned myself as I headed for the stairs.

I FOLLOWED the siren call of sizzling bacon down the stairs to the kitchen the next morning. My steps slowed at the first notes of feminine murmurs and I debated retreating, offering Lola space. And then a second, clearer, female voice sounded, and my heart stuttered.

Shit. Carolyn.

I hurried down the stairs and into the kitchen, pausing at the sight of Carolyn's back to me. Her red hair was plaited in a thick braid, and she was dressed casually for a woman who didn't own jeans and didn't believe leggings were pants. Rake and Lola stood across the island from her, Lola's head turned to watch Leo cooking with a trace of a smile on her lips and her light hair rumpled around her head. Rake was the first person to see me and he smirked, brow raising slightly.

I wiped the panic off my face just before Lola twisted and caught sight of me too. She was dressed in a combination of men's clothing, slightly dwarfed in fabric, and she didn't look startled to see me, although she leaned into Rake's side as she glanced over me.

"Carolyn brought pastries," Rake said in greeting.

Carolyn twisted in place, leaning against the giant steel island, and her smile reached her eyes as she took me in. "There you are. I didn't realize you were such a late sleeper."

I wasn't usually up half the night tossing in my sheets.

"I wouldn't have slept in if I'd known you were coming," I said, crossing the open space to her side and leaning in for a brief kiss against her lips, aware of Rake's amusement across from us.

"Coffee?" Rake asked.

"No."

"Please," I said at the same moment Carolyn refused.

"I thought I'd come and check on you since things sounded kind of dire last night when you canceled," Carolyn explained.

I resisted the urge to grimace, but I couldn't stop my gaze

from flicking to Lola, seeing her lips flatten and her eyes drop to the counter. Leo shot a soft glare at me over his shoulder before returning to his cooking.

"You can always come to the house, Carolyn, you know that. Especially with pastries," Rake added, softening the scratch of his mild taunt. "Lola, would you grab the almond milk from the fridge?"

Since when did my eyes have such a mind of their own? It was like I was physically incapable of pulling them off the younger woman. When she moved away from the counter and headed for the fridge, I got the first glimpse of her bare legs. I put my back to the open room and met Carolyn's stare with another smile.

"How long have you been waiting?" I asked.

"Not long. Just getting formally introduced to Lola. How is everything today?" Carolyn asked in return.

"Everything today is peaceful," Leo answered for me, pushing bacon out of a skillet and onto an open plate before cracking eggs into a pan.

I nodded at Carolyn in support of his answer. Lola's scent was faint under the smells of cooking and Rake's perfume, and her sweet acidity contrasted with his rich scent and Carolyn's faint florals. Lola's smell reminded me of the paper cups of flavored ice I'd had as a child, and it gave me a similar impulse to *lick*.

I cleared the thought out of my head and nodded to the paper bag in front of Carolyn, waggling my eyebrows at my girlfriend. "Do I smell butter?"

Carolyn's expression brightened. "Your favorite croissants, yes."

"And bacon and eggs? I feel very spoiled this morning," I said.

Brightened by her success, Carolyn resisted the urge to glare at the cup of coffee Rake slid to me. She never admitted to disliking my omega, and as my relationship with Rake wasn't sexual, I could only assume that Carolyn resented my need of him at all. But that was the thing with my pack, I didn't *need* them. And they didn't really need me. We were just happy together, as we were.

Carolyn was the most accepting woman I'd dated when it came to my pack, but I couldn't help wondering if there wasn't something better than this compartmentalized version of a relationship.

"So, Lola, how did you meet Rake?"

Restraint slipped through my fingers, and I turned to find Lola sitting up on the counter near Leo, looking perfectly at home in our space. I smiled unconsciously at the picture.

"On set for a *Designate* photoshoot. I'm a new hire in the beauty department."

"Oh! So you're all tangled up in the pack then," Carolyn mused.

I knew my girlfriend wasn't doing an intentional job of antagonizing Lola, but I was scrambling to think of the best way of getting the two women separated as quickly as possible.

"Where are the others, by the way?" Carolyn asked, looking around the kitchen as if it might've been possible to hide Wes anywhere in the room. Unlikely. The man was a giant.

"Plates please," Leo announced. Rake rushed to follow the order as Leo broke off a piece of bacon and hand fed it to Lola. They shared a gentle look that made my heart twist, and I was relieved to study the feeling and find it wasn't jealousy, just a kind of appreciative gratitude for them both.

"Would everyone like a croissant? Matt says the ones from Armand's are the closest thing in the city to a good Parisian."

"Two please," I said, earning an eye-roll from Carolyn as everyone echoed a 'yes.'

"You eat like a garbage disposal," Carolyn muttered.

I shook my head. "No. My taste is far too good for that."

Lola huffed a soft laugh and drew my gaze again like a magnet, but this time I tore it away before she noticed.

"What do you think of taking our plates out to the garden deck?" Leo asked, and Rake nodded quickly. "You're welcome to join us," Leo added to me, carrying the skillet to dole out greasy eggs and bacon on every plate.

"No, we'll leave you to it," I said before Carolyn could speak.

Leo nodded, and Lola slid down from the counter, miles of long leg ahead of her. Rake draped his arm over Lola's shoulder, the trio left the kitchen, and awkward silence followed in their wake.

Carolyn nudged her food around her plate, and I glanced at my own. Only one croissant, but Carolyn wasn't likely to finish her own, so I could take it. She wasn't very likely to eat much of anything on the plate. Leo had cooked comfort food to satisfy a salty craving. Three years into our relationship, and I'd discovered a very small collection of things that Carolyn craved.

Quiet.

Shower sex.

And red wine with Diet Coke, although it'd been a year into dating before she'd revealed that one.

"You work awfully hard at ignoring that gorgeous young woman, Matt," Carolyn murmured softly.

That was true. And I debated taking the hit, letting Carolyn see the worst of the situation, but the urge to defend myself rose up quickly.

"She's uncomfortable around alphas. I suspect the others are giving them space," I said, offering an answer to her earlier question.

Carolyn's eyes widened. "Oh. *Oh*. I see." She blushed and shook her head, tearing off a piece of flaky croissant and slipping it into her mouth. "I wondered why she was here when you said there was a pack emergency but it's…it was something to do with her?"

I frowned and studied my own plate, and Carolyn nodded.

"It's all right, I don't need to know details. I understand. I guess I got…" Carolyn let out a soft laugh. "I got jealous."

"Did you think I was fooling around with them?" I asked, brow furrowing.

Carolyn visibly swallowed, green eyes going wide. "Maybe…maybe a bit."

"I've told you, my relationship with Rake is—"

"I know, I know," Carolyn said, nodding. "I suppose, if she were a link between the two of you."

A link *between*? Something feminine for me to enjoy with Rake, like a toy?

"It's just that you insist on your life with your pack—"

"Because they are my *pack*, Carolyn." I held my hand up, the alpha in me stretching. "Stop. This is disrespectful to all of us. Lola and Rake, as well as you and I. The link between Rake and I is our friendship, our… It's a different kind of bond, I know, but it is a bond. We've never needed someone else to complete it, and that's never what I've looked for in a partner."

"Yes, you're right. I'm sorry, Matt," Carolyn murmured. Her hackles were up, nerves grated after being chastised.

I relaxed and pulled a stool around to sit and enjoy my breakfast, trying not to let the guilt of knowing Carolyn was at least right in suspecting my interest affect my appetite.

Lola
17

"Where did you put my clothes, by the way? I need to get going soon."

Leo and Rake exchanged one quick look, and then Leo answered, "No."

"No?"

"It's almost dark, you should just stay the night," Rake reasoned.

"I have to work tomorrow," I said, eyebrows raising.

Rake made a dismissive sound, but Leo said, "We can get you to work."

It had been easy to indulge the day away with Leo and Rake, first on the lush green 'garden nest' that faced out over the park, and then in Leo's rooms snacking and watching movies together, talking aimlessly.

I checked my phone. It was almost eight, and I was starting to get hungry. If I stayed to eat with the guys, I'd be getting home even later. It was hard enough to think of facing my apartment after two days in this palace of a house, it would be better to rip the band-aid off. I made to sit up, but Rake's head was in my lap and Leo's arm around my shoulders circled close.

I snorted and shook my head. "Come on. I'm not going to work in your boxers and sweater. It's a look, but not the one I aim for in the beauty department. I need to get home and shower and sleep and…"

"If you had something to wear for tomorrow would you stay the night?" Rake asked.

"You're *not* buying me an outfit," I said, catching the gleam in his eye. Was that even possible this late on a Sunday? Probably, if you were Rake.

"We could easily get you home in the morning. With a driver to the Stanmore, you'd save time," Leo bargained.

I twisted to look up at him and regretted it immediately. Leo had a pleading gaze down pat.

"I have to go back," I said. Maybe not tonight but…eventually. Soon.

"Then Leo and I will come with you," Rake said.

"No! Fine. Just tonight," I said in a rush, heat rushing up my cheeks at the thought of Rake walking into my apartment. It was bad enough now, knowing Leo had been there. And I was definitely going to unpack my fucking boxes before he came over again.

Leo grinned in triumph, and I was certain I'd just offered a future tool for him to use in this kind of argument.

"Just tonight," I repeated. "And I need to be up and on my way home at like five-thirty tomorrow."

"No way. Seven-thirty."

"I cannot go into *Designate* with this face," I said, waving my hand over my bare face.

"I like this face," Leo murmured, bending down and nipping at the tip of my nose and then traveling down to my lips for soft, persistent pecks.

This had been my day. Endless cuddles. Constant kisses. All very PG too, which was somehow even more indulgent? Naked in Rake's arms in the bath yesterday, his intentions had been chaste, even while we were hip to hip and his erection had pressed between us.

I hummed and arched into the kiss, aware of Rake rolling against my side to watch, his chin resting between my ribs. Leo was facing upside-down to me and I liked the new angle, sucking on his bottom lip and humming as he did the same. His hands were cupped over my shoulders, fingers brushing softly against the collar of his t-shirt. A moment later, I gasped into the kiss as Rake pushed the shirt's hem up, scooting down to kiss over the sensitive skin of my stomach before dipping his tongue into my belly button.

I moaned at the unexpectedly erotic touch, and Leo's mouth traveled to a sensitive spot on my jaw that he'd discovered. I squirmed between the two men, body shivering under Rake's playful exploration, tongue flicking out to taste me as he moved toward my hip bone. He hooked the waistband of the boxers I was wearing with one finger and tugged it down, mouth latching on the skin there and sucking hard.

My eyes squeezed shut as the feeling pulled at my center. Leo's hands slid beneath the v-neck collar of the shirt, covering my breasts and then gripping gently as Rake hummed, teeth scratching against my skin and tongue soothing.

"He's trying to mark you, I think," Leo rasped, amused by his omega's antics.

I swallowed hard, my heart hammering in my chest, and I squirmed, trying to sit up and catch my breath. Rake and Leo followed, Leo's hands leaving my breasts for my hips, his fingers sliding down under the fabric to stroke on the inside of my hips. Rake sat up on his knees, hands cupping my jaw and dragging me in for a deep, licking kiss, his hesitation from the day before gone as his tongue fucked my mouth. My core throbbed and my body rolled between them, grinding against Rake's hips and then back against Leo's, but my chest was tight and uncomfortable.

When Leo pushed my hair aside and leaned in to suck along the muscle of my shoulder, I shuddered again. Rake's heavy perfume went from rich and sweet to charred and bitter, and there seemed to be hands in too many places.

"Lola?"

"Um," I whimpered against Rake's kiss, and gasped as Leo's touch rose up to my waist, gentling as he scooted back.

Rake pulled away, brow furrowed, and I sucked in a deep

breath. His eyes widened, and I wondered what he saw in my expression.

"Hey, gorgeous," Leo murmured at my back. "It's all right. You're with us."

I swallowed on air and nodded, reaching to draw Rake closer, but he only caught my hand in his and settled on his heels.

"What is it? Is it my perfume? I can shower."

"No. No, it's not that," I said, bending and kissing him firmly on the mouth, the confusion of the moment passing. I reached behind me for Leo, but the second his back was against my chest, my whole body tightened.

Rake, with his gaze fixed to my face, noticed immediately. "Aww, Lollipop. It's us together?"

Leo settled and pulled me down so I was facing the rest of the room, my breath immediately coming easier.

"I'm sor—" I said, eyes welling up.

"Don't you dare," Leo murmured, kissing my temple.

"Yeah, Lola, seriously. A threesome is intimidating for like, literally anybody," Rake said, waving his hand through the air. "And if it's something you experienced, you know…"

"With them," I said, words rasping.

Rake paled but nodded. "It's not me though?"

"*No*, Rake, it's really not," I said, tugging him closer and cupping his jaw to kiss him again. He settled against my side, and having them both close returned to being comforting.

"It's like the elevator, probably. Being closed in that way," Leo said gently, his hand rubbing over my bare thigh.

"I think I'm still a little shaky from yesterday too," I admitted.

"Do you guys want me to go, though?" Rake asked, fixing his expression into something stiff and neutral. "If you want to like, connect, and everything, I would totally understand. There's plenty of time for us to figure this out later."

I glanced at Leo, even though I was pretty sure I already knew the answer. "No. I want to be with you both," I said.

"Same," Leo said, smile stretching back into place.

"Today has been a good day."

I nodded in agreement and Rake settled back against me, pulling one of my hands up to his lips to press a kiss against the palm.

"Come on," Leo said. "A little more cuddle, and then we'll go make dinner."

I made myself cozy between them, Rake returning his head to my lap, and tried to ignore the sinking feeling in my stomach. This was a hiccup, if not a really fucking unfortunate one. But I wanted to believe that Rake was right. We had plenty of time to figure it out between us.

LEO DROVE me himself back to my apartment early the next morning, two big portable cups of coffee between us. He parked his car illegally in front of my building and insisted on walking me in, frowning at my unlocked street door.

"I'm gonna track down this landlord of yours," he muttered.

I opened my apartment door and winced as I realized I'd left all the lights on when I'd left for the police station. "Okay, well, home sweet home," I said, staring down at my shoes with Leo behind me.

"Don't make that face. I'm really fond of this apartment," Leo said.

"Fond?" I asked, scoffing at him.

He grinned and nodded, looking over to my couch. "Good memories and all that."

I cracked a laugh and accepted Leo's triumphant kiss, giggling against his lips. "Thank you for the ride."

"Can I come over tonight? I've gotta fly back to the west coast tomorrow morning, and I meant it when I told Rake I was fine not having you to myself last night, but..." Leo trailed off, raising his head and waggling his eyebrows.

I laughed again. "But you want me to yourself? Yeah. Come over tonight. How long will you be out of town?"

"Couple days. You should plan a sleepover with Rake while I'm gone."

"Are you the cruise director of my sex life now?" I asked, tilting my head.

Leo hummed and grinned. "I accept the position, thank you."

He bent for a kiss and nearly had me up against a wall before I remembered that I needed to be getting ready for work. "Go. Go, you're very distracting."

"We can shower together," he growled sweetly.

"You talked me out of an hour and a half of getting ready time, Leo, *go*. Save it for tonight."

He laughed and released me, moving to the door. "Okay, but just prepare yourself because I'll take you up on that."

I was giddy by the time he left, and I flicked my lights off on the way to get ready for my shower.

"ALL OF THESE ARE GOOD," Cyrus said, tapping the images in my fashion week layout, while the rest of the team and I sat around the conference table. "Most of these are *amazing*. But…"

He glanced at me and I shook my head, folding my arms over my chest. "Don't be nice for my sake. Not if it means Wendy's gonna dole it out later."

Betty grinned at me and Cyrus' smile flickered on. I wondered what he'd done all weekend while I was in his house. I hadn't even seen him or Wes once. Not that my run-ins with Caleb and Matthieu hadn't been awkward enough.

"Okay. These two. The photos are gorgeous, the makeup is impeccable, but it's definitely something we've seen before. Even if it's a trend that's coming back…"

"*Designate* isn't here to recycle old trends," I said, and Cyrus nodded in approval at me. "Got it. There were two others. I think the looks are kind of hideous to be honest, but they're brave."

"Show me."

It was Zane that pulled my images out, laying four of the more controversial looks. One was especially bland, a sort of dull dewy look. Another was striking, but presented entirely on pale models. Cyrus pushed those both away and stared at the remaining two. One was the gold makeup I'd done for Rake's show in Odette's studio.

"You didn't like this one?" Cyrus asked me.

"It's a beautiful image, but using gold leaf in a makeup look? The whole thing is really inaccessible. But it's definitely a statement."

"Though, it's more common now for people to try really outrageous makeup. Even if it becomes a social media challenge for laughs—" Corey started.

Cyrus pointed to her. "That! Yes. How do we do that?"

"We can promote it on the site, on all our own social media. I'll make a video of my own," Anna said with a shrug. "I've got over ten thousand followers."

Damn. Not bad. I'd been nearing those numbers before I stopped making videos. But Anna loved a dramatic look and social media loved the dramatic.

"Good. Do it. We'll pitch it with the layout," Cyrus said, standing up to stare down at the added photos and nodding. "Lola, you can replicate this for a shoot?"

"Of course."

"Good. Put that together as quick as you can and we'll add it all to our next pitch pack. Now. I have a challenge for you all. Highlighters are back in," Cyrus said. Betty let out a massive groan and he nodded. "I know. And of course, we are *Designate*, so we can't rehash the same drivel about opening up your features and shaping. We need to look at this from a new angle."

"Get shimmer literally fucking everywhere," Zane muttered.

"That's not a suggestion, and if it is, it was a terrible one," Cyrus answered. He pulled a box up from under his chair, opening it and tossing onto the table a collection of thin iridescent pens. "Here's their new twist. They're really thin. You draw on the area and then take your brush of choice to blend them out. I'm looking at you, Betty."

Betty, queen of blending, floundered for a moment. "So we do a cross-comparison of different highlighting strengths?"

"Betty, we'll come back to you when you're ready," Cyrus droned, and the table chuckled.

"We go…celestial instead of the mermaid thing? Celestial is in," Anna said.

I wrinkled my nose, and Zane grinned at me. "Lola disagrees. Share with the table, killer."

"I… Celestial is just an inspiration to add to the highlighter, it doesn't change its function," I said, reaching for one of the pens. I shrugged at Anna in apology, and she waved her hand in answer, no offense taken. I uncapped the pen, its color a delicate shimmering blue, and studied the fine wet brush end.

"Come on, killer. You're like two for two so far, aren't you?" Betty asked. Sometimes my nickname was a compliment, and sometimes it was just a way for Betty to goad me.

"There are five of you sitting at this table, Betty," Cyrus warned gently. "Corey, got anything?"

I drew a faint spiral on the back of my hand, looking at the pretty trace of color. I smudged the swirl into a soft glow and frowned as I rolled my hand in front of me. Just highlighter.

"Umm, we can try layering it over mattes?"

"We did that the second time the companies pushed it," Betty said immediately.

My eye caught on a thin scar on the back of my thumb, a long line running from one knuckle over the next all the way to my nail bed, when I'd stuck my hand into a hole in the school wall on a dare, and caught my skin on an old nail.

"What if it's not about how it's used but where it's used," I said.

The table had moved on, and I was pretty sure as I looked

up that I'd just interrupted Zane, based on the flat annoyance of his expression.

"Like...what if we highlight scars?" I asked.

"Scars?" Betty repeated frowning.

I took the pen and used it to paint the line of my scar, the blue standing out brighter against the shiny pale skin of the scar, adding decorative dots on either side and then turning it to show the table.

"Highlighting imperfections," Anna mused. "It's a statement for sure."

"Where are we going to get models with scars on their face?" Zane asked, frowning.

I looked to Cyrus and watched as the light bulb went off behind his eyes.

"Omegas," I said. "Their bondmarks. Betas too. But not just bondmarks, because plenty of people don't have those. It doesn't have to be their face."

"Reinventing the stretch mark under a crop top," Corey said, smiling. "Giving so-called imperfections a different lense."

"Ahhh, an inclusivity approach," Zane said, nodding slowly.

"I love it," Anna said with a shrug. "We need to find models."

I looked to Cyrus, who'd been quiet through the discussion, and found him already staring back at me, eyes warm with a secret smile.

"This is exactly what we need. Start looking at models now. When we know what we're working with, we'll take it to the fashion team too. Make it an airbrush-free shoot," Cyrus said with a nod. He pushed up from the table and raised an eyebrow at us. "Well? Go grab the portfolios. Start thinking designs too. Test some patterns."

Betty raced to the wall to pull down binders of models, and Anna pushed up her sleeve to draw directly onto her skin. Cyrus flashed me his full, brilliant smile on his way out the door.

Lola
18

"I feel weird that your alphas go into hiding while I'm here," I said to Rake as we took the elevator up from the first floor to his rooms. With Leo out of town, I'd picked up two giant orders of ramen for Rake and me.

"I mean, honestly, sometimes we're all so busy doing our own thing it feels like I'm home alone," Rake said with a shrug. "Other times we make sure we're home for family dinners and movie nights. I can put out an alert to them to quit tiptoeing around you, if you want."

I swallowed. Did I want that? Maybe not, but it only seemed fair. Between Leo and Rake, I was bound to be spending more time at the house. If the rest of the pack had to vanish just to accommodate me, there'd be tension about it eventually.

"Do it," I said with a nod.

Rake pulled his phone from his back pocket and sent out a text. A pack group chat, of course. I wondered how many times I'd been the subject of that chat and then pushed the thought away.

I was going to be cool. In control. Calm and flexible.

I'd spent one night with Leo at my apartment, and then one night alone catching up on the sleep I'd lost, before giving in to Rake's pleads to come back to the house. This time, I'd been smart and brought an overnight bag too, and it was currently slung over Rake's shoulder. An omega and a gentleman.

The elevator dinged and we got off on Rake's floor. Caleb's rooms were dark, so maybe everyone was doing their own thing on the family floors below us and I wasn't too much in the way for the night.

"I can see you worrying," Rake said, arching an eyebrow.

"Get used to it," I volleyed back, and smiled when I made him laugh.

We walked into his rooms, and I bit at my smile. The first time I'd been here, the space had been overtaken by a stylish kind of chaos, clothes and photo equipment and books were strewn about everywhere. Now it was spotless and organized, with a few candles burning around the room that seemed to replace some of his heady perfume with a clean citrus smell. The curtains were closed to his bedroom, making the space feel comfy and close.

I sat with Rake on a dense loveseat in front of a long coffee table, pulling our food out of the paper bag as I glanced over at the corner of the room that was set up like a mini photo studio.

"Do you do shoots here at home?" I asked Rake.

He was quiet and I turned to find him blushing, stirring chopsticks through his ramen. "Um. Not for like...not professional ones," he said, cheeks darkening.

It took me a moment of staring at his growing blush for it to click. "You do sexy photoshoots at home?" I asked, my grin spreading. "For your alphas?"

"*Of* my alphas, and my beta," Rake said, laughing at my dropped jaw. "Okay, sometimes for them too. For us all."

"Ohmigod, that's so...*hot*," I said, staring down at my food and wondering if I could ask...

"Do you wanna see some?" Rake asked me, face wicked and eyes warm on my face.

Now *I* was the one blushing. "I...I mean, would they mind? Are there ones with just you and Leo?"

"Oh for sure. And to be honest, Cyrus probably couldn't care less, even if you are his employee. I'll be very selective,"

Rake said, jumping up and pulling a heavy leather-bound book from the shelves across the room.

It looked professionally printed and I wondered how they'd managed it, or if Matthieu had done it with some of his publishing connections. I would've assumed it was a coffee table art book if I'd been browsing the shelf.

"Okay, let's see. Um…nope, not that one." Rake flipped through pages with an almost smug smile on his lips as I slurped noodles and watched brief glimpses of skin flipping by. "Ah. Okay, umm…huh, this feels sort of weird to show someone, actually. I didn't think it would."

"You don't have to—"

"Nope, here." Rake flipped the book around, setting it down on the cushions between us. A little bit of broth dribbled down from my lips, and I caught it on the back of my hand before it could hit the full-page photo of Rake.

It was just his bare torso and his face, but it was explicit even showing so little, his skin wearing a sheen of sweat, muscles strained and face torn with a silent cry of pleasure, eyes squeezed shut.

"I set up the camera and just let it take shots to see what it'd get while we…you know."

My mouth was dry. I wanted to see that look on Rake's face for myself. I wanted to watch someone else put it there. "It's beautiful," I breathed. "You're beautiful."

"Thanks," Rake said, his foot nudging against mine as he picked the book up again. "Okay, what's next? Oh, this one I like."

He turned it again, and the next photo wasn't explicit at all, but it was intimate—a black and white photo of Matthieu in profile, shadows catching all the lines and texture of age on his face. Rake turned it long before I was done studying the man, it was easier in a photo than in person when I might be caught. I wasn't sure what exactly about Matthieu Segal was so appealing to me, only that I wanted to trace the outline of that profile with my finger, memorizing all the angles.

"Here's Leo," Rake said, and the photo brought an immediate smile to my face.

Leo reclining in white sheets, body on display but relaxed and languorous, the aftermath of lovemaking in his lazy, drowsy smile.

"Yeah, I knew when I met him. It's just…he's just like that feeling of coming home from a long trip away, but it's every time I see him," Rake said, and I bit my lip to keep from agreeing. I didn't know Leo the same way Rake did. I wasn't part of his pack. But he *did* feel a lot like home already and I was trying not to let it terrify me.

"Okay here's a juicy one. But I just really like it," Rake said.

I held my breath to keep from gasping, but even that didn't prepare me for the visceral shock and ache of seeing the next photo. Cyrus was there, mostly covered by Rake's sprawling, tense form, the omega's back arched and mouth open on a moan, his hips in Cyrus' darker hands. Leo was there too, bent over Rake, licking down his chest, his hands wrapped around Rake's length and hiding it from view. Altogether, the lines of their bodies filled the page in muscle and stretch. It looked as much like a Renaissance study in oil as it did a racy photograph of a pack.

My sex pulsed at the picture, and I blushed and turned away from the sight. "I…don't think I know enough about art to tell you how impressed I am."

Rake laughed and pulled the book away, closing it and sliding it onto the coffee table. "That's enough of a compliment for now. You can congratulate me on my super hot pack if that's easier."

I laughed and nodded. "Yeah, um, sexiness is not something this house is lacking in, for *sure*." I looked up at Rake's wicked grin and drew up some courage. "So…how does it work?"

"Being surrounded by hot men? Fine, I'm a big fan. Ten out of ten, would recommend," Rake said.

I snorted and shook my head, drawing in a deep breath. "No I mean...um, a male omega. With male alphas?"

Rake's lips formed an 'o' and he nodded slowly. "Ah. Right. Like, do they knot me?" I lifted my ramen container high to hide my blush, my eyes wide, and Rake laughed. "Um. So, yes, they do. Although it's not... Biology is a bitch, honestly, and it's not quite the same. Do you know much about female alphas?"

"I know about knots, and that's kind of it," I said.

"Right, so a female alpha doesn't have a knot, she has a 'lock.' Basically, when she's...uhh, ready, she locks down on the male omega. And just like a female omega is extra sensitive and prepared for pleasure from a male alpha's knot, a male omega is um..." His head wobbled side to side, and he searched the air for the right words before meeting my eyes and shrugging. "I can come a lot, basically. Like...*a lot*. It's all about breeding, I guess."

I slurped noodles and Rake laughed, pulling veggies from his own bowl, the pair of us munching and staring at one another in the ensuing awkward silence.

"So with you and the guys..."

Rake sighed and shrugged. "You know, I uh...had an opportunity to be with a female alpha once. But they don't do super well with packs, because they're rare and I guess they have a hard time with male alphas. And this one didn't want shit to do with my pack, so it seemed like a risky idea. So yeah, my guys and I, we just adapt a lot. There are some toys that mimic an alpha-lock and we use those, although—I mean, the lock feels fucking awesome, but sex feels fucking awesome too. I'm not that picky," Rake said, grinning.

"Does it hurt you to be knotted?" I asked. It had hurt me, but that had been Indy's intention, hadn't it?

Rake's eyebrows jumped. "I mean it could, but it never has. Or not more than I might like it to. The guys are really careful with me. We love each other. It's not...it's not about alpha and omega with us. It's just about us," he said.

I smiled at that and turned back to my food.

"Leo...Leo told me about the night you met," Rake said, drawing my gaze back up. "Have you...have you only been with betas since you left those assholes?"

I nodded. "Just betas. Just in clubs. Just once. Until Leo, obviously."

"Man. Leo would've given you hell if you'd had sex with him in the bathroom and tried to leave without his number," Rake said grinning.

I shook my head. "That whole night went wildly out of control."

"Control? Is that what you like?" Rake asked, setting his food aside.

I shrugged and set my own down, staring back at him. "I...guess it's what I thought I needed to survive, at the time."

"Lola, if you want control, I'm your guy," Rake said, his eyebrows raising slightly, focus firmly glued to my face.

We were facing one another on the loveseat with just a few feet between us, and Rake's invitation was like a rope around my chest, tugging me closer, begging for my attention.

"It doesn't have to be like that," I said, watching him.

He grinned. "I mean, like I said, I'm not picky. But if you wanna tie me to the bed and have your way with me, I sure as hell wouldn't ask you to stop. Honestly, I'd do just about anything you asked me to at this point."

My breath stopped, but my heartbeat picked up, thumping so hard in my veins I could feel the pulse between my thighs. Or maybe that was just pure desire. Rake's tongue flicked out over his bottom lip as he watched me. He was so... easy going, so open. I was bundled up in my spot on the loveseat, but Rake was sprawled open, thighs and arms spread over the furniture, making room for me against him if I was brave enough to take it.

I concentrated on my own body, forcing my shoulders to soften and relax, my spine to straighten. I sat up on my knees and crawled closer until one knee was pressed to Rake's groin. His chest was rising and falling faster now, eyes hooded as he watched me, and he pushed his hips against my leg, riding it slightly and drawing a smile up on my lips. I braced my hands behind his shoulders, hovering my face over his as his head leaned back, warm breath fanning against my neck.

"So where'd you put all those sex toys I saw last time?" I asked, grinning.

———

RAKE TASTED LIKE CARAMEL, rich and buttery and sweet on my tongue. And he wasn't kidding. I'd already made him come once, on accident, on his own stomach while I'd been fiddling around with a toy in his ass, teasing him for all the sounds he made—perfect whimpers and sighs and moans.

After that first experiment, I'd become more careful and better at being able to tell when he was about to lose control.

Like right now. I drew the textured roller away from the base of his cock and slipped my fingers out of the handle of the sleek glass prostate stimulator, rising up on my knees.

"Fuuuuck, Lola, please," Rake moaned, wiggling in the dark sheets of his bed, cock weeping profusely. His cock was surprisingly thick, not super long, but I had no doubt it would give me a stretch I'd be feeling for the next day at least, whenever I got around to being done teasing and ready to ride, that is.

"You were right," I said, staring down at Rake's pleasure torn expression, the sweat clear on his brow. "This feels really good."

"Woman, you are literally killing me," Rake gasped. His eyes were almost fully black and his cock jumped as I ran my finger up its side, gathering the seeping fluid and drawing it up to my lips to suck.

I'd discovered Rake's second bite mark early, down in the crease of his thigh, and I dipped to lick over the spot now, making Rake's leg shake in response. Caleb had picked a fairly traditional if not subtle spot on Rake's shoulder—the mark I'd covered up in Rake's photoshoot—but evidently Cyrus had opted for somewhere more unusual. According to

Rake, it also meant that Cyrus had his head between Rake's thighs for a torturous two days after the bonding while the mark healed.

"You're fine," I said, looking up and grinning. "But if you really need me to, I can give you a break."

"Fuck no," Rake growled, one hand flying out of the pillows he'd been clenching down on, to reach out and cup my hip. His fingers caught in the side of my panties, tugging slightly. "But maybe I could have a taste?"

I bit my lip, wetness slipping from my core as I imagined staring down between my thighs to watch Rake feasting on my sex. It was…tempting, to say the least. I shimmied out of my panties, and Rake sat up to watch me expose my pussy, his expression wild.

Just when I'd made up my mind to let him eat me out—gosh, what a hardship—Rake's phone on the bedside table rang.

"Shit," Rake said, twisting on his side and then groaning as his swollen cock rested against my thigh. I scooted back out of the way with a laugh when he started to grind against my leg, his eyes rolling back in his head. "Shit. Oh! It's Leo," he said, lifting the screen. He glanced at me and gave me a wide grin. "Wanna torture him too? He wants to video chat."

Shyness, or worry, welled up in my chest, and Rake held out his free arm, offering me his side to curl into. I took him up on it, crawling up and hiding my breasts against his chest.

"Maybe," I said. "If he wants to."

Rake hummed and kissed my forehead, and then swiped across his screen to accept the video call. Leo popped up immediately, propped up against a headboard in a hotel room, pillows high behind his back. In the top corner of the phone screen, a little image of Rake and me was there, and I realized how totally mussed my hair was from Rake holding onto it while I'd treated his candy-flavored dick like…well, candy.

Leo's eyes widened, and he let out a long sigh. "I have

never hated business trips more than I do at this moment. You two look like dessert, Jesus. Hey, gorgeous."

Leo's smile was so wide that my worry evaporated almost immediately. "Hey," I said, a little whispery from some remaining reserve.

"Lola is murdering me, slowly and divinely," Rake said. "She's a secret Domme in the bedroom."

I laughed at that, and Leo nodded. "I had my suspicions. But your hands are free so she's taking things slowly, I guess?"

"She mastered orgasm denial in like two minutes," Rake said, a faint whine in his tone.

"Fuck, well if I wasn't jealous before, I am *now*," Leo said. "Don't let her break out the whips and chains before I get back."

"Ohmigod, shut up," I said, laughing and burying my face against Rake's throat as the men grinned. "I might like to listen to Rake beg, but it doesn't make me a sadist."

"Have you gotten a taste of her yet, babe? Our girl is fucking heaven."

"You *just* interrupted us, as a matter of fact," Rake said, flashing me an evil grin as I lifted my head.

Leo was quiet for a minute, and I looked to the screen to find him settling into the pillows more. "Any chance I could convince you two to pick up where you left off? Without ending the call?"

I nearly swallowed my own tongue, and Rake looked to me. Of course he did. I stared at Leo through the small phone screen and licked my lips.

"Are you going to join us?" I asked.

"I think I would have a hard time keeping my hands off my cock if you give me a view like that, gorgeous," Leo said in his rasping growl.

This lucky bitch had found herself a beta who sounded like an alpha. My thighs pressed together and I looked back to Rake, nodding. He beamed at me and wiggled in excitement.

"Oh, hell fucking yes, Lollipop," Rake said. "You be the camerawoman. I'll do the work."

I laughed at that and took the phone from him, rising up. Rake didn't even wait for me to crawl up to him, he just slid right down the sheets.

"God, I miss you," Leo hissed. He was shifting on his hotel bed, pushing his boxers off his hips probably, although I couldn't see it yet. "Miss you both. Lola, gorgeous, can you be at the house tomorrow night too?"

Rake was handling me from below, making me giggle as he pawed at my legs, desperate to make room for himself between my thighs.

"Yeah, I'll figure it out," I said, watching Leo's face light up.

Good thing I never got the cat I'd wanted, I guess. Poor Mr. Kibbles would've been cramping all this sleepover style I had going with my new boyfriends.

I tapped the screen to flip the camera and blushed to myself at the new view. Leo had a vividly explicit picture to enjoy, right down my stomach to where Rake was grinning up from between my thighs, his tan contrasting against my ultra pale skin.

"Lola, you're fucking soaked," Rake said, waggling his eyebrows.

I opened my mouth to answer, but Rake arched his neck, lifting his head and swiping his tongue directly up my center. Leo, Rake, and I all moaned at the same moment.

"Leo," I gasped. "I wanna watch you too."

Leo nodded and then rolled, setting the phone down on a table and then shifting into frame. He tore his t-shirt off with one arm, over the back of his neck, until he was naked in front of the camera, a hand fisted around his cock. Up in the tiny right-hand corner of the screen, Rake grinned up at me.

"Ready?" Rake asked.

"Mhm," I nodded.

"Fuck yes," Leo echoed, tugging on his own length and then smearing the pre-cum back up.

I whined and the shot blurred as Rake wrapped both arms around my thighs, and pulled me down to his mouth. I cried out and Leo huffed, his stomach jumping as he started to fuck into his hand.

"Ohmigod, it's like watching porn," I said, giggling breathlessly.

"Best porn ever," Leo agreed.

It was. Best porn ever and one desperately greedy mouth on my aching pussy. For all the teasing I'd done to Rake, I'd been making myself just as needy and excited. Rake's mouth was already smeared with my wetness as he lapped and sucked over every inch of me.

"Fuck. Fuck yes," I whined. It was a strange mirror, watching Rake eat me out on the screen, watching Leo's brow furrow and fold as he watched, his chest heaving. My brain knew what I was watching corresponded to the delicious sensation of Rake's lips and tongue on me, but I could almost pretend that the two were separate, that it wasn't my hips that were rocking and rolling and pleading for more.

Jesus fucking Christ, Rakim Oren was eating me out. I was so used to the playful, sexy man I'd gotten to know, I'd genuinely forgotten that he was, well, *famous*.

"Don't be so fucking shy, Rake," Leo gasped on the line. "Fucking devour her."

Rake puffed a breath against my sex, and then I was shaking, barely able to keep the camera turned in the right direction as Rake's tongue thrust up into me, his nose burrowing against my clit.

"That's it, gorgeous. Gush all over our man. You wanna ride him too?"

If I was a Domme, then Leo was like the King of Dirty Talking. "Yes," I whined, although I was totally already riding Rake.

"His cock's gonna feel so good in you. He's gonna make you so slippery and soaked, but I want you to fucking ride him until he begs you to stop," Leo said.

I shivered as Rake pushed me up slightly, taking a deep

breath and sucking hard on my clit, tongue swirling over the spot. Fuck. *Almost*, I wanted to say, but I didn't want him to stop, to return the teasing I'd done earlier.

"Don't go easy on her," Leo said.

Rake moaned against me, and I echoed the sound as it vibrated through me. My breasts ached and I lifted one hand, squeezing them hard in turn. Rake's tongue returned to my center, thrusting against my entrance, forcing the tip in, and he nuzzled roughly against my clit.

"Your thighs are shaking, gorgeous. She's ready."

I was so fucking ready.

Bright lightning pops of pleasure burst inside of me, and Rake held me with an iron grip, suckling and drinking and gorging on me with open-mouthed hunger as the orgasm flooded through me, rushing like lava through every muscle up into my head and then back down again, all the way to my toes.

"That's it. That's it. Slower now," Leo purred, and then he broke out in laughter.

My eyes had fallen shut, and Rake pushed me from his mouth as I started to tip forward, he and Leo laughing as the phone slipped from my hands back onto the bed.

"Fuck. Oh my *god*," I moaned, catching my fall by my palms and pulling in a deep breath.

"Put the phone somewhere I can watch," Leo said.

I tried to shake the daze out of my head, and it was Rake who wriggled up from beneath me, face glossy with my release. He picked the phone up and put it sideways on the table against the lamp, turning it until Leo could see us both, me braced and bent on the bed, with Rake beneath me. Leo turned his own phone, laying on his side, still pumping his cock just enough to keep himself hard without ending the game.

"Gorgeous," Leo said.

I grinned at him and then looked down at Rake, mussed and flushed and panting. A mouth like his deserved a reward. I bent and Rake moaned as I folded his lips with mine, dragging one kiss after another, tasting myself on his lips. It was like the first time with Leo, but Leo was here, or close to it.

"You do taste like heaven," Rake murmured.

I pecked his lips again and then reached past the phone on the nightstand for the condoms Rake had put out for us. His eyes tracked my hand, and he bit his lip.

"I'm clean. I dunno if you're on birth control but..." Rake trailed off and glanced at the phone where a grinning Leo was watching us, giving his own cock lazy strokes.

"I started up again recently, and I'm clean too," I said, shrugging. I usually used condoms anyway, and Leo had never brought up going without.

"It's just that I...I get kind of, um, messy," Rake said, eyes widening. "And they don't really make condoms that accommodate..."

My eyebrows jumped. Fuck. So that was what Leo meant by Rake making me slippery. *Why* did that sound so hot?

"But I know scents are hard for you—" Rake started.

I dropped the condoms on the bed and rose up, checking to make sure Leo could still watch as I took Rake's bouncing, dripping cock in my hand. Rake's words died on his tongue. The flirtatious, deviant, sexual man of the past few weeks stilled, and all that was there in front of me was a desperate, breathless creature. I lined him up at my entrance, teasing the head of him against my soaked flesh, and Rake moaned, eyes blinking slowly.

"Watch," I said to him, and to Leo too, for that matter.

I sank down and gasped as Rake slipped in. He was...soft. Not *soft*, but like...for all of his girth it was almost pillowy. He went in easily, and he filled me up without any of the sting of the stretch.

"Oh my god," I breathed. "Holy shit."

I bounced experimentally, and Rake's hips rolled to chase me as I retreated.

"Come on, gorgeous," Leo called, his tone rough, his pumps more insistent. "Come on, let go."

I groaned and started to rock, to twist and bounce my

hips on top of Rake. Maybe no one had mentioned this to Rake, but it seemed pretty fucking significant to me. His cock was like fucking...pussy magic. I giggled at the comparison, but I couldn't think of how else to describe it. There was the friction I craved with sex, but every movement was so *easy*.

"Fuck, god, Lola, you really worked me up. I'm gonna... I'm gonna come again, but don't fuckin' stop okay?"

I nodded as Rake's hands cupped my hips and he moved me over his lap. I braced my hands on his shoulder and joined him, rolling my hips so I could grind myself against his lap. The pace was fast and deep, the slap of skin wet and noisy. I watched Rake's furrow of concentration as he gazed at where we were joined, the wet dew of sweat on his upper lip. I leaned down and sucked it into my mouth, and then whined and rocked into him harder.

Rake shouted beneath me, body tensing, and he swelled inside of me, that first moment of stretch as he came.

"Don't stop, gorgeous," Leo gasped.

I nodded and fucked Rake as he shuddered, watched his throat flex as he struggled for breath, his grip loosening on my hips. That was all right, I'd found my rhythm. I pulled his hands up to my breasts, showing him how rough I liked it, and Rake swallowed, focusing on pinching my nipples as I took over the pace. I let myself fall roughly down his length, wet heat leaking out between us with every thrust, the crash tickling at my clit.

Shit. Rake would be really good at rough sex. All the force with less of the day-after pain.

"You like it, don't you?" Leo asked, grinning.

"I fucking love it," I gasped.

Rake moaned, his heels bracing against the bed so he could meet my thrusts, bodies pounding together and making me cry out every time we joined. He was perfectly deep, beautifully plush and thick inside of me, velvety soft as his cock pumped.

I was babbling some combination of their names, and Leo was praising me as Rake got wilder. He came again, and the rush inside me made me shiver, almost made me come. It would be all right if I did. I had to keep going until Rake said stop, wasn't that what Leo said?

Arousal pooled on Rake's groin, dripped down between us to the bed. Fuck. It was messy. It was messy and it was hot, and I laughed breathlessly as the slick slide of us made every twist and rub of our bodies smoother.

"You tired?" Leo asked.

My thighs were *burning* from effort, sweat dripping down my body, but I shook my head.

"Good girl. Rake, get her off."

Rake's hand dropped from breast to my clit, and with a quick flick and rub of his fingers I was arching back, shouting high and bright. Rake groaned and sat up with me, his arm circling my waist, fingers persistent on my clit.

"Keep going, gorgeous. Squeeze tight around him, so tight," Leo said. His words were unsteady now too, broken by the force of his hand on his cock.

I was draped backward over Rake's knees, my whole body weak with exhaustion, but I kept pushing. I did every damn kegel muscle trick I knew, rewarded by Rake's long howls and wild bucking beneath me. Squeezing down on him didn't force him out, but instead just gripped him tighter, and I realized I was doing something similar to a female alpha's lock. My hands flew to the back of Rake's head, and I pulled his mouth to mine, pressing a vicious biting kiss to his bottom lip.

My clit burned with his attention, and the fire exploded through me as Rake flooded me once more, totally out of control, movements broken. Leo called our names in broken pleasure from the phone. Rake whimpered against my lips and dragged me down with him as he fell to the bed. My own orgasm left me limp and shuddering on top of him.

"'Nough. Enough," Rake gasped as I tried to keep moving. I sagged gratefully, and Leo chuckled.

"Damn. Damn, I fucking wish I'd been in the room for that," Leo gasped.

"Shit, Lola, you *wrecked* me," Rake said, chest heaving for air.

"Think I wrecked myself," I said, totally collapsed on his chest. I wiggled, and Rake grunted as I moved just enough to smile at the phone screen. There was a little splash of white on Leo's chest and I licked my own lips, wishing it was him I was tasting.

"Tomorrow night," Leo said. "Even if we're just all watching each other wack off, I don't care. Just can't wait to get back to you guys."

I snorted and buried my blush against Rake's chest. "Love you, babe," Rake said to the phone.

"Love you," Leo echoed. There was a pause, and he added, "Miss you both. So much."

"Miss you too," I answered, looking back to drink up Leo's heavy stare until he disconnected the call.

Rake sighed, his arms circling my back and his lips pressing a series of kisses to my forehead. "Give me like… twenty seconds to catch my breath, and then I'll carry us to the shower."

I wiggled to start to roll away and stopped immediately at the first sensation of thick slick seeping out between us. It was a startling feeling, but also strangely erotic, a faint tease to start all over again. Rake waggled his eyebrows at me, and I broke out into peals of giggles.

"Mm, okay, you squirming on top of me feels too good. We better get into the shower now," Rake said, sitting up and bundling me against his chest, never pulling out as he raced out of the warm bed and for the bathroom.

My laughter echoed over the tile until it turned to moans under the steam.

Lola
19

Rake was snoring softly, sprawled out face down on the mattress like a starfish, one of his arms and legs draped over me. The clock on the nightstand only read eleven thirty-eight, and while I was physically exhausted from the night, my mind was running one hundred thoughts a second.

What was I getting myself into with Rake and Leo? My experience with Buzz had shattered me, but the potential emotional fallout with these two might be devastating. They weren't cruel, and I hadn't become addicted to them as a filthy fun secret. Leo was...Leo was perfect, too good to be true. And Rake was outside of even my own wildest dreams; sweet and sexy, and as persistent in his affection as I'd dreamed an alpha would be.

It sounded great on paper, but I knew better. Eventually, things between us would hit roadblocks, and what would it cost me to have to walk away from them?

Your entire fucking heart, idiot.

My pounding, racing heart. I needed to get out of the bed before I let myself spiral into a full-blown panic attack and had to explain myself to Rake. I didn't want to ruin the night we were having. Stupid as it was, I had already decided to see things through with these men to the bitter brutal end, even if there would be nothing left of myself when it was over. The destruction was too sweet to resist.

Gently, watching his face for any sign of waking up, I

lifted Rake's arm up from my chest, settling it into the pillows behind my head. Inch by inch, I slid myself out from under his stretched leg and then off the bed. My clothes were strewn over the floor on the way into the bedroom, but I'd brought sleep clothes with me in my bag in the other room. I tiptoed out to the open space, half expecting one of Rake's alphas to appear suddenly. But no, they were too good at giving me space.

I dressed and grabbed the takeout containers. I could take them down to the kitchen, it would give me a good excuse for nighttime wanderings and the space I needed at the moment.

Caleb's rooms were still dark, and my heart actually ached for him. Had my presence totally chased him out? Guilt hung like a collar around my throat, dragging weight behind me with every quiet step to the stairs. Caleb seemed... He seemed *sweet*, which was not something I'd ever associated with an alpha, even before Buzz. I didn't want to be the cause of any discomfort for him.

It seemed kind of early for the whole house to be silent, so I wasn't surprised as I crept down the stairs to hear music coming from the third floor. I paused on the landing, looking out the front window to the dark street, an orange street lamp across the road casting spiderweb patterns through tree branches onto the blacktop. A solitary guitar strummed through a familiar blues melody, and it wasn't until the notes broke off and corrected themselves that I realized this wasn't music playing over speakers, but one of the alphas.

I continued down to the kitchen, almost sorry not to see anyone else up, tucked the ramen into the fridge, and allowed myself a little indulgent exploring. I'd never been anywhere where everything was so *nice*. Not that it was all brand new— there was an old retro café model espresso maker, and Caleb seemed to have a taste for Art Deco antiques—but everything was high quality. You couldn't call the house 'understated wealth' because the money involved was clear, but it definitely wasn't gaudy or flaunted either.

Unsure of what to do with myself, I wandered back to the

third-floor landing, hanging at the edge of the hallway and listening to the musician. I had an inkling of who it might be, and curiosity won out, leading my steps past an office and one of Rake's tucked away nests. The rooms were more private and closed off on this floor, and I stopped in front of one open door to see a narrow room with floor to ceiling bookshelves and the walls cluttered with paintings. There was a book left open on the couch and the blanket I'd snuggled up in draped over the arm.

I continued to the back of the house, the guitar growing gently louder, and hesitated in front of a sliding door. A light was on inside, soft glow angling out across the wood floor of the hall. The blues were set aside, and now I was fairly sure I was listening to a slightly clumsy but intricate version of an old pop hit, something angsty and familiar that had come out when I was a kid.

I stepped up to the doorway, pausing in the shadow as I got the first glimpse of Matthieu Segal, hunched over a beat up, sea-foam green electric guitar, sitting on a squashed leather stool. A lock of salt and pepper had fallen over his furrowed brow as he studied his own fingers in their work. The room was a strange collection, a desk cluttered with business papers in one corner—a pair of glasses left open in front of a black computer screen—and the other corner filled with shelves loaded with records and CDs. There were music posters on the wall, as well as a few magazine covers and framed awards.

The song ran down to an aimless end, and Matthieu looked up, frowning as if he were disappointed or frustrated in his own performance. My lips were quirked in a smile, and I knew the second he saw me in the doorway. His back straightened and the guitar pick in his hand scratched awkwardly against the strings, a howling chord ringing over the small amp sitting near the stool. His eyes were wide and open in surprise, and I was perversely pleased to have snuck up on him.

"Lola!"

"Hi, sorry," I said in greeting, giving him a tiny wave. "I heard you while I was taking some stuff to the kitchen. I almost forgot you were a musician."

Matthieu's shock vanished in a grimace. "I was in a punk band, so I'm not sure the word applies," he said with a wry shrug.

My eyes turned to one of the posters on the wall, the words 'Washed Up' bold in a splattered hand-drawn font. The picture on the poster was bold in black and white, pixelated and a little hard to see. But the resemblance between the young man screaming into a microphone while holding a guitar, and the older version sitting on his leather stool in his beautiful city home was faint. Honestly, if it weren't for the same hook in his nose, I probably wouldn't have ever connected the two. Matthieu was so…polished when he was at the Stanmore.

Not now though. Now he was in a pair of sweatpants worn out over one knee, and a t-shirt that had been well-worn to the point of its original art being totally obscured, and I could see a hole in one of the armpits.

"I'm pretty sure if I'd known at nineteen where I'd end up, I would've given myself a massive 'fuck you,'" Matthieu mused, his own eyes turning to the poster.

I snorted. "How did it happen, anyway?"

"Um, George and I started Broken Record," he said with a shrug, referring to the now famous music magazine enterprise. "It took off. George sold his take, I kept mine, we got bigger and then…I suppose everyone assumed I knew what I was doing."

I grinned at him, my expression freezing as I realized he'd been watching me closely. Matthieu was observant, that much had always been clear. He'd seen my reserve around him and Cyrus in that very first moment in the hall at the Stanmore. He'd always been careful around me too.

"Do you miss just being in a band?" I asked him, hoping to distract his focus on me by turning it back to himself.

Matthieu's nose wrinkled, and he looked down at the

guitar in his hands. "No, I don't think I do. Touring and partying was fun at the time, but thinking about it now makes me tired," he said. He looked up at me with a sly grin. "Anyway, no one wants to watch an old man jump around in chains and spikes."

"Oh, but the mohawk! *Designate* could probably bring it back if you wanted to give it a second shot," I said.

Matthieu's laugh was warm and surprised, his face lighting up and deep grooves digging into his cheeks as he smiled. My stomach flipped and a deep tug in my center urged me toward him. I crossed my ankles, pressing my legs shut, and tried to force the mental image of replacing Matthieu's guitar in his arms with my own body.

Haven't you learned your fucking lesson, Lola? Just because Matthieu didn't act like a predator to me, didn't mean he was safe. And I knew perfectly well that Rake hated it when people used him to get close to his alphas. I'd meant it when I said I didn't want that, but my body seemed to have other ideas.

"I think I'm lucky to still have my hair, and I better not tempt fate," Matthieu said, still grinning.

I was biting at my own grin. He wasn't *that* old. In his late forties probably, although I suppose plenty of men started balding before then. His hair did look thick though, and it was longer than Leo's or Rake's. It would feel nice to dig my fingers through—

Oh, you're fucked in the head.

"I should go try and sleep," I said, pushing myself away from the door.

Matthieu's stare took one long track over me, and for the first time I saw hunger in his gaze instead of only study. The ache echoed in me and he turned his head away, nodding slowly, eyes blinking. When he looked at me again, his expression was mild.

"I'll play you out," he said, settling the guitar back into the cradle of his arms.

"G'night, Matthieu." I turned away with the first subtle, falling notes.

I stopped on the landing, the music playing at my back, and leaned against the wall, sinking down to the cool floor and letting my eyes fall shut as I took slow, deep breaths.

Get your shit together, Lola.

I WOKE to a warm mouth on my collarbone leaving wet messy kisses. For a hazy moment, I didn't know where I was, and strangely enough I wasn't *frightened*. And then I took a deep breath, chocolate heavy on my tongue, and I smiled.

"Morning," I said, voice scratching.

"Hello you," Rake breathed against my shoulder. His erection was pressed to my hip, his hand passing up and down on my side, thumb caressing the underside of my breast with every pass.

"What time is it?"

"Early. Early enough," Rake said with a soft nudge of his hips.

I grinned and giggled, leaving my eyes shut against the sunlight warming my face. I'd sat on the landing for a few more quiet songs from Matthieu before his guitar went silent and I realized I was at risk of being caught. When I'd tried to sneak back into the bed with Rake, I'd accidentally woken him up. Not that he'd minded, based on the way his mouth had immediately latched onto mine. By the time I'd fallen asleep, it was nearing two in the morning.

"'Kay," I said to Rake, stretching out on the bed and letting him roll on top of me. "But you do the work this time."

He snorted, breath puffing against my throat as he slid his cock against my entrance, weeping pre-cum making his work easy. That really was convenient as hell.

"Deal. Can I use this too?" Rake asked. A moment later, a

soft buzzing sounded and Rake's chest pulled away from mine.

I gasped, eyes flying open and back arching, as Rake pressed the vibrator directly to my clit. "God, yes!"

He pushed into me and I moaned as he settled, the vibrator perfectly nestled between us, stimulation rolling over every sensitive inch of me as Rake fucked me with slow, shallow thrusts.

Three divinely intense orgasms and a thorough shower later, and I finally looked at the clock.

"Shit. That was not early enough," I said, turning my back to Rake for him to pull up my zipper for me.

"You've got ages. The guys are still down in the kitchen, and if you leave with them you know you won't be late."

"Assistant beauty editors are supposed to be early, not on time," I said, glancing over my shoulder at Rake. "And definitely not arriving at the same time and in the same cars as their bosses."

He snorted and nodded. "Okay, yeah, fair enough. We'll get you a separate car then."

"Or I just get moving faster and I grab the bus," I said.

Rake wrinkled his nose. "I think we can do better than public transit, Lola. I'll run down and get you some breakfast and arrange a car."

"I'm presentable," I said. "I can come down for my breakfast."

Rake was on his way to his door, and he stopped and looked at me over his shoulder. He was dressed in sleep pants and nothing else, his floral tattoo twisted over the muscles on his back. "The guys are probably all there," he said.

Oh. *All* the alphas. But the idea of the four of them didn't make me tense the way it had even a week or two ago. I was already surrounded by their scents in this house, I should be able to face them over the kitchen island.

"Will they mind me being there?" I asked.

"Of course not, but—"

"Then I won't mind either," I said, squaring my shoulders

as Rake's smile bloomed over his face. I crossed to him and took his hand, following him out of the rooms and to the stairs.

"We can plan a car to pick you up from work too," Rake said, wrapping his arm over my shoulders.

"Don't worry about that, I have to run back to my apartment to grab a new change of clothes since I'm coming back tonight."

Rake shrugged. "That's fine. And you might as well grab a few changes, since I can guarantee Leo will want to talk you into staying the weekend."

I chewed on my lip as we headed down to the second floor. "I think I should spend another night at my place after tonight. No, listen," I said as he started to object. "Don't you think Caleb and Cyrus will start to get jealous?"

Rake scoffed and then grew quiet, staring into the distance as he thought. He glanced at me and sighed. "Not *jealous*. But I suppose they might start to miss us. Caleb especially."

I tried to swallow around the lump in my throat as I nodded. "So there. I'll get some downtime on my own, and you guys will get some quality time with your alphas. It's only fair."

Rake grumbled something unintelligible, and then we reached the kitchen. All around the room, the four previously relaxed and slouching alphas straightened, eyes fixed to me, coffee cups halfway to their lips.

"I-err-we can-umm…" Caleb stumbled, a spatula in his hand as he stood in front of a skillet, eyes darting around the room looking for an escape route.

"Don't mind me," I said, offering them a tight smile.

"Mind her enough to get her a cup of coffee," Rake corrected, squeezing my shoulders with his hands.

Tentatively, with a few calculating looks in my direction, he slipped to Cyrus sitting over a bowl of granola and fruit. Cyrus leaned in immediately and I watched them kiss, a firm press of lips and Cyrus' dark hand holding Rake to him by the center of his back. It reminded me of the beautiful picture I'd seen the night before, and I passed them with a blush on my cheeks, nearly running into Matthieu.

The alpha stood in front of a steaming mug of black coffee, looking over to me. "What do you like in it?"

"Black," I said, wiggling my fingers for the mug and sharing a smile with Matthieu as he slid across the counter to me. I hummed my thanks with the first sip. Along with everything else in this house being high quality, their coffee was especially good. I needed to ask Rake or Leo where they got it.

"Would you like some pancakes, lo- Lola?" Caleb said, and I watched as he flipped one small pancake in the air back into the skillet.

He and Leo must share their morning sweet tooth. "Yes, please."

"Sit," Matthieu said, nodding toward the last open stool at the island. Which would leave him without a seat.

"I don't mind standing," I said, looking at him. He arched one eyebrow in challenge, and I found myself sliding into the seat next to Wes, blinking at my cup of coffee. Had he just alpha'd me? Either I had a particularly weak will or Matthieu was an especially potent alpha.

Probably both.

I glanced to my left and found Wes sitting, tense with his arms locked in tight to his side, even though there was a good foot of space between us. In front of him was a plate loaded with egg whites and spinach and whole wheat bread. He didn't have coffee in his cup, but what looked like grapefruit juice. A health nut then. He also had a paper folded in front of him, pen resting beneath a half-finished crossword.

"Wow. Risky move," I said, pointing to his pen.

Rake laughed on Wes' other side. "Not sure the word 'risk' has ever been used in association with Wes before."

Wes' lips quirked, and his massive shoulders softened slightly. "I wait until I'm sure," he said.

I looked over the clues and at his answers briefly before

grinning. "But you got thirty-eight down wrong. It's Coe, not Poe."

"'Edgar Allen blank's *Ravenous*'?" Wes read aloud.

"Edgar Allen Coe is a rapper with an album called *Ravenous*," I said, smiling up at Wes' baffled response. "They tricked you on purpose."

He cursed, and Caleb slid a plate in front of me with three perfect sand-dollar sized pancakes, already dressed with strawberry preserves.

"Thank you. These look delicious."

"Of course, I'm glad you joined us," Caleb said, sharing his smile between me and Rake.

"We need to order Lola a car to the office," Rake said, digging into his own plate of food. "She wisely pointed out that she probably shouldn't arrive in the same car as Cyrus."

Cyrus choked lightly on his breakfast. "God. Imagine Betty's face," he said, leaning over his plate to grin at me.

"I really don't want to," I admitted, and he laughed again.

This was…easier than I expected. I was at the end of the counter so I had room to move, but honestly, Wes had the kind of sweet and bright and *fucking delectable* scent that made me just want to lean into him. Except that wasn't freaking me out. These alphas knew the boundary between us, and they respected it. I was safe, just like Leo had promised.

"I could drive you," Wes said, and the kitchen went quiet. He cleared his throat and shrugged gently. "It's on the way for me. You can sit in the back if you want."

I glanced at the rest of the quiet men. Caleb's eyes were on his immobile fork, and Matthieu was staring over my head at Wes. Rake and Cyrus were watching me.

"I don't want to treat you like a hired driver, but if you're sure you don't mind offering a ride," I said.

Wes nodded. "Definitely not. The service we use has a few alpha drivers, and I wouldn't want you to end up with someone unfamiliar. As long as you're—"

"I'm sure," I said.

He's huge. He could overpower you so fast. You don't know what he wants. He could hurt you.

But he won't.

I shut down the argument waging in my head with another bite of pancake, and Wes relaxed, digging into his own plate.

"Perfect," Rake said. "Leo's back tonight, and Lola will be here. Family dinner?"

"You'd better plan the meal though, and not leave it up to Leo to figure out at the last moment," Caleb said with a playful glare at Rake.

And the conversation moved away from its awkward pause.

WES WAS DRIVING us out of the garage in his sleek black sedan, turning onto the road, when I looked into the backseat for the third time and it finally clicked.

The foggy morning, and the shining black shoes waiting in front of me. The long back seat of the dark car, and the close-cut blond hair of the driver.

"It was you," I said, barely audible.

Wes' hands flexed on the steering wheel, and his head twitched in my direction.

"You... Wasn't it? You picked me up from the Hangmen's club that morning?" I asked, staring at him in profile. "How is that... Why would it be you?"

I didn't remember very much of that morning, and I wasn't sure if it was because of whatever I might've been dosed with the night before, or that I didn't want to remember. I couldn't recall the face of the man who'd driven me away from Buzz and to the safety of David's apartment, but I remembered the thick black sweatshirt I'd worn on the ride. My lungs were clogged with alpha scents, covering my skin, and it had taken most of the drive before I realized I was with another alpha.

Wes nodded and swallowed hard. "It was me. David called in a favor."

My heart sank like a lead weight. "So the others—"

Wes' head shook, his hand closest to me leaving the wheel and hovering between us like he'd meant to touch me and thought better of it. "No. No, I never said anything to them. It wasn't anybody's business but yours. I…"

I turned my face away from his, the city a blur outside of the window as I scrambled to control my breathing, keep my focus on the present and not the past.

"I'm sorry, Lola," Wes whispered.

"Sorry? What are you sorry for?" I asked, my head whipping to stare at him. "I should say I'm—"

Wes let out a low growl. "Don't you dare." My lips snapped shut and Wes' cheeks reddened, his eyes flicking to me. "I'm sorry for not going back to that place and burning it to the ground like I thought about doing when I dropped you off with David. Then you wouldn't have this asshole sending you texts. The whole mess would've been over."

His knuckles were white and red around the steering wheel, jaw ticking with tension.

Burning that motel and bar to the ground sounded like a beautiful idea. The very mention of it, and I craved the view, imagining flames eating away at the peeling wallpaper and turning those awful mattresses to ash.

"You didn't know me then," I said, studying him.

Wes was all squared angles and thick muscle. If Leo was bulkier than my usual type, Wes was about three of my usual type put together. He wasn't *handsome* necessarily, but he was the definition of strength. The anger he'd revealed a moment ago was already bleeding away, leaving me in the car with the gentle giant I'd sat next to at breakfast.

"I had a guess of what had happened to you, and I knew what those men deserved," Wes muttered darkly. "I'll find him, and I'll make sure he never so much as looks sideways at you again."

Simple as that. Wes' promise was plain and his voice was

confident. I believed him too. I didn't know *why* he was so determined to see me safe, but I believed him.

"Thank you," I said.

His jaw clenched again and his shoulder jerked in an uncomfortable shrug. He glanced at me and the corner of his mouth twitched with an offered smile. "Dig into the front pocket of my laptop bag. Take a look at fifteen across for me?"

I reached down and pulled the newspaper out and Wes' scent sweetened in the car around me, heady and syrupy. I relaxed into the deep seat, slipping my feet out of my heels and curling them under me.

CALEB
20

It wasn't easy to be an alpha around Lola.

She was curled up in an armchair in the den while Leo made them each a deep bowl of ice cream and fresh out of the oven chocolate chip cookies. She had my blanket draped over her, even though the house was warm and her cheeks were flushed. I wanted to tear the blanket away from her and replace it with me. If she liked my scent so much, then I would've been more than happy to let her steal it directly off my skin.

I pushed up off the couch and headed for the kitchen before I accidentally planted myself in her lap.

This was the issue. Lola might not realize it, but she thrived under care. I'd seen the way she responded to Leo and Rake's attention, even the little brief attentions the rest of us were brave enough to offer. And as an alpha, I thrived in *offering* care. It was starting to drive me a little crazy not to pick the woman up and carry her into a nest for a good cuddle.

She's not an omega, I reminded myself for the thirtieth time this week. And even if she were, I already had an omega. It maybe didn't help that Rake and Wes were out of the country for a quick international photoshoot.

"Want one?" Leo asked, waving an ice cream coated spoon at me and nodding to the bowl.

I released a low purr as I surrounded his back, wrapping my arms around his middle and dropping my forehead to the back of his neck. I sucked in a deep lungful of my beta and released my breath slowly, resisting the urge to groan as I found Lola's slightly tart flavor on my tongue.

"Hey," Leo soothed in a whisper, stroking his hand over the back of my arms. "You miss me?"

"You know I do," I said.

Leo sighed. "I'm sorr—"

"No, no I didn't mean it like that," I said, kissing his pulse and then releasing him, leaning against the counter to face him. "I miss you, but I don't begrudge you or her the time you spend together. I just…"

Leo smirked and looked down at the ice cream carton. "For the record, I think you could be a *little* less careful around her."

My eyes widened. "I don't want to ruin this for you."

Leo nodded and smiled. "I know. I appreciate that, honestly. But if this is going to work, it can't be a lifetime of you guys walking on eggshells."

"A lifetime?" I whispered. My heart gave a happy thump. Leo was thinking of Lola long term? *Long* long term.

I didn't mind my pack's tendency toward dating around; it didn't change how we felt about one another. I was just less inclined to pursue physical gratification with strangers when I didn't already have emotional groundwork laid down. Rake and Leo had been dating for three months before I got to know him well enough to realize I was as attracted to the beta as my omega was. And it had been Leo who'd given Rake and I our real introduction to one another. Rake had been afraid I'd try and tame and domesticate him, and I'd been afraid his emotions were too flighty for me to weather. We'd both been wrong.

With Lola, the attraction at the moment was more of a biological impulse. Take care of the vulnerable, nurture the one who needed tenderness. There were signs of a woman I wanted to know tucked away in the shyness—her wit, the moments of intense sensuality she revealed when she didn't realize the rest of us were watching. If Leo was thinking of her as a permanent part of the pack, then I might have a chance to explore the interest.

"I..." Leo blushed, but he looked giddy too. Maybe he hadn't thought that far ahead yet.

I swallowed hard and folded my arms over my chest to resist the sudden inclination to go running back into the den and start petting the poor girl and purring in her ear. I needed to be the opposite of a pushy alpha.

"I'll try and be more...natural around her," I said, and Leo beamed at me.

"She *wants* to be comfortable around you all. It's happening."

I nodded. "It just takes time. I know."

Leo slid spoons into the prepared bowls and then wrapped his arms around my waist, our noses brushing. "Love you."

I sighed, and my hands cupped his jaw, our mouths grazing softly together. I wanted more, but with Lola in the next room, it was not the time to start something with my beta that I wouldn't get to finish.

"I love you too," I rasped.

Leo leaned back, lips parted like he was about to speak, but instead he smiled and nodded, slipping away and taking dessert to Lola in the den. Cyrus walked into the kitchen as Leo left, his eyes slanted in a private smile as he moved to me.

"Struggling?" Cyrus asked.

"I don't know why. It's not like they haven't had their share of relationships I wasn't a part of, didn't need to be a part of."

Cyrus nodded. "Yeah, but Lola's not taking them for a ride. This one's more serious. I do okay with it at the magazine. She's different there. I don't see the cracks while we're working." Cyrus looked me over with a slower stare. "You need to get out for the night? We could go...for drinks? Find some music maybe?"

I shook my head and combed my hair out of my eyes. "No, I...I prefer to be here. Is that perverse?"

"It's a little masochistic," Cyrus said fondly. He stepped in close and I accepted his full kiss. "But I understand."

I grabbed my own loaded bowl of sugar and cream and chocolate, and returned to the den with Cyrus close at hand, my eyes immediately turning to the bundled young woman in the arms of my beta.

"CAN I HELP YOU?"

My head whipped around to find Lola hovering in the doorway of the formal dining room. Her hair was damp from a shower, but there was no mistaking the scents. Rake and Leo had kept Lola to themselves all afternoon. She was dressed in something a little sleeker than the usual woman's standard of a Little Black Dress, a more contemporary and boxy silhouette, but the fabric leaned into her curves, giving away hints of her shape.

"I'm…I'm trying not to overdo it," I said, looking back to the table I was dressing. "But do you think candles would be nice?"

The dinner party, if it could be called that, was my idea. It was just a few extra seats shy of being a family dinner, but the nature of the event had convinced Carolyn to come, as well as Lola's cousin, David. Lola had been slipping in and out of the house for the past two weeks—basically as often as Rake and Leo could convince her to come—and while she joined the pack for meals, she still seemed slightly ill at ease. I was hoping tonight might change the atmosphere just enough for her to feel less like she was intruding on the pack, and more like she could see herself as a part of the company.

The dining room was long and somewhat narrow, thin mirrored panels along the walls to give the space more depth and warm sconce lighting. We'd have more than enough room at the table with just the nine of us, and I'd taken advantage of the extra space with careful floral arrangements.

"I like candlelight," Lola said with a nod. She padded into

the room barefoot and stood across the table from me. "These are beautiful," she added, reaching out to touch the flowers I'd pulled from the gardens, spindling ferns mixed with low dark buds and blooms, and thin long-stemmed herbs hanging out of vases. "You've taken so much time on this dinner."

"I have more fun planning than I do at the events, to be honest," I said, and then rushed to correct myself. "Not that tonight will be stressful, of course. David's an old friend."

Lola smiled at that and shrugged. "I'm already a little nervous."

"Because it's the whole pack?" I asked, frowning. She'd seemed more at ease in the past week, less watchful of her surroundings in the house and less inclined to stiffen when one of us entered the room.

"No. Because I don't think I've ever been to a dinner party before. Not one that wasn't really a potluck," she said, grinning.

I glanced down at the plates and tableware I'd already laid out. Maybe I needed to simplify a little. We didn't need the *full* set of china.

"If you go to the mirror three to the left of you and press in, you should find the candles inside," I said.

Lola turned to the wall and moved to where I pointed, pressing against the surface. "Oh, that's cool!"

"If you choose a mix of lanterns and candlesticks, I'll make us both a drink to help burn off our nerves. How does that sound?"

Lola hesitated, her face barely in profile, and a dark cloud settled on my shoulders. She didn't want an alpha making her a drink. That monster Wes was hunting had turned her inside out, had shown her the worst of my designation. And I didn't know how to prove to her that I wasn't a threat.

"A drink sounds nice," Lola said, reaching into the hidden cabinet. "Better not make it too strong though. I don't drink much."

The cloud evaporated. "Two very mild drinks coming up," I said, hurrying out of the room to head for the bar.

Trust would come with time and good experiences. That was what tonight was for.

LOLA WAS TUCKED between David and Leo in the corner of the long couch—red lips curled in an almost permanent smile, cheeks rosy from dinner, and a long series of drinks. There was a glass in her hand against her lap, ice melted and the contents forgotten.

"You're watching her," Rake whispered in my ear.

My eyes flicked to him, his chin landing on my shoulder and Cyrus close on his other side.

"I know," I whispered back, face flushing.

"Cute," Rake said, his smile smug. I shook my head minutely.

Rake *probably* wouldn't announce my interest in Lola. He wouldn't want to jeopardize her comfort with our pack. But he wouldn't let me forget he knew either.

"...So I let them carry on trying to fit that juniors dress on their horrid mannequins..." David rattled on in his story and Lola's giggle sounded from the corner, her head leaning against Leo's shoulder.

David's attendance at the dinner had been a roaring success. Rake and Leo didn't seem surprised by Lola's almost effervescent mood, but it was clear on Matthieu and Wes' faces that they were as awed to see the generally subdued young woman in stitches and smiles. Lola took another sip of her drink, one of many I'd made for her throughout the night by her own request.

She wiggled forward between the two men, Leo's hand wrapped around her side, and set the drink down with a thunk before dropping back into Leo's chest, allowing him to pull her closer. Her gaze was drowsy and warm, body limp and relaxed, and I realized with a quick glance around the room that it wasn't just me staring. My entire pack's focus was drifting to her.

With a quick glance at Carolyn, I wondered if there was a subtle way to remind Matthieu to pay attention to his girlfriend.

"Would anyone like another drink?" I asked, rising up from the end of the couch.

Carolyn raised her wine glass, lips pressed in a thin line, as a few voices echoed their thanks.

"I should actually be going," David said.

"Oh, David," Lola cried, smile falling.

David rose and smoothed down his suit, reaching out his hand to his cousin. "I know, but it's late. Downtown streets will be a mess with the partiers if I stay any longer."

"I'll walk you out," Lola said, swaying as she rose up from the couch.

She'd worn heels for the dinner but kicked them off almost immediately when we moved to the couches, and now she bounced along behind David as he made his goodbyes and they headed for the doors, a little drunk but not terribly so. I wasn't sure if it was all women in formal wear and bare feet that I found arousing, or just Lola.

I carried a tray of glasses with me to the bar, and realized from where I stood I could see out of the living room and to the front door clearly. Lola and David were standing close at the door, Lola's smile easy as David said his goodbyes. I poured wine, refreshed Matthieu's bourbon and ice, and when I looked up again the cousins were still speaking. Except this time Lola's head was dropped, her smile gone. David had her hands in his, his head cocked to try and catch her eye.

Liquid splashed against my hand and I shook myself, wiping tonic water away with a rag and spilling some of the drink back into the sink. Rake would forgive me.

I took the drinks back to Carolyn and my pack, Carolyn relishing the undivided attention of the moment by telling some story regarding her and Matthieu at an event. I slipped away before Rake could pull me back down the couch and headed for the front door where Lola was watching David meet a cab on the road. Her lips were turned down as she stared out the window, but when she caught my reflection in the glass a new smile bloomed.

"Are you all right?" I asked, soft enough the room of people nearby wouldn't hear us.

She nodded and turned away from the door. "David just got me in the feels is all," Lola said with a soft shrug.

Her lips were a vivid red, eyes shadowy, but her hair was down and mussed with waves I wanted to run my fingers through. Instead, my hand was caught by hers, a gentle squeeze of her fingers around my palm.

"Thank you for inviting him, by the way," she said.

"Of course," I said, giving in to the urge to pull her closer by her hand, leading her back to the others. I was holding her loosely, she could pull away if she needed to, but Lola followed along at my side, warm shoulder brushing against my arm.

"I suppose I should've expected as much, dating one of the city's most desirable alphas," Carolyn continued, rolling her eyes at Matthieu.

"Just the city's?" Matthieu joked, his shoulders tense, eyes tracking Lola as her hand slipped free from mine and she practically skipped back to Leo's side.

"You have a constant flock of sycophants, Matt," Carolyn said. "I didn't realize I'd have to defend our relationship so much."

I glanced to Rake just as he rolled his own eyes.

"The one I don't understand is Wes," Lola said, before Rake could say something petty to Carolyn.

Wes, who'd been left to his own quiet devices in an armchair facing the couch, raised his eyebrows and glanced at us in question.

"Wes?" Carolyn echoed with a puzzled frown.

Lola stretched her long legs out on the couch as she leaned back into Leo's chest, nodding and grinning wickedly. "Where are his sycophants? With the way he smells, I would've thought he'd have a non-stop pussy parade following him around."

Matthieu choked on his scotch, and Cyrus belly laughed at the announcement. I found myself laughing too as Wes shifted nervously in his armchair while Carolyn gawked at him.

"*Bravo!*" Rake cried, leaning forward and clapping his hands together. "I concur. And on that note, how *does* he smell to you?"

Lola sat up, adorably puzzled. "Why? Does he smell different to you? Like…sex on the beach, but not the drink."

Leo's eyebrows shot up, and his grin was giddy as he glanced down at Lola. She was expressing interest in one of us. Or maybe not interest, but appreciation. An alpha. *Wes.* Our too often overlooked protector.

"Amazing," Rake said with delighted awe. "He smells sweet and fresh to me, but it doesn't make my mouth water."

"Doesn't make my *mouth* water either," Lola said in a soft mutter with a slight giggle as Leo barked a laugh and dragged her up onto his lap, burying his smile against her throat.

I wanted to dive in next to them, to soak up their sweet faint scents. I joined Rake, let him anchor me with a hand on my thigh, and Cyrus stretched an arm out over both our shoulders.

"Oh *now* I understand it," Carolyn said with a twist of her lips as she stared at Lola. "I couldn't picture you with Rake at all, you seemed so timid. But now it makes sense! Anyway, every time I see you, I get that song stuck in my head. The old silly one, umm…" Carolyn hummed and waved her hand with thought while Matthieu frowned at her. "You'll know it. Um, 'Her name was Lola, she was a Show—'"

Wes sat forward, a sudden growl echoing in the room, startling Carolyn into silence. I glanced at Lola, and dread landed heavily in my lap. She was sitting up, stiff and pale, scooting away from Leo quickly as he reached for her, her back heaving with breaths.

"Lola, it's all—"

And then she was up off the couch, legs scrambling clumsily as my entire pack stood as if we might catch her. She ran for the bar, straight to the sink, and heaved. Leo raced after her, framing her back and stroking her hair away from her face.

Carolyn sat gaping at us all as the warm, happy mood of the party suddenly died.

Not a very good idea after all, I thought.

Lola
21

I kept my face buried in the pillow long after waking. I had a slight pinching headache from drinking more than usual the night before. Mostly though, I had a serious case of 'never going to look anyone in the eye again' for how the dinner party the night before had ended.

A warm hand stroked up my back beneath my t-shirt, the bed sinking under added weight.

"So are we hiding in here all day?" Rake asked, curling up against my back.

I was in Leo's room, sprawled out on his mattress. I'd felt Leo get up out of the bed earlier in the morning, but I'd been pretty determined to be ignored. Not that I could reasonably expect Leo to let me just waste away in his bed for days on end.

I rolled over and winced at the sun. Rake pulled a pillow from the pile behind my head to lay over my eyes.

"I should go back to my apartment," I said.

"Hey. No. I'm not here to drag you out of bed, okay? I just wanted to see what was on the agenda for the day. You want something for your stomach, or coffee for your head?"

I swallowed hard. "I want everyone to stop feeling like they have to see if I'm okay all the time."

Rake was quiet for a moment. "Really? Because this seems like a pity party. And those usually like a bit of extra coddling."

Fuck. I threw the pillow off my head and sat up, trying to

ignore the pound in my head and the wobbling churn of my stomach. I glared down at a smirking Rake, and a moment later my lips twitched in answer. Sneaky omega had called me out. And he was right too.

"Okay, fair," I said with a slight nod.

"So ginger ale or coffee?"

"Both. I'm gonna go brush my teeth eight times in a row."

"Want me to bring it up to you?"

"No, I'll come down. I want to apologize to everyone," I said, moving slow and careful to the edge of the bed.

"*Lola*, that didn't call for an apology!"

I waved my hand back at Rake as I jogged for the shower. I loved Leo's shower, a deep blue tiled corner of his bathroom with a waterfall shower head and more thick glass tiling for the wall to let light in. I grabbed the spare toothbrush I'd been using while I spent the night and stripped quickly, turning the water on just shy of scalding before stepping under the spray. I'd gotten more used to having Rake's scent on me, but I went ahead and used the scent cancelling products Leo had in the shower for me. Rake didn't seem offended when I did, and they helped clear my head when I was feeling shaky.

I wrapped a towel around myself and stepped out of the shower to find Leo sitting on his sink counter waiting for me, a can of soda in one hand and a mug of coffee in the other.

I opened my mouth, and he shook his head. "Don't do it, gorgeous."

"You don't even know what I was going to say!"

"Yes I do," Leo said, arching an eyebrow.

I swallowed hard and crossed to him, stepping in between his open legs and letting him pull me to his chest, my chin resting on his shoulder. "But Carolyn… I should explain."

"Matt took Carolyn back to her place last night, and no, you really don't need to do that. Carolyn was trying to antagonize Rake or Matthieu, or…I dunno. She didn't realize what she was stepping into, and I'm sure if she were here she'd want to apologize to you too. So just let it go."

"All right."

"All right. Now, everybody wants to see that you're okay for themselves, and Wes went and got groceries first thing this morning, *including* those seasoned potatoes you're weird about—"

"Potatoes are a *vital* corner of the food pyramid," I said, leaning back to defend my spuds.

Leo grinned and shook his head. "They don't have their own corner, Lola."

I reached up between us and made a triangle with my forefingers and thumbs. "The three main food groups are noodles, pizza, and potatoes. The chunk in the middle is your baked goods."

Leo leaned back with his loud laugh. "I'd be really worried about you if I hadn't seen you eating asparagus like it was going out of style last night."

"I'm an equal opportunity eater. And you're a really good cook. Now let me finish getting dressed. I need to chug this ginger ale and belch in private."

"That's my girl," Leo murmured, pecking my lips and then sliding away and out of the room.

I sighed and stretched as the door shut behind him. *Keep it together*, I thought, staring at my own reflection. For Leo, Rake, and the pack, if not myself. I could crack when I was alone like this, but I was sick of making Leo patch me up when I was wobbling.

When I made it downstairs, dressed in a t-shirt dress and my hair a wet mess on the top of my head, I found that Caleb had brought up the flower arrangements from dinner. Wes and Leo were at the stove, and I moaned at the perfect morning smells of grease and meat and good rye bread.

"Hey there, sunshine," Cyrus said from the counter, beaming at me and holding out his arm.

I hesitated for a moment and then tiptoed forward, accepting the half hug, his dizzy scent bringing back the bright, happy buzz I'd had the night before without the same queasiness. He released me quickly, but warmth prickled over my skin. Caleb passed behind me, his hand touching my shoulder briefly as he leaned around me and left another ginger ale fizzing in a glass in front of me, along with a plate holding two crispy strips of bacon.

"Morning, love," Caleb murmured as he passed.

Wes looked over his shoulder at me and we blushed at the exact same moment. I'd sort of…hit on him the night before. Not that Wes didn't deserve to be hit on. But from *me* of all people?

"Hey, sweetheart," Wes said, voice cracking slightly and his cheeks turning even redder, then he turned back to his skillet.

"Hey, sex on the beach, can I get another slice of bacon?" Rake asked, grinning.

"Fuck off," Wes and I shouted at the same moment.

I could see Leo's smile from my stool as I leaned into Rake's side and passed him a broken piece of my own bacon. No one mentioned the night before, aside from Rake's playful teasing, and every chance one of the men had, they touched me. Casually and in passing, but each moment was a subtle reassurance. I was safe here, and in spite of the weakness they'd seen from me last night, I was accepted.

Painless, I thought. *Or nearly there.*

"SO IT'S NOT a professional grade photo, I know, but this is my friend, Baby," I said, showing Zane a shot of Baby one of her guys had taken. She had a cheesy grin on her face and her hand was raised to show the bite mark on her palm. "She's got one on her bottom lip too that you'd see with the highlighter effect. And one on the side of her breast, which would show with the right shirt."

"Jesus, five bite marks? They practically tenderized her," Zane said, eyebrows jumping.

We were at our desks taking a brief brain break from copy editing and photo touching when Baby sent me the photos I'd asked for. I was hoping to recruit Baby and her plethora of bondmarks for the highlighter makeup concept.

I swiped the photo quickly to Seth, and Zane whistled. Yeah. Seth was like…model pretty. I'd noticed it before too. "He's got a mark as well. They'd look good in a shot together."

"I mean, obviously we have Rakim on board, but most of the other models we found who were interested in the shoot have scars or birthmarks rather than bites," Zane said. "It would be nice to have their bondmarks. She'd be great for the purpose of the shoot, and he's gorgeous."

"Hey. She's gorgeous too," I said, pulling back.

"Sure," Zane said with a shrug. Right. Zane probably wasn't real concerned with Baby's looks in general. "Hey, so…has Betty talked to you?"

I dropped my phone to the desk and tucked a loose strand of hair behind my ear, glancing between Zane and my computer screen. What had I forgotten? Or was Betty pissed with me?

"Nooo," I said slowly. "Why? What's up?"

"It's nothing," Zane said, too fast. I raised an eyebrow at him, and he sighed, staring into the distance. A moment later, he gave in. "Okay. It's not *nothing*. But it's something you need to keep to yourself if I say anything, okay? Just like…just between you and me. And then Betty when she says something, but don't say I said something. Act surprised. Well, not *surprised*, just act the way you act when I tell you—"

"Zane, ohmigod, *what*?" I laughed and stared at him, eyes wide.

Zane leaned in and double checked the room. There was no one but us, just as there had been no one but us when he started rambling incomprehensibly. The other girls had all gone out for Thai food, but I had a packed lunch—thanks, Leo—and Zane said he was fasting.

Which was concerning too.

"So, Wendy really likes your work," Zane whispered.

"Oh. Good," I said, nodding, still not entirely sure where this was going.

"It's just, I don't know if you noticed, but Wendy has issues with some of the magazine staff."

"Cyrus you mean?"

"Yeah, well, yeah, that's a personal thing, but actually, it's way more widespread than that. It's just, you know, *Designate* has been around for *forever*. And for every policy or layout or point of view Wendy successfully convinces the magazine to reinvent, there's like fifteen more that Voir won't let her touch. Like the paper model instead of focusing on digital content to bring us out of the dark age."

"Oh." My eyebrows jumped. I'd wondered about *Designate*'s general lack of digital content in the past, but Cyrus had jumped on board with the idea of the gold leaf challenge. "Yeah…that makes sense."

"Basically, Matthieu Segal has his boot on Wendy's throat and is keeping the magazine five years behind in media format," Zane said, and I was glad he was rolling his eyes and missed my stunned expression.

That didn't *sound* like the Matthieu I'd seen, but I had to remind myself that I knew him in his home, not in his office.

"What does this have to do with me?" I asked.

"Well, right, so it has to do with Wendy's interest in you. Wendy is…taking special note of those working here who are actually forward thinking, coming up with fresh content and not just relying on tired old tropes. There's nothing concrete yet or anything, it's just…you know, if she ever leaves *Designate*, the next thing she'd do would probably be to start her own magazine. She's a big deal." Zane watched me, his expression on lockdown as he waited to see my reaction.

"She's a major deal," I said immediately, my voice bright as I nodded. I scrambled to speak, to sound excited. Zane was talking about a serious betrayal to *Designate*. I may only have been at the magazine for a month, but David pulled a favor with the very people whose backs I'd be sneaking behind if I took this offer seriously. And how *long* from now would it be before Wendy was ready to leave *Designate*? All that time I'd be here waiting and knowing that I was going to walk out on Cyrus?

"That would be just—" I fumbled, and Zane nodded, wide eyed.

"I know, killer. But lips sealed, yeah? I mean, we don't even know if it would ever happen, right?"

"Right, totally, lips sealed," I said, miming my lips zipped shut.

God, I was lucky Zane didn't know I was in a relationship with Rake and Leo. There was no way he would've brought this to me. Or maybe it would've been better if he had known and never said anything. Now I had to decide what to do.

MATTHIEU
22

"Do you like the wine?"

Carolyn hummed and nodded. Of course she did; it was her favorite. That's why I'd ordered it for dinner. I was just searching for some way of starting a conversation with my suddenly silent girlfriend. I scanned the restaurant for the third time since we'd sat down.

It wasn't a recent development that Carolyn and I had started to run out of things to say to one another. That'd been going on for almost a year. But I'd considered us comfortable up until…

Lola.

No, until the dinner party really. I could admit that I'd been short with Carolyn, insisting on taking her home, away from Lola before she tripped into another sensitive subject. But I was doing my best to make up for the rocky weekend. Favorite flowers, favorite restaurant, favorite wine—minus the Diet Coke.

"How's the symphony?" I asked.

Carolyn hummed again, swirling the wine in her glass. Oh good, she wanted me to suffer in silence. *Perhaps less of a punishment than she thinks*, I thought, frowning at myself for the bitterness. If Carolyn didn't want to dive into the latest gossip of the Metropolitan Symphony's finest where she was first chair cellist, then I was officially in the dog house.

"Caro," I murmured, leaning across the table, my hand

outstretched between us in offering. I needed to make the effort, didn't I? And not a half-hearted one.

Green eyes slanted down to my palm, and I prepared myself for another chastising hum. Carolyn sighed, and her free hand lifted from her lap, settling over mine. Her eyes flicked up to mine and I smiled.

"I think it's time, don't you, Matt?" Carolyn murmured without returning my smile.

My brow furrowed. Time? "I…" I shook my head, missing her meaning, although a slow dread trickled cooly down my spine, some subconscious part of me aware of what was coming.

"I do…I do love you," she said slowly.

Time for what? Not marriage, surely? She couldn't stand Rake, and she knew I would never leave my pack.

"It's just that I don't really *need* you," Carolyn said, my spinning thoughts grinding to a halt. "And I think that you need to be needed. Or that you want badly to be needed, at least."

"I'm…I'm an alpha," I said shrugging and staring back at her. "It's in my nature, Caro."

She nodded. "It's just…Rake is so blasé, I kind of assumed that wasn't something you looked for in a partner. But I think I need to be needed too. And that's just not what we are to one another anymore, if we ever were."

I sat back in the deep booth in Carolyn's favorite corner of her favorite restaurant, staring at a glass of wine I didn't even really care for.

"You want to break up," I said. *Slow on the uptake these days, aren't you, old man?*

"You're always going to be a dear friend, Matt. I'm not angry, and I do care for you. It's just taken me this long to realize that what we have…"

"Isn't enough," I said, looking up at her.

Carolyn's shoulders squared, and I shut my mouth. She needed to say these things. And for the sake of her peace of mind, it was probably better if I didn't mention feeling the same way for a long time.

"No, it's not," Carolyn said, nodding and taking another sip from her glass of wine.

The waiter would come back to take our order soon. Would we sit here together and eat a last supper, or call it over by the end of our glasses? I might've preferred to get up and walk out now, but that was just my bruised ego and I was pretty sure I could do better than a display that would leave Carolyn embarrassed and holding the check.

"I'm sorry you didn't find what you were looking for between us," I said, hoping it was a diplomatic version of my thoughts.

"I did. I really did, and then I guess I wanted more."

Yes, that was it exactly. I wanted more too, I'd just gotten complacent. And truth be told, I was never very good at splitting up with women. Too afraid of their tears, or too disappointed in myself for causing them. But you could still cause someone pain by trying to hold things together. Carolyn was doing us a mercy.

I glanced at Carolyn and noted with relief that tears were not an issue at the moment.

"I hope you find what you're looking for too," Carolyn said, a wavering smile on her lips.

I opened my mouth, maybe to be gallant and say that I had been happy in our relationship, and she shook her head.

"Don't lie to be sweet, Matt." Her eyes narrowed slightly, and the sharper Carolyn appeared. "I understand why that girl falls into your pack so neatly where I never did."

"Carolyn—" I started, close to a bark.

"Matt, you look at Lola like… God, you look at her like she's an omega."

I scoffed and turned my face away, jaw ticking. "I am nearly twice her age, Caro. Do you really think I'm trying to relive my youth or one of those other ridiculous cliches?"

Carolyn leaned forward and dropped her voice. "I think that she *needs* someone to care for her, and that is an irresistible siren call to you. I like you, Matt, I really do. But you can be kind of impossibly *alpha* for a man who has some strange platonic role with his own omega."

I breathed out slowly, Carolyn and I glaring at one another from either side of the booth, neither one of us wanting to attract the high profile stares of the other diners. Maybe a dinner in would've been better. Carolyn could've really let off some steam shouting at me and I…

No, I didn't like to lose my temper. That was one alpha habit I made sure not to indulge in.

Buying gifts, pampering…sexual appetite? I thought Carolyn had liked those qualities, but maybe not.

"I'm not judging you. I'm just saying, look in a mirror. You are just waiting for that girl to glance twice at you," Carolyn said. "Just be careful with your own heart. Lola needs your pack now, but there will be a time, someday in the future, when what's happened to her is in the past and it's not about needing you anymore."

I gaped at Carolyn, stiff in my seat, my brain skittering to a stop. Being transparent was one thing, but being cautioned…

The waitress arrived in her black dress and placid smile. "Have you decided what you'd like to order?"

"Yes, I'll have the scallops," Carolyn said, a cool, crystal-perfect smile on her lips. "And I think I'd prefer a dry chardonnay for that dish."

I swallowed my pride and shook off my stupor. An awkward dinner it was, then.

I HAD three days to mull over Carolyn's accusations or advice or whatever I could call her words. And then Lola returned to the house.

I was so busy watching Lola and Caleb, their heads bent together and faint smiles on their lips as they spoke to one another in hushed tones, I didn't notice Rake calling my name.

The toe of Wes' boot nudged my ankle, and I snapped my stare away from the girl. Lola had been absent from our house for the past few nights, and I was both relieved and nervous to see her again. She seemed subdued, and unless Rake, Leo, or Caleb were coaxing a smile to her lips, she was wearing an anxious expression most of the night so far. Had that Indy character sent her another message? She would tell us, wouldn't she?

"I'm sorry, I was…" I cleared my throat as Rake arched an eyebrow at me, lips slanted in an attempt to stifle his laugh at my expense. He knew what I was doing. I recovered awkwardly with, "What were you saying?"

"I said I was surprised Carolyn could spare you so much this week," Rake said, slicing a thin strip of his steak and dipping it into the bèarnaise sauce I'd made. "You haven't missed a family dinner."

Ah. I wondered when they'd notice.

"Carolyn and I split up," I said, focusing on my own plate so I could ignore the sudden quiet that fell over the table like a blanket, conversations dying off at my announcement.

"What? Matt, when?" Rake asked, hushed, as if it were meant to be a private conversation.

"On Tuesday, when I took her out for dinner."

My pack looked more distressed by the news than I had probably felt when Carolyn eviscerated our relationship.

"Matthieu, I'm so sorry to hear that," Caleb said gently.

"Are you all right?" Rake asked, brow furrowed.

"I am," I said, nodding. When Rake's eyes narrowed, I added, "Honestly. She said it was time, and she was right. If we'd both been happy with where our relationship was at, it might've been a different story, but neither of us really was."

"She knew you were a part of our pack—" Rake said, hackles rising and hands fisting around his fork and knife.

"She did, and when we started dating, that wasn't an issue. The pack will always come first for me," I said, holding

Rake's gaze so he would know that whatever regrets I had with Carolyn, giving her up for my pack was never going to be one of them.

Rake's lips pursed, and he dipped his head in agreement.

"I'm sorry for any pain it caused you, but I am happy to know you'll be at more family dinners now," Leo said, and I raised my glass to him.

"To the pack," I said.

Around the smaller family table, my packmates raised their own glasses, echoing my sentiment. Only Lola hesitated, pink on her cheeks and her fingers on her own glass, but uncertain on whether or not to join the toast. Rake's arm wrapped around her shoulder and he leaned in, pressing a kiss to her temple and chinking his glass against hers. She wasn't a formal member, but how long would that take?

Perversely, and perhaps unwisely, I hoped it didn't take long. Leo and Rake might not be able to claim her formally, but with the approval of us alphas, no one would question her place with us. And maybe, with enough time…

I swallowed and dragged my eyes back to my plate. The thought of claiming Lola was so far-reaching, and possibly even violating to the young woman, I was ashamed of myself for letting it cross my mind. Caleb made more sense. He was Leo and Rake's alpha, he would provide her with a bond to both of them. Not to mention, he was one of the gentlest and most patient alphas I'd ever met.

He's not twice her age either, I reminded myself.

"Is it wrong of me to say I'm a little relieved?" Rake asked.

"Rake," Cyrus cautioned in a low tone.

I huffed at my plate and shook my head. "You would not be the man I know if you didn't," I teased back, gifting Rake the tired smile he'd be striving for.

Satisfied, he relaxed, his arm slipping from Lola's shoulders as we returned to our dinners, conversations finding their way back to their usual patterns. Wes watched me, and I met his stare.

"You're a bit relieved too, aren't you?" Wes asked, quiet enough that only Cyrus on my other side might hear.

"A bit," I said with a shrug. "I didn't like that she never warmed up to our pack as a family. I'll be glad not to worry about that tension."

Wes nodded. "You'll find someone that fits in with us," he said.

Wes was often impossible to read. He could crack a smile or a joke like the flip of a switch, but he could hide his worry and anger beneath an impenetrable stone veneer. Only a decade of living with him gave me the sense that I was being laughed at. His eyes never left my face, but it was like he was pointing a finger down the table to where Lola sat at the corner. I glared at him, and just like that, his grin flashed and he returned to his dinner.

Successfully made paranoid about my transparent interest in a younger woman well out of my reach, I ate the rest of my dinner with my head down. Wes collected our plates as we finished up, and chairs started to scrape away from the table.

"I made a cheesecake that's in the fridge whenever anyone feels ready for dessert," Leo announced. "I think I need a walk around the gardens before I dive in. Lola, want to join me?"

"I'll help you clear away," I said to Wes.

Lola stood from the table, hands wringing in front of her. "Actually, I...I was wondering if I could grab a word with Cyrus and Matthieu."

I was half out of my chair, spare glasses in my hand, my eyes caught wide in surprise. One look at Cyrus, and I knew he was equally caught off guard, as were Leo and Rake.

"Of course," I said. "Here? Or..."

"Um, private, maybe," Lola said, voice losing courage with a wobbled note, her shoulder twitching with a shrug. "An office?"

Cyrus and I nodded to one another, and I set the glasses back on the table. "We'll go to my office," I said with a nod. Cyrus' was more of an art studio, and there wasn't anywhere to sit or speak really. "Or we could use Leo's, I'm sure," I said, when I realized Lola might prefer a space that didn't belong to an alpha.

"Yours is fine," Lola said.

"Do you want me to wait for you?" Leo asked her.

She shook her head and rolled her shoulders back, fixing a tight lipped smile to her face. "I'll find you when this is done. Save me a slice of cheesecake."

The room watched Lola's back as she headed for the stairs, Cyrus and I following quickly behind her.

Lola

23

I fiddled with the cuffs of my blouse, wishing I'd changed before dinner into something more comfortable. But maybe it was better to be dressed this way, bound up in professional clothing rather than facing Matthieu and Cyrus in leggings and one of Leo's sweaters.

I entered Matthieu's office and the room looked different in daylight. Less cozy, maybe, more professional. I'd snuck down a couple more times to listen to his nighttime strumming, although I hadn't peeked my head in again. Now I hovered in the center of the room, surrounded by the deep, velvety scent of him on every surface. Behind me, Matthieu and Cyrus entered.

"Sit," Matthieu said gently. I opened my mouth to refuse, and he settled into his own worn-out armchair. "Sit, you'll make Cyrus anxious."

Cyrus scoffed lightly, leaning against Matthieu's giant oak desk with his ankles crossed.

The only seat in the room that wasn't Matthieu's footstool was a newer version of the armchair Matthieu sat in, its leather still in high shine. It faced Matthieu and Cyrus with plenty of open space between us, and it smelled more like an armchair than the alpha who owned it, but when I sat I sank deep into the cushions.

"I take it it's about the magazine if you wanted to see the two of us," Cyrus said. He wore a smile, but it seemed tense, like the one he wore during meetings with Wendy. "If I've made you at all uncomfortable—"

"What? No! God, no," I said, perching on the edge of the chair. "It's nothing like that at all."

Maybe Cyrus had made me uncomfortable in the beginning, but only by being an alpha, nothing he'd done. I felt terrible that he'd even question his own behavior. I took a deep breath and squared my shoulders.

"It's about Wendy," I said.

Matthieu and Cyrus exchanged a glance, guarded and unreadable, and Matthieu sank back into his seat.

"What about Wendy?" Cyrus asked. "She sings your praises. Well, as much as she does anyone's."

I swallowed and nodded. "No, I know. She's…it's not her directly, but I've been…approached," I said, wincing. "By Zane at first, and then today by Betty as well."

"Are they harassing you?" Cyrus asked, a slight growl in his tone.

I moaned and reached up, digging my fingers into my roots briefly. "No one is *harassing* me. This isn't even about me, honestly. They're talking about leaving *Designate*."

"Who are Zane and Betty?" Matthieu muttered to Cyrus. "Would it matter?"

"They're in my department, and no, not really," Cyrus said with a brief grimace. He looked back to me, that smooth dark skin furrowing over his brow. "What does this have to do with Wendy?"

"It's not just Zane and Betty leaving," I explained. "It's Wendy and whoever she successfully taps. From *every* department of *Designate*. And today Betty said something about them taking contacts with them?"

Finally, the news registered. Matthieu sat up sharply while Cyrus sagged, shoulders slouching.

"When?" Matthieu asked, leaning forward and propping his elbows on his knees. He'd lost his suit jacket before dinner, and his button-down stretched across his chest, a slight glimpse of chest hair in the v of his collar and fabric straining over surprisingly muscular arms.

Jesus, focus you idiot.

I shook my head. "I don't know. *They* don't know. But Betty told me that Wendy wanted to meet with me privately, that she'd get in touch with me through Betty for a dinner." Matthieu's hand scrubbed over his jaw and he looked to the floor as Cyrus rolled his neck, eyes on the ceiling—equal but opposite gestures. "I didn't know how serious Zane was, or I would've said something on Monday."

"You didn't need to say anything at all," Matthieu muttered, frowning at me. "You haven't been with *Designate* long, and if Wendy starts her own project—I take it that's where this is headed?" I nodded, and he continued, "If she starts her own and gives you a position, it can only help your résumé. Getting in on the ground of something like that leaves you an entirely vertical path on the board of that magazine."

I clenched my jaw and stared back at Matthew. "I have three very good reasons not to take Wendy's offer."

Cyrus sat up, a soft smile stretching over his lips. "Rake and Leo?"

I shrugged. "My relationship with them and my friendship with this pack, yes. But the most important reason is that I *love Designate*. I have ever since I was a little girl. Wendy thinks that the magazine can't change, so she wants to tear it down on her way out," I said, and Matthieu's eyes flinched briefly. "But I know *Designate*'s history. It *has* changed. Several times, and it can do it again. I don't think *Designate* deserves to be carved open to make room for something new to grow. Wendy's magazine can succeed or fail on its own without leaving scorched earth behind."

I caught my breath for the first moment since I'd started my speech and found the two men stunned into silence. Warmth flooded my cheeks, and I waited for them to speak. Cyrus was smiling at least. Matthieu fell back into his cushions, palms braced on his thighs.

"Well," he started, and then failed to finish the thought.

"David told me you loved the magazine, but I definitely wasn't expecting that level of devotion," Cyrus said. "So... Matt, what do you think?"

Matthieu reached up a hand and stroked his fingers over the slight scruff of his beard, eyes distant over my head. "When you say change, you mean..."

"More unique digital content, a wider look at the products we market being accessible to the audience we actually have, better diversity in models and media. Also, *Designate* should really consider opening its content to subjects outside of fashion and beauty. We're the last hold out, and our audience is ready."

Cyrus was beaming now, all but laughing. "I told you. She's editor material."

Matthieu sighed and collapsed. "Is this what Wendy's been saying all along?" he asked.

"Some of it, the digital content and adding in politics, yes," Cyrus said.

"It wouldn't have to be politics, although I think our audience has a clear leaning. But that's been done. *Designate*'s focus could be...society. Discussions about sex and gender that aren't just, you know, weird tip lists of how to take care of your man," I said, shrugging and ignoring my blush. I had more ideas on that topic after playing around with Rake and his incredible collection of sex toys, but I wasn't sure I was prepared to share them with Matthieu and Cyrus at this exact moment. "There's a whole community of non-binary and queer people who would be happy to be targeted in a fashion and beauty magazine like *Designate*. And that would bring—"

"An additional demographic," Matthieu said, eyes lighting up.

There, talk numbers and business with the man and he caught on quick.

"Lola, feel free to say no, but...how would you feel about a little corporate espionage?" Cyrus asked, crossing his arms over his chest.

My eyes widened. "I... What do you mean?"

Matthieu nodded. "I see, yes. You would take Wendy up on her offer of dinner, at the very least. See what she outlines for you. And if you're willing to play along with her, you might be able to give us more. More names, more of Wendy's plan."

I bit my lip. "Can I think about it? Telling you the truth, I'm comfortable with. Playing a spy game...I'm less sure about."

"Of course," Matthieu said, nodding. "I respect your decision either way. Now that we know..." He looked to Cyrus who nodded. "We can do our own snooping around if we need to."

"Thank you for the heads up, sunshine," Cyrus said, standing up and crossing to the door. "And for looking out for the magazine. Wanna come down for cheesecake?"

"In just a minute," I said.

Matthieu was still deep in his chair, eyes out the nearby window and lips turned down in a frown. Cyrus left for the hall, and I waited until his footsteps were quiet.

"Matthieu?"

"Hm?" He blinked, eyes landing on me and widening slightly, surprised to find me still here maybe.

"I have a question. It might be dumb," I said, wincing.

"Don't say that. Ask anything, it won't be dumb."

The room felt too huge between us, and my question was too personal to share with all the empty inches. I stood up from the chair and Matthieu sat up straighter as I moved to him, settling on the footstool.

"Things with Carolyn...it didn't have anything to do with what happened on Saturday, did it?" I asked, nearly whispering.

I hadn't seen Matthieu since I'd broken up the party, sick to my stomach and on the edge of yet another panic attack before Leo got me into the elevator and up to his rooms.

"What? Lola, *no.*" Matthieu leaned forward, warm calloused fingers catching my hand, folding one of mine between both of his. "No, it was nothing to do with anything that happened at the dinner party. It was a long time in coming."

"I just wanted to make sure," I said. "I wanted to apologize but—"

"You had nothing to apologize for," Matthieu urged, vivid pale eyes on mine. He sighed, head dropping, and I got a good look at the threads of silver that ran through his ash brown hair. "It was probably a mistake to think that either one of us could stay happy long term in a relationship outside of my pack. But it's done now, and we are… We will both be fine. Sooner than it might be polite to admit."

His touch was gentle on the back of my hand and his scent was heavy in my nose, coaxing and reassuring at the same time, both powerfully masculine and reassuringly gentle. I waited for the panic to rise, for the edgy nerves to crawl under my skin. I wasn't peaceful, here with Matthieu. My skin was hot and sensitive, and my heart was racing faster, pounding heavily in my veins. But I knew what those symptoms were from, and it wasn't discomfort.

Dangerous, I thought.

He cleared his throat, cheeks flushing, and the soft strokes on my skin stopped, Matthieu pulling away slowly.

"I'll see you downstairs," he said, a slight rasp in his faint accent.

I nodded and wobbled up on numb legs heading for the door.

Rake hates when betas chase his alphas, I reminded myself. But I didn't feel like I was chasing Matthieu. I didn't feel like he was hunting me either. More like I was sliding gently in his direction, waiting for the soft collision.

"SO WHAT HAPPENS if I'm completely terrible at this?" Baby asked. She didn't sound worried. She might even have sounded excited, or maybe that was just because she was busy staring at everything around her—the racks of clothes waiting for her to try on, the models running around in their underwear and tank tops from one booth to the next, the dozens of assistants trying to wrangle the room into some semblance of order.

"Not fuckin' possible, kitten."

Baby had brought one of her alphas, a giant one with a messy top knot of honey brown hair and a thick beard. He was covered in tattoos, dressed in leather and denim with asskicker boots, and he smelled like roses. He stood respectfully distant from me, but I was getting used to his presence the longer he hovered and said adorably supportive things to Baby *and* Seth.

His name was Bullet, and he wasn't what I was expecting at all. Maybe Baby was right and I needed to come by the Howlers because Bullet wasn't gruff—well, his voice was—or overbearing. He was cheerful and *endearing* and disgustingly devoted to Baby.

"You're going to be amazing, and I'm going to make sure you look perfect for the shoot," I said. I smiled at Seth. Bomber. I was going to use their road names now that Bullet had said they preferred them. "You both will look perfect. I really appreciate you coming and helping with this."

"I always knew I was too pretty to just bartend," Bomber said, grinning and making Baby giggle.

"Lo, this is the coolest ever. I can't believe you came up with this plan and they just, like—"

"Listened to me?" I joked. "I know! And for it to be a full shoot and not just a little mini-article. I can't wait to see the clothes. I think it's gonna be an avant-garde club look."

"You hear that, Bomb? Gonna put you in pleather and mesh," Bullet called.

Bomber made a dismissive 'pft' sound, and I decided not to warn him that Bullet might be right.

Bullet had been Baby's pack's only concession when it came to doing the shoot, and the magazine had been happy to comply. He was like their security guard and considering

Rake and Wes were due to arrive any minute, Bullet was just another bit of scenery. One the other models seemed *riveted* by, based on their scampering past us every few minutes and giggling.

I finished wiping down Baby and Bomber just as the models let out a chorus of squeals and greetings.

"Lo?" Baby hissed, eyeing the door. "Is that a celebrity?"

I glanced over my shoulder, an unwelcome blush blooming on my cheeks immediately. "Um, kind of. In the fashion world, yes. That's Rakim Oren. He's the other omega for the shoot that I'll be working on. And that's Wes, one of his packmates. Will that be, umm..." I twisted my lips in a frown and glanced at Bullet.

He shook his head, shrugging easily. "Not an issue, sweetheart," Bullet said with a smile that I automatically returned. Bullet was so easy going, he reminded me of Cyrus in a somehow totally opposite way.

Rake's chocolate perfume grew stronger, the flurry of activity from the models settling down as he neared my station. His scent was richer than usual, and we'd spent the night before in one of his nests, Leo and I taking turns wearing Rake out until all three of us were too tired to continue. When I woke, Rake had been missing, and Leo explained he'd probably gone to Cyrus or Caleb in the night rather than wake us again. His heat was due in less than a week and it was already starting to show.

"Hey, Lollipop," Rake said, wrapping an arm around my waist and pressing a brief kiss against my jaw. Baby's eyes widened as Rake barely nuzzled against me before drawing away in a cloud of chocolate and heady omega.

"Hey, Rake. Hi, Wes," I said, smiling at the pair of them. Rake's seat was on the other side of the station I'd set Baby and Bomber up at, and he went to collapse in the chair.

Baby was gawking at me. "I thought you were trying out a new perfume," she hissed, leaning forward to whisper yell at me. "You're dating an omega?!"

I shrugged and then since that seemed kind of unfair to me and Rake, I nodded.

"Ohmigod, Lo," Baby said, voice rising.

"Shit," Rake said from the other side of the mirrors. He reappeared, eyes a little wider and smile a little less sleepy. "I just realized, you must be Baby! And you two must be some of her sexy bikers." Rake winked at Bullet. "Lola never tells me enough about you, to be honest."

"I know the feeling," Baby said, overemphasizing the words and glaring at me.

"Baby, this is Rake and Wes. You guys this is Baby, Bullet, and Bomber. Baby and I are old friends," I said, rushing through the introductions.

"Bullet and Bomber?" Wes asked, eyes narrowed.

"They're just road names. His is purely fashion, but mine I got in the army. Sniper," Bullet said, holding out his hand to the other alpha.

Wes' eyebrows jumped and he looked Bullet over, shaking his hand. "I think I might've heard of you. You need a job by any chance? I work in personal security."

"I got one," Bullet said, pointing his thumb over his shoulder at Baby. "She's full time. Plus over time."

"Watch it," Baby growled, feigning an alpha snarl with bared teeth. Bullet just blew a kiss back at her and grinned.

"Rake and I met at a photoshoot," I said.

"And she's double dating my beta, Leo," Rake added, grinning at me.

"Shut the fuck up," Baby said, reaching out and *tit punching* me.

"Ohmigod, Baby, we are adults," I said, a laugh falling out as I resisted the urge to grab my boob and comfort it after the abuse from my overly caffeinated best friend.

"Adults have communications skills, *Lollipop*," Baby answered back. I glared at her, and Rake bounced on his heels, a manic grin overtaking his face at our exchange.

"I knew I wanted to meet her," Rake said to me. "I told you."

"I have to get started on this makeup before I get fired," I answered, shaking my head.

"Here," Bomber said, standing up from his chair and offering it to Rake. "That way you and Baby can compare alphas and things Lola fails to tell you."

"Oh wow, you're dead to me," I said, glaring at Bomber.

"So tell me about Leo," Baby said, settling into her chair. "Also tell me about Wes. Wes, you smell delicious. If you aren't bonded—"

"Kitten, say one more word. You have *plenty* of alphas," Bullet growled.

This was fucking *chaos*.

"That's interesting. Lola also finds Wes' scent delicious. She described it as Sex on the Beach," Rake said.

"This is why no one lets omegas out to play," Wes grumbled.

"Definitely the sex, yes," Baby said with an authoritative nod. "I'm getting syrup too. I wanna lick him."

"*Baby*," Bullet growled.

"You, lay back. Close your eyes. I'm doing your face, and I'm starting with that loud ass mouth of yours," I snapped at Baby.

Her back straightened and she tilted backward, lips twitching. "Yes, alpha," she replied in a purr.

I huffed, and Rake cackled, his perfume curling provocatively around my head. I was going to be dizzy with the scents by the time I was done with the two of them.

"She's a fuckin' handful and a half," Bullet said to Bomber, who hummed in happy agreement.

"WANT ME TO WASH YOU OFF?" I asked as Baby returned to my station after being promptly removed from the gauzy twisting dress she'd worn for the shoot.

"Nooo, leave it," Baby said, eyeing herself in the mirror, lip pouting and revealing the decorative enhancement I'd given to her bonding bite. "I kinda love it, and it'll either flip Green and Scorch out completely or drive them wild. Either way, I'll have fun. So..."

I swallowed hard and studied the brush I'd been cleaning as if that could keep Baby from asking too many questions. Bomber was with Bullet and Wes near the door of the studio where the photos were being taken. Rake was inside working with a gorgeous model who had alopecia and let us give her an intricate crown with the highlighter.

"Are you happy?" Baby asked.

I looked up, a little surprised by the question. I'd expected more along the lines of her wanting to know about the pack, about how I was doing near alphas maybe, or even another omega.

"I...am, yeah," I said, nodding. "It's a whole process, I guess. It's more stressful than just shutting out the rest of the world, but..."

"It's good to be alone when you need to be alone. But I think it's better to find people you can be happy with," Baby said, sweet and simple.

I nodded and relaxed, dropping my supplies in my case and shutting it. I leaned onto the counter of the desk, letting my shoulder rest against Baby's, happy to have hers lean back against me.

"So what's it like to have sex with an omega?" Baby blurted out.

"Ohmigod, babe. Seriously? You *are* an omega," I said, laughing and glancing around us.

"I know, but I don't get to have sex with like *myself*, I mean, not like that." She frowned in thought and then shook her head. "Anyway, tell me. Tell me, or I'll ask Rake himself."

"You've gotten very uncooperative in your old age," I muttered. I glanced at the door. Wes wouldn't hear me, right? Oh well, Baby would never let it go. "So do you...like, come a lot?"

Baby's eyes lit up and she squealed softly, head nodding wildly.

In for a penny, I thought, taking a breath. Anyway, it was nice to do this with her again. Be weird and gossipy and silly together like we used to. Even if things couldn't be exactly the way they were before Baby's heat came in, it was good to get some pieces of my old life back

CYRUS 24

Matthieu and I had barely made it to the family room, and I was planning on breaking off to go and paint, when Rake came racing out of the kitchen, eyes wide.

"Good! You're finally home. Come on, I'm calling a family meeting," he said in a breathless rush.

"Rake, I—" Matthieu started.

"It's important," Rake called, turning immediately back to the kitchen.

My lips twitched with a smile, in spite of the interruption to my plans. Whatever Rake was excited about, his enthusiasm was usually infectious. I followed my omega to the kitchen, Matthieu at my back with a weary sigh. Things at *Designate* were tenuous at the moment, now that we'd learned about Wendy's insurrection, and I suspected Matthieu was carrying the majority of the burden privately rather than alert the board yet.

I blinked as I walked into the kitchen. I'd assumed when Rake said 'family,' he meant whoever was on hand. Our pack wasn't often all home at the same time—let alone in the same country—but it seemed like lately, we'd been more available to one another. Still, it was a shock to see Wes home before nightfall.

"What's this about?" I whispered to him as I slid up to the counter.

"He's been keeping us in suspense," Wes muttered back.

Leo and Caleb were sitting on the stools, Leo's arm around Caleb's shoulders, and Matthieu took a spot at the corner. Rake stood across from us, bouncing on his toes and all but glowing in the spotlight of our attention.

"All right, you have us," Caleb said, amusement twisting his lips. "Now what is this about?"

Rake took a deep breath, squared his shoulders, and met each of our eyes before speaking. "I want Lola to be pack."

My brow furrowed at the words, and I expected to see the same confusion on the other's faces. Wes was impossible to read, as usual, but I thought I was seeing a glimpse of something like relief on Caleb and Matthieu's faces. Leo looked equal parts elated and worried.

"Is that even possible for her?" I asked, staring at the others.

"What do you mean?" Rake asked, his smile faltering as he stared at me.

My eyes widened. "Well…she has her…"—*Don't say issues*—"aversions to alphas."

Rake made a sound of dismissal, his hand waving through the air. "That's just a matter of time, don't you think? I mean, she likes all of you," he added with a shrug.

"But if she isn't bonded," I tried again.

"She would be accepted," Matthieu said with a surprising amount of readiness. Our heads all whipped in his direction, and even Rake looked surprised to hear the words. Matthieu blushed but held our gazes. "Our pack has never been conventional. If Lola accepted an offer that came without alpha bonds, why should it make any difference to us?"

Rake sighed and nodded. "Exactly, although I think, with time—"

Leo held up his hand to halt our omega's words. "Wait, Rake. You know I'm as much in favor of this as you are, but when are you planning on bringing this up with her?"

"Tonight," Rake said, with a firm nod. "That's why I'm glad you were all on time for once. She'll be here soon and—"

"No." This came from all of us. Well, all of us but Rake. His mouth fell open, and his face twisted with offense.

"What? But—"

"Rake, Lola isn't ready to hear this yet," Leo said, leaning forward, his eyes wide. "I absolutely agree with you. I want her to be pack. She belongs with us." I wasn't sure if Leo meant him and Rake specifically or us as a whole. "But I don't think there's any version of this offer that Lola is prepared to accept."

Caleb cleared his throat and nodded at Leo, continuing to reason with Rake. "She's only just getting to know the pack, and her progress is wonderful already, but I agree with Leo. It might be difficult for her to see a future with us at the moment."

"There's no rush," Wes said, catching Rake's eye.

Rake grimaced. "I mean…there kind of is. We leave for my heat tomorrow and I…I want Lola there."

Silence fell in the wake of that announcement, and it wasn't until I saw Rake's crestfallen expression that I realized I was shaking my head. "I'm sorry," I said, trying to organize my thoughts as quickly as I could so I could give Rake a better answer than the flat 'no' on my tongue. "I don't object to the idea. Just…I just can't imagine her saying yes."

"Would you want Cyrus and I out of the nest, love?" Caleb asked Rake.

"No! No, of course not, I just…" Rake sighed, and his shoulders sagged. His elbows landed on the steel island, and his hands covered his face.

"My instincts say Lola is pack," Matthieu said in the quiet that followed. It was a big announcement. Matthieu was unofficially the head of our household, our pack. He could overrule us if he chose, although that wasn't how Matthieu led us.

Not us, I realized. *Just me*. I was the only one who didn't seem to be prepared for Lola to join our family. I *liked* the girl. I understood her appeal. She was just…fragile at the moment. Maybe our pack would give her strength. Or maybe, if she wasn't ready for us, we would become an oppressive weight on her shoulders as she tried to shape herself for us.

"So do mine," Wes said.

Rake's hands dropped from his face, expression brighter. Wes rarely made any waves in our pack. He and Matthieu making this declaration was an interesting twist too. It should have been Caleb and I supporting Rake; we were his bonded alphas.

"I would like to see Lola in our pack. I just want her to be ready to accept," Caleb said.

Which left me. Rake's eyes found mine, hope winking along our bond. He was trying to keep his end quiet too, to avoid influencing me. That alone told me how seriously he was taking this discussion. Rake was not above wheedling and begging when he wanted something.

I moved around the island, wrapping my arms around Rake's shoulders and pulling his back to my chest. His scent was so thick right before a heat, and it drew out an automatic response in me to suck and fuck and drag him off to a nest. I stamped that down and focused on the discussion.

"Invite her to the heat," I said slowly. "If she comes, I think Caleb and I can behave ourselves."

"Of course," Caleb said quickly, almost eagerly.

Rake was giddy, but I pushed caution back to him as I nuzzled his temple and kissed his nearly feverish skin. "I like Lola, but I'm not prepared at this point to call her pack," I said gently. "And I don't think she's prepared either. So can we table that for now?"

"Yes," Rake said with a quick nod.

I sighed and kissed his throat. Leo's phone chimed on the counter and he flipped it over, a smile mixing with a little tangle of worry on his brow.

"She's on her way here."

Rake's grin was nervous, and he stared back at Leo. "You better coach me on how to talk to her about this, so I don't blurt everything out at once."

Lola and the Millionaires

I WAS MEANT to be painting. Or maybe not meant to, but that had been my goal for the night. At least until Rake snuck out of Leo and Lola's embrace and came slipping into my bed, needy and frosted in their scents.

Leo's scent had never done much for me, too soapy. But Lola's?

I'd been licking it off Rake recently. *Does that mean I want her as pack?* I wondered. I enjoyed women, enjoyed falling in love with women, especially ones who guarded their emotions. But I didn't have the best track record of romances with women. With anyone who wasn't Rake, actually. Was I impossible, or did I have bad taste?

I stared down at the neglected palette of colors I'd prepped, and then back at my canvas, grimacing at the shadows of buildings waiting to be illuminated. *A cityscape. How original*, I thought spitefully. This is why I was still at *Designate* in middle management. Not that I wanted Wendy's job like Matthieu had been hinting. But I was never going to break out of the magazine and into galleries with *cityscapes*.

"Oh!"

I spun on my stool to find Lola in the doorway of my studio, her eyes wide and traveling around the room, taking in the clutter and the canvases and the art on the walls. She blushed as she met my eyes, her smile more cautious than the one she wore at work.

"The door's always been closed before and I wanted to snoop. Sorry," she said, grinning a little.

"Snoop away." I jerked my head in invitation, watching as she stepped in without hesitation. Rake was right. Lola had already overcome a lot of her fear of the alphas in this pack. Still, I was sure she was a long way from imagining herself taking a permanent place with us.

"I didn't know you were a painter," she said, moving slowly around the room. "Oh, Cyrus! You painted the angel on the stairs didn't you?"

I sat up a little straighter at that. "I did, ages ago. I'm surprised you noticed."

"The brush strokes are the same. It's absolutely beautiful," she said, spinning and beaming at me.

It hit me then like a punch to the gut, a *craving* for her. If she had been any other girl, any one of the ones Rake had been interested in in the past, I would have reached out for her and dragged her between my thighs. I could've dug paint smudged fingers into her hair and scratched my teeth along her jaw until she was whining and begging for me.

But she was Lola, so I kept my hands to myself.

It wasn't the first time I was attracted to her. Lola was stunning and had a kind of crystalline femininity that tempted me. But it was the first time it came with questions bigger than the usual physical ones. *Is this girl pack?*

I was lost in my own head when she stopped at a stack of paintings, pulling one forward to peek behind at the next.

"Is this…is this Wendy?" she asked.

I cleared my throat and slid off my stool, moving to stand at her side. She didn't flinch, even when my arm brushed her shoulder.

"You've found my old lovers," I said, studying her expression as she looked up at me.

She had Rake's scent all over her, and I wondered what he was doing if Lola was out of his bed.

"You paint your lovers?" she asked, a wicked little grin on her face.

"I paint my break-ups." I leaned in and Lola remained still as I moved the paintings out of their usual stack so she could see a few sitting side by side. I pointed to the one I'd painted of Wendy, trying not to look too closely and get lost in old emotions. "It reads left to right, like a sentence. All the optimism of the start of a new relationship. The way the person kind of shines to the point you can't even see them clearly," I said, gesturing to the bright glow of the left side of the portrait's face. "That kind of midland clarity of falling in love where you think you know the person's faults but embrace them anyway. And then…"

"When the glow wears off," Lola said, crouching down to look closer at the wince in Wendy's gaze on the right side of her face, the cruel turn of her mouth, the almost wolf-like angle of her cheek.

"Normally, I am pretty self-forgiving of my wayward romances. Wendy was an especially great mistake on my part. I never learn not to rush." I hadn't waited to see what Wendy wanted from our connection, and when I realized…things had started to fracture quicker than I could reach to hold them together.

"Because you work for her," Lola said.

"Because she wanted me to leave Rake. To leave my pack."

Lola gasped and looked up at me, and I stepped back from her as she rose up. "But you're bonded!"

"Yes," I said. It had been an impossible ask, and something I might've seen coming if I'd been even the tiniest bit more cautious. I'd learned some care since then, at least.

Lola frowned and then glared down at Wendy's portrait again. "She strikes me as someone that wants the world to prove to her how important she is, rather than deciding so for herself."

My eyes widened, and I stared at Lola. "You're a good judge of character then."

Her face went pale and her eyes dropped to the floor. "No. I'm really not."

She needs us. Lola needed us to prove to her that not all alphas were monsters, but also that some would recognize and cherish her value. And she needed time to prove to herself that her trust in us was well-placed. Maybe she related to Wendy's fight for validation, but instead of injuring others, the only harm she'd done had been to herself.

"You're so talented," Lola murmured, glancing around the room again and then up to me, grey eyes direct. "But these are painful and *moving*."

I grew warm at the compliment. My packmates had seen my work and encouraged me, but there was something about someone who had made no vow to support me that made the weight of the praise heavier.

"If I was going to show any of my work, it would be these," I said, and then shrugged. "But I'd probably end up in a lawsuit if I tried."

Lola's lips twitched. "They're not very flattering, no. I don't think break-ups often are."

I hummed my agreement and moved back to my seat to give Lola space. No, mostly it was to resist the urge to find an excuse to touch her. "I'm surprised you escaped Rake's clutches for the night," I said, and wondered if that was crossing a line.

Lola blushed but shrugged. "I needed a minute. Leo has him distracted until I get back. You know he'll end up with you eventually."

Rake wasn't going to get much sleep until the heat broke this weekend. "He invited you to join us for the weekend," I said, as if it was just a trip to the country, and not a *heat* with a pack.

"He did," Lola said slowly, eyes sliding back to the floor.

She turned him down. I realized it with a surprising pang of disappointment. Maybe the others weren't so far off with their feelings for Lola. Heats were pack-only events, and I hadn't expected to be let down by the idea of Lola not being there. But it was there, a little sour note that told me our family wouldn't be complete if Lola was staying in the city without us. I bit my tongue before I said as much.

"I should get back to them," Lola murmured, a little shy pinkness in her cheeks. Her eyes glanced at my canvas and then up to me. "You should paint the city like you paint your love affairs. I'd like to see that."

I stared at her, the cryptic suggestion teasing my thoughts as Lola retreated from my studio. My eyes slid down to my palette, and I picked up my brush.

Lola
25

"Are you sure you wouldn't rather I stay?" Leo murmured.

Rake had moved to his alphas in one of the nests for the night, and in the morning the whole pack was set to leave for their *country home*—I was still wrapping my head around that—to spend a long weekend together for his heat. A heat I had been invited to, leaving me speechless for a good five minutes while I caught my breath from the offer.

"I'm gonna be fine, Leo," I whispered back, grinning. It was dark out, but the city's glow let ambient light in through the brick glass ceiling above, enough for me to see Leo in blurry blue and gold and shadow. "Isn't a heat a big deal? Rake would miss you if you weren't there."

Leo sighed and nodded, his arm nudging against me. I sat up a little so he could slide it under my back and tug me against his chest. His skin was warm under my cheek, and I burrowed closer.

"I wish you were coming," Leo said, so soft I wasn't sure I was meant to hear it.

"I thought heats were for pack," I said, trying to stay relaxed.

Leo snorted, breath puffing against my shoulder. "That… wouldn't matter in this case. To Rake or anyone else. But…"

"I'm not ready for that," I said, more gently, and sighed when Leo nodded. "Anyway, I've got that dinner meeting thing with Wendy tomorrow night. I can hardly miss it and tell her I'm going to Rake's heat, right?"

"Are you sure you wanna get into that pool of sharks? I mean I love Matt and Cyrus, and I know this is important to them, but you don't deserve to be a rope in a tug of war," Leo said.

"I think I want to hear from Wendy herself though. Like, are Betty and Zane putting a poisonous spin on things, or does Wendy really want to rake *Designate* and Matthieu over the coals?"

Leo hummed, head turning and lips pressing to my forehead. "I was gonna say they're lucky they hired you, but to be honest *I'm* lucky they hired you, otherwise I might not have found you again."

I gasped and pressed my face firmly into Leo's throat, trying to hold a tight grip on my emotions. No waterworks tonight, not even for happy reasons.

"I'm having a hard time knowing I'm gonna be out of town again and this stuff with…you know, isn't really taken care of yet."

Indy.

I soothed my hand over Leo's chest. "Wes tracked the phone to pretty far west of here, didn't he?"

Leo nodded. "Still. Any chance I could talk you into staying here while we're gone? Matt will be home, but he'll stay out of your way if you want him to."

"I don't mind Matthieu. I don't mind any of you," I said. "But Wendy's sending a car to my apartment and—"

Leo let out a heavy sigh and I laughed, wiggling up against his chest to hover my face over his. "Tell you what. You guys get back Monday, right? I will be here then. Maybe even sooner. I'll keep in touch with you *and* with Matthieu if it makes you feel better."

"It makes me feel much better," Leo said, smile stretching. His arm tightened around my waist, pulling me over his hips, my legs falling open to either side. "Having you on top of me like this makes me feel *great*."

I grinned and dipped down, sucking on Leo's lips and rolling my hips, catching his moan on my tongue.

―――

IT WAS weird to overthink what you wore to a dinner meeting with your boss. It wasn't a *date*, but there was an aspect of trying to impress involved. I wanted to look professional, but not stuffy, and at *Designate* professional kind of ran the gamut of styles. I settled on a long, black, jersey t-shirt dress and a red leather jacket, pairing it with sharp makeup and dressy accessories just in case we were going somewhere a little nicer.

I didn't need to worry though. Wendy had chosen a trendy but informal fusion restaurant, and she was sitting in the booth dressed in a t-shirt and jeans. Granted, they were obviously tailored to fit her perfectly, but that was probably a given with fashion people.

"Lola, nice to see you out of the office like this," Wendy said, rising from the booth just long enough to shake my hand.

"I'm happy to be here," I said, and tried to make sure I looked it.

Any sensible brand new assistant editor at *Designate* should be *ecstatic* to be asked to dinner with Wendy, and I needed to remember that. It was just a little more difficult after my conversation with Cyrus the other night, seeing the pained expression on his face as he talked about her. I would be in some kind of serious shit if Wendy realized I was here to dig up information for Matthieu or Cyrus, and not because I was genuinely interested in her plans.

"I've always wanted to come to this restaurant," I said, since that was true.

I had always wanted to, but it was constantly booked.

"Let me know next time you want to come. Niko is a friend of the family, so I'm a little spoiled," Wendy said, shrugging. "Restaurants always hold a few tables if you know who to ask."

"I'm surprised *Designate* hasn't branched out into stuff like this. Not just restaurants specifically, but new cultural landmarks," I said.

Wendy took a sip from her water glass, eyes watching me over the rim. She had pretty, thin rings stacked on her fingers, different metals and gems winking under the raw lighting.

"You have the mind of an editor in chief, you know that? Thinking of the magazine as a whole instead of just your beauty pages," Wendy said. "Don't get me wrong. You're very good at your specialty, but you should consider starting to map the ladder you'd like to take up your career."

"Thank you," I said blushing. Before getting the job at *Designate*, a Head Beauty Editor position was as much as I'd dreamed of. More than that was a tempting but unknown route of fantasizing about my future.

Wendy sighed and looked down at the table. "I don't know if you've noticed, but Voir is run by a bunch of dusty old white men. They've decided *Designate*'s place is to tell a woman how to see herself in a mirror and nothing more. They're determined to leave the magazine a dinosaur, rather than let it breathe and change with a new generation of women. Not to mention a new age of publishing."

I opened my mouth and wondered if I could debate her point of view. Matthieu hadn't tossed my ideas out the door when I blurted them out in a run the other night after dinner. What was the real rift between Wendy and Voir? It was as if she was taking her anger at Cyrus out on the entire company.

"Betty said you're interested in starting your own magazine," I said instead.

"Mmm, more like a website devoted to fashion, to beauty, to culture," Wendy said. "The age of paper and ink is over, and there's so much more money to be made with online advertising. So much less money to be spent too. We wouldn't need offices, wouldn't need to waste a fortune on floors of a place like the Stanmore."

My heart sank at the thought. Maybe it was superficial of me, or maybe I was more old fashioned than I realized, but I loved working at the Stanmore. I loved the beautiful old building, and I loved sitting at the table brainstorming with the beauty team. God, I *loved* playing with the samples of everything.

"Sounds like an entirely different kind of beast," I said, nodding slowly.

"Absolutely. A sleek, efficient, globally available beast. I want to hire some of the biggest names in the social media beauty trends to work directly with us, reel in some of the independent figures that provide a place like *Designate* with competition, and turn them into my allies," Wendy said.

It was smart and it was cutthroat, and it would deliver a major blow to *Designate* if Wendy succeeded in that alone, never mind taking some of the magazine's contacts with her.

"Are you a picky eater?" Wendy asked as a waiter approached our table.

I was a little queasy with nerves now, but I shook my head. "Never. Everything here sounds amazing."

Wendy nodded. "It is. Yes, hi, Marco. We'll have one of everything, just bring sharing plates. And can we get two glasses of champagne please?"

I swallowed hard. Had I already agreed to take part in Wendy's plan just by telling Betty I'd come to the dinner? Either way, I had a long night ahead of me, and after hearing Wendy's broken down, streamlined version of *Designate*, I was pretty sure I needed to see this whole thing through.

ALL DAY FRIDAY, with Cyrus out of town for the heat, our department kept busy with more of the menial tasks. Zane and Betty were in and out of the office, and I couldn't tell if they were running errands or just helping themselves to a lot of breaks, but I was happy to be able to work alone for most of the day. My head was still reeling from the dinner with

Wendy. She was powerful, in a brutal kind of way, and her vision of the future of fashion and beauty reporting sounded uncomfortably impersonal and disparate.

To make matters a little worse—or a lot, if I was honest—I was missing the guys like crazy. Not just Leo and Rake, although my nightmares decided to come calling again now that I was back at my apartment alone. But I was missing seeing Cyrus at work and then again at dinner. I was missing Caleb and his warm scent and his careful words and his constant habit of finding new ways of making me comfortable. I missed helping Wes with the crossword and curling up in the passenger seat of his old Plymouth when he would drop me off at the Stanmore.

And Matthieu…

It was less *missing* and more *craving*. I was nervous at the promise I'd made to Leo to return to the house sometime during the weekend. I trusted Matthieu, but I didn't trust myself around Matthieu. He was a wholly unexpected temptation, and I wasn't blind enough to ignore the stares he made in my direction. He'd just ended a relationship. Maybe I was just a convenient side piece? An easy rebound opportunity, and a beta to boot, so no real threat to the stability of his pack.

My phone rang at lunch and I grinned when I saw Leo's name on the screen. I'd called the night before but he hadn't answered, and it'd been hours later before he'd responded with a series of deliriously tired but sweet texts.

"Hey, I miss you," I said, the words falling out easily.

Leo sighed, low and long over the line. "God, gorgeous, I miss you too. And I'm not the only one."

"How is he?" I asked, glancing around the office. Corey was in, so I was probably better off not saying Rake's name specifically. Rake had been cuddly at the photoshoot, but not much more than most models and omegas usually were.

"He's… I mean, he's good, of course. Heats are fun," Leo said slowly. "But…um…okay, so he's been asking for you a lot."

"Oh." I tried to ignore the twinge in my chest. I'd assumed when I'd turned down Rake's invitation that would be the end of the idea. That'd he happily move on to enjoy his heat with his pack.

"Whining. Begging, really," Leo said, voice dropping in my ear, and heat thrumming in my core. "I know you said you weren't ready to come to a heat, and I *totally* understand. But I... It's hard to see him like that, and I said I would ask again for him."

My jaw hung open and my eyes flicked around the room without really seeing my surroundings. "He's not... Is he *okay*?"

"It's almost like pain, but not quite. Like the pain of, you know, *wanting* someone but without the satisfaction. I mean he's satisfied, and then two seconds later, he's asking for you. Caleb and Cyrus could stay clear-headed enough to keep their hands off you if you changed your mind, but I don't think they'll be able to leave the nest," Leo said. "I know, Lola. I know it's a big ask. And it's just a few more days, really. Maybe by the time the next one comes..."

Maybe then I wouldn't mind being part of an orgy with my alpha boss and another alpha packmate of Rake's?

Caleb and Cyrus, I reminded myself. Caleb was basically a friend. Cyrus was too, aside from the whole I reported to him at work thing.

"Say no if you need to, gorgeous," Leo prompted gently. "Rake would never begrudge you that, and as soon as his head is clear—"

"How would I get there? I don't have a car."

Are you fucking serious right now? Leo's voice died off abruptly as my brain sputtered to a halt. Was I really considering going? And if I was, why *now*?

Because it's Rake, and he doesn't just want you there. He needs you. Badly enough that Leo felt pressured to ask, which Leo would never otherwise do.

"Matthieu was going to come up tonight so the whole

pack was together. He would pick you up if you decided to come. It's kind of a long drive," Leo added gently.

That alone might've been a strong enough warning to change my mind if I'd been thinking straight, but apparently I wasn't.

"I can't guarantee Rake won't try and talk you into more, but if you catch him in some downtime, the cuddles alone would help," Leo said. He was obviously tiptoeing over his words, expecting me to spook and refuse.

I wanted to prove him wrong, to prove myself wrong really. I wanted to be strong enough to be there for Rake when he needed me. Cuddles would be nice. I *missed* them; it felt like I was missing limbs as I tried to fall asleep, I was so used to having someone to curl up against now.

"Okay. I'll need to run to my apartment after work first."

"Okay?"

"Okay."

"Are you sure?"

"Not *really*," I said. "But I'd like to try."

"Try is fine, gorgeous. If anything changes, you let me know. It's—I can't wait to see you," Leo said, wistful and warm.

"Ditto."

I swallowed hard as Leo made his goodbyes, and we both hung up. I was going to Rake's heat. I was going to *try* and be there for Rake's heat. Where Caleb and Cyrus would also be.

I needed to think of something, anything else. Anything but what my boss might look like naked and fucking Rake.

What the hell are you doing, Lola?

Lola
26

"So what are the chances of me being in the room and *not* having sex?"

"Umm...when one of my alphas tried to give me space, I went and hunted his ass down," Baby said. "But this isn't Rake's first heat. I—"

"Honest opinion, babe," I said, stuffing clothes into a bag in my apartment.

"Fuckin' slim to none. None. You're gonna have heat sex. Bomber says it'll feel a little like you're getting high with all the pheromones flying around."

Shit. That was probably the thing I was least prepared for. The sense of being out of control, of things starting to happen and me not knowing what would come next, or where it would go, or who would touch me or—

"If Leo is there and you need to leave, he will make sure you can, right?" Baby asked, voice cautious.

I huffed out a breath, the slow tensing of my shoulders collapsing at her question. "Yes. Yes, he will." That I trusted completely. Leo had texted three times since he'd called during the day to make sure I was still okay with coming, and he'd already told me that he hadn't said anything to Rake yet in case I needed to change my mind.

"Are you at all excited, or just nervous?" Baby asked.

"Ehnnn, yeah, I mean, I'm a little excited," I said laughing. "I'm always a little excited when it's the three of us. Just now it's the three of us plus two and those two are—"

"Try not to think of them as alphas. They're nice guys, right, and they won't play grabby hands with you? So they'll be like…sexy air fresheners. Mood enhancers. Sound effect machines. Spare dicks if it comes down to it."

I was wheezing with laughter, yanking on the zipper with one hand and holding my phone with the other. "I was planning on saving it for when he got back, but I got Rake a surprise and I figured now is probably a good time to gift it to him."

"Ooo a naughty courting present? I love it!" Baby sighed. "My little Lola's first heat. Gosh, how they grow up."

I scoffed and shook my head, pulling the phone away and then seeing the time. Shit. I ran to the window and looked down to the street. There, in the no parking zone, a long, sleek black car waited, red tail lights still on.

"Baby? Car's here, I gotta go."

"Okayiloveyoubaiiiiiiii," Baby rushed out.

I slung my bag over my shoulder, patting the bottom to make sure my recent purchase hadn't been forgotten, and then ran out the door, locking it behind me. Matthieu was halfway up the stairs, a long brown wool coat on over a cozy looking sweater and jeans. He smiled as I nearly ran into him and then he pointed down to the door.

"Why isn't that locked?"

"It was supposed to be, but the landlord hasn't done anything yet," I said with a shrug. "I think he's pretty absent."

"Wes will take care of it when we get back in town."

"Wes isn't my landlord," I said, frowning.

"He will *speak* with him," Matthieu bit out as we reached the landing. "Do you need your bag? I can put it in the trunk for you."

I shook my head and Matthieu was there, slipping his hand under the strap and sliding it off my shoulder before I needed to say anything. Standing at the backseat door, a tall beta in a black suit waited for me to slide in.

We were taking a driver to the country house? The car

wasn't quite a limo, but there was more than usual amounts of legroom in the back seat, as well as a small fridge and a privacy window up to screen off the front seat.

I caught a glimpse out of the window on my left as I slid in, my stare freezing on a figure in the dark. Across the street, leaning against a light post, someone was standing under the glow, wearing a dark hoodie. Even with the shadow of the hood and the head lowered, the body was facing me directly.

"Would you like me to sit up front?"

I whipped my head around to see Matthew ducked and looking at me through the car door.

"What? No, you don't have to do that."

"You're sure?" Matthieu asked.

It seemed strange to insist on him sitting in the back with me, and there was something vulnerable and nerve-wracking about the privacy window and the knowledge that we would be entirely alone in the small space. Still, I nodded, and Matthieu slid into the backseat.

"I think Leo's waiting until the last moment to give Rake the news," Matthieu said with a soft smile. "Otherwise, he might try to make Wes meet us on the road or…" Matthieu cleared his throat and shook his head, the slow blush rising to his cheeks just barely visible in the dim light of the backseat.

Through the partition, the car twitched with the driver's door shutting, and a moment later we were moving away from the curb. I glanced back out my nearby window and startled. The figure was still there, but now the face was turned up, revealing a cheesy Halloween skull mask. A moment later, we were out of sight, and I tried to settle the nerves the eerie image had left in me. Maybe my neighborhood was getting a little sketchier, or maybe it had just been a teenager playing to scare.

If Wes *did* talk my landlord into finally fixing the lock on the front door, that would be a relief.

"Leo said the drive was long?"

Matthieu hummed and nodded, eyes fixed on our reflection in the partition glass. "A few hours. I made sure there was food in the fridge, but if you'd like to stop, we certainly can. I thought…this way, you could relax," he said, words fumbling as he went, voice gaining a rasp. He cleared his throat and ducked his head.

Right. Just relax. In the backseat of a not-quite-limo with an alpha that made me forget why I avoided alphas, and instead left me wanting to climb on his lap and—

"Thanks. And thanks again for picking me up," I said, pressing my thighs together and trying to get my brain *under control*.

"My pleasure," Matthieu said, nodding and looking out his window.

I mirrored him, watching the city streets pass. A few hours in the car with Matthieu, and then I'd be at the house for Rake's heat. Nothing to worry about.

THE RIDE WAS TORTURE. We hit bumper to bumper traffic on the freeway out of the city, and an hour had already passed without us hitting the suburbs. With every passing minute, Matthieu's scent grew stronger, silky edges showing a bitter frayed edge with nerves. Neither of us had so much as twitched over into the middle seat, but even so, I was fairly certain I was coated in his scent. This wasn't a normal amount of alpha pheromone either, it was *flooding* the confined space, which meant whatever Matthieu was feeling that triggered the response was *strong*.

I was getting less and less worried about the prospect of the heat the longer I sat surrounded by Matthieu's pheromones. I was aroused. Hell, I was *soaked*. I was taking thin brief breaths to try and keep from sucking down dizzy lungfuls that might make me do something regrettable. Like thigh-ride Matthieu for the remainder of the drive. I would definitely be ready for whatever Rake needed when I got to the house, and I was only a little nervous about what that would mean. If it satisfied this hunger, I'd deal with the repercussions later.

Suddenly, it occurred to me what Matthieu's scent might be about.

"You must be anxious to get to Rake," I said, relieved to sound halfway human and not have all my words fall out in a needy whine.

"Hm?" Matthieu startled, turning his head to me with his brow furrowed. "Rake?"

"For his...his heat," I said, swallowing. Leo hadn't mentioned Matthieu being in the room too, but maybe the alpha was more possessive with Rake and wanted one on one time with him? I didn't really know enough about the whole thing, and I wished Rake and I had discussed it more before I ended up deciding to come.

"Rake's heat?" Matthieu stared at me blankly, my own lips parted in confusion and his eyes darting down to glance at them. All at once, comprehension lit up on Matthieu's face. "Oh! No, no I... Rake and I aren't bonded in that way. I go to the house when I can so he has his whole pack around, but we have a-a platonic romance," Matthieu said with an amused smile, a little line of confusion left digging into his brow.

I stared straight ahead at our reflection in the partition. "Oh."

Then why was he filling the car with his scent right down to the stitching in the leather seats?

"Oh," Matthieu echoed softly, his own stare moving forward until we were holding each other's gaze in the black glass. He cleared his throat and my eyes fell to his hands over his knees, gripping until his knuckles were white.

You know exactly why, I hissed to myself.

It was like when I'd worn Baby's scent and caught Buzz's eye, except this time there was no omega perfume to explain Matthieu's reaction to me.

"I'm sorry," Matthieu murmured, shifting to face me. "I didn't realize how difficult it would be. Would you like me to move up front?"

I bit down hard on the inside of my lip, studying his earnest expression, the clarity in his gaze. I shook my head slowly.

"Are you sure? I don't want you to feel uncomfortable, Lola, and this is entirely my own issue."

That hawkish nose. The lines around his eyes and lips from years of deep smiles. The broad shoulders. It wasn't just Matthieu's alpha scent that had such an effect on me, although it certainly didn't help. That was just the siren song. Matthieu was the cliff I wanted to throw myself from.

"I'm sure," I said, words breathless. I twisted to face him too, our knees bumping together, and then I parted my thighs, cool air sliding up under my skirt and making the arousal against my panties even more obvious.

Still, I was only a beta, and it took Matthieu a moment to notice. I watched the exact moment my scent reached him, his nostrils flaring and pupils blooming black. He let out the softest vibration, the lowest combination of an alpha's hungry growl and satisfied purr, before swallowing the noise. Not fast enough to stop goosebumps rushing over my skin and my nipples hardening to points.

"Lola."

I caught my breath, eyelashes fluttering at the slow, round notes of my name on his lips. It was a caution, or a prayer, musical and deep in my ears.

The hand on his leg slipped over to mine, ducking beneath the soft fabric of my skirt, fingertips sliding down to the hypersensitive skin of the back of my knee. An embarrassing broken moan slipped from my loose lips at the faintest touch. With a gentle nudge from him, I slid my leg up onto the seat, spreading myself wider, the tart whiff of my desire growing stronger.

I lunged forward and Matthieu caught me, sliding over squeaking leather to meet me halfway. Our foreheads bumped, and then my mouth was suckling and searching over rough stubble to find his lips. His tongue swept in immediately, bringing with it a drunk and heady flavor burning on my tongue that left me craving and searching for more. The kiss was rough and messy to start with, but soon Matthieu's hands were on my back, sliding up to hold my head. He took the lead, guiding and working my lips with his—teeth scratching and tongue soothing—until I was twined around his body, whining and writhing. This is why the French were famous for kissing, or maybe Matthieu had just had the best practice. Every touch was masterful and affectionate and left my pulse thrumming from my head to my toes, my clit pounding and begging for attention.

He was getting hard. I could feel it against me, and I started to grind against him, my core already tingling with pleasure like I'd been waiting the entire ride for just a little bit of touching to push me over the edge. This was the high I'd been doing everything I could to avoid for the past year, the dizzy drunk desperation. I would do *anything* to keep Matthieu's hands on me, keep his attention.

It was like someone had turned up the volume on life. I was more sensitive, more aware, more alive.

"Lola," Matthieu growled, mouth pulling away as I tried to chase him for more. His teeth nipped my chin, and then I was arching back as he sucked kisses on my throat, strong pulls against my skin that echoed in my cunt. "Lola, tell me this is all right."

"Matthieu, I want—" I whined and rolled my hips against his, one of his hands coming down to my ass and squeezing.

"Anything," he hissed, licking over my pulse. "Anything."

I sucked in a breath, and it was a struggle. I was on a dangerous edge of arousal and panic, and for every delicious perfect sensation, there was heightened anxiety to match it.

"I need control," I said, stretching and bracing my hands on the back of the seat.

Matthieu was under my shadow, eyes nearly black with desire, lips wet and chest heavy with breath. I lifted one hand

and hesitated, wanting to slide my fingers into his hair. His head tilted in the direction of my hand, inviting me to touch, and his hands fell to the leather seats. My knees were on either side of his hips, my back to the partition. Matthieu must've turned us and pulled me onto his lap during the kiss, and I hadn't even noticed in the haze.

"It's yours," Matthieu murmured, a scratch in his words and his gaze heavy-lidded. "Anything you want, Lola."

My breath hitched. Well now I felt like I'd just been left in front of a massive buffet table of all my favorite foods. Where did I start?

"The driver can't see, right?" I asked.

"No, but he might hear if we aren't careful," Matthieu said, lips curling.

That was all right then. I planned on keeping my mouth busy.

I reached down, my fingers looping around Matthieu's wrists and drawing his palms up to the back of my thighs. "Touch," I whispered, lowering my head to brush my lips over his. "But don't push."

Matthieu started to purr, but he choked on the sound as my fingers reached for the hem of his sweater, dipping underneath and stroking at the soft skin of his stomach. I kissed him again, trying to take sips of his flavor instead of guzzling the moment down like an alcoholic reuniting with their favorite poison. Matthieu's hands were warm on my skin as his fingertips, calloused from playing the guitar, slid up between my thighs. Up and down he stroked, tempting me to sink down into his touch and let him feel how badly I wanted him.

Remember what Rake said? a warning voice asked.

I did, and that was the worst part. I wouldn't stop. God, they would smell Matthieu all over me when I got to the house. Maybe that would be the end of all of this. Rake and Leo would see who I really was.

I still wouldn't stop.

My fingers on Matthieu's stomach moved down, cupping his erection over his jeans. Matthieu groaned, a purely sexual sound, and his hips bucked as I massaged him through layers of fabric. Unable to resist the call of my warmth or trying to reciprocate my touches on him, Matthieu's hands under my skirt grew brave, pushing against the damp fabric of my underwear.

"Fuck," Matthieu hissed, eyes squeezing shut. "Jesus Christ, what are we doing? Fuck you're so wet, Lolotte."

I whined at the coaxing pet name and rode his fingers, the pair of us handsy and probably louder than we should've been if we wanted this to be private.

"Fuck, if I'd known," Matthieu gasped out, leaning back to catch my eyes, a perfect silvery-blue ring of color surrounding his full pupils.

Decision made, I pushed his hands away and then moved backward until I was off the seat of the car and down on the floor. Matthieu's head shot up as I moved his knees aside to make room for me between them. His eyes were wide on my face, breaths panting.

"Are you—" He stopped on the words, swallowing hard and searching my face. He let out a long breath and smiled at me. "Are you trying to kill me?"

I sighed in relief. I really hadn't wanted him to check on me again. I didn't know if I was all right, but I knew what I wanted. And that was to tear Matthieu down one piece of pleasure at a time. To own him in the moment and to pretend I was in control and not just a slave to old habits.

"*Un petit mort*," I quoted. A little death.

Matthieu huffed a laugh, hand reaching up to slide over his face. He stiffened and then pressed his fingers to his nose, a soft growl echoing in the small space as he smelled me there. Distracted, Matthieu didn't notice as I leaned in, rucking his sweater up. His stomach flexed as I sucked a kiss on his ribs, my hands returning to the crotch of his jeans, one working at the top button while the other stroked the ridge of his length through the fabric.

I kissed my way down his right side and then again down his left, my hands keeping busy over his erection. His own hands were back on the seat, fingers digging into the cushions, flexing with every strained puff of breath. When I undid the zipper and reached to the waistband of his jeans, looking up at Matthieu, his vision was glazed with hunger, cheeks and throat flushed red.

He muttered something in French as he lifted his hips and helped me pull his jeans and boxer briefs down his thighs. It'd been a long time since I was in a French class, but the few familiar words I caught combined with his tone led me to think he might've been insulting himself.

"I want my mouth on you. My hands on you," Matthieu breathed out as his cock bobbed free, long and uncut and red with angry arousal. He blinked slowly at me, stomach exposed and twitching as I teased my fingertips over the insides of his thighs. "This is your show. But just know I'm desperate for you."

I swallowed at the words, at the ragged tone of his voice, and nodded once. I wouldn't be able to resist him. I wanted those things too. But first I needed or wanted to know if he would—if he *could* let me have the control when it came to his pleasure.

Matthieu cursed again, a rough combination of English and French, as I wrapped one hand around his base. He had a curve in his length, bowing toward my face, one I was pretty sure would feel fantastic brushing inside of me. The head of his cock was weeping, and I sat up on my knees, lapping my tongue over the slit to catch the fluid. Velvety and burning, like a shot of good alcohol. Matthieu snarled and froze at the touch, his breathing loud in the small space.

I did it again and he released a long, quaking groan, thighs flexing and stomach jumping, his entire body fighting the urge to pounce and take control. But he held still, even as I took him deeper in my mouth, pumped his length with my hand and cupped his balls.

I didn't usually go down on the betas I met in the club. I wanted to make sure that *I* got off on those excursions, not the random partners I met. This also wasn't something I'd been bullied into with Indy. It might've been Matthieu who was groaning and moaning at the feel of my mouth on his pulsing cock, but I was getting wetter too, the longer he held still and let me have my way.

This was something I'd never asked for with an alpha. Alphas didn't give up control, and to be honest, I had been so determined to catch one because I'd wanted that thrill of surrendering. Matthieu's surrender was twice as heady as any of the early nights with Buzz or any other alpha who'd given me an hour of their time.

I licked stripes up his length, sucked at his tip until he was shaking in my hands, and then pulled him deep into my mouth with long drags and bobs of my head till he hit the back of my throat. Underneath my hand at his base, his knot grew swollen and pulsing, begging for attention.

"Fuck, *merde*. Lola, *Christ*," Matthieu chanted a long litany of expletives and pleas as I toyed with him. His fingers squeaked over the leather, leaving sweaty handprints behind.

I wanted him to touch me again. I wanted his hands in my hair, tugging. Or even on the back of my neck, guiding me to the right pace, forcing me deeper on his length. He never so much as bucked, even while I rolled his sac in my hand and mouthed down to his base where they met.

"Touch," I said, lifting my head just long enough to catch my breath.

Matthieu's hands flew off the seat, but they weren't forceful. They scooped my hair up away from my face, piling it on the back of my head in one of his hands, the other resting gently over the back of my neck, thumb stroking my cheek. I squeezed my hand harder around his knot and sucked, hollowing my cheeks and taking Matthieu as deeply as I could. Matthieu moaned and then purred as I pulled slowly up, licking a swirl over his head and mouthing down the underside of his length. When I made it back to the tip, there was a small dribble of fluid waiting for me.

"I'm so fucking close," Matthieu rumbled.

So I did it all again, Matthieu stiff as a board in the seat as he sank into my mouth until my nose was against my own gripping fist. A long line of curses fell from his lips as I drew back up, panting gasps as I teased his cock with kisses and licked away the pre-cum. On the fourth slow deep thrust into my mouth, he gave in.

"Don't stop, Lola. Please, please don't stop."

My hand left his sac just long enough to give an encouraging squeeze to the back of his hand. And then Matthieu was urging me faster, deeper, both of us desperate to see him crashing over the edge.

"Now," Matthieu hissed, tugging on my hair.

I forced myself to relax and kept sucking and pulling as Matthieu arched and let out a long shattering, low howl of pleasure as he exploded on my tongue, knot pounding his pulse against my palm. He was fiery down my throat, the warmth spreading through me even as I gagged a little. I eased up and caught my breath, slowly pulling away, careful to catch every drop. When my tongue flicked over his head, Matthieu growled.

His hands grabbed me by my neck and arm, dragging me back up against his chest. I met his lips in a rough kiss, trying to keep all his flavor to myself as his tongue ravaged my mouth. He turned me on his lap, almost like a bridal carry, so that I was laying in his arms and against the side of the car. Suddenly, his hands were everywhere—squeezing on my breast, gripping the back of my bare thighs, and then up, hooking under my wet panties and thrusting into my aching sex.

I shouted at the sudden intrusion, and Matthieu swallowed the sound, tongue stroking against mine, his fingers pumping roughly into me, thumb hunting for my clit. I thrashed in his hold and his free hand clamped on the back of my neck, holding me in place. Panic spiked, but so did ecstasy as he found my clit and my g-spot at the same moment, thumb and fingers manipulating me into a sudden, shocking orgasm.

The anxiety melted away as I arched and then collapsed

under the thick and drugging feeling that followed the orgasm. Matthieu's kiss softened into gentle presses and pulls, and my arms twined around his shoulders, fingers slipping through silky strands. His touch was careful too, slowly guiding me through sweet aftershocks.

"That's it," Matthieu murmured. "You didn't think I'd leave you wanting, did you, Lolotte?"

The name made me shiver, as did the shallow but steady pumping of his fingers.

"You *almost* followed the rules," I said, leaning back against the car and sharing a smile with him. I wasn't mad, I was just—

I gasped as his thumb brushed my over-sensitive clit again. I tried to scoot back, but Matthieu shook his head, touch following.

"No, not done yet," Matthieu whispered, curling his fingers inside of me and then pushing in his ring finger too to stretch me wider.

My mouth and eyes opened wide on a silent gasp. "But—"

"I want you dripping down my wrist," Matthieu said, gazing down at me, hair mussed from my hands. "I want your legs to shake as you walk into that nest. If you want to come, you can ask and I'll make sure you do. But I want to fuck you with my fingers—hm, and maybe my mouth too, I think—until we get to the house."

My heart skipped a beat and my legs fell open, involuntary permission for Matthieu to do whatever *the hell* he wanted to me.

"Is that all right, Lola?" Matthieu's head ducked down, cheek nuzzling against mine, scent-marking me in a way that was meant to happen *before* you had your cock down a girl's throat, not after. "Would you like that?"

Alphas were dangerous. That was still true. It's just that the danger of Matthieu wasn't that he would hurt me. It was that I was already addicted to how *good* he made me feel.

His thumb rolled over my clit and my head lolled on my

shoulders, a soft whimper escaping. Matthieu dragged a wet kiss over my jaw up to my ear, sucking on the lobe. I rocked into his touch, hands clutching his shoulders and the nape of his neck.

"Yes, I want that," I whispered.

Lola
27

My legs *did* shake as we walked into the house, and the insides of my thighs burned from the friction of Matthieu's beard. Once again, the house wasn't what I was expecting; it was cozy and the halls Matthieu led me through were tighter, the building clearly historic and made from stone and mortar. It was a large but humble house, with worn wooden furniture and a brighter interior to make up for the smaller spaces. It was built on the top of a hill, the rooms cascading down to make a bigger home out of what looked like a two-story Tudor style.

Matthieu's thumb stroked the back of my hand as he guided me down the stairs. Rake's nest was on the last floor, and with every step, worries plagued me.

Matthieu stopped us at the bottom of the stairs, sliding my bag off his shoulder and dropping his coat over the arm of a chair, turning to face me and pulling me against his chest. The hall was dark and it was quiet. Was everyone else in the house asleep or were the walls thick? The driver had dropped us off and left, and I'd expected to see Leo or Wes when we got in, but there was no sign of anyone.

"What's wrong?" Matthieu whispered, head bending to rest against mine. "Are you afraid of the heat? Or upset? Lola, if I—"

"I'm worried Rake will be angry," I answered, keeping my eyes down. "Or Leo will be hurt. I should've thought of it before. No, I *did*. It just didn't stop me."

Matthieu was quiet for a long time, his hands stroking over my back. He lifted his head, and I forced the courage to look up at him. There was a light on in the stairwell overhead that illuminated half his face, and his expression was... thoughtful maybe.

"I hadn't considered it, if I'm honest. I was so..." He shook his head, lips twitching, and then sobered again. "For what it's worth, I don't *think* you have anything to be worried over."

My brow furrowed. "Rake is so used to people using him to get to his alphas."

Matthieu's eyebrows bounced. "Is that what you did? Are you no longer interested in Rake and Leo?"

"No, of course noooot..." I narrowed my eyes and cocked my head as Matthieu grinned. "Okay, that's...a point."

"Hmm," Matthieu hummed and pulled me up to my tiptoes, mouth slanting over mine for a deep and lingering kiss. "Sore?"

I shook my head. Matthieu had been thorough and considerate in every aspect. "Weak in the knees, yes. Still wet? Yup. But not sore."

Matthieu purred, his stare hovering over me, eyes warm and holding a hint of his smile. He sighed and stepped away. "If I keep you locked away for my own purposes Rake *will* be angry," Matthieu said, taking my hand again and picking up my bag. "Do you want me to come in with you?"

I bit my lip and thought it over. It was tempting. Matthieu might keep my head distracted from the fact that there were two other alphas there. But it might also make Rake feel like I was there for Matthieu and not for him. Plus, if Rake was angry, it needed to be with me and me alone.

"No, I think it's better if I go in alone," I said, squeezing his hand.

The door to the nest was at the end of the hall, a few doors open on bedrooms.

"I'm on the next floor up," Matthieu said. "And there's a bathroom here just before the nest."

Even the bathroom was comparatively small to those in the city house, but there was still a decently sized glass shower stall in the corner, and a clawfoot tub.

"There's a short hall after the door, just to help make the nest more private, and it's...cozy from what I remember," Matthieu said. His eyes were on my face as I stared at the heavy wooden door. "I'm sure I could take Leo's room on this floor if you'd like me to be nearby?"

It was only that he sounded as anxious to be near as I was to have him, that made me nod. "If you don't mind, that would be nice."

"Of course," Matthieu said, stepping in close. I rose on my own, meeting him halfway for the kiss and then again for another.

It had been two, maybe three hours in the backseat of a limo, not weeks of dating, but something between Matthieu and I already felt...settled. It was probably just the high of his scent and the over-generous amount of orgasms he'd gifted me with on the drive.

"You walk into that nest now, or I'll have you in bed with me in two minutes," Matthieu whispered against my lips before sucking the bottom one, dragging his teeth over its fullness.

I caught my breath and Matthieu stepped back, smiling with a tightness around the corner of his eyes. I took my bag from him and fumbled at the doorknob, sneaking in and stealing one last shadowy glimpse of him before shutting the door behind me. All it took was a full breath alone in the space, and my eyes widened. The short hall was dimly lit, small bulbs offering a soft glow, and there were thick soft robes hanging from hooks along the wall. It was also oppressively thick with Rake's perfume, Caleb's warmth, and Cyrus' champagne bubbles. Any hints of Leo were buried under the rest.

Voices bled through the next door, gentle and calm sounding from where I stood, and I took a moment to adjust to the blend of alpha and omega. I sniffed my shoulder, and

Matthieu cut through everything else. My heartbeat was rioting, but my core already throbbed, some memory of Matthieu and the prospect of what I'd walk in on. I set my bag down on the floor and crouched, rifling through the contents until I found the 'lock' I'd ordered online. I tucked it and its remote into my pocket and then stood, preparing to knock on the door.

Instead, it opened, Leo ducking furtively into the hall and then stopping suddenly with the door cracked behind him. God, the air was so much heavier already, leaving me gasping and wavering in place. Leo snapped the door shut and then jumped forward.

"Lola," he sighed, scooping me up in his arms. He was a little sweaty, and his skin was hot, and he was covered in Rake and Caleb. He hummed, taking a deep breath of me, and then paused.

Matthieu. My throat was tight, waiting for him to push me away, but instead, Leo's arms circled tighter around my waist.

"Did you…have a nice drive?" he asked, and then he let out a soft laugh.

"Leo, I-I'm so sorry—"

"Hey." His head leaned back, eyes searching my face. He looked tired but happy, and his smile only grew as he took me in. "Hey, I was only teasing." He pecked my lips, and I swooned into the kiss until it deepened. "It was nice, right? You aren't… Matthieu wouldn't have—"

"No, nothing like that, I-I dunno who leapt first but…" I cleared my throat, stroking my cheek against Leo's. "You're not mad."

"I'm not mad, Lola," Leo soothed, kissing my forehead. "It's hard to explain, but pack is…it's like an extension of myself, right? Matthieu and I may not seem as close as Caleb and I, but we're pack. If you're happy, I'm happy. Now, Matthieu texted to say you were probably freaking out in here. Any second thoughts? I can sneak you out, you know."

I let out a long breath through pursed lips, steadying myself, and shook my head. "No, I'm good."

"Yeah?"

"Yeah," I nodded.

"He's been...kind of working up to another round I think," Leo said. "Seeing you will probably set him off for real."

It was a gentle warning. If I went in now, Rake would need more than just a cuddle. *But what'd you put the lock in your pocket for if you thought you were just cuddling?* I reminded myself.

"I'm ready."

Leo leaned in for another kiss, licking and sweet and lazy. He pulled away grinning. "You smell like an alpha. He's gonna beg so bad."

I blushed and then Leo took my hand, turning back to the door. *Just breathe*, I told myself.

Except I took a breath as the door swung open, and it was like being slammed under a wave of sex and chocolate and champagne, a caress that stroked directly between my legs and made me whimper. Leo pulled me along through the doorway and stepped aside, and I choked on the sight before me.

Rake was on his side between his alphas, their hands and mouths stroking up his sides and over his chest, tongues licking down his stomach and up his throat. Rake was twisting and moaning between them. Damn, Cyrus was *ripped*. I blinked at his shining, ridged chest and then tore my eyes away from the trio before I could get too enraptured with Caleb's perfectly rounded ass. The nest was smaller than I expected, with dim lights around the room pointed almost like spotlights at the center of the pillowed floor where the group was clustered. The ceiling was so low, I suspected Caleb had to duck when he stood up. There was no furniture, just an endless mattress of a floor cluttered with pillows and blankets pushed aside, and the three busy bodies.

"Hey, baby. I brought you a surprise," Leo said.

Rake whimpered and then gasped, wiggling out from between his alphas as he caught sight of me.

"Lola! Ohmigod, Lola," he jumped up on wobbling legs, heading straight for me. Behind him, Caleb seemed to roll away with a grateful gasp, collapsing against the wall, soon joined by a panting Cyrus.

And then all I could see was Rake, wrapping himself around me, body slick with sweat and skin feverish, his dark curls plastered to his head. He was hard against my stomach, already soaking pre-cum through the thin fabric of my dress as he nudged unconsciously against me. With one deep breath in my hair, Rake moaned, his hands on my back clutching.

"Fuuuck," he breathed, arms immediately trying to drag me down into the bed.

I met his wet, licking kiss, steadying him with my hands on his jaw, trying to gentle the hungry ravage of his teeth and tongue.

"Easy, Rake," Caleb said in a firm tone from the corner of the room.

Rake sighed into my mouth and softened, Leo helping guide me down to my knees, his presence safe and welcome at my back.

"You smell so good," Rake whined. "I *knew* Matt was interested in you, that quiet French bastard." I hiccuped, worried Rake was angry, but when I pulled away he had a drowsy grin on his lips. "Was he sweet to you, huh?"

I swallowed hard and nodded, overly aware of the stares from the alphas on the other side of the small room. I tried not to think about the fact that I was alone in a room with four men, all of whom were naked.

Leo. Rake. Caleb. Cyrus. I played their names over in my head. They weren't strangers. I was safe.

"Are you sore?" Rake asked, leaning in again and burrowing his face into my neck. His hands slid down my back to my ass, and he rocked himself against my hips, working his cock in the folds of my skirt.

Rake smelled like chocolate warming over the stove, and

every breath I took was like drinking down thick syrupy spoonfuls of his scent. I slipped my fingers into his thick strands, scratching my nails over his scalp and smiling as he shook against me.

"I'm not sore," I answered into his cheek.

"Will you stay?" he rasped.

Leo's hands were gentle on my back, mostly holding me up as Rake leaned heavily into me, body moving in small unconscious thrusts like he was just *waiting* to get inside of me. I had a chance to change my mind. I could wait and come back to the room when Rake was a little less amped up. He would understand.

But in that small nest room, surrounded by perfumes and pheromones, with Rake's hands roving and pleading with me, I wanted to stay.

"Yes," I said, and then Rake's tongue was in my mouth, fucking against my own tongue, his hand rucking up my skirt.

I grinned and laughed into the kiss as he started to whine and rut against me, trying to push me backward into the mattress.

"You smell like an alpha, and it's driving me fuckin' crazy," Rake rasped.

I stroked my hands down to his shoulders as he butted me up against Leo's chest, and then I gripped and pushed. Rake was pliable and with one nudge from me, he let himself fall back, dragging me over him with his hands on my ass. I crawled over his lap, laughing as Rake's hips bucked under my skirt, searching for my core.

Matthieu had my panties somewhere, they'd gotten in the way at a certain point in the car. *Probably while he was wearing your thighs as earrings*, I reminded myself, a flash of heat in my core at the memory. Twice as tempting was the picture of Rake below me, glowing with flush and sweat, face torn in the agony of heat. I settled down, sliding myself along his cock as he tried to burrow inside of me. My palm on his chest held him still as the other reached into my pocket, pulling out the toy remote first.

I turned and held it out to Leo, whose eyebrows bounced as he took it from my fingers.

"You'll get the hang of it," I said, smiling at him as he grinned back. Then I pulled out the lock next. It looked fairly innocent, almost like a thick rubber bracelet, with ridges for decoration. I'd gotten the sleek black version, the 'Cadillac' of locks according to the site, and when Rake's eyes tore away from my skirt to see it in my fingers, they grew wide.

"You didn't," he gasped.

"I did," I said, waggling my eyebrows.

"Fucking *Christmas*," Rake whispered, settling beneath me.

I glanced over to the corner of the room, remembering our audience. Cyrus and Caleb had both covered up slightly with a blanket, and Cyrus was curled into Caleb, sucking on his throat, hands above the blanket. Caleb was watching me, one hand holding Cyrus to him but the other making the blanket bounce slightly. He stopped as I caught him, our gazes locking, and I almost wanted to tell him to toss the blanket aside, to let me watch.

But I wasn't the *real* alpha in the room, even if I would play one for Rake.

"Unzip me," I said to Leo.

Rake moaned and rocked up, his cock weeping against my sex as Leo pulled the zipper down and helped me out of the dress. The lock was a tight fit over Rake's cock since he was already plenty aroused, but he pushed into the sleeve, the fluid already seeping down his length making the glide smoother. When it sat snugly around his base, almost seamless with his girth, Rake guided me to balancing above him.

"I missed you," Rake murmured, brow furrowed and chest heaving, trying to be sweet even when I knew all he really wanted was for me to sink down and surround him.

So I did, gasping as he filled me. Matthieu had been prepping me for almost two hours, making the way just the right amount of easy for Rake and I.

"What should I do?" Leo asked.

"Anything," I gasped, rocking and feeling the perfect fit of

Rake inside me, and the slightly less giving texture of the lock at my opening. "Everything."

A moment later, the 'lock' started to buzz, Rake and I both shouting at the sudden vibration. Leo laughed behind me.

"Oh, this is going to be fun."

I bent and Rake arched to meet me, our mouths connecting in a fierce latch of lips as I started to bounce and grind, the vibration teasing my sensitive opening.

"Oh *fuck*," Rake cried. "Oh, god, Lola. I'm gonna—" His body bowed, throat flexed and strained as he let out a strangled cry, heat and slick bursting inside of me.

I giggled and rode him harder, letting my clit crash against his skin. He bucked into the feeling, one arm wrapping around my hips while the other reached a hand up into my hair, tangling it in his fist and pulling the way I liked.

"Get her bra off. I wanna suck her pretty tits," Rake rasped.

Leo followed the orders quickly, dropping the bra down my arms, not even pulling it off me before Rake was bowing forward, lips wrapping around one nipple. He sucked like he was trying to pull an orgasm up from where we were connected right through my breast, and a moment later I thought he might succeed, a throb starting in my core that made my toes curl and my hands clench in the mattress.

"Turning it up," Leo said, and I gasped on a silent scream as the vibration thrummed, harder and fuller, even deeper inside of me.

Rake's knees bent, heels in the mattress forcing himself up in rough thrusts, his hands holding me for the taking. I heard a groan from the corner and my eyes fell shut, resisting the urge to look, to see Cyrus and Caleb watching me with their omega. Their stares were hot on my side, Leo's hands soft on my spine, helping me keep pace even as my legs trembled.

Rake switched breasts, teeth scraping roughly, his angle shifting deeper inside of me, and I came in a sudden crash, like lightning snapping through my veins, tickling and scorching at the same time. Rake joined me with a moan against my chest, the wet rush gushing out between us. He pushed up, wanting me on my back, but Leo helped me hold him down.

"Not yet, babe," Leo said.

Leo's hands soothed my trembling back, and then cupped my ass. They moved lower again, making Rake moan and thrash, and then trailed up. His fingertips slid between my cheeks, and I stiffened as Rake carried on fucking up into me, breathless moans hitching with every slapping connection of our skin. Leo teased a slick finger against the sensitive skin of my ass, pressing softly against my hole.

"More or less?" Leo spoke into my ear, settling close and making sure I could see him when I turned my head.

I held my breath and looked down. Rake was underneath me, falling back into the mattress, his hands moving to my chest to hold my breasts and massage them as his pace slowed, and he stared at where we were joined. And it was Leo behind me, offering me more, more connection with the both of them, more pleasure. I was safe.

"More," I said.

Leo's lips pressed to my spine, and his fingers took the same path, gathering the combined release that slipped out from me and using it to dip the tip of his finger into my hole. I relaxed onto Rake's chest, the vibration of the lock humming against my clit as he stroked steadily inside of me, and sighed as Leo teased me open.

We'd been testing this next step for ourselves for weeks now. I wasn't shy about the idea, although the reality of being pinned between two bodies sometimes threw me back into dark places. But there was nothing about this moment that reminded me of my nights with the Hangmen. Rake's nest was too full of the scents of people I cared about, people who cared about me.

"I want you, I want you both," I moaned, rocking off of Rake and toward Leo, ready and waiting.

LEO
28

I swallowed hard, watching my fingers sink into and stretch Lola. Caleb had tossed me the lube, and I was using it liberally on her and myself to get her ready.

She'd said that she was open to this, to taking me and Rake at the same time—and I'd nearly had a heart attack the day I'd seen her and Rake in the shower together, a little bright pink plug peeking out of Lola's ass. It was now just a matter of whether or not any unexpected anxieties crept up. Looking down at her as she whimpered and rocked on top of Rake, their mouths fused together and hands holding tight to one another, I was fairly certain tonight was a good time to test the idea. The room was thick with the sexual frenzy of the days of heat, and the last time Lola had looked at me, her eyes had been dilated with arousal.

I wished I had a bond connecting me to her the way I did with Caleb and Rake. Rake was like a constant pulse in my cock, refusing to let me escape the frenzy of the heat until he was done with it too. And Caleb…

I glanced at him, found his lips parted and tongue darting out to wet them as he watched me kneel between Lola and Rake's legs. He was like a sensitive nerve in my heart, aching to be closer, to be in the midst of our trio. I'd caught little snippets of wanting from him for the past month or so, and with it confusion and worry, even little moments of jealousy. It was coming together now. Caleb wanted Lola. I could've crowed with happiness.

Lola was falling into an open place in our pack that I'd previously only thought of as comfortable breathing room. We loved each other, but we gave each other space to move in and out of the pack. We revolved around Rake the way packs did around their omega; he was our sun to orbit. But Lola was like a magnetic force, drawing us in and holding us together, creating one planet out of many.

She had no idea.

"God, Leo, please," Lola whined, rocking back against my fingers. The heat was riding her now too, removing the usual anxiety of this act from her shoulders.

"That's it gorgeous," I said, beaming down at her as she started to race over Rake's cock. She was working up to another orgasm, and there was no way I was gonna miss that feeling. I pulled my fingers free, and Lola gasped. "Ready?"

"Yes," Rake moaned, thrusting up and trying to push Lola against me.

She rose up on her palms and shot a smile over her shoulder. She was trying to keep her head turned away from where Caleb and Cyrus were together in the corner, and as much as I wanted to push her into connecting with them, I knew pushing was the exact opposite of what she needed. She and Matthieu had fallen together naturally, it seemed. The same might happen with the others when she was ready.

I took my slippery cock in hand, pumping lightly, holding Lola steady by her shoulder, and lined myself up at her ass. I pressed to her opening, stroking her back gently to remind her to relax until the head of my cock nudged into the tight ring of muscle.

"Fuck," I whispered at the first clasp of her around me. I sank in with gentle nudges, Rake unable to resist echoing them with soft thrusts from beneath until I was deep enough to feel him and the hum of the vibrating lock. "Oh, god," I hissed.

I gathered Lola up from Rake's chest and wrapped my arms around her, pulling her to my chest as I bent slightly over her back. Rake and I were brushing against one another inside of her, separated by a thin wall. Lola shuddered, head rolling and exposing her neck to me, and I latched onto her throat, sucking and swirling my tongue over the pounding drum of her pulse.

"Lock," Rake gasped. "Lock, please."

"Let me," Caleb said, sitting up from the wall.

If Lola heard Caleb, she didn't show it, or at least she didn't care. God, I wanted to feel her, to know if she was still nervous now or if she was as deeply absorbed in the heat as the rest of us. She seemed like it, rolling her hips, grinding against Rake, and then rocking back to meet my careful thrusts.

Caleb studied the narrow little remote with interest, lips curved and his cock bobbing with interest. I knew the moment he tightened the lock. Rake bellowed on the mattress, taking Lola's hips in his hands and rutting up inside of her. I stopped moving, the feel of him striking against me and making Lola squeeze and flutter almost more than I could stand.

"Yes, yes, holy shit," Rake muttered, riding Lola from below.

She let out a soft sob, almost making me pull her off Rake in case he was hurting her, and then I felt her clamp down on us both, shuddering and sagging with the force of her orgasm. My teeth sank into her throat, and her hand flew to the back of my head, holding me there. Rake groaned and twisted, eyes rolling back in his head briefly as he came.

"More or less, love?" Caleb asked, reaching out to us.

My eyes widened as Caleb's fingers took Lola's chin, not mine, turning her head to look back at him.

"More," Lola moaned, lifting her face to him, eyes blinking.

I shared a brief glance with Caleb, my head nodding to encourage him, and then he bent and grazed his lips over Lola's, pulling away and letting her chase him. I arched, pressing into her, and tilted her head to catch the corner of her mouth, satisfying the kiss he'd left her craving.

"Can you take me like this?" Caleb asked me.

"Yes," I breathed against Lola's lips. "Is that all right, gorgeous?"

Lola nodded, head limp on her own neck, falling forward as Rake struggled to sit up. With a few fumbles and laughs, Rake was on his knees, Lola pressed between our chests as we peppered her shoulders and neck and jaw and lips with kisses.

After days of the heat, it didn't take much work for Caleb to have me ready. I'd been lubed up and fucked every which way, but *this*? This was absolutely about to be my favorite moment in my entire life. I sucked on Lola's ear lobe, moaning as Caleb entered me from behind, every sensitive nerve in my body firing at all cylinders. Lola squeezed around my cock, and I learned that strange and magical sensation of nuzzling against Rake inside of her, while Caleb filled me up until I thought I could taste him in my throat.

The air was hazy. Matthieu's scent was different on Lola's skin, sweeter and brighter. Her voice added a new harmony in the chorus of moans that was so familiar to my ears. When Cyrus couldn't resist the siren call of us together, he wrapped himself around Rake's back, taking his dizzy begging omega with one stroke. Lola cried out, her hands fluttering and catching one of mine and one of Cyrus', eyes wide and unseeing on the ceiling. She came with a long shout, dragging Rake over the edge with her, wetness running down the inside of her thighs and dripping over my sac.

Snaps of ecstasy were biting at my spine, warning me I was close.

"Don't stop," Lola gasped.

The vibration grew stronger and she arched with a shout, head falling back onto my shoulder, Rake leaning in to kiss me. I sucked on his tongue, felt him shudder against Lola, throb inside of her.

We were falling into a rhythm, two opposing and equal forces rocking gently to meet inside of the beautiful woman in our arms.

I loved her. I loved her so much, and I'd been biting the

words on my tongue for weeks, waiting to look into her eyes and know the moment was right. That she would believe me and *believe* she had a place with us. It was so obvious. She was *pack*. I was only a beta, and I'd known it. Rake's begging for her during his heat was proof too. Based on the way Cyrus was staring avidly at her face, he was over his reserve of just days ago.

We just needed Lola to be on the same page.

I pushed one hand down between Rake and Lola to roll her clit. Her voice was a constant and exquisite collection of shattered, pleading sounds, and she was so slick everywhere I touched, my fingers slipped out of place.

"Nearly there," I rasped in her ear. "One more time, gorgeous."

Tears rolled out of her eyes but she nodded, pulling away from Rake's kiss and searching for mine. Caleb's hand was on her waist, Cyrus' fingers still locked with hers.

It wasn't a rough union, but it was deep and intense, my own emotions high in my throat as color flashed behind my eyes. I pressed in deep, Rake sinking in and settling, the alphas taking charge of the thrust and soft pound until Lola shattered, the sweetest, trembling sound on her lips as she clamped around me. I came, biting on her lip and trying to swallow my groan as hot spikes of pleasure burst out of me.

She was ours. If she didn't see it now, she would soon. Lola was pack.

Lola

29

The others retreated, and I collapsed back onto the mattress with only Rake. He was still bucking and whimpering, still hard. He was on top of me, brow furrowed and throat flexed, and I stretched my neck as he held my thighs around his hips. I latched onto his throat, and Rake groaned, pace hiccuping.

"Release the lock," Leo rasped, settling down near me.

"Not yet," Rake gasped. He turned his head down to meet my eyes, face pleading. "Please. Please a little more."

I had no strength, and his thrusting inside of me was almost a numb feeling. Not painful, but not exactly stimulating either. I was pretty sure I was used up. But I nodded and pulled his face to mine, sucking on his lips. Still, whoever had the remote turned the vibration down, and the burning pulse against my clit settled and softened into something pleasant. I hummed and Rake whimpered.

I stroked my hands over his sticky skin, the wet squish of our releases splashing a little against my sex and stomach every time he thrust in.

"Lola," Rake mumbled against my mouth. "Oh, god, Lola."

"It's all right," I whispered, combing my fingers through his hair.

"Fuck, it's fucking heaven," Rake groaned, and the burst of another release warmed me and left a soft echo in me that made me shift into him, as if I might still have it in me to come again.

How was that even fucking possible? I had to be high as a kite. I'd just been the center of the most insane sexual sandwich, there should've been no room left to want more.

Rake landed heavily on top of me, body still working, trying to drag more from the both of us. The pressure and the heat of him was stifling, but I buried my face into his neck, wrapped my arms tight around his back, and held on as he rocked and twisted. Leo was close, kissing my shoulders, my arms, Rake's back, touching us both. Rake came again and I gasped as a soft, teasing flutter rushed through me.

"Again," Rake whispered in my ear, and I whined, turning to catch Leo's kiss.

He fit his hand back between us, fingertips pressing over my clit as Rake created the perfect pressure with his shallow thrusts. The orgasm came on in a soft slide over my skin and I was under it before I realized, fingers pulling on Rake's hair, legs tight around his hips.

"Now," Leo said.

And then Rake was gushing and groaning, shaking on top of me, one wet burst after another, his mouth finding mine to shout into our kiss. It was filthy and explicit and noisy, but it was also satisfying. I'd given Rake this experience he'd never really had before. I wasn't an alpha, no, and I wasn't even good at pretending it, but I'd made him desperate and animal and demanding more from me and I'd delivered everything he'd asked for.

Rake's lips slid away and he panted into my hair, finally still aside from his heaving breaths. Leo reached for his shoulders, and I caught his hands.

"Let him stay for a minute," I said, breathless from Rake's weight, from the whole extended experience, but happy in the moment.

"Only a minute," Leo murmured, kissing my forehead. "He can't hog you. Or crush you."

Rake sighed and kissed my throat, lowering my legs down

to the bed and making me wince as he shifted inside of me. Just one more minute.

I'D SLEPT hard for at least an hour or so, but when I woke again, pressed between Rake and Leo, I was restless. And shivering, despite the heat of them on either side of me. The air was a little stale now, less perfume and more pungent, and I was keenly aware of Cyrus and Caleb on either side of my boyfriends.

Caleb had kissed me. Barely, but it was still a kiss. They'd both been up close and personal with me now, even if we hadn't had sex directly. Kind of. Where *were* the lines on this sort of thing? In the haze, it had seemed natural to have them close and now…

I wasn't *upset*. I was overwhelmed. And in the quiet pause of the night, being overwhelmed was more than a passing feeling. Every second I lay awake while the others slept, it grew stronger, a steady pressure on my chest.

I knew what came next. A few more minutes of lying here and letting my brain run like a car without a driver, and I'd be gasping for air and hitting a panic attack.

It was tricky to slide out from between Leo and Rake, their limbs were scattered on top of me, and even one of Cyrus' hands had landed near my ass. I did it in slow shifts, my eyes closed as I felt my way carefully out of the tangle of men. When I was up and kneeling between their legs I looked back once to find Leo and Caleb wearing twin frowns, their brows folded in the same troubled expression, as if Leo could sense the loss of me and shared it with Caleb.

I crawled to the entrance of the nest, glancing back and pausing as Rake scooted into the empty space I'd left, Leo's frown smoothing away. *There, like you never needed to be there in the first place.* I forced the poisonous thought back and stumbled my way out of the room and into the short hall. There were only four robes hanging up, and I'd just left my dress inside the nest, so I grabbed my bag from the floor and snuck into the hall, running for the bathroom. Rake's cum was dripping out of me, and I was sore and weak, every muscle calling for mercy.

I cranked the hot water on in the shower, twitching as it came out cold, smacking against my tender skin. My knees shook and I sank down to the tiled floor of the shower, the glass door swinging shut behind me. The spray grew warm and misty, rolling into my tangled hair, running in thin rivulets down my back. I sat there, the anxiety of the nest going numb and quiet until my hair was fully soaked.

A light went on in the bathroom, footsteps scuffing, and I huddled under the water, stiff and staring at the fogged glass.

"Lola?"

Matthieu.

"I-in here," I said, voice weak.

The glass door cracked behind my back, and a moment later Matthieu was inside the stall with me. He knelt, arms scooping around my back and under my knees, pulling me onto his lap. One hand reached up to push my hair out of my eyes, and I stared up at him. There was a pillow crease on his cheek, and he was wearing soft cotton pants that were rapidly growing soaked.

"What's wrong?" Matthieu asked, shifting me in his lap.

I glanced down and frowned. "Matthieu, why are you in the shower with your pajama pants on?"

"Because I saw you curled up on the tile. What's happened?"

I gaped at him and shook my head. "Nothing. Not *nothing*, I just…woke up and felt, I dunno, edgy, I guess. Overwhelmed."

Matthieu sighed and nodded, relaxing around me and snuggling me close, pressing his lips to my forehead.

"Are you sore? Weak?"

"A little sore. Mostly weak. I was working up the energy to wash off."

He leaned back, stretching across the space of the stall so

his feet rested against one wall and his back against the other. The water ran over us both, soaking the fabric of his pants, and into his hair. He had gray curls over his chest and my fingers studied them greedily, thoughts clearing as the water rinsed away a whole collection of scents, giving me room to breathe in my own head.

Matthieu's hands smoothed from my shoulders, over my breasts and around my waist, down to my hips, massaging there gently as I sighed and softened into his chest. The ache of my muscles after so much fucking made me groan and close my eyes. There was a brief flare of Matthieu's scent, but he kept his touch caring rather than stimulating and it felt too good to pull away.

"Let me help?"

I nodded immediately. Matthieu bundled me up again and then stood by some massive feat of strength and balance, holding me to his chest and tipping my head back for water to run through my hair.

"Head to toe?" he asked.

"Please," I whispered.

I don't know how he did it, holding me up and reaching for bottles. I braced myself against his shoulders sometimes, or rested my head on his chest as he scrubbed shampoo in my hair. He was tender and thorough and kind. Occasionally his lips would brush my cheek or my shoulder, once even my knees, but never more than briefly.

Any other moment, and I might've dragged him against me and begged for sex, but I meant what I said. I was sore, I was weak, I wasn't in *pain*, but I was well and truly done for the night if not longer. Matthieu seemed to understand. Even as he cleaned between my legs, his touch was careful, efficient, and gentle.

I sighed as the suds ran down my body, Matthieu finished with his task and simply holding me under the water.

"Better?"

I nodded.

"Still anxious?"

The man was a little *too* good at reading me. "I don't think so. Maybe after some sleep I will be, but I think I'm too tired for it right now."

He hummed in agreement, and the water shut off. "Let's get dried off and into bed. Do you want company or privacy?"

"Company."

He picked me up, arms around my hips, and carried me out of the shower, shaking his pants down his hips and leaving them in the stall. There was a small closet just to the left of the stall, and Matthieu pulled out what had to be a full-sized bed version of a fluffy cotton towel, wrapping it around us both like a cloak. It was warm too. The closet was heated.

Fucking rich people and their amazing toys.

"Thank you," I said, my arms around Matthieu's shoulders.

He smiled and lifted his chin to me, and I dipped my head to kiss him briefly.

"Even your lips are swollen, Lolotte," he murmured. "Time to rest. Are you hungry? I can get us a midnight snack."

He carried me across the hall and into the bedroom he'd said was Leo's. It smelled clean, but not in a Leo way, and I figured Leo had probably been in the nest for most of the visit anyway.

"A little hungry," I admitted.

Matthieu set me down on the bed, gave me a quick rub down with the towel, and then whipped the covers back, watching me slide in.

"Wait here. I'll be back with something to tide you over until breakfast."

I hummed and pulled the covers up over my bare skin, the mattress soft and giving beneath me. I smiled at Matthieu's back, the towel wrapped around his body like a toga, and then my eyes fell shut. I never even woke up for the snack.

THE BED DIPPED, and a chapped kiss met my lips. I woke from a heavy, dreamless sleep with warm skin pressed to my back, and found Leo hovering in front of me.

"Can I slide in with you?" he whispered. His eyebrow cocked and he added, "It is my bed after all."

"Mm, please," I answered, scooting back against Matthieu's chest.

Matthieu purred and his arm circled my waist, lips mumbling in my hair. "Want me to go?"

I glanced at Leo anxiously, but he only smiled. "You're fine. Just wanted to check in on our girl."

Matthieu hummed, and his nose burrowed through tangled strands of hair to kiss the back of my neck.

Leo's laughter faded slightly and he scooted in closer, slipping his hand under mine that rested on the pillow. Our fingers tied, and Leo squeezed lightly.

"I was worried maybe last night got to be…too much," Leo whispered. "I know the haze can be pretty powerful and—"

I leaned in and rested my lips against Leo's, hushing his worry. Even my lips were still tender from the night before, and the rest of me was badly in need of some good stretches and maybe a longer soak in the tub.

"I did have a little…fritz afterward," I admitted, pulling my hand free of Leo's and soothing away his wince. "But I'm good now. And I'm good with everything that happened. I just needed to grab some space and…clean up after. How's Rake?" I wanted to offer to check on him, but there was no way I could do another marathon session like the one during the night.

"Still sleeping," Leo said, grinning. "I think you broke the heat, actually. His temperature is down, and Caleb turned on a vent to recirculate the room just a little. Having a 'fritz' is okay, though?"

I nodded. "I'm learning it's part of processing. I'm just going to need to step back sometimes to organize what's happening and separate it from what already happened, yeah?"

Matthieu's arm tightened around my waist, and Leo sighed, his eyes blinking slowly as he nodded.

"Mmkay, as long as you're good now. Wes texted to say breakfast is in progress too, by the way," Leo hummed, eyelids fluttering slowly.

My stomach growled, and Matthieu huffed a laugh against the nape of my neck, goosebumps rising in answer.

"Want me to try and bring you breakfast in bed?" Matthieu asked.

"Please," Leo mumbled.

I twisted under the blanket, remembering very suddenly that Matthieu and I were naked together as my hips brushed against his. Before I could overthink that I'd found myself in bed with an alpha, Matthieu's hands were on my neck, guiding me up his chest to take soft kisses from my mouth.

I pushed myself up, trying to take the blanket with me, covering my bare chest. "I need to get up and move around."

"We'll let Leo sleep then," Matthieu said, sitting up and sliding out from under the covers.

We, just like that. And it was a relief that Matthieu wasn't even asking, actually, surrendering control simpler under the circumstances.

If I'd been aware of Matthieu's body next to mine last night, it was nothing to seeing him naked in front of me. He was surprisingly muscular, although the forms were softer than Leo or Rake's. His legs were delicious though, sculpted like a runner's. He cleared his throat, lips smirking, as he set my bag down on the bed. I glanced back over my shoulder as if that could hide the blush I was sporting, and found Leo face down into the pillow, head turned to me just enough to reveal his parted lips, breath puffing in steady beats.

I pulled the covers up under my arms and flipped open the bag, taking stealthy glances of Matthieu's back and legs flexing as he dressed. He'd already seen me naked, I reminded myself that I didn't need to feel bashful. He'd had a more than thorough opportunity to study me while he'd washed me off in the shower. Still, it seemed different with sunlight falling in through the narrow windows along the ceiling and my head on straight.

He got you off like seventeen times in the back of a limo, idiot. It's a little late for dignity.

I huffed and found myself a change of underwear, giving up on modesty and getting out of bed to dress, groaning slightly as my body reminded me that I'd overdone it with the whole group sex idea. I had brought a comfy old sundress with me, and Matthieu pulled it out of my bag, raising it over my head for me.

"I leave for the city tomorrow night, a bit earlier than the others," Matthieu said, his hands following the path of the fabric, over my shoulders and breasts, around my waist and down to my hips. "Will you stay that long?" I nodded, looking up at him as he stared at his own hands cupping my hips. "And will you come back to the city with me? And stay at the house?"

I went to bite my lip and then immediately remembered why that was a terrible idea. Ouch.

Matthieu, catching my hesitation, hurried to smooth over the moment. "It wouldn't have to be *with* me, if you—"

"I'd like that." I smiled as Matthieu's words halted, and rose up to my tiptoes, his hands guiding me against him as his head bowed for the grazing kiss.

I'd expected Wes to be making a spread of oatmeal, egg whites, and fruit for us, since that was his usual leaning. Instead, I caught the whiffs of grease and meat and fat as we stepped into the rustic, cozy kitchen. I moaned, and Matthieu purred at my back, his hands moving aimlessly over my shoulders.

"Wes, my hero, what are you making?" I sighed, taking in the bright space and the low ceiling, a large yard calling to me through small windows.

Silence followed my question and my eyes moved back to Wes at the stove, only to find him staring back at me, watching as Matthieu's arms twined around my waist and his head dipped to nuzzle my temple. Wes looked... somehow both more and less surprised than I'd expected. Like he knew this was coming, but hadn't expected it so soon. My blush flooded my cheeks and throat as Matthieu pulled away.

"I'll start your coffee," Matthieu murmured.

Wes cleared his throat and shook his head subtly, clearing the awkwardness of his shock with a rare, dimpled grin. "Biscuits, gravy, eggs, and potatoes. From *scratch*, not that frozen shit."

My stomach roared in answer, and I swallowed hard. "God that sounds *amazing*. I'm so hungry," I moaned.

Wes blushed, head nodding jerkily, and he turned back to the stove. "I'll bet."

Matthieu grinned wolfishly at me, and I grabbed the mug in his hands to help hide my blush.

"You should've been around for the pack argument about what Wes cooks for the post-heat meal," Matthieu said, drawing me to his side again.

Wes huffed a laugh and shook his head, and I wondered how I had it in me to admire the shift of muscle that happened under his t-shirt as he moved. "I've given up trying to protect the pack's cholesterol. But there is grapefruit, if anyone has the sense to eat it."

I slipped out from Matthieu's hold and crossed to the basket on the old wooden hutch by Wes, grabbing up one of the heavy grapefruits and flashing him a smile. His curiosity was almost palpable, and he watched me return to Matthieu's side with a keen eye, but he never questioned what had happened.

If he had, I honestly had no idea what I would say. I'd found one more man in this pack of perfection that I was hopelessly unable to resist. One more way to break my heart.

"GETTING ANTSY?" I murmured into Rake's ear later that night.

The entire pack and I were out on the screened-in back porch, shutters turned to reveal the sunset beyond the old mill. The porch was cozy, with a small wood stove and deep, pod-like seating. Caleb, Rake, and I were piled together in a pod, my legs draped over Rake's as he leaned into Caleb's chest. Caleb's hand was resting over my knee, thumb brushing my skin in a warm repetitive path, and Leo was leaning against the tangle of the three of us, sitting on a dense cushion on the floor.

"Not yet," Rake said, although he'd started squirming every few minutes. He must've been resisting the urge to get back to his nest.

I'd napped with him there earlier in the afternoon while the alphas took the opportunity to shower, and it had turned into sating a minor flare-up with Rake fucking me lazily as we lay spooned together. He'd been gentle, but it definitely hadn't left me *less* sore.

"Want me to swap with Cyrus?" I whispered, resting my chin on Rake's shoulder.

He frowned, bottom lip pouting slightly. "I wish I was more…cube shaped."

Leo snorted softly on the floor and I squinted at Rake, who shrugged in response. "I just want you all directly next to me, but there's only one of me and four of you and it's… The geometry's not working out."

Caleb hummed, and I caught his eye. He lifted his eyebrow, arm shifting back to offer the open space of his chest and lap. I only hesitated for a moment, pulling myself out of Rake's arms as he whined, and tiptoeing around Leo to resettle onto Caleb's lap. He was kind of vibrating, and it took me a moment to realize it was a silent purr rumbling in his chest. Leo's neck was arched to grin up at us and with a few shifts, Caleb and I had Rake bundled against us, our arms crossed over his chest.

"Cy!"

"Yes, hun? Aww, you made room for me?" Cyrus pushed up from his armchair in the far corner, immediately wedging himself into the small space left in the loveseat.

It was a miracle the little couch hadn't broken between the four of us. I tried to stifle my giggle, but it drew the eyes of the room. Matthieu's gaze was on me, as hot as the small fire he sat next to. But so were Wes'. He'd been watching me all day, ever since I'd come up for breakfast with Matthieu. If I'd ever had any question about the interest of Rake's unbonded alphas, it was gone now.

You're just a convenient hole to fuck since they can't—

I shut down the nasty words. There was affection between Rake and his two unbonded alphas, friendliness and ease. I hated thinking that Matthieu or Wes might simply be trying to replicate any sexual relationship they were missing with Rake. If that were the case, Matthieu probably would've been all over me in the shower while I'd been coated and full of his omega's scent, not extra careful to avoid hurting or alarming me.

Caleb's purring grew stronger at my back as Leo leaned back against us. His scent was strong and thick, as sweet as an omega's but without creating the pit of hunger in my stomach. I snuggled into him, reaching my free hand down to comb through Leo's hair. My own head tipped back onto Caleb's shoulder, that heady dense blanket of warmth right in front of my nose. Three gulps down, and I was fast asleep.

Lola
30

"Are you *sure* you shouldn't call off work tomorrow and stay one more night?" Rake asked, resting his cheek on my bare breast. He and Leo had talked me into a nooner without any of the alphas, but in another hour or so, I would be heading back to the city with Matthieu.

"I am already walking funny," I said, and Leo huffed. "Plus, I dunno, with this whole corporate espionage thing going on, I probably shouldn't be absent from work at the same time as Cyrus."

"How serious is this thing with Wendy?" Rake asked.

"I'm not sure, honestly. I haven't even told Matthieu everything she and I discussed at dinner. But I feel more confident that I don't want to work for her if she leaves *Designate*."

"Speaking of Matthieu…" Rake said, waggling his eyebrows.

Leo chuckled at my back, and I grimaced and braced myself.

"Lola, don't look like I'm about to bite you. I just wanna know how it happened. And if it'll happen some more. And if maybe I can watch sometime?" Rake laughed at my gobsmacked face. "What? Matthieu and I annoy each other as much as we love each other, but I do still have eyes. I would *love* to see him go to town on you."

"Ohmigod, Rake!"

"I bet he's all like intense about making sure you come

first and—oh! What's that face, what's that?!" Rake wrestled himself up, and Leo helped him roll me onto my back, the pair of them catching my hands and keeping me from hiding my blush.

"Um… It might've…gone the other way," I said, trying to wiggle away.

Rake grinned maniacally above me, teeth gleaming in the faint glow. "Spill, Lollipop."

I huffed and fessed up, explaining about Matthieu filling the car with his scent, and me thinking it was for Rake.

Rake frowned at that. "Wait…why did you think Matthieu and I were a thing?"

"You'd never said you *weren't*, and there was all that stuff between you and Carolyn," I said.

"Pft. That was just because Carolyn never wanted to spend time with Matt around the rest of us. Like she was trying to pretend he didn't have a pack," Rake said, shrugging. "Matt and I don't fuck. We just love each other."

"Right, well, yeah. He explained that," I said. I blushed, and Leo and Rake both raised their eyebrows waiting for me to spill the rest. I swallowed hard and then blurted out that I'd taunted Matthieu with my own arousal and then demanded he let me suck him off. Rake was back on the mattress, curled into my side, and half-hard by the time I finished the story of the drive here and my plentiful orgasms.

"So you guys haven't had sex yet?" Rake asked, licking his lips.

"Not officially, yeah." I released a nervous giggle and then stared at Rake, his gaze intent. "Does it bother you if I do get involved with Matthieu? I don't want to risk—"

Rake leaned forward and kissed me, rocking against my side and letting me feel his arousal, sticky on my skin. "Who's your favorite?" Rake asked.

"What? My favorite? Rake, I…" I frowned at Rake, and then it dawned on me. I shared a quick smile with Leo, and then a long kiss, before I turned back to Rake, pressing my lips to his before answering. "I don't have one."

"Hmm...well, that wasn't the *right* answer. Obviously, I should be the favorite," Rake said, wearing a wicked grin. "But it wasn't wrong either. You are more than welcome to sex it up with Matthieu as much as you like. And, you know, date and be romantic and stuff too. As long as it doesn't mean you don't want to do those things with me."

"We should do more dating and being romantic and stuff with Lola," Leo murmured.

"We should," Rake agreed. "Matt's gonna woo the shit out of her. And probably Caleb soon too. So we have to keep up. In the meantime, though, my manhood feels challenged. Does yours, Leo?"

Leo sat up, rubbing his palms together. "It definitely doesn't, but if you're proposing what I think you are, I'm on board."

A nervous flutter warmed in my belly as Leo moved one of my legs to make room for himself between them, and then settled down onto his stomach.

"What are you two planning?"

"We're planning on beating Matthieu's record," Rake said.

Leo hummed his agreement, head dipping and mouth kissing my soft stomach.

My laugh was breathless. "I have to get ready to go soon. He had, like, an hour more time."

"Yeah, but there's two of us," Rake said, reaching to my chest and cupping a tender breast.

"And we know what sets you off better," Leo said, words rough in my ear.

His head bowed again, lips finding their target immediately, and my eyes squeezed shut. Probably better to let them make their point, right? I gasped as Leo sucked my clit and flicked it with his tongue, fingers diving into his hair.

Definitely. It's good for their egos.

I arched into Leo's kiss and offered up my breasts to Rake. I'd just help them along a little.

"LOLA? WE'RE HOME?"

I woke up frowning, a little pool of wet drool under my cheek, and I sat up so fast my head crashed against the top of the car.

"Oofuck."

Matthieu laughed, sitting up from beneath me, his hands cupping my head. "Aw, shit. Apologies, Lolotte."

My eyes were fixed to the wet spot on his dark t-shirt, and I reached up to quickly wipe my mouth. Maybe he hadn't noticed? Except those perfect crows feet were wrinkling in the corners of his eyes and his lips were twitching.

I sighed and tugged at the collar of his shirt. "Sorry about the…drool thing."

"Forgiven," he said, grinning. "You were talking in your sleep, you know?"

I frowned and sank back on my heels. Matthieu and I had curled up on the deep bench seat of the limousine for the ride back to the city. Since my sleeping had been pretty irregular all weekend, and Matthieu purred like a motor every time we touched, I'd slept nearly the entire way back.

"Was it a nightmare?" I asked.

Oddly enough, Matthieu's smile grew even wider. "No, I think it was a confession of love. To french fries?"

I laughed, pulling my hair off the back of my sweaty neck and into a ponytail, pushing myself out of the limo and stumbling onto the sidewalk. Dreaming of french fries? For once, I regretted not remembering my dreams.

"It gave me an idea for dinner," Matthieu said, sliding more gracefully out of the back of the car and heading for the trunk to grab our bags. "Have you ever had properly French fries? *Pommes frites*?"

My mouth was already watering. I shook my head and he nodded, passing our driver an envelope, probably a generous cash tip. "We'll drop our things inside, and then I'll take us for a drive."

I followed Matthieu up the front steps and into the house, laughing as he took my hand and ditched our bags by the elevators.

"Don't you want to change?" I asked, tugging on the back of the t-shirt I'd drooled on.

"No, we'll... We won't go in. It'll be like a drive-thru, kind of."

"*French* french fries from a drive-thru, in the city?"

"Kind of," Matthieu repeated.

I'd only been down in the bottom level once for a quick swim, and we'd used the elevator to drop us off right by the pool. It was in a long and narrow space with optional jets for resistance, and a beautiful starlight speckled lighting feature on the ceiling. From the stairs with Matthieu, we passed the pool room, and a giant glassed-in gym with workout mats and two of every kind of exercise equipment.

"How much does the membership cost?" I asked, teasing Matthieu and eyeing the serious weight system.

"I'm pretty sure Wes would happily sneak you in anytime," Matthieu said. "So would I for that matter."

"No wonder you're all so hot. I'd have a six-pack too if I had an onsite gym," I said.

"Given the state of the rest of your building, I'm pretty sure you'd get tetanus if not something worse. Here we are." Matthieu opened the door to a garage, four of five spaces occupied by the kind of beautiful pieces of machinery that anyone would stop to stare at if they saw them passing.

There was a lean polished black motorcycle at the far end of the room that surprised me, as well as several sports cars. But my favorite by far was the one Matthieu headed directly for, a vintage mint-colored convertible that was all curves and a long nose. It had a cream soft top up for the cool weather, and rounded cat-eye headlights.

"Is that yours?" I asked, jogging down the metal steps to the garage floor.

Matthieu opened the passenger door, his eyes busy admiring the car. "It is. The '72 XKE."

"Is that a serial number?" I asked, staring blankly back at him.

Matthieu snorted. "It's a Jaguar. My favorite child," he said grinning.

"You know, I know how to drive stick," I said, waggling my eyebrows.

Matthieu's eye twitched slightly. "I'm resisting the urge to make a terrible joke. Get in. *Passenger* side, please."

MATTHIEU DROVE us to the trendiest district of Old Uptown, full of little boutiques and galleries and eclectic restaurants. We passed an upscale vintage store that I used to regularly window shop at, and then turned into a narrow alley.

"Umm, is this a legal maneuver?" I eyed the dumpster we passed narrowly with a slight wince. But it seemed unlikely that Matthieu would risk his precious convertible.

"It is, technically, a thoroughfare," Matthieu said, his own gaze cautious on the wall near him. After the length of one deep building, the alley opened up and there was enough room for us to pass without holding our breath.

"Not one an SUV would fit through," I said.

Matthieu stopped the car at a backdoor in the center of the block, and I got the first perfect whiff of salt and spud and grease.

"How have I missed this place? I used to live around here and I was on this block all the time."

"Napoleon is in the basement level. They do most of their business while the clubs are open," Matthieu said, pulling his cell out of his pocket and shooting off a text.

"And they take back alley orders?"

"They do from investors," Matthieu said with a sheepish smile. "Normally I'd go in, but I'm in the mood to eat with a better view than exposed brick and a lot of hipsters."

Before I could think of what to say to that, the back door

Lola and the Millionaires

opened and a young black man with a large grin and a white chef's apron came dashing over to the car. Matthieu rolled the window down and shook his hand.

"Segal," the man greeted, his accent thicker than Matthieu's. He dove into rapid French and passed Matthieu a thin menu.

"*Deux grande, s'il vous plait,*" Matthieu answered with a nod. "*Et un petit poutine.*"

The chef ran back inside, and Matthieu passed me the menu. It was a long list of entirely sauces.

"I ordered us both a large order of their fries. The large comes with six sauces, but you can choose more if you want. I can never make up my mind. They have little cup carriers and Paul will just fill them up for us."

"Matthieu. You're telling me I lived near a restaurant entirely devoted to dipping French fries in flavored dips and I never knew?"

"Double fried french fries," Matthieu said. With a brief frown, he added, "Remind me to take my cholesterol pill when we get back. And don't tell Wes or Leo. They'll be on me about this."

I made a soft dismissive sound. Leo couldn't really talk. He had a sweet tooth that deserved at least two cavities, even if he was meticulous about flossing.

Between Matthieu and I, we ordered just about every flavor of sauce on the menu—including bordeaux wine, figs, and sage!—and poor Paul had an extra set of hands help him bring everything up to the car.

"What if I accidentally drip?"

Matthieu shrugged, a massive cone of french fries settled between his thighs as he pulled the car back down the alley and onto the street. "I'll get Bertha detailed. Don't worry. Now tell me what happened with Wendy?"

I gave Matthieu the full rundown of the dinner with Wendy while he drove, and I helped him navigate the complicated chart of dips we'd collected. He didn't take us back Uptown, but over to the western docks, pulling up to an empty spot and a view of the harbor, freight ships at a distance and the sun setting to our left.

"She didn't give me a concrete timeline or names or anything," I said. "Just a very clear picture of how she plans on building her business and what she plans on taking from *Designate* to do so."

"Hmm, maybe I'm a little old fashioned for the publishing industry now," Matthieu mused, twisting in his seat to face me. "I know her plans make sense financially, but I can't imagine running a company all through social media, with so little actual socializing involved between my employees."

"That was what I thought too actually," I said, pointing to Matthieu with a fry. "I *love* walking into the Stanmore. And getting to know the other people in the departments. Plus… maybe it's silly, but if *everything* is digital I…" I hummed and blushed under Matthieu's intent stare. The sunset was burning over the harbor behind him, creating a strangely romantic picture, and I was about to admit something that seemed a little childish. "When I was little, I used to cut out the things in magazines that I loved and tape them up on my walls. I think most girls did probably. And I just wonder about stuff like that. Like how do you make a wish board to put up on your bedroom wall to wake up to without magazines? Print things out from the internet? It seems weird to me."

Matthieu was only smiling. "A wish board? Is that…things you want to buy someday?"

"No, I mean, maybe. Kind of. Mostly, it's like…" I twisted my lips and looked out to the water to think of how to explain it. "I guess it's like a representation of who you'd like to grow into being? Not necessarily what you own, but an example of the kind of confidence you'd have to have to be the woman who walks down the sidewalk in a red velvet trench coat, or gold lamé lace-up boots, or—oh, you know! Whatever you want," I said as Matthieu laughed.

"Is that who you wanted to be when you were younger?" Matthieu asked, grinning.

That was who I wanted to be three years ago when gold

lamé was still in style. I shrugged in answer and Matthieu dipped another fry, waggling his eyebrows at me.

"A bit," I admitted. "Mostly I... It wasn't just clothes. I think I had little collections for everything. Houses. Pictures of guys. Nests, and things I'd learn to cook, and places I'd travel."

"Nests?" Matthieu's head tipped to the side, face blank with surprise.

I choked lightly on a fry and winced. Had I said that? I had said that. Keeping my stare on the harbor, I shrugged. "I was definitely one of those betas that wanted to find out they had surprise omega genetics. Even as I got older and it became pretty clear I didn't."

Matthieu was quiet, watching me. His foot stretched across the floor to tap mine, encouraging me gently.

"You don't still want that?" he asked.

A painful stillness took over me, weighing me in my seat, and I turned to meet Matthieu's gentle gaze. "Last year when Baby's perfume came in, I think I just realized finally that it wasn't happening. I'm not special. It was like...it was almost like she took it from me." Shame burned in my eyes, and I blinked it away. "Or at least, it sank in that it was statistically impossible that two beta friends in their twenties would both suddenly discover their latent omega designation."

"Why do you think it matters?" Matthieu asked, frowning. "Being an omega?"

"It means you're wanted," I said simply, swirling a fry in a peppered parmesan sauce and then glancing up.

Matthieu's eyes narrowed at me. "You assume that means you aren't?"

My skin flushed hot, and I stared down at my lap again. "I think it's just not a guarantee for the rest of us. Alphas are always waiting for something better."

Matthieu set his food aside, grabbing a napkin from the pile and wiping his fingers. "What are betas doing then?"

The mood was souring in the car, the food heavy in my

stomach and the last of the perfectly delicious fries growing cold.

"Waiting to turn into alphas or omegas," I said. "And then moving on when that doesn't happen."

"Hm." Matthieu didn't say anything else. He didn't need to. The quiet sound was enough condemnation. He turned the key in the ignition, and we left our quiet moment by the water.

Lola
31

His voice was mumbling in my ear, singing tunelessly to the stupid song my parents had cursed me to carry for the rest of my life.

"Her name was Lola..."

I tried to keep my breathing even as the mattress sank at my back. Would it even matter to Indy if I was asleep? Couldn't he just leave me alone? Where was Buzz, and why was I always stuck with Indy now?

"Wake up, bitch, I know you're faking it. Like usual."

"Lola. Lolotte, wake up."

My breath hitched, and I stiffened in Leo's bed. My heart was pounding, but my mouth wasn't dry. Matthieu was kneeling on the bed at my back, and he coaxed me with a gentle touch to my back.

"Was I screaming?" I whispered, looking up at his dark shadow

Matthieu froze for a beat, and then his hands slid underneath my shoulders. "No, no you weren't screaming. I...came in to ask you to come to my room and sleep next to me. Is that all right?"

I nodded, and my arms circled Matthieu's chest as he pulled me up from the bed, arms cradling me. The rest of the night had been awkward. Matthieu had held my hand for most of the drive back to the house, but when we'd made it up to the top floor, I hadn't known where to go. He hadn't issued an invitation, so I trailed back to Leo's rooms, cursing myself for my dinner confessions.

"Nightmare?" he asked, leaving Leo's rooms and heading for his own across the hall.

"Just the start of one," I said, my head foggy with sleep.

Matthieu's room was brighter than I expected and compared to Leo's vast island of a bed, his was a relatively cozy four-poster king. He had a lamp lit on the nightstand, and he left it there as he settled us together under the covers. I remained curled against his chest with one of his arms draped over my back and the other hand combing gently through my hair.

"I don't want to lecture you about designation," Matthieu murmured. "But please don't think you being a beta has any bearing on the very simple fact that you *are* wanted here."

I clamped my eyes shut. Matthieu was not going to deal with my tears on top of managing my warped headspace of the evening.

"I shouldn't have said that. The way Leo is here, my relationship with him…it's not lesser," I choked out.

"I know," Matthieu said, still stroking my hair into a smooth rush down my back. "Someone's been pouring poison in your ear, Lolotte."

My lips twitched. "What's that mean? Lolotte?"

"Hm? Oh, nothing really. It's just a…a name for someone precious. I like the way it fits your name."

"I do too." The soft curls of Matthieu's chest hair were against my cheek, and I pursed my lips, blowing against his skin and smiling as he twitched beneath me. Now that it was safe to open my eyes again and not leak on him, I shifted and raised slightly so I could look down at him.

His hand took a fistful of my hair in a careful grip, the ends teasing my back above my loose tank top. "What do you think it means to be wanted?" he asked, head tipping, light catching in the gray hairs of his stubble. "Nests and fancy clothes and traveling?"

My chest tightened, and I shook my head. "I don't want to talk about—"

"Tell me, Lola," Matthieu said, eyes darkening. His arm

lowered to my waist, voice grunting slightly as he pulled me to lay over his chest. "Do you want to be spoiled? Given presents?"

I swallowed hard, breaths thin and even. I nodded once.

"Say it," Matthieu said, lips curving.

"Yes, I want presents."

His hand slid from my waist down to my ass, and he smiled wide enough to give me a glint of his teeth, gentling the command in his tone. "Pretty things or french fries?"

"French fries are pretty things," I said, squeaking and squirming as his hand slapped lightly, just along the hem of my shorts. "Both."

"Do you want a spectacle of it?" he asked.

I shook my head, face flushing and breaths starting to pant. When I let my legs slide down on either side of me, I realized I was poised perfectly over his groin. Another little spank, another wiggle, and I'd be grinding against him. My pussy burned with wanting and tried to squeeze around nothing.

Matthieu's eyebrow arched. "I'm not sure I believe you on that one, but we'll start gently and in private."

The innuendo was not lost on me, and I couldn't help but shift against him, happy to find him growing stiff against me.

"Matthieu, I don't want you to—"

Matthieu's hand in my hair tugged, and my words were torn by a moan and a wanton roll of my hips over his.

"Don't. Not everything needs to be about beta and alpha and omega nonsense," Matthieu said, echoing my shifting with a little of his own from below. "And you don't need to be ashamed of wanting material things to go along with emotional affection. We won't trade one for the other, but you'll have both if you want. Yes?"

His fist twisted in my strands, and I rubbed myself against him, breasts scraping pleasantly inside of my tank top.

"Say yes," he purred, a wave of that welcoming familiar fragrance washing over me.

"Yesss," I hissed, eyes sliding shut as I not-quite-shamelessly humped Matthieu.

"Ungh. Very good, Lolotte," Matthieu growled, rising up into my motion. "Keep going."

It was a cherry on top of the sundae to have his permission, not that I probably would've been able to stop.

"You like this?" he asked, taking a better grip on the roots of my hair. It was never painful or punishing, just the perfect grounding pressure to sing through me. I nodded and whined as I rocked on top of him. "Did you used to do this as a girl with your boyfriends?"

I moaned, and my cheeks were full bonfire flames, I was certain of it. I shook my head. "Not boyfriends. But…"

"Tell me."

"Blankets. Pillows and stuff like that," I admitted in a whisper, gasping for breath as I moved faster.

Matthieu grinned back at me. "Ah. Yes, I think I fucked a fair bit of bedding when I was a teenager too. My poor mother."

I snorted and had to take a break to catch my breath. When Matthieu's hand on my ass cheek swatted again, perfectly light and purely playful I whined and jumped back into motion.

"You like that too," Matthieu said, repeating the teasing action and tugging on my hair at the same time.

My mouth was hanging out open, my voice thin and whimpering as I started to rut desperately, heat growing in my core, flaring in small doses to hint at what was coming.

"I like it like this, with you here where I can see," I said. I still had a hard time with a lover behind me, leaving room for my head to replace them with ugly memories.

Matthieu hummed in understanding. His hand moved to cup my hip, pushing me up even as I tried to grind down.

"Up, Lolotte," Matthieu said, firm and warning.

I growled back at him and he laughed, happy lines digging into his cheeks as I wiggled up, hovering a few inches above him. He tugged my shorts and underwear down, smiling at the wet dew coating the lips of my sex, and then pulled his own sleep pants down, cock bobbing against his stomach.

"There, now get me wet with your juices," Matthieu said, pushing me back down and hissing as my hot pussy slid over the length of his cock. "That's it. Make me ready for you, hm?"

I moaned and tucked my face into Matthieu's neck as I obeyed him, the heat of his thick, stiff cock against me guaranteeing I'd be coming fast in another moment or two.

Matthieu's lips pressed to the shell of my ear, making me shiver. "Use me like one of your blankies," he whispered.

"Ohmigod!" I burst out laughing, pounding the heel of one hand against his shoulder in retaliation for his dirty teasing.

Matthieu purred in response, twisting my hair and pushing my bare ass down to press me harder against him. I squeezed my eyes shut, sucking down deep lungfuls of his scent as I rocked over his length. I hit a bump at his base and realized it was his knot, and it felt fucking *fantastic*. Matthieu groaned in earnest as I stayed there, the sound vibrating against my cheek.

"Fuck, Lola, you'll undo me and I have plans for you," Matthieu rasped.

With that promise I came, my hands fisting over his shoulders as my thighs trembled, and I slowed into little twitches of my hips. Matthieu sighed and bucked gently beneath me, coating his length in my release.

When his hand guided my hips to line himself up at my entrance, I patted his shoulder limply.

"No?" he asked, and I marveled that he didn't even seem frustrated by the thought I was refusing sex.

"Oh, no, I definitely want to. But I want you on top," I said.

I pushed myself up to see Matthieu's surprise, his cheeks flushed and his throat bobbing. "You're sure?" he asked.

"Definitely sure." I wanted Matthieu's weight on top of

me and his scent surrounding me. I wanted him driving into me and holding me in his arms. The only thing I *wasn't* sure of… I bit my lip, and he waited. "I just…don't think I'm ready for your knot."

"Mmm, not an issue," Matthieu said. He released my hair to hold my shoulders, rolling us on the mattress and making me gasp as he nestled back between my thighs.

I sighed. He hadn't even blinked. Instead, Matthieu nestled close on top of me, our chests pressed together. He kissed my chin and both my cheeks and then over my neck, licking my throat until I was wiggling beneath him. He rucked my tank top up and then over my head.

"Kiss," I begged, all but devouring his mouth when he finally offered it.

Matthieu hummed again, pulling away just enough to reach between us, guiding himself to my soaked entrance. "Still sore?"

I shook my head and then arched as he pushed in slowly, never stopping until his knot rested against my opening, nudging my clit just enough.

"Oh, fuck, yes," I breathed, my eyes falling shut and my legs spreading farther open for him.

His lips landed on mine, swallowing my gasp as he pulled out and then stroked in again, from tip to hilt, slow and steady, letting me feel every thick, long inch of him. He sucked my tongue, arms around my back holding me as close as he could, our chests pressed firmly together. Every stroke nudged his knot against me, but he never pushed, never tested me, and soon I was rising up into his thrusts, enjoying the friction of the ridge against me.

Matthieu was close, intoxicating and heavy and encompassing. My legs twined around his hips, and I swallowed his groan in our deep kisses. His purr resonated against my breasts, body pinning me to the bed, anchoring me in the blissful connection.

His mouth tore away, pressing to my cheek, and I caught that first rewarding mutter of French on my ear. I dug my fingers into his back and arched my own, turning my hips so the head of him dragged along my walls.

"God you feel good, Matthieu," I moaned. He did, he felt fucking amazing, but I wanted to play it up a little too. "So fucking good. Ah! Yes, just there, there. Oh, fuck, please!"

Every little word of praise made him thrum and growl in my ear, the bed starting to rock as his thrusts were quicker.

"I'm not a school boy, Lola," Matthieu rasped, teeth scraping along my jaw. "And I plan on feeling you gushing around my cock at least twice before I finish."

I whimpered and squeezed my thighs around his hips, meeting his thrusts, marveling at the thrill of his knot striking gently against my opening. Could I take him? All of him? Would he howl for me if I did? Bite—

Matthieu pushed up just enough to cup behind my shoulder blades, his own back arching so his lips could cover my breasts in sucking, biting kisses that made me beg.

"Please, please, *harder*," I cried.

Fingers tangled in my hair again, a rougher tug, and Matthieu fucked me in earnest, hips slapping against mine. I drew my knees higher, planting my heels into his ass and gasping as Matthieu chuckled against a nipple.

"Come for me, Lola," Matthieu growled, pinching my other nipple in his fingers.

I came with a cry, body trying to twist out of reach, but Matthieu held me tighter in his arms. He purred with a roar in my ear as I shuddered over his length, riding me into the bed even as I shattered. His forehead was against mine, breath panting on my lips.

"You sure you can make it?" I teased when I caught my breath. His body was almost frantic on top of mine, every muscle tensed and restraining.

Matthieu grinned and nipped my full cheek. "Touch yourself for me, Lolotte. I want to come together."

That was too sweet an offer to resist, and I wiggled my hand between us, fingering my clit roughly and digging my free hand into his hair. Matthieu's tongue licked against mine, mimicking the long thrusts of his cock inside of me. The longer he lasted, the heavier he got, until my hand was trapped between us, cursory nudges against my clit made by his shallow thrusts rocking us both. Sweat stuck our chests together as we begged and praised and moaned into one another's mouths.

"*Belle. Ma Lolotte.* Come. Come again," Matthieu pleaded.

My legs had fallen to the bed, and I spread them as far as I could, suddenly wishing I'd never said a word about his knot. I wanted him to consume me, or vice versa. I wanted us tied together completely and permanently.

"Come, darling, please," he said, sucking on my bottom lip.

I squeezed myself on his length, forcing my orgasm to come crashing over me, and Matthieu wedged his hand next to mine, fucking me frantically and gripping hard on his knot. His orgasm overlapped with mine, our voices broken as we broke the kiss, heat filling me. Matthieu was slack on top of me, breathing hard against my jaw, scenting me with gentle nuzzles. His purr was broken with his panting, and he groaned as he turned us, holding us joined together as he rolled onto his back and draped me over his chest.

His hands squeezed my ass and I shuddered, making him grunt. "Lie together with me?" he asked.

I nuzzled his temple and Matthieu's purr thrummed heavily, echoing in my sex and flaring soft heat. "Yes, please."

"Mmm. You'll be very easy to spoil, Lolotte," Matthieu said, kissing my throat.

LEO
32

Rake's foot nudged mine as we sat on the couch, his eyes popping slightly, trying to urge me to speak. Deep in his own armchair, Matthieu sat innocently drinking his scotch with a book open in his lap. Cyrus was painting in his studio, and Wes was…doing Wes things—working out maybe, or working in his office.

"Ask," Rake hissed.

"You ask," I whispered back.

Rake was a master of the faintest use of his bottom lip. It was absolutely a pout, but not one you could reasonably call him out on. I sighed and cleared my throat, catching Caleb's attention on my left but not Matthieu's.

"Maybe later, in private," I said to Rake.

He huffed and twisted toward the end of the table. "Hey, Matt."

Ah, shit.

"Hm?" Matthieu's eyebrows bounced, drink held to his lips.

"What's up with all the gifts you've been sneaking Lola?" Rake asked, leaning forward on the couch.

Matthieu turned to stone at the question, although I was pretty sure there was a little hint of a smile in his eyes. "What gifts?"

"The flowers," Caleb said immediately, smiling when I glanced at him in surprise. "What? You think I haven't noticed too?"

"And that chocolate cake you brought home for dinner last night that made her make sexy sounds," Rake said.

"And the hair clips," I added.

I hadn't noticed them at first, the pretty twisted silver pins she'd used to twist her hair up, ones that matched her usual silver earring posts. She hadn't had them last night but she'd been wearing them as she left this morning. Rake and I had already noticed something was up. Matthieu was practically bouncing as he walked, and Lola had a near permanent blush on her cheeks and a glitter in her eyes that I usually only caught right before sex. It might've been explained by sex too, except I knew Lola's anxiety started beating her up after the post-coital endorphins wore off. This was different. It lasted longer, and I wanted to know how to make it happen for her as well.

"Are you trying to seduce her with money? Because I don't think that's Lola's style," Rake said.

Matthieu straightened at that, his smile vanishing. "Of course not. It's not…" His jaw clenched, and he stared out the dark windows to the balcony.

"Are you courting her?" I asked, staring at him.

Matthieu blushed. Aha!

"I…hadn't thought of it like that, but yes, I suppose I am," he said slowly, brow furrowing. He pushed up from his armchair and crossed immediately to the ottoman in front of the couch we all sat on, planting himself in front of Rake. "You are my omega but—"

Rake shook his head. "Don't. Don't ask me for permission, you have it. You know I already want Lola to be pack. If her connection to us includes you, then I'm even happier for all our sakes."

Matthieu sighed, and his shoulders softened as he nodded. "Good. I assumed that's what we were all thinking. She said something that bothered me on Sunday, that she didn't think a beta was wanted. But I don't think she meant all betas."

I nodded. "She meant herself, I've caught that from her too."

Lola and the Millionaires

"Is it because of them?" Matthieu asked, growling faintly. "Those men?"

I groaned and reached my arm behind me to try and dig the tension out of the back of my neck. "I'm sure they didn't help but...a lot of betas have insecurities about self-worth. Alphas have a very clear purpose, and our whole culture is built around the concept of cherishing omegas."

"You want to treat her like an omega," Rake said softly, staring at Matthieu. "Oh, Matt, I love that idea."

"I intend to treat her as she deserves to be treated," Matthieu said with a shrug. "But I did get her to admit that she craves the kind of attention that comes with courting an omega. Don't share that," he said, pointing sternly at all three of us. "That was information I gained with a great deal of persuading. I don't want her to feel like all we do is gossip about her when she's not here."

"It is all we do," Caleb said with a soft laugh. "Leo, you should swap the name on my ticket for hers. Take Lola to Malta with you."

My eyebrows bounced. I had a trip to Malta planned over the weekend to see a property my firm was interested in for a possible resort site. Caleb and I had planned to go together months ago, but the idea of taking Lola was equally appealing. Lola was sharing her time at the house between Matthieu, or me and Rake together. As happy as I was to see her falling into a place with our pack, I was a little nostalgic for those early moments with her.

Just us.

"You don't mind?" I asked, and Caleb shook his head. I turned to Matthieu and he blinked in confusion. "Do *you* mind?"

He scoffed. "Do *you*? Not that men should say things like 'dibs' about women, but I have been horning in on your time with her recently."

"You've been making her happy," I said, smiling as he sat up straighter. I turned to Rake to make sure he was on board, and instead found him scrolling furiously on his phone. "What are you doing?"

"Shopping."

"*Now?*"

"I'm sorry, but if anyone is an authority on spoiling an omega, it's the omega in the room. Besides, Lo and I talked about fashion and makeup for hours during fashion week. I have an actual wishlist I compiled for this exact moment."

"*Subtlety*, Rakim," Matthieu growled, reaching for the phone as Rake scooted quickly out of his reach and into Caleb's protection.

"*You* be subtle! Anyway I can just…stuff it in my closet until I think she's ready," Rake muttered, adding a pair of leather-like leggings to his cart.

"You're just going to keep women's clothing in your closet and assume Lola won't wonder why?" I asked.

"Gender is a social construct."

Matthieu groaned and left the ottoman, heading out of the living room.

Rake smirked at me and Caleb. "He just knows I'm going to out-do him on the presents."

"Call her now," Caleb urged me.

I dug my own phone out of my pocket, reaching my arm back behind Rake to squeeze Caleb's shoulder in thanks. He had his own reasons for wanting Lola comfortably and permanently entwined with our pack, and it made my heart ache beautifully to watch the way she was falling into the center of us. Even Cyrus, who had balked at the mention of making Lola pack a week ago, had spent every dinner she was with us since flirting shamelessly with her. And Lola hadn't seemed the least bit skittish in response.

"Can't manage even one night without me, can you?"

My whole body melted into the couch at the sound of her voice, teasing and sweet. Lola had come a long way from the guarded woman I'd met at the club who'd lured me in like a siren. Every glimpse I got of the happy, witty, talented girl that had been buried under terror, made me want to dig for more, help her excavate herself from the rubble.

"Barely. Hey, do you have a passport?"

"Um? Yeah, if it's not expired."

"Check for me," I said. *Take the dumb grin off your face, she can't even see you.*

"Ugh, but packing boxes. Okay, hold please."

I listened in the quiet to her shuffling through her barren apartment. I leaned into Rake's side, watching him shop on his phone. "You're overdoing it," I whispered to him. Lola didn't need a lot of formal wear. Unless Caleb finally found his theater event partner...

"I'm just brainstorming," Rake whispered back.

"It's still good," Lola said on the phone.

"Great. I hope you don't have plans this weekend."

"I promised Rake I'd watch that new reality show."

"He'll forgive you for canceling."

"Wait...this weekend? I thought you and Caleb were going to—Oh!"

"Last-minute appointment," Caleb whispered to me, and I nodded.

"Caleb has a last-minute appointment with a client he needs to meet. I need a date for the trip. It's only a little bit of business, and you can hang out at the hotel pool—"

"Oh! Swimsuits," Rake whispered.

"—or come with me to the property and tell me what you think. We'll be back late Sunday night."

"I..." I held my breath as Lola hesitated on the other end of the call. Caleb and Rake both stared at me, eyes wide and hopeful, waiting for her answer. "I don't really have any reason to say no," Lola said, giggling. "God, that sounds amazing! Are you sure?"

"Positive! Fantastic. I'll pick you up from work on Friday. And you'll be here tomorrow night won't you?"

"Mm, maybe I should pack—ah, fuck it, I'm totally packing tonight. Yeah, I'll see you tomorrow night."

"Great. See you tomorrow! Lo-Lola," I said, choking over the words I'd nearly said and scrambling her name instead.

"'Night!"

She hung up and Rake reached up, poking my flaming cheek with his finger. "Smooth recovery, babe."

"Don't tease him. And pick her out a swimsuit for the weekend. That's an easy one to sneak into her suitcase," Caleb said, winking at me.

Lola

33

All of my internet searches hadn't really prepared me for Malta. I couldn't imagine a place so old and so bright, without stepping onto its warm streets myself. The entire city of Valletta was built from the same beautiful golden sandstone, but the architecture shifted from one era to the next, creating unity and diversity at the same time.

"I feel bad that Caleb is missing this," I said. "I'm sure he'd have loved the inspiration for his own work."

Leo hummed and smiled, face tilted up to the sun's rays as we walked the tiled city roads, little narrow paths through nestled buildings. "We can always come again with him," Leo said. "Do you like it here?"

The flight had been overnight with a blurry stop in London I barely recalled. We'd only been off the plane for a few hours, dropping our bags off at the hotel and arriving in Valletta just in time to catch the fish markets open. We'd stopped in a cafe for Turkish coffee and 'hobz biz-zejt'—a delicious flatbread spread with roasted tomatoes, tuna, capers, and onion—and now we were on a search for cannoli.

"I love it," I said.

Maybe it was jet lag, or maybe it was the exquisite lack of clouds in the sky or the fact that there was water the actual shade of aquamarine like something you'd see in a photograph, but I really meant the words. I wanted the whole pack here. It would be fun to see Wes unwind a little on a vacation, and I was sure Cyrus and Rake would be able to sniff out the best nightlife, or at least the best swimming holes. And Matthieu...

Matthieu was just someone I wanted to be around. I felt steadier with him and more open; he made me feel transparent and strong at the same time, encouraging honesty with him and with myself. I wanted to be holding Leo's hand on one side, and Matthieu's on the other, grounded between them. I'd worried it would be awkward, balancing my time between the three men in the pack, but either it was naturally easy or the guys were making sure it felt that way for my sake.

"What else are we doing aside from your business?" I asked, bumping my hip against his.

"I booked us a wine tour on our way to the open house. Which is less about the house than it is about the land. And then if we can keep our eyes open after that's done, there's a great dinner reservation here in Valletta tonight too. Tomorrow we can be lazy until we have to check out?"

I nodded and squeezed Leo's hand in mine. I was tempted to ask if I could call off work on Monday or even Tuesday too, and see if we could stay a little longer. We were really only here for thirty-six hours, and that suddenly didn't seem nearly long enough. But Leo had already covered the expense of putting Caleb's—*first class*—ticket in my name. A whole new flight and more nights at the hotel was too big an ask.

"Ah! *Dezerta*," Leo said, pointing to a sign in a glass window. In front of the first-floor shop, two small tables with chairs sat waiting for customers. "I think we just found your cannoli."

WARM AFTER OUR wine tour and day of sun, and cuddled into Leo's side in the back of a small taxi, I watched the sea curving around the edge of the island.

"Seeing this property at sunset seems strategic," I mused.

"Oh, definitely. There aren't a lot of places in Malta that

don't have a good view of the sea, but I think this one adds some serious weight to their asking price," Leo agreed.

"And it's the land, right? That you want to develop?"

"It is, but it comes with an old salt farm and a homestead. That's the tricky part of my job on this. The owners would prefer it be kept a private property, but they haven't found a buyer willing to meet their ask because of how much property there is, so now they're looking at commercial real estate possibilities," Leo said. "My pitch is going to be a fairly small resort with the intention of keeping the salt farm intact. I'm hoping that'll beat out some of the bigger offers."

I nodded along to his explanation. I was mostly in it for the wine tour and five-star hotel room I'd gotten a peek of earlier. Plus this time with just me and Leo.

"I'm glad you asked me to come," I said.

Leo turned and caught my eye, dimples winking in his cheeks. "Aw, look at you. You're a little wine buzzed, aren't you? I'm thrilled you agreed to come with me. I haven't *missed* you, but I've missed…" His brow furrowed so I finished for him.

"Us," I said, nodding.

"Mm, yeah. Just us," Leo said smiling. "Don't get me wrong. The more tangled up you are with our pack, the happier I am."

"I get it. Things to do feel simpler today," I said, resting my head on his shoulder.

"Do they? Are things complicated with you and Matthieu?"

"Shouldn't they be? He's twice my age. He's my boss. Like *Boss* boss. He just broke up with someone he was with for *years*. I'm seeing his packmates, but it's not like with you and Rake where we can all just curl up in bed together, right? And how long is it going to take before this whole 'poor little damaged beta girl' thing wears off, and you all just get *tired* of me?"

Leo startled as my word vomit ran to a close. Thank god our cab driver had barely any English under his belt. Leo's hands reached for my shoulders and he pulled me upright, head ducking so we were eye to eye.

"You're worried about *all* of that?" he asked softly.

"Tip of the iceberg," I said with a single nod.

Leo's lips twitched, and I huffed a nervous laugh out.

"All right, I'm just gonna cover one thing for now, and we'll get to the rest later, okay? Your trauma is neither part of your appeal, nor is it a detriment to our feelings for you. End of story." Leo's eyes held mine for every word, hands rubbing my shoulders slowly, working away a tightness I hadn't noticed on my own.

"Okay," I said, nodding lightly.

"Okay. Good. And you never know about the dynamics thing. I'm sure if you crooked your finger, Matthieu would jump in the bed, regardless of who else was sharing it," Leo said, shrugging and pulling me back into his side. "Also, don't worry about the boss thing, he's too far up the food chain at the magazine. Or Carolyn. That was a dead weight relationship they were carrying."

"So just don't worry?" I said, smiling.

Leo kissed the top of my head firmly. "Exactly. Hey, I think this is it."

I sat up, leaning over Leo's lap to watch the house come into view. "Oh, it's so sweet!"

The home was on a low cliff overlooking a long stone bench of salt pans—shallow man-made puddles of salt water shimmered in the carved stone, reflecting the sunset like panes of stained glass. The house itself was built in stone brick and mortar, the same tan stone like the buildings in Valletta. It was humble and squat, with dusty pink shutters, and it looked out of place on its own property, surrounded by sports cars and men and women in business attire.

"Will the owners be here?" I asked, as our driver stopped next to a bright red, compact sports car.

"I think it's just the agent tonight, which is good considering that commercial real estate fighting over land like this can be a swarm of vultures. Go ahead and wander, and I'll manage the handshaking?"

I slipped out of the car, following Leo to the mass of suits before splitting off on my own. There was a set of well-maintained stairs carved down the cliffside that led to the salt pans, and I followed it down, holding onto the rope handle. Malta was cool in early spring, especially at night, and I had grabbed one of Leo's sweaters to wear over my sundress, but I enjoyed the salty bite of chill that licked at my legs from the sea.

I was halfway down the steps when I saw the couple by the cliffside, and paused on my way down. They were older, and mostly shadows against the sunset, but the man propped himself up with one hand on a cane, his other arm wrapped around the woman's shoulders. They stood together, balancing on the grooves of the salt pans and watching the sun paint the water red. They definitely weren't part of the suit party up by the house, and I guessed from Leo's description they might've been the owners. Seeing them together like this, a wave of melancholy washed over me. They were selling their home. It looked as though they were savoring a sunset like this one for as long as they could.

The man turned slightly, and spotting me, bent his head to his wife, who waved me down the stairs. I was more interested in the view here than the negotiations Leo was in the middle of, so I finished my way down the steps, meeting the couple at the bottom.

"*Ełow*," they greeted with a dip of their heads.

"Hello," I answered with a smile and a nod.

And then, impossibly, the woman took my arm and started off in a steady and incomprehensible stream of Maltese, accompanied by thorough gesturing to explain the salt farming process. I followed her tugs on my arm with confused laughter, letting her lead me through the shallow pools of the pans, to where the sea came in toward the shore.

I didn't understand a word she said, but I could guess the process somewhere between the motions of her hands. They brought the seawater up from the grooves in the stone near the shore, let it bake in the pans under the sun, rotating the regions of the stone bench to keep track of how long it had been. She scooped a handful of salt in soft, gnarled hands, and then captured my hand again and forced the large granules into my palm.

"*Tiekol*," she said, pushing my hand up toward my lips, leathery tan cheeks grinning at me.

I popped a morsel in my mouth, sharp and tangy and immediately making me salivate. I hummed, and she laughed and nodded, pulling me back to the stairs where her husband was perched on low steps.

I followed the couple on their slow journey back up the cliff, watching the sun sink until the steps were just visible as we reached the top. Most of the cars were already gone now, and Leo stood by the picturesque little house with a handful of others. His gaze immediately landed on me, his professionally smooth expression cracking under a grin. He made a quick escape from the group and joined me with the elderly couple.

"You made friends," Leo said.

"I think these are the owners," I explained as they offered him a more cautious greeting than the one I'd received.

"Grech?" Leo asked, beaming at the man's nod. "Leo Santoro."

"Look, I've farmed salt now," I said, holding my hand in front of Leo.

"Oh, good, I'm starving." Leo popped a quick pinch of the salt into his mouth and just like that, hearts were won over as he hummed with pleasure.

A tall black man in loose linen pants joined us. "Leo, you've met the Grechs."

Mrs. Grech made a quick announcement which made the new man laugh. "She likes your woman, Santoro. And your taste buds." Leo grinned at me as the real estate agent waited while Mr. Grech added to his wife's statement. "Ah. Marcellino says that now that the vultures have left, you're both very welcome to stay for dinner. He's a good cook and I'm a decent translator, so I'd recommend saying yes."

Leo took one look at me as I bounced on the balls of my feet and nodded. "Yes. Absolutely."

"*IL-LEJL IT-TAJJEB!*" I said, bending to accept the kiss on both cheeks from each of the Grech's as Leo shook the hand of David, their real estate agent slash old family friend.

"*Il-lejl it-tajjeb,*" they echoed. 'Good night.'

I wasn't going to hold onto much of my new Maltese I'd learned over salted smoked fish, rabbit stew, and more warm fresh bread smeared with roasted veggies, but I liked the pretty rolling sound of the language. I blinked away tears as I stepped back, and Leo took my place, hugging the elderly couple.

I loved this sweet little house, so close and warm, everything centered around the kitchen and the small dining room table. And I loved this welcoming old couple who hated to give up their salt farm and have their home torn down to make room for another fancy hotel for tourists.

"Come on, I'll give you two a ride back to Valletta," David said, ushering us out the door and to his tiny four-door sedan. It was modest compared to what the visitors tonight had arrived in, and David scrambled to move kids' sports gear out of the way of the back seat for me.

"You didn't mind wasting the reservation?" I asked Leo as we got into the car.

"Are you kidding? Did you see me undo my belt after the stew?" Leo asked, laughing. "Home cooking like that can't be beat."

I leaned forward from the back seat to kiss his cheek as David slid into the driver's seat on the right.

"Well, Santoro. You're family now. You could put a Hilton on this property, and they'd probably only downgrade you to cousin instead of adopted son," David said, pulling away.

I waved out the back window to the small couple under the tiny front light over the door. "That would be a horrible waste. I don't blame them for wanting to keep this place private. It seems like a shame to bulldoze it just for a hotel."

"Mm, the house needs work," David allowed.

"It could be renovated. The bones could be kept," Leo said to him.

David's eyebrows bounced. "Are you getting sentimental? Aren't you here for the sake of a resort?"

"I'm here for the potential of the property," Leo said carefully.

I slipped my arms over Leo's shoulders, scooting forward so I could rest my chin on Leo's shoulder. "It should be a home."

"If it were owned privately, I know there are other salt farmers on the island that might add the pans to their roster," David said, smile growing sly.

"This seems like a setup," Leo muttered, turning to butt his forehead against my temple. "Did that adorable elderly couple put you up to this?"

"You mean Mama and Papa Grech?" I asked, grinning. "I'm sure they would've if I'd picked up the language faster. Maybe your firm can think of a better use for the place than just a hoity-toity resort?"

"Hmm, maybe." Leo kissed my cheek and I sank back, mildly victorious and leaning to the window to watch the stars go by.

I WOKE up the next morning to a warm breeze coming in from our vast hotel balcony and the slight chink of china as Leo set a cup of coffee down on the nightstand. He climbed over me, bundling me into his arms, the sheets rumpled and barely covering my breasts.

"I arranged us a late check-out, so we have plenty of time," Leo said, kissing the shell of my ear.

I shivered and nodded. "Thas' nice."

"There's...there's something I want to talk to you about while it's just us," he added.

I stiffened in his arms and Leo kissed the corner of my jaw. That sounded like *serious* talk, and yesterday had been so...so easy. Like I was able to be myself, totally forgetting about everything that came before, free of all the drama and the memories.

"It's not bad, gorgeous," Leo said, kissing the same spot again. "I just wanted to say something before someone else did, I guess."

I wiggled and he loosened his hold, letting me roll to face him. "Still ominous, Leo."

"Right. Sorry," he said, grimacing. "Okay, so...Lola, I think you need to reconcile yourself to the idea that..."

I held my breath and forced myself to keep my eyes on him and *not* cry.

Leo sighed and finished, a soft smile curling on his lips. "The idea that the pack is going to want you to stay. To be one of us."

A bird called from the hotel courtyard, and a woman laughed down in the pool. A breeze kissed my back while I waited for Leo's words to sort themselves out in my head.

"I don't understand."

"I'm talking about you being a part of the pack, Lola."

I scooted backward and leaned over the side of the bed, reaching for my nightshirt. This kind of conversation warranted clothes.

"Leo, that's so...why would I—" I wrestled into the shirt and then flipped my hair off my face, finding Leo sitting up cross-legged in the middle of the bed.

He reached for my hand, and I could tell he was fighting laughter now. "Lola, Rake adores you. I've never seen Matthieu so happy in all the time I've been with the pack, and I... Lola, gorgeous, I love you."

Oh, thank god.

"Hey, there's that smile I've been waiting for," Leo said, grinning.

It faltered almost immediately, and Leo frowned in answer. "This can't work," I whispered, throat squeezing and eyes stinging.

"Lola," Leo said slowly, cautioning me. "I know that ugliness in your head that says this can't be for you, but please, just give yourself a chance to believe in it a little bit."

"What happens when Matthieu doesn't want me anymore?" I ask, dread coiling like a viper in my gut.

"You don't know that's what will happen. Even then, it's not gonna change how I feel. Or how Rake feels," Leo said.

"That's Rake's alpha. Or what if it's Rake who loses interest? Leo, your pack doesn't *need* me."

"Lola, you were there for Rake's heat. That's not for outsiders, that's not how packs work, not even ours. His needing you there was as good as a declaration. And the way Caleb and Cyrus responded was just further proof." Leo held up a hand to stop my next refusal. "Okay, listen. This is what I mean. I need you to give yourself a little hope on this idea, gorgeous. I know you're trying to protect yourself. I've been there, believe me. But this can't happen if you won't let it."

I sighed and drew my knees up under the blanket, folding myself into a tight ball and lowering my head, trying to listen to his words. Except just one part kept ringing over and over in my head.

Fuck.

I looked up and saw the lines of stress digging into Leo's forehead, the frustration pressing his lips together, and the worry in his gaze. That was my fault, and I'd jumped into the conversation at entirely the wrong angle.

"I love you too," I said.

Leo's high shoulders sagged and just like that, *so easy*, Leo was beaming again. I squeezed his hand that waited for me on the bed, and he tugged on it, drawing me into his lap.

I kissed his chin and then softly against his lips, a little bit of a coffee flavor in his answering sigh. "Sorry. That was the important bit, wasn't it?"

"Mhm, this is more of the reception I was looking for," he murmured, resting his temple against mine and wrapping his arms tight around me. "I never really talked to you about Odette, did I? To be honest, after hearing everything with Buzz and Indy, it just didn't seem right to compare."

"It's not like that."

"I know," Leo said, nodding. He sucked in a deep breath and moved us to lean against the padded headboard. "And there's a relevant bit in all of it, about how I work with the pack—"

"Leo, I *know* you belong with them," I said.

"Yeah, I do, and your logic on why you wouldn't doesn't hold up," Leo said, arching an eyebrow at me. "But for now, let's skim through the Odette saga. Um, let's see… So, she hired me before I even had my license or anything. She said a lot about me having potential, but I think she just saw something she wanted in me. She's into young, vulnerable betas. The relationship happened…quickly, probably within my first month working for her. There was a rumor going around the firm that Odette had been rejected by several omegas, but later Matthieu said she wasn't ever a member of the Omega Center. I think she might've circulated the rumor herself as emotional bait. Made us feel like she *needed* us."

Leo huffed and rolled his shoulders, brow furrowed, and I turned in his lap to face him. His hands settled on my hips and he continued, eyes watching his own fingers stroke my skin. "She was more careful, but she fed me a lot of the same bullshit that those assholes gave you. She needed me, but I would never be *everything* she needed, that kind of shit. Enough to make me feel valuable but also worth less than others. When I first met Rake, I kind of hated him, but I was also curious because he was exactly what I was supposed to be. Rake saw right through her shit, knew exactly how she had me pinned, so he kept getting in touch with me."

"Nothing if not persistent," I said, and Leo nodded. I dug

my fingers into his neck and shoulders, and his eyes fell shut, the tension melting away off of his features.

"The more time I spent around Rake and, you know, his magical ability to just *shine* on you, the more fractures there were with my relationship with Odette. He was feeding me the self-worth she'd tried to starve out of me. And then Rake started inviting me to the house, and I met Caleb and… I think I was already in love with Rake, but I noticed it right away with Caleb. Rake was only bonded to Cyrus at the time, he and Caleb were friends, but Rake was trying to prove he wouldn't be Mr. Omega At Home for the pack. Caleb is such a steadying influence, I think he spooked Rake or vice versa.

"I felt like a bridge between them at first. Rake and I started having sex, I broke up with Odette and *immediately* got fired, and Caleb was just…he was there, but he was careful with me. He knew he and Rake had to cleanse me of all of the bullshit Odette had fed me before I'd really see that I wasn't a stand-in for Rake." Leo widened his eyes significantly at me, and I pinched the back of his neck to make him continue. "And while they were helping me, they fell in love too. I would say I knew for certain that Caleb loved me as much as he loved Rake before the three of us bonded, but to be honest I probably still had doubts. The bond eliminated those completely. And before you say anything about bonds, I am cutting you off *right now*. Neither of us can know how your relationships will develop with anyone in the pack, but you've got to stop telling yourself they're dead in the water just because you're a beta, or whatever it is you think makes you not good enough for us. If it weren't for me, Caleb and Rake might never have fallen in love. Without you—"

Leo sucked in another breath, and I stopped him. "You're right."

His mouth hung open, words frozen in a pause and his eyes narrowed, making me laugh at his suspicion.

"I'm letting Buzz do the talking in my head, but before all of that, I was still…pretty brutal with myself," I admitted. "He just confirmed—"

"He did not *confirm* anything, he twisted—"

"Okay, yes, he *preyed* on anxieties I'd been cultivating for a long time," I said, and Leo nodded and sighed. I opened my mouth to tell him about my mother and then changed my mind. "I'm going to start looking for a therapist."

"I have one I can recommend."

I resisted the smirk. "I'm going to start looking for one I can afford."

"But—"

"Leo, you can check in on this with me, but I'm handling it," I said, firmly.

Leo's lips quirked. "Yes *ma'am*. And you're gonna let this pack thing marinate in your head? I just, I don't want it to overwhelm you and make you…"

"Fritz?" I suggested, the word I'd used before in a similar situation.

Leo nodded. "No one's going to toy with you, Lola."

I could still get hurt, even if it was done innocently. I could hurt them too; there were no guarantees in this. But if that was only anxiety talking, then I owed it to myself to get that shit *sorted*. There was no one in the world more perfect than Leo and his pack. I needed to know if the dread that beat in my veins—that I would inevitably disappoint them and have to live with that knowledge every day—was more than just my imagination.

"I will work on it," I said.

Leo patted my hips and grinned. "I'll take it. Now, what should we do with our last hours in Malta?"

I blew a soft breath out and imagined it was the stress I was carrying. It wasn't a perfect fix, but it helped a little.

"I think you should tell me you love me again, while we shower. Maybe a few times? And then I think I'm going to need a few more rounds with cannoli," I said.

Leo laughed, and his arms tightened around my waist, lifting me with him as he got us off the bed and toward the yummy tiled en suite bathroom.

"I love you, Lola," he said in my ear, nipping the lobe.

"I love you," I answered, taking a deep breath of his scent on his neck, finding the faintly sweet, clean breath of him twice as soothing. "So much, Leo."

"I've been biting it off for weeks," Leo said, laughing. "Time to make up for all those times I didn't say it."

The words grew soft under the steam of the shower, Leo and I entwined from head to toe. Every repetition of the words, the feeling, brought a little spike of worry in my heart. What if I broke this? What if Leo had to choose between me and his pack? I would walk away just to save him that.

But first, I'd fight to keep hold of him, and of the others. For my own sake.

Lola
34

"This isn't you running, right?" Leo asked as I moved to slide out of the car that was idling in front of my apartment. We'd gained a little time coming back from Malta, although it was still midnight on a Sunday, and my neighborhood was dead quiet.

"It's not like that," I said, shutting the car door again and turning to face him. "I'm not trying to *avoid* you or the pack. But if I come back to the house tonight, I'm going to fall right back into the cycle of enjoying one moment and panicking about the inevitable end in the next. Also, I *really* need to do laundry. But I promise I'll come tomorrow night. I just need to do some thinking, and start looking at therapists."

"Okay, well now I sound unreasonable," Leo said, laughing. "Fine, get some rest tonight. Hey, wait!" He caught my hand, and I raised an eyebrow at him until he grinned and said, "I love you."

I bit my lip and a bubble of warmth rose up in my chest. That feeling definitely hadn't gotten old yet. "I love you too."

"See you tomorrow," Leo said, leaning in for a last kiss.

Wes had given me the key to my new front door lock right before I left for Malta with Leo, and I used it gleefully now. No one in the building would know I was the catalyst for our landlord finding his motivation at last, but at least we now had a functioning lock and buzzer system on our front door.

Desperate to fall into my own bed, even if it was just for a minute before I gathered up my laundry, I raced upstairs and unlocked my door. It wasn't until I was inside, sliding the chain into place, that I caught the first whiff.

Just a whisper, bitter and sour, but enough to stir a painful onslaught of memories.

Indy.

My brain spun in circles, fingers gripping on the chain as I faced the door and debated running back out into the hall. Was I imagining his scent here? The apartment was dark at my back, street lights glowing from the outside and casting my own shadow on the wall to my right. Was I *alone*?

My heartbeat pounded in my ears as my hand slid down the door and over to the light switch, fingers trembling as I listened for the slightest shuffling step, waited for the breath on the back of my neck. When it never came, I flipped the switch—eyes wincing at the sudden light—and turned slowly around to face my living room. There was no stirring in the apartment, no sound but my own rushing pulse. The only sign of the disturbance, the only *proof*, was the scent burning in my nose and the soft scattering of yellow feathers trailing down the hall to my bedroom.

I whimpered behind pinched lips, digging into my purse as my travel bag dropped to the floor. I pulled my phone out and moaned at the dark screen, the room blurring as tears rose to my eyes. My breath hitched as I sucked in a gasp and held it in my chest, trying to gather control again. My phone was dead, of course, and I had barely thought about it for the whole weekend. A weekend that seemed so distant from this moment. So impossibly *safe*.

I slid down the wall in front of the door, fingers fumbling in my bag for my charger.

He's not here. He's not here, I repeated to myself, a steady refrain that failed to soothe me at all. He *was* here. Indy had been here. He'd not only made it back to the city, but he'd *found me.*

I crawled down the hall to the nearest outlet, ridiculously and humiliatingly terrified of those stupid yellow feathers. I fumbled the plug into place and hooked up my phone, squeezing my eyes shut and trying to organize my mind.

Lock the door. Call…Leo. Leo was closest.

The phone buzzed to life and I jumped in place, gasping and eyes flying wide as if I expected to see Indy standing in front of me, looming over me, hands reaching with those awful rings on his fingers.

There was a voicemail from UNKNOWN waiting, and I swiped with a shudder, bile rising in my throat.

"Her name was Lola, she was a showgirl…" Indy's voice droned softly over the phone, the whisper scratching at my skin and dragging another whimper from my lips. My eyes fluttered, but it was too easy to imagine him at my ear if I couldn't see for sure that I was alone, so I forced them open.

"Hey Showgirl, gotta say I'm disappointed. Came all this way to see you. What're you doin', Lola? Avoiding me?"

My hand clapped over my lips as I gagged. Get it together, Lola. Come on. Hang up and call Leo.

"Wanna see you again, Showgirl. Wanna feel you strangling my knot as I…" Indy chuckled, a poisonous sound. *"See you soon, babe."*

The phone beeped and I dropped it to the floor, pressing my back to the wall and taking deep breaths, gulps of air to keep down the urge to be sick. Except with every breath came a little taste of Indy on the air, faint and clawing, a single fingernail scratching down the back of my throat. When had he been here? Friday? Or just last night?

"Fuck. Fuck. Come on, Lola," I whispered. I grabbed my phone with shaking hands and tried Leo first. Straight to voicemail. "Noo," I whined. "No, come on. Please."

I puffed little breaths and swallowed the next whine. Call…the police. Or Baby. Or David. Or…

There was really only one person, more than all the others, I wanted to see at this moment. I couldn't have explained it, only that I knew he would know what to do. That he would be here, with me, as fast as he could. I scrolled through my phone, praying I'd saved the number and then pressed to call right away.

"Please. Please, please, please."

"Hey, sweetheart. What's wrong?"

I gasped at the sleep gravel in his voice and sobbed once before putting a stranglehold on my control again. "Wes? Indy was in my apartment. He's in the city."

Wes cursed and shuffled over the phone as I swallowed hard, staring into the dark of the bedroom.

"He's not there now, right?" Wes asked, sleep cleared away to a sharp and efficient tone.

"I...I don't know. I haven't gotten farther than the hallway."

"I'm on my way, sweetheart. You call the police yet?"

"No."

"Okay. Okay, I want you to stay on the line with me. Can you do that?"

"Yes," I squeezed out.

"Where's Leo?" Wes' pounding footsteps down the stairs matched the still rapid beat of my heart.

"He's in a car on his way home, but his phone is off. He left a voicemail...he said he's coming back."

"Indy? Fu—did you delete it?"

"No."

"Good girl. Is your door locked?"

I forced myself to stand and finished sliding the chain and bolts in place. "Yes."

"Okay, you hang tight, and you stay on the—" There was a voice in the background, and Wes answered with my name, the voice rising. "—Stay on the line with me. You're sure he's not in there, right?"

"I...his scent is faint but I...don't want to go into my room."

"Do you have a weapon, sweetheart?"

I turned the phone onto speaker and let it rest near the charging port. Wes' voice was doing wonders for me being able to move around, to breathe evenly. I opened my tiny coat closet and pulled the old baseball bat out from the corner.

"Yeah."

"That's my girl."

My shoulders squared at that, and I peered into the kitchen. It looked relatively untouched, but I turned on the lights and found that Indy had helped himself to something, new dishes in the sink.

Fucking asshole.

"I think I'm alone," I said as an engine roared on Wes' end.

"I think you are too, but if you wanna wait by the door for me, we'll both feel fine about it, okay?"

I nodded, even though he couldn't see me. "Okay."

"I'm on my way. I freaked Matthieu out on my way out, so the cavalry might be on the way too."

My couch was what was carrying the heaviest layer of Indy's scent and I avoided it completely, taking Wes' advice to sit down by the door, on the floor with my phone in one hand and the baseball bat in the other.

"Talk to me, sweetheart."

"Leo tried to get me to stay the night at the house, and I wish I had. I would've seen the voicemail first and—"

"And passed your phone to me so I could scour it and deal with this mess," Wes growled softly.

I hummed, and my eyes drifted back to my bedroom. "He sang that stupid song," I said. "And left feathers on my floor. They go to my bedroom."

"Wait for me, Lola," Wes said, more caution in his words, and then added, "It's gonna be okay. I'm ten minutes away. Less if I get a little liberal with the stoplights, okay?"

The song was stuck in my head, or at least the part of it Indy knew.

…yellow feathers in her hair and her dress cut down to there…

I knew the rest of the song, the lyrics haunting me all through adolescence every time someone thought they were being clever singing it to me, just because it matched my name. There were better choices, but that was always the one they knew. It was those first few lines that haunted me now, in Indy's almost tuneless hiss in my ear.

"Lola," Wes said sharply.

"I'm here, I'm okay." I was calmer now, but it was a kind of drugged calm, the adrenaline wearing off and creating a toxically dreamy effect in combination with the jetlag. I made myself ramble, more for Wes' sake than my own, about cannoli and my laundry and the elderly Grechs of Malta.

"I'm here, sweetheart. Ready for the buzzer?"

I scrambled to my feet, wavering slightly. "Ready."

I still jumped at the roaring blare of the buzzer, immediately hitting the button to let him in and fumbling with the locks. His steps thundered up to my door and I hung up as soon as his scent reached my nose, that candied sex smell oddly comforting in the moment. Even more comforting was the enormous figure of Wes running up my steps to my open door.

"I'm already to her place. I gotta call the police, okay? Oof," Wes puffed as I ran into his chest, the baseball bat clattering to the floor and propping my door open. His arm wrapped around me, holding me tight, and I cleared the last remnants of Indy out of my lungs with every breath I took while my nose pressed to his chest. "That's fine. See you soon. Hey, I got you, sweetheart."

I wasn't crying, just shaking a little.

"Look at me." I tilted my head back, and Wes brushed his hand over my hair, his eyes searching my face. "You wanna wait out here for the others, or go back inside with me?"

I wanted Wes to pick me up off my feet, take me out to his car, and then burn my apartment down to the ground behind us both.

"With you," I said, settling on the simplest compromise between the two.

Wes frowned and nodded, guiding me back into the apartment as he called in the break-in to 911. "They're gonna be forever," Wes said with a sigh as he hung up. "It'll move things along a bit if we can figure out if he took anything. You've got the voicemail to prove he broke the restraining order request at least. Want me to go look?" Wes asked, glaring at the trail of feathers down the hall.

"Can we just...just stand here for a minute?" I asked.

"Of course we can," Wes murmured, arms open as I turned into his chest again, folding them over my back.

He was warm and solid and purely alpha, and if I'd made one real advancement over the past two months, it was getting over my aversion to alphas. Or at least Rake's. Wes vibrated with a silent purr, my eyes falling shut and the apartment going distant in my head.

"I think Matthieu and the others caught Leo on their way out," Wes said.

"Others?"

"Sounded like a full car," Wes said. "You're gonna take tomorrow off, okay? And you're going to stay at the house for a while."

I slid my hands under Wes' denim jacket and clutched at his back, planes of muscle thick under my fingers. I could fall asleep like this. I was definitely on some weird kind of high, floating in a hazy middle ground of panic and exhaustion.

"You're all right, sweetheart," Wes said, stroking my back. I was trembling, and I nodded against his chest. "Okay, you wait right here. Matt and the others will buzz any second."

Wes peeled me off his chest, propping me up by the buzzer and bending to kiss my forehead briefly before heading down the hall. I watched his steps as he carefully avoided stirring the feathers, although they skirted away from his boots like they were alive. He stopped in the door of my bedroom, his broad back blocking the view as he flipped the light on.

"Fuck."

Queasy churning returned to my stomach as I watched Wes' shoulders rise toward his ears, hackles up and anger making the citrus in his scent sharper.

The buzzer screamed at my ear and I flinched, turning and smacking it hard in answer. My door was still hanging open, and I heard their voices immediately. Matthieu's dulcet tones, and Leo's gravel. Rake's rapid whispering, and Caleb and Cyrus with smooth, low answers.

"Lola," Leo called.

But I was watching Wes as he stepped aside, leaning against the door.

Fabric was everywhere in the room, like a bomb had gone off in my closet. I stared at the innocent carnage, my feet carrying me mindlessly down the hall. Wes stepped into the room and bent, picking up the closest piece, my bright purple dress from the night of the fashion week party, torn down the middle. I made it to the door, a chaos of voices at my back, and the puzzle of the scene fit together as I saw another old dress of mine, sweet and white with eyelet flowers over a pale blue slip, now shredded down the center.

And her dress cut down to there...

"That's not what the song meant," I breathed out, a little stupidly.

Wes looked up at me as a storm of men calling my name burst into the apartment. Arms grabbed me from behind, and even though I *knew* it was one of my guys, I jumped and tried to spin away. But Leo's grip was firm and the second I faced him, my flight response vanished.

"God, Lola," he gasped, pressing me to his chest.

Just as quickly, warmth and velvet enveloped us both, Matthieu pressing to my back, his hands on my shoulders and his lips on the crown of my head.

"All right, back up," Wes said gently. "We're gonna leave this area for the police to go through first."

"Let me through," Rake snapped, squeezing under Matthieu's arm against my side, nuzzling my cheek and neck.

Tension unwound in me, and I drooped into their embrace.

"Give us a minute, Wes," Matthieu said, words thick with a low combination of a purr and growl.

"I'm okay," I offered in a mumble.

Physically I was fine, give or take the desire to pass out or be sick or just curl into a ball wherever was most conveniently available. Rake pulled me loose from between Leo and Matthieu, and then Caleb was there, all but knocking me out with his heady sweetness. His hands cupped my jaw, lifting my face, and I realized everything was blurry, eyes spilling over with steady tears. His thumbs wiped them away before I could and he leaned in, blocking the hallway out as he pressed a kiss to my forehead.

Cyrus wiggled into the limited space left in the hall, arm around my shoulders in a firm hug. "Wes, where can we wait in here?"

"Living room, I think," Wes said.

"Not the couch," I added, words thick.

Matthieu and Leo took my reins again, shepherding me to the warm radiator bench in front of the windows. Matthieu set his coat down on top of the old frame and they settled me between them, broad shoulders as close around me as they could be. Caleb was by the couch, nose wrinkled and a surprising, whispering growl in his throat.

Wes stood at the end of the hall, staring over the group of us as Cyrus and Rake drew my bar chairs in close to me. "It's going to get even more crowded in here when the police get here. It might be better if some of you—" he started before Rake cut him off.

"We're not leaving her."

"You should go," I said, and my head drooped to Matthieu's shoulder as I fiddled with Leo's hand in mine. "You've got work and—"

"I'm not leaving, Lola," Leo said, fingers squeezing mine. "And you're coming to the house and staying until this fucker is in jail."

"I can go to David's."

All four alphas released small, brief growls that were quickly cut off, and it was Caleb who spoke, kneeling down in front of me. "You can stay wherever you're most comfortable, of course. But please don't turn the offer down for our sakes. We'll feel better having you close."

Matthieu was breathing deep and slow on my right, Leo's

hands tense but gentle around mine. Caleb had seen right through me. I knew where I wanted to be, right now, and who I wanted to have around me. I knew where I would feel safest.

I nodded and gazed back at Caleb, speaking softly. "All right, I'll stay."

I just hoped I didn't bring trouble with me.

To be continued in Lola & the Millionaires - Part Two
Now Available!

Also by Kathryn Moon

COMPLETE READS

The Librarian's Coven Series

Written - Book 1

Warriors - Book 2

Scrivens - Book 3

Ancients - Book 4

Summerland Series

Welcome to Summerland: A Reverse Harem Romance - Part 1

Secrets of Summerland: A Reverse Harem Romance - Part 2

Leaving Summerland: A Reverse Harem Romance - Part 3

Standalones

Good Deeds

Command The Moon

The Sweetverse

Baby + the Late Night Howlers

Lola & the Millionaires - Part One

Lola & the Millionaires - Part Two

Sol & Lune

Book 1

Book 2

SERIES IN PROGRESS

Sweet Pea Mysteries

The Baker's Guide To Risky Rituals

The Rooksgrave Manor Series
Esther: A New Beginning - Book 1

Acknowledgments

Well 2020…this is no thanks to you.

This is absolutely thanks to my family, my friends, my Moongazers.

Thank you to the readers who let me run around in genre playgrounds, rearranging all the pieces into something completely different, and are still happy to come and play with me after I've made a strange and interesting mess of things. My books will never be for everyone, but if *this* book was for *you*, then I'm so happy!

Now specifically onto the people who keep me on track and in the best possible shape-

Gorgeous cover compliments to Kellie Arts for the art and Lana Kole for the font work!

Proof-reading amazingness thanks to Bookish Dreams Editing!

My alphas - wink wink - Chloe, Lana, and Desiree, who chased me down for more every day (cough, Chloe, cough)

My beta babes who absolutely devoured and protected this story; Jami, Ash, Kathryn, and Helen, thank you so much for all of your input and for making Lola so much stronger as a book!

I also just want to say to all of the above women that if I

ever wanted to commit a crime, I would just present it as a book idea and you'd probably all let me get away with it, cheering me on from the sidelines the whole time. And I really appreciate that! Not that I plan on committing a crime…

About the Author

Kathryn Moon is a country mouse who started dictating stories to her mother at an early age. The fascination with building new worlds and discovering the lives of the characters who grew in her head never faltered, and she graduated college with a fiction writing degree. She loves writing women were are strong in their vulnerability, romances that are as affectionate as they are challenging, and worlds that a reader sinks into and never wants to leave. When her hands aren't busy typing they're probably knitting sweaters or crimping pie crust in Ohio. She definitely believes in magic.

You can reach her on Facebook and at ohkathrynmoon@gmail.com or you can sign up for her newsletter!

Printed in Great Britain
by Amazon